CW01649452

THE THREE PROMISES OF JOHN COAKLEY LETTSOM

THE THREE PROMISES OF JOHN COAKLEY LETTSOM

by

John Whitehead

CONCHSHELL BOOKS

First published in 2024 by Conchshell Books
conchshellbooks@gmail.com

British Library Cataloguing-in-Publication data
A catalogue record for this book is available from the British Library

ISBN 978–1–3999–8275–7

Printed and bound in the UK by Short Run Press

The artwork on the cover of this book has been created by Lucy Frontani and combines photographs of Little Jost van Dyke island taken by the author with an engraving first published in the *Gentleman's Magazine* in 1814. The latter was taken from a painting of the Lettsom family home by William Thornton which was in turn based on sketches made by the artist on a visit to the British Virgin Islands in 1791.

When any sick to me apply,
I physics, bleeds, and sweats 'em;
If after that they choose to die,
Then I, John Coakley, Lettsom!

PREFACE

The Three Promises of John Coakley Lettsom is a story concerning real people. It makes extensive use of the main character's own writings, of what other people have written about him, and even of archaeological excavations of his former home on Tortola. His personal life and his feelings about those around him are less well recorded, and available information about the lives of the enslaved people with whom he interacted is minimal and mostly formal. Intrigued as much by what is missing from the record, as by what is known, my story fills in the gaps using imagination while striving to remain credible. Details of which aspects are fact, and which are fiction, are provided at the end of the book. I recommend that readers wait until they complete the story before looking there, in order to avoid spoilers.

The story concerns an era in which violence, cruelty and injustice were widespread. Much of the action occurs in what was then the epicentre of transatlantic slavery: the Caribbean. In order to be clear about the brutality that the characters would have suffered, inflicted or just been aware of, certain appalling incidents are described. I have not intended to dwell on these at unnecessary length, and for the most part I have used details from contemporary records rather than attempting to invent such scenes myself. The people of that time suffered immensely, and I hope that readers will not be too upset by these passages.

In terms of language, I have alluded to characters using foul words to describe enslaved people, but I have not reproduced those words in the text. Some characters do make slurs about enslaved people, and they are not always immediately called out by one of their more enlightened companions. However, over the course of the book I have tried to ensure that such generalisations are shown to be clearly false.

ANTI-SLAVERY INTERNATIONAL

All of the author's profits made from the sale of this book will be donated to Anti-Slavery International.

Anti-Slavery International is the world's oldest human rights organisation. It exists to ensure all people, everywhere are free from slavery. Since 1839, it has challenged slavery in all its forms and helped to make slavery illegal in every nation around the world. Today, it challenges modern forms of slavery wherever they exist by tackling the root causes of slavery and creating lasting freedom for all.

Anti-Slavery International is a UK registered charity (No. 1049160) and a company limited by guarantee, registered in England and Wales (no. 3079904). For more information visit https://antislavery.org.

PART I: 1750–51

Childhood

CHAPTER 1

The black girl curled up into such a tight ball that no part of her could be seen from outside the cave. Not really a cave, but a natural dark cavity with two entrances under a huge boulder propped up by surrounding stones. She heard her pursuer approaching through the scrub and held her breath. She saw his grubby white legs just outside the larger entrance as he paused to look for clues. Then he was gone. She breathed again and stretched out her aching limbs in relief. At once he was at the smaller entrance, grasping her foot and dragging her out. She shrieked, and then leapt to her feet and gave him a great big hug.

"You're the last", he said, "and mother is giving us sugar cane juice back at the house".

They ran up the hill together, John taking long purposeful strides and Teresa having to work hard to keep up. On a bench under the tamarind trees that grew in front of a neat white wooden dwelling, a woman was holding a large earthenware jug full of the sweet juice extracted from crushed sugar cane. Ed and Sam were sitting on the ground, hoping for a refill of their cups.

"I found her! I found her in the cave", shouted John as they approached. "I knew that's where she'd be, so I went straight there".

"No you didn't!" said Teresa, with a giggle. "I saw you searching around. You didn't have a clue where I was till I moved."

John and Ed were twins. Identical at their birth nearly six years before, they were now easy to tell apart. John was the lucky one.

Tall for his age, athletic and strong with luxuriant wavy blond hair, he had quickly shrugged off the childhood illnesses that had come his way. Not so Ed. He was born second and had been a difficult delivery. Lengthy bouts of illness had then left him shorter and weaker than John – although he was fit enough at this moment as he wrestled with Sam and succeeded in stealing his second helping of juice.

Sam and Teresa were half-siblings, he slightly older than the twins and she a few months younger. Their father, and owner, had sent them to the island of Little Jost van Dyke following the death of Sam's mother and the sale of Teresa's to a plantation owner on a distant island. Sam was a powerful young lad with a dark complexion and tight curly hair. Teresa was slighter and paler and had fine, straight black hair. She was a healthy, inquisitive and pretty child. Mary Lettsom, the twins' mother, was delighted to have two additional children to look after: she had wanted more of her own but had suffered a series of miscarriages and lost numerous infants before John and Ed had been born.

"John", said Mary, handing him his cup of juice, "your father wants to see you in the house. He has a visitor he'd like you to meet".

*

Little Jost van Dyke island, where the children were playing, is a tiny speck in the Caribbean, just one mile long and half a mile wide. At low tide it is connected by a sand bank to the larger Jost van Dyke island, to the west. To the east of both of these islands lies the largest of the archipelago making up the British Virgin Islands – Tortola – being all of twelve miles long and up to three miles wide.

The whole of Little Jost was owned by Edward Lettsom, the father of the twins, who was doing his best to make a living farming the poor Caribbean soils. His small cotton fields were scattered around the island in raised plots enclosed by stone walls, furnishing excellent hiding places or opportunities for ambush when the children's game changed to Pirates.

Between the cotton fields were plots where fruit and vegetables grew, and the higher and rougher ground was covered with trees, bushes and cacti. Impenetrable before the island had been settled, this wilderness was now criss-crossed by paths made by Edward to link his fields, trails carved out by field-hands for hunting wild birds or reaching coves and beaches for fishing, and by smaller tracks made by foraging goats. More cotton fields were tended on the tiny islands known as Green Cay and Sandy Cay to the east, and Edward also owned a sugar plantation at Cane Garden Bay on Tortola itself. Sam and Teresa's father, Samuel Taine, acted as a part-time overseer for this part of Edward's holdings.

Most of the labour on these small properties was provided involuntarily by two or three dozen slaves. Numbers varied with the seasons, with the passage of fevers and diseases, with Lettsom's fluctuating fortunes, and with the arrival of fresh supplies of Africans at Road Harbour on Tortola. Most of these workers, including nearly all of the women and children, lived in a small settlement not far from the Lettsom's own house. They, together with the four Lettsoms and their two young guests, formed the entire human population of Little Jost van Dyke.

For the last year Little Jost had become a paradise for John. First Ed had become healthier, recovering from a long illness and becoming able, first to walk, and then to run with John along all the island trails. Then Sam and Teresa had arrived so that there were four playmates to explore the island together. John and Ed loved the animals and birds that were abundant on the higher ground and by the sea shore, especially throwing stones at them and occasionally – when their aim was good – hitting and killing them. A prize collection of turtle shells and birds' eggs and feathers accumulated.

With Sam, most games involved sailing boats in tidal pools and then in the shallow waters of the island's sandy bays. Sam showed John how to assemble small model boats from driftwood and stolen firewood, and later taught him how rafts made from tying together various assemblies of logs, planks and branches could support two small boys venturing out into the waves. They learnt how to float, how to ride the incoming waves, and, after a fashion, how to swim. Their terrors, when waves swept them too far out and when their return to the shore seemed impossible, faded as soon as they were safe again. But the thrill of the adventures remained.

John enjoyed gentler pursuits with Teresa. They amassed a collection of shells of all colours, shapes and sizes, augmented with corals and sea ferns. They picked and pressed the most colourful of the wild flowers that they found. They crept up on nesting bananaquits and observed their egg laying and hatching, the determination of the adults in feeding the chicks, the mortality of the unsuccessful, and the fledging of the survivors.

Much of the time, all four children played together. They soon knew every square inch of the small island, creating their own geography of Lookout Point, Pirate Hill, Dead Hog Cliff, Sandy Beach, Rocky Harbour – all secret names meaning nothing to the adults. To the north of the island Atlantic breakers would crash against dark cliffs, but to the south the gentler waves of the Caribbean lapped against sandy beaches.

The waters between the Jost van Dyke islands were clear, and appeared purple from the abundance of corals, sea ferns and sea eggs that grew there. The last were a form of prickly sea urchin which, if opened very carefully, provided a small and tasty treat. Paddling, wading and swimming were quite safe when the sea was calm, but the children – being blissfully unaware of risk –

would go out in all weathers. Fish could easily be caught in nets, and balanced on small branches of driftwood for cooking over an open fire. Sharks were rare, but sucker fish looking in vain for sharks or rays to latch onto could switch to childish bodies instead, causing panic, disgust and pain on removal.

When they were not playing together, the children were working together. Mary Lettsom was not a woman of leisure. She went about her work assisted by slaves, but she was not in a position to delegate everything. A house slave named Rosett helped her with cooking and cleaning, and the children fed the small flock of chickens that patrolled the yard just outside and collected their eggs. Tending the fruit trees, herb gardens and vegetable plots was a joint venture with the female slaves – with input to the heavy work from the men – and these provided the subsistence diet of all of the island's residents. The twins and Sam and Teresa would join children from the slave village to help with the lighter and more delicate parts of the gardening work. Most tasks could be turned into games or competitions and their contributions were not especially onerous nor, it must be said, particularly efficient.

As for studying, there was very little time for that, although it had been one reason why Taine had entrusted his children to the Lettsoms. When the twins' father was at home, he would read from the Bible to the four children, and he had taught them to count up to twelve, and to perform simple additions. Mary had taught them to recognise and pronounce the letters of the alphabet, and to read and write a few short words. Practical skills of gardening, sewing, looking after animals and so on formed a greater part of their curriculum.

These then were the activities that allowed John and his companions to grow and thrive. As he ran towards the house to meet his father's visitor, he was unaware that they would all soon be coming to an end.

*

“This is my son John”, said his father proudly as the boy entered the living room. Edward Lettsom was addressing a tall, well-built young man of around twenty-four years of age. They were seated cosily around the dining table, smoking tobacco from clay pipes, each with an unfinished glass of dark red wine in front of them.

“Pull up a chair, John, and say hello to Captain William Lindow whose ship arrived in Road Harbour just yesterday.”

“Wow!” said John, climbing onto a chair that had been made high enough for him to reach the table easily. “Did you sail all the way from England?”

“Aye, with stops in Madeira to get wine for your father and Antigua to pick up slaves for the Pickering plantation”, came the reply. “We had good winds and a calm crossing, and made it in just seven weeks.”

“What’s your ship called?”

“She’s the *Abigail,* named in honour of the sweet little daughter of the man I sail her for.”

“How big is she?”

“Enough questions”, said his father. “What we want to talk about is school. Would you like to go to school?”

“Yes!” answered John immediately. And then, “What’s school?”

“It’s a place where dozens of boys get together and learn how to read and write. How to add and multiply. The names of all the Kings and Queens of England and all the cities and countries of the world. And, of course, about the Bible and the teachings of our Lord Jesus.”

“Do they learn about animals and birds and fish?” asked John.

“Oh, I don’t know”, said his father.

“I’m sure that they do”, suggested the captain.

“Where’s the school?”

"In Lancaster", replied the captain.

"That's in England", added John's father.

"Gosh!"

"So, you'll go with Captain Lindow when he returns to England next month, and stay with his employer, Mr Abraham Rawlinson in Lancaster. He'll arrange a place for you, and off you'll go to study at the school there."

"Wow! Will you and mother come too?"

"No".

"Will Ed come?"

"No".

"Can Sam come? He's very keen on boats and ships, and he'd love to sail across the ocean."

"No".

"Can Teresa come? She's very good at adding up and can even write her name – and mine."

"No, son. It's just you. The future of the Lettsoms depends on you getting a good education and coming home to earn a living for us all."

"When would I come home? Would it be for three months? Four months?"

"Ten years, we reckon", said his father.

That's when it hit him. That's when the penny dropped. This was not a jaunt or a holiday. He was being sent away. Forever. Away from Ed and Sam and Teresa, just as he had got used to their friendship. Away from his parents. Away from Lookout Point, Pirate Hill, Dead Hog Cliff, Sandy Beach and Rocky Harbour. His father and the captain continued to talk, but he was no longer taking it in.

"Did you go to school?" he suddenly interrupted.

"No", said his father. "I never had the chance. I wish I had".

"Did you?" he asked the captain.

"No", came the reply. "I went to sea. But the Rawlinson's boy, Henry goes. And his cousin. They'll be about seven and twelve years old now and they love it. Even Abigail goes to school. She's Henry's sister, and ten years old. Very clever girl she is too".

Other boys whom he would get to know. Girls too. Perhaps this wouldn't be too bad. Now he began to feel conflicted. Torn.

"Lancaster's a very fine town", the captain continued. "By the sea, surrounded by high hills, warm in summer but cold in winter. They get snow there, especially on the hills."

"What's snow?"

"In winter it gets so cold that water freezes solid. The rain freezes and comes down as snow."

"Doesn't that hurt when it hits you on the head?"

"No", replied Lindow, laughing. "The snow comes down as gentle white flakes, very soft and very pretty. It covers all of the hills, all of the streets and houses. You wake up one morning and find that everywhere has been turned bright white. It's a lovely sight. But it's so slippery! You go out and try to walk but you slide all over the place. Old men, young women, sliding and slipping and falling over. But it's soft when you fall on it. People make statues out of snow, and throw balls made out of snow at each other. And the lakes and ponds freeze over with a layer of solid ice, so that people can walk out over them."

"Just like Jesus on the Sea of Galilee?" suggested Mr Lettsom.

"Not really. It's solid when the ice is thick enough. It's not a miracle! And people don't just walk. They put skates on their feet – special shoes with blades like knives underneath – and they glide across the ice. Very elegant."

The captain tried to demonstrate what skating looked like, which is quite difficult on a wooden floor.

Snow! It sounded wonderful. How much he would miss Little Jost. What an adventure to go across the sea. Ten years would be forever. But then he would become a man. Like this fine young captain who had now sat down again at their table.

"So, what do you think, John?" His father's question brought him back to the conversation.

"Yes! It'll be great! I'll go! Can Sam come too?"

"No".

"Just as far as England, so he can sail in a ship and see another country."

"No, that won't be possible. Captain Lindow might not come back here for years."

"Well, I'll be able to tell him all about it when I get back."

"Yes, you'll have so much to tell".

The adults now signalled that John could leave them, and he scurried outside to tell his friends all about his forthcoming adventure.

"Guess where I'm going!" he called as he approached. "To Tortola", "To Uncle John's", "To Hell", they tried. "No. I'm going to England. I'm going to school in England. I'll make lots of new friends, meet pretty girls, and slide around in the snow." His second-hand demonstration of skating was even less illuminating than the captain's. He enjoyed explaining how wonderful it would all be. They received another message: "I'm leaving you. You'll be staying here. I'll be having a great time." He was very disappointed when, one by one, they wandered off to do some chore, collect more shells, or find driftwood to make a new model boat, even before he had finished explaining again what snow was and how people skated on ice.

CHAPTER 2

John leaned back and looked up into the clear blue sky. High above him could see three great black frigate birds gliding effortlessly. He had been told that these birds could fly vast distances. Might they be able to fly all the way to England? Where he would be going soon. Since learning of his forthcoming adventure the day before, he had been able to think of little else.

It being the First Day, as the Lettsoms referred to Sunday, the whole family were in their shallop sailing to Fat Hog Bay on Tortola for their regular weekly observance at the Friends' Meeting House. Although not of the Quaker persuasion himself, Captain Lindow had been invited to join them as a guest. While Edward Lettsom took the tiller, Lindow trimmed the sails. In his expert hands they caught every ounce of breeze and the boat moved gracefully and speedily eastwards along the southern coast of Tortola.

Mary took the opportunity to attend to some overdue repair work on her husband's shirts while John and Ed, having given up on attempts at fishing due to the unusual speed of their passage, relaxed at the bow. Sam and Teresa did not join these gatherings: their father was not a Friend and besides, neither slaves nor people of colour had yet been admitted to the community.

John listened as Lindow explained his fascination with the Quakers and their beliefs. They had a strong presence in Lancaster and his employers, the Rawlinson family, were staunch members of the local Meeting.

"Did you know the first Meeting House in the West Indies was founded as far back as 1655?" his father asked. John did know that, but Lindow shook his head.

"That's only three years after George Fox established the Society in England", continued Edward. "Two amazing women brought it here: Mary Fisher and Ann Austin. They convinced a good friend of the Governor of Barbados of the truth of the message, and before long there were five Meeting Houses on the island! George Fox himself came over and preached at them."

John knew that too. Mary Fisher was his favourite amongst the early Quakers whose stories he had so often heard. "Tell him how she went to Massachusetts next", he thought idly, but instead his father had moved on to the decline of the Meeting Houses on Barbados and the establishment of the one on Tortola: "About ten years ago, a Quaker trader from Lancaster persuaded John Pickering of the message."

"Is that the planter I delivered fresh slaves to yesterday?"

"Yes, he's the one. He was Lieutenant Governor at the time, so he was very influential! He established the Meeting House we're going to on his own plantation and converted the first half dozen Virgin Island Friends. It just grew from there and now we've around a hundred members regularly attending meetings. Mary and I joined about eight years ago, so John and Ed were born into the Society. It's a central pillar of our life here, and you'll understand how marvellous our little community is when you meet them."

"How can John Pickering be both Lieutenant Governor and a Quaker?"

"Ah yes. Well, there was no problem at first. But when war with France broke out he had to relinquish his office as he wasn't prepared to organise the military defence of the island. He said his faith came first."

John has always admired Mr Pickering for making this principled choice – while at the same time enjoying the thrills of leading his own little squad in daring and bloody military victories over imaginary French invaders of Little Jost.

As they approached Fat Hog Bay, the Captain called on the twins to help him control the sheets and explained to them how to set the ideal course for the jetty. They approached it perfectly, and John leapt ashore and wound the rope around one of the bollards.

*

The congregation emerged from the Meeting House into the sunshine, and made their way to tables set up in the shade of a grove of tall almond trees. After an hour of earnest devotion, they were eager to gossip and hungry for their lunch. Provision of food for these occasions was rather competitive. The women supplied the best of their produce while trying to give the impression that it was their normal fare. Mary Lettsom had killed and roasted a plump chicken the day before and this was central to her contribution. More prosperous Friends provided beef, pork and lobsters, and everyone brought along the finest produce from their fruit and vegetable plots. There was always too much, and plenty spare to be taken home. To drink there was weak ale, although excessive alcohol was frowned upon and so no wine or rum was available – not on the top of tables anyway.

Normally, John was one of the first out, running to find his cousins and play some energetic games while the men talked and the women laid out the food. On this Sunday, however, John did not go with Ed to seek out his playmates. Instead he stuck close to Captain Lindow, who took a place alongside John's parents. They were joined by Phoebe Smith and Mary Evans who had travelled together from Pennsylvania to preach to this offshoot of their faith, and by Mary Nottingham, Mr Pickering's sister. Her new husband, Samuel, took the last place at their table.

"Again, you told us there is something of God in everyone, and urged us to love our neighbours", said Samuel Nottingham, addressing Phoebe Smith who was helping lay out the cooked meats. "But when you say everyone, do you include those amongst us who were torn from their homes in Africa to labour here?"

This was a question that Phoebe had to deal with regularly. "George Fox taught that slaves should be treated kindly and persuaded to share with us in the fear of God", came her practiced answer. "Eventually, of course, they will be free."

"And how long is this process supposed to take? Mr Fox also said that Africans and Englishmen are of one blood, and of one mould. How is it then that no Quakers have yet brought their captives to God, to join with them in worship – as free men?"

"You must forgive my husband", interjected Mary Nottingham. "He's an Englishman, unfamiliar with our ways. Our plantations would not survive a day without our African brethren. Cultivating sugar is just too hard work for free men to consent to. We must be as considerate as possible, but without them we would all perish."

"Ten years back there was that dirty little dwarf who burst into our Yearly Meeting with a pig's bladder and stabbed it to squirt bright red berry juice over us all as a protest against slavery", said Phoebe.

"Benjamin Lay", recalled Mary Evans. "The juice was supposed to represent the blood of the Africans."

"Yes, him. He wanted immediate freedom for slaves, and called slave-owners apostates. It took us weeks to get those nasty stains out."

"What's an apostate?" John had been following the conversation carefully. The realisation that some people were free and some were slaves – including his friends Sam and Teresa – had come to him only recently and he still could not make sense of it.

"An apostate is someone who renounces his faith", answered his father. "So Mr Lay believes that owning slaves amounts to abandoning the teachings of the Society."

"Is that right? We own slaves. Does that mean we no longer follow the teachings of the Society?"

"It's more complicated than that", suggested his mother. "We must first persuade our slaves to walk with God. That's very difficult. They believe in witchcraft and idolatry. They dance and sing to their false gods. They need us to look after them and to protect them from harm. George Fox was a very loving person, but he never really lived with Africans. This Benjamin Lay was also an incomer from England, and he was disowned for what he did."

"Anyway, Africans are basically lazy", contributed Captain Lindow. "Without discipline, they wouldn't even be able to feed themselves. But if they're controlled firmly, dealt with fairly, fed well and kept healthy, then they will work hard, multiply, and increase in value. The slaves I brought over from Antigua for John Pickering are from Sam Martin's plantation. They're splendid fellows, and Martin is a shining example of how to manage these people in a modern and businesslike way."

"Well, the Martins certainly learned their lesson the hard way", observed Edward Lettsom. "His father treated his slaves atrociously, and in the end they murdered him. The last straw was when he cancelled Christmas."

John could appreciate how hard that would be. At Christmas, island tradition was to give slaves three days off, and to provide a feast for them. Roast hog, boiled chickens, fresh seafood – all served by the master and mistress. Washed down with full-strength beer and rum. Everyone put on their best clothes: clean and plain for the owners, bright and colourful for the slaves.

They exchanged hand-made presents they had worked on for months before. In the slave village, there would be music and dancing – last year he had slipped out to watch. One holiday amongst twelve months of labour. Yes, cancellation of that could make men murderous.

*

Back on Little Jost, Teresa and Sam had no time for religious discourse. Nor could anyone accuse them of being lazy! Whenever Mary was away, they were put to work under the supervision of Rosett who had the knack of inspiring them to great efforts through her own example and through her wit, humour and love. Entertaining Captain Lindow the evening before had lasted late into the night and seemed to have involved using every plate, glass and utensil in the house. Teresa was given the job of washing the dishes while Sam swept the floors.

Teresa had no reluctance to do chores. Although sewing and tending to the chickens were her favourite tasks, even doing the dishes, standing on a box so she could reach the tubs of hot and cold water prepared for her by Rosett, was pleasant. She was free to let her imagination wander. Where it went that morning was back to the days before she had come to live on Little Jost.

She and Sam used to live in their father's chaotic household in Road Town, the main settlement on Tortola, accompanied by his slaves, whichever captive females or free black women from local bars were his current favourites, and her grandmother – known to one and all simply as "Grandma" – who did her best to act as housekeeper. It was a frightening place for a little girl. Strange women wandered around the rooms, sometimes kind to her, sometimes shouting at her to go away. Belligerent men came to play cards or to drink with her father, and were either rather too nice to her, or violent and abusive, or both. Most terrifying were the large dogs Taine owned. Both she and Sam were attacked and bitten several times, only to be advised to be firmer with the animals and not to show their fear.

Teresa could hardly remember her mother. She had been a favourite of Taine for several years until his affections were transferred to a new purchase. When Teresa was about three years old, her father made a good profit selling his cast-off to a planter on Anguilla. Sam's mother had never recovered from the trauma of his birth and died when he was a few months old. Grandma protected the children as best she could, but her health was failing and her strength fading. Eventually it was she who had persuaded Taine to ask the Lettsoms to take them in to provide the care she could no longer manage and to give them a rudimentary education.

So here, washing the dishes, secure in the knowledge that no-one was going to suddenly start shouting at her or to hit her for no reason at all, and that there were no dogs on the whole island that might come and bite her, Teresa felt safe and at peace. Later, Rosett would make some sugar juice drink for the children and sit with them and tell them amusing stories of the latest goings on in the slave village.

Teresa was just beginning to make some sort of sense of the society in which she lived. There were clearly the white people who had the authority and gave orders for others to carry out. They could whip and beat the black people, who for some reason did not seem able to fight back. The latter did most of the hard physical work, and could be suddenly sent away. That much was easy to understand. But where did she and Sam fit in? They were neither white nor black. They lived with the white people, but they could not go to the Meeting House with them.

When the Lettsoms returned, there would be still time to play out with John and Ed for an hour or so before dark. To play! An activity she and Sam had never imagined, let alone experienced, while they lived in Road Town. Now, as she dried the last of the dishes and started to put them away in the tall kitchen dresser, she began to ponder what might happen to her when John went off to school in England. That thought punctured her serenity.

Fear began to return, not fear of what might happen right now, nor tomorrow, but of what lay ahead after John had gone. She did realise that she was the quickest of the four children to learn, both in formal studies and in the practical tasks of work and play. But she knew she would never be able to go to school. Even Sam – a boy, slightly stronger and slightly fitter than John and not much behind him at reading and writing – would never be able to go away to school.

Teresa saw in John's parents the happiest, fairest and most reliable adults she had met. Her ideal future? Surely to live in the same way as his mother in a pretty little house on an island paradise – alongside John and their own children, of course. But now it seemed likely that she and Sam would be packed off to live in Road Town again, with Taine, his women, and his dogs, and such a happy outcome would be further out of reach.

*

The conversation outside the Meeting House continued, becoming repetitious and argumentative. John wandered away to join Ed and their three cousins who were sitting a few tables away with his Uncle John and Aunt Margery. They were already talking about his forthcoming voyage and education, although he was not quite sure why this was provoking laughter. They asked him about snow, and he was pleased to explain it all over again, and to demonstrate how people skated.

"I saw snow once", claimed his Uncle John. "Up high in the Blue Mountains of Jamaica."

"What on earth were you doing in the mountains?" asked his wife.

"Well George Fox had a vision on Pendle Hill, wherever that is, so I thought I'd climb those mountains and converse with our Lord myself. But He wasn't there and it got very cold, so I started to come down. Then it started to snow. Just like young John says, big fluffy white bits like cotton, floating gently to the ground."

"Did you skate?"

Uncle John laughed. "No, I came down as quickly as I could. The sun came out, and the whole hillside was white, but by the time I got down it had all melted away. It was so beautiful while it lasted. As good as a vision!"

John saw his uncle quickly pull a bottle from under the table and reinforce his beer with rum. He was already in a jolly mood, and John and Ed found him entertaining when he was like this. Later, he would become morose and withdrawn, but for now he entertained them with his yarns, many of which they already knew by heart. John began to realise that there was a lot that he was going to miss.

Eventually, his father called the twins over and the family and their guest took their leave. As they approached the harbour, they were accosted by Taine, who had been drinking at a waterside bar while waiting to intercept them.

"When are you going to pay me, Lettsom?" was his aggressive opener. The payment in question was for overseeing sugar cultivation at Edward's plantation at Cane Garden Bay. Samuel Taine described himself as a cooper, and indeed if any barrels for wine, rum, sugar or salt beef required repair, he was the man for the job. But few barrels were actually made on Tortola, and Taine plied several trades besides. He grew a little cotton, had a small kitchen plot, and kept a few chickens and hogs. He owned slaves to help him in his work and to hire out to planters needing extra hands. He undertook general carpentry tasks and assisted planters who, like Edward, had no overseers.

Taine now launched into a catalogue of woes about how hard the work at Cane Garden Bay was, how lazy and stupid the workers were, what an unsuitable site it was for sugar anyway, and so on and so on. His language was not the polite dialogue of the Meeting House lunch, but a stream of invective, spiced with words that were uncommon even on Captain Lindow's ship. The terminology used to refer to the captive workers was particularly repulsive. Mary asked him to restrain his language in the presence of John and Ed, but with little effect. Edward reminded him of their agreement to settle up after the harvest. This brought Taine to his main point. As the work was so much harder than he had foreseen, and as the workers were so useless, his payment should be increased. Lettsom refused. Taine persisted. Eventually, Lettsom offered a modest increase and Taine accepted it with exceptionally bad grace. Taine was not yet finished.

"And how do you expect me to get work out of them without beating them?" he asked.

"I've never found that a problem", replied Edward. "The Quaker way is encouragement through fair treatment and rewards for hard work. I've always found they respond well. No physical chastisement is needed." This evoked a sneer from Taine, spitting on the ground to express his contempt for the notion. Both men knew that physical abuse, of the sort that left little in the way of external marks, would continue.

"And when are the half-breeds coming home?" This was a reference to Sam and Teresa. "I bet you're just getting free labour from my children and not teaching them anything. I'll come and check on them soon." With that, Taine slouched off back to his rum.

"What an unpleasant man", said the captain when Taine was out of earshot.

"Yes, but there's very little choice when it comes to hiring help", responded Edward.

"He's coarse, that's for sure", admitted Mary, "but he does get the work done. We can't expect everyone to live up to our standards."

"Will he really come and take Sam and Teresa away?" asked John, anxiously. "They weren't happy when they lived with him."

"Well, he is their father", replied Edward curtly.

CHAPTER 3

Superficially, life on Little Jost van Dyke returned to normal once Captain Lindow departed. Ed, Sam and Teresa were cool towards John for a few days, but couldn't keep it up. They even began to show an interest in his plans, and to speculate on what he might find in England. Teresa was concerned about his voyage. Her understanding of crossing the Atlantic was gained from her grandmother who had come across thirty years before in very different circumstances.

"Grandma said it was horrible! The men were all chained up, and everyone was crammed together. People were thrown overboard. Some jumped into the sea and drowned. Everyone was sick. How could you want to make a journey like that?"

Sam understood that the crossing would be different for a white boy. He had watched ships dock in Road Harbour and seen sailors climbing to the tops of the masts, heaving on the ropes and controlling the sails as they left the harbour and disappeared over the horizon.

"Will they let you climb the rigging? Sit at the top of the masts and watch the islands go by? See the dolphins and the whales? I'd love to do that."

Ed's main pre-occupation was with school. Spending all day learning to read, write and add up. He was the only one of the four who could not yet recite the alphabet or add up any but the simplest numbers.

"Uncle John says they all sit in rows doing sums all day, or copying out verses from the Bible. If you make a mistake, or talk to anyone, or don't scrub your face, then they beat you with a stick."

Before, time had had no meaning. The sunny days came and went, and it seemed as if they always would, with games and laughter interspersed with light chores that never got them down and short lessons that only Ed hated. But now, there was an end in sight. Captain Lindow had said that it would take him six or seven weeks to continue his voyage to Jamaica, complete his business there, and then return to collect John. It was now clear that Sam and Teresa would then have to return to live with their father. Ed would be left on his own. They all began to realise that they must make the most of the disappearing days that remained.

When John went off with Ed, they now sought more challenging quarry to hunt. Turtles and pigeons were easy to trap and kill, and they never fought back. But amongst the undergrowth and up in the trees lived racer snakes, up to three feet long, brown in colour, and vicious. When cornered, they would rear up and strike at a person, inflicting a venomous bite. Slaves would run from them. Planters would beat them to death. Such a creature would make a worthy adversary for their last hunt together.

Someone, probably Uncle John, had told the twins how he used to catch a snake. You need a long stick with a loop of thin rope protruding from the end. Just slip the loop over the snake's head, and pull it tight. This had been explained, but not demonstrated. Their father's shed held pieces of wood for every conceivable purpose, and ropes of varying widths for use in his vegetable garden and for his shallop. The boys had already been taught how to handle knives safely and how to tie some basic knots, so it didn't take them long to construct a "snake catcher" as they called it. Then off to the quiet far end of the island, where they might find a victim, out of sight of their mother or other observers.

For three afternoons, they searched and searched. They were sure that they had seen snakes in the area every time they had been there before, but now there was none. On the fourth attempt they were luckier, but they did begin to understand why they were called racer snakes. One quick sighting and they were off into the deep undergrowth. Then at last, just before sunset, the boys came across a fine specimen basking in the light of the evening sun at the centre of a clearing.

"I'll creep up behind it", whispered John, who was carrying the snake catcher. Then you step in front. When it rears up I'll slip the loop over its head."

This was the plan that they had had from the outset, but now it seemed rather scarier. John successfully crept around behind the snake without disturbing it, and raised the snake catcher. Ed stepped out in front of it, and the snake reared up ready to strike. Down came the loop, right over the snake's head as intended. But John lowered it too far, and was too slow in pulling the rope tight. The snake shot up and through the loop and slithered away from them. Instinctively Ed jumped and landed with his feet on top of the creature. Before it could raise its head, John was standing on that. Ed was carrying the knife, and he stooped and with some effort separated the head from the body. John kicked the head away, and they both surveyed their trophy: the scaly brown body of the snake, about two feet long.

"I'm going to keep this for as long as you're away", promised Ed. "I'll hide it under my bed, where mother won't find it." They ran down to the nearest beach to wash their prize, which was only slightly damaged by the struggle, and then home. Ed hid the body within his shirt as he slipped past their mother and into the bedroom. The next day, they showed it to Sam and Teresa. John demonstrated the snake catcher, and explained how he had caught the snake by looping the rope over its head. Teresa thought it a very brave thing to do.

*

Sam's longing to sail with John to England was eventually channelled into one ultimate maritime ambition – to build a large raft and take John over the ocean himself. During the few days it took for him to develop this project, he revised its scope downwards several times. Eventually, he decided that while Little Jost would play the role of itself, the role of England would have to be played by Green Cay – the tiny island about a hundred yards east of Little Jost. Nevertheless, this was to be the first time that the boys attempted a crossing to another island.

They stole away at dawn one fine sunny day when the sea was calm, carrying bags full of raft-making equipment and food and drink for the voyage. A busy morning on the easternmost shore of their island culminated in the creation of a fine and sturdy craft, and by lunchtime they had safely landed in England, which was fortunately completely deserted that day. They discovered Lancaster, Pendle Hill and London before setting off for home. This was when Sam nearly lost John. He underestimated the current pulling their craft northwards and overshot the gentle southern flank of Little Jost.

Now the boys' furious paddling was taking them to the shore, but to the sharp black rocks of the northern coast. For half an hour they struggled as the sea swell repeatedly pushed their vessel away from the land, until at last a huge wave hurled the raft against a cliff, smashing it into pieces and depositing its crew into the foam. They were very lucky that day. Both were swept towards a tiny pebble beach up which they were able to scramble to safety. After a few minutes they were able to stop trembling, and after several more John was able to thank his captain for a successful expedition and explain that he had never doubted their safe return.

*

Teresa wanted to spend time with John collecting shells. They had the same ideas about which were the prettiest and the most impressive. Teresa already had an extensive collection of conch shells. When they found a live shell, she and John would make a hole in the sharp end to break the vacuum, and then tap out the raw flesh: a delicacy for which they had acquired a taste. They would clean inside the shell and admire its beautiful pink interior. John's father had taught them how to shape the hole into a mouthpiece and blow into the shell to produce a mournful sound that could be heard across the island, the note being varied by inserting and removing a hand inside the shell. Their lungs were not yet strong enough to produce a consistent blast, but they enjoyed the softer sounds that they were able to make.

Now Teresa's quest was to find the perfect triton shell. One with intricate colourful patterns and without any blemishes. They set off along the southern beaches to search.

"I want my last shell to be the prettiest on the island", she said.

"The prettiest in the Caribbean."

"The prettiest in the whole world!"

Then John picked up on the important part of her statement. "Why your *last* shell?"

"Oh, I won't be doing this when you're gone. I'll be back with Mr Taine. I'll be his slave. I'll be tidying his house, digging his garden, cleaning his pig-sty!" Now the tears started. Her tears. His tears. She was inconsolable. He felt helpless, and guilty. They hugged each other tight and then she broke away. They continued along the shore in silence.

Then suddenly: "This is the one!" Triumphantly, Teresa held aloft a large, brilliantly patterned triton shell. They examined it together. It was perfect: not a mark or a chip. John took it in order to make a hole to release the vacuum and pop out the creature inside.

"No!" cried Teresa. "Don't make a hole there. I'll dig out the snail from the big end. Then we can make this into a lamp for your mother. She can pour oil in and light it every night until you come home." John went back to the shore and came back with three pieces of driftwood about nine inches long.

"I'll lash these together with string to make a stand", he said, demonstrating what the finished product would be like.

They carried the parts for their present carefully back home and hid them away.

*

Time passed. The Lettsoms attended more Meetings for Worship at Fat Hog Bay. Mr Pickering spoke to young John about school, and how important it would be for him to make the most of it. He stressed the importance of keeping his faith, and gave him a Bible to take with him. Samuel Nottingham had actually been to school himself, and told John of the discipline needed for study and of the punishments inflicted on those who fell behind. Nevertheless, he stressed that it was worthwhile in the end as it helped in understanding God's teachings and God's will. He warned John about the perils of sailing across the ocean, and told him of storms and attacks by pirates.

After that, it was good to talk to his Uncle John, who dismissed the boy's new found concerns about the voyage. John was already used to storms and gales, and Captain Lindow could easily negotiate bad weather. He could also use his superior seamanship to evade attacks from pirates, even though – as his employers were Quakers – he carried no guns or weapons on his ship. John would have splendid adventures, make his fortune, and return home an educated, wealthy gentleman.

Time passed. Mary taught John how to write his name. First, "John". Then, "John Lettsom". Finally, to show off, the full "John Coakley Lettsom". "Coakley" was Mary's maiden name, the name her forefathers had brought with them from Ireland. Teresa laughed at John for having so many names. She was just "Teresa", and she had been able to write that for months already. Mary told her that she was actually, "Teresa Taine", but the little girl was not interested in trying to write that out.

Edward passed on his geographical knowledge of the other side of the Atlantic Ocean, explaining the shape of the British Isles, where England, Scotland and Ireland lay, and the positions of London and Lancaster. He was vaguer about Europe and the locations of France and Spain, and even more hazy about the position and shape of Africa. But he was confident where to find Bethlehem, Nazareth and Jerusalem.

Time passed. The sixth birthday of John and Ed was celebrated with a party, attended by his Uncle John, Aunt Margery and his cousins from Tortola. Much food was consumed, sweet drinks were enjoyed, and competitive games were played. Uncle John was not content with sugar juice, and sought out Edward's rum supply. The games proved rather boisterous for the visiting children, with the home team of John, Ed, Sam and Teresa outrunning, outthrowing and outwrestling their opponents. The visitors left in some disarray. Uncle John rather tipsy, and sulking after a dressing down from Mary Lettsom. His children in tears having lost all of the games, bearing grazes and bruises, and swearing never to visit again. But Aunt Margery had had a splendid time, gossiping with Mary about other Friends and sharing tips about cooking and making clothes.

*

News of Captain Lindow's progress in Jamaica filtered back to Little Jost van Dyke. Every ship's crew calling at Road Harbour seemed to know something about the whereabouts of the *Abigail.* Either they had been to Jamaica themselves, or met with a ship that had, or received their information via a longer chain. The Lettsoms were updated when they went over to Tortola for Meetings or business, or by anyone passing by from the main island. Stories arrived in a jumbled order: difficulties in repairing the ship in Jamaica were reported before tales came in of incidents on the voyage to get there. Eventually, a reliable forecast was given that Lindow would arrive back at Road Town the very next day.

The news made a deep impression on everyone on Little Jost. What had been an event that belonged to the distant future was suddenly just around the corner. John's excitement reached fever pitch – everyone else began to prepare themselves for life without him. His mother helped him pack for the journey: just the few good clothes that he possessed, his favourite knife, some letters of introduction from his father and from Mr Pickering as a senior member of the local Friends, and some mementos – feathers from a dove that he and Ed had killed, a small wooden boat carved by Sam, and half a dozen shells collected with Teresa. That afternoon, Rosett caught him alone and told him he must go to the slave village after dark. They were preparing something special for him.

John was familiar with the slave village, and had been made welcome there and given tasty treats whenever he visited. But he had never been there at night. His parents had never forbidden him to do so, but he had always assumed it would be wrong. However, this time, he was determined to go. Rosett had been very insistent.

That evening, as they prepared for bed, John told his friends of his invitation and asked whether they wanted to join him. Ed said that they shouldn't go as they would get into trouble. Sam was being moody and predicted they would be given revolting food and have to watch people shuffling around doing boring dances for hours. Teresa was the only one up for it, and seemed pleased at the prospect of it being just the two of them on this special night.

After he heard his parents go to bed, John waited to give them time to get to sleep. Then he got up quietly, found Teresa had been observing him and was ready, and the two of them crept past the adults' room and out into the warm night. Hand-in-hand, they negotiated the short path, and as soon as they rounded the corner taking them out of sight of the house, they saw that a torch had been lit to guide them. Round another bend, they saw the village, with a large fire burning in front of the cabins and about two dozen people sitting silently around in a semi-circle on the ground. Rosett rose to greet them and guide them to a space at the centre of the semi-circle, right at the front. Everyone welcomed them, in a variety of accents and languages.

Once they were settled, the oldest of the slaves, whom John knew was called Cudjoe, rose and stood before them. He spoke in a clear voice for several minutes, but in a language they did not understand. Then he called to two of the women, who approached the children and presented each with a full cup to drink from and a plate of food. Rosett explained that Cudjoe had welcomed them as special guests to join their community for the evening, and that they should express their gratitude and sample the refreshments. John stood and thanked Cudjoe on behalf of both of them, and offered his hand which the older man solemnly shook.

He sat down again, and sipped at the drink. It was sweet, strong, and undoubtedly alcoholic. He looked at the food, and saw fish, shellfish and pieces of chicken. Taking a piece of the last of these, he started as its spiciness overwhelmed him. After the shock subsided, he proclaimed the food to be good and gave Cudjoe a great beaming smile. Upon that signal, drums began to beat, and the sound of stringed instruments was heard. Food and drink was distributed to everyone, and people began to sing.

Rosett explained that the songs were in many African tongues. Most of the people in the village did not understand more than one of the languages and some understood none, but they learnt the sounds of the songs by heart and had been told what most of them meant. Every time new people came to work on the island, they brought new songs, either directly from Africa, or from other islands. Many songs would have deep religious meaning back home, and some would be reserved for priests or holy men, but here they were sung for pleasure and as a link with "home". John and Teresa were taught the words of a couple of simple, repetitive songs, and joined in to great acclaim.

Then singing moved on to dancing, and then to singing and dancing. The dances also came from Africa, with modifications and refinements on the way. At first, John and Teresa just watched the bodies moving to the music, illuminated by the light of the fire. Music, singing, and especially dancing, had no place in Quaker tradition. Indeed they were frowned upon, and so John had no experience of rhythm and coordinated movement. Eventually, however, the children became bolder, helped no doubt by what they had been drinking, and joined the dance. Their hosts beamed great smiles, corrected their moves and encouraged them to lose themselves to the beat.

Eventually, the music stopped, and Cudjoe gave a great cry. Everyone sat down again. Cups were refilled with drink. Cudjoe gave another speech. Rosett smiled at John, and explained that this was what he had been invited for. A special song and dance had been composed in his honour, to wish him good fortune in his travels. Cudjoe sang the song solo to begin with. It was simple and repetitive, but somehow distinct from what had gone before.

"The words mean: May this young man travel safely across the sea towards the rising of the sun", translated Rosett. "May he prosper in the land that we came from. And may he return and take us with him, back towards the rising sun to the land we came from." John and Teresa learnt the African words, and recited them back to Rosett. Once they had got most of them right, the music started again, and everyone joined in the song. Then they all rose, and performed the dance that went with the words.

John and Cudjoe moved like a ship towards the east. After some swaying, they returned to the fire and motioned the rest of the people to join them. Then they led everyone towards the east. Back to Africa. Then they returned and repeated the steps. Again and again, with the music going faster and faster and the words getting louder and louder. Finally, Cudjoe stopped. Everyone was safely in Africa for the last time. He raised John in the air, and said some words that amounted to a blessing. Rosett told them that the evening was now complete, and that they should return to the house. He saw her tears as he kissed her goodnight.

"I'll do it", he told Rosett and Cudjoe. "When I've made my fortune in England, I'll come back and take you all to Africa!"

Then he and Teresa ran off back to the house. Creeping up to the door, only Teresa noticed Edward, standing under the tamarind trees smoking a clay pipe and checking they had got back safely.

CHAPTER 4

The next morning seemed the same as any other morning. The children got up, ate breakfast, and got on with their chores. Teresa was helping Mary wash sheets and clothes, and John and Ed were working with their father making repairs to his shallop. The conversation was strangely normal, focussing on the jobs at hand. So it continued until shortly after midday, when the semblance of routine was shattered by the arrival of Captain Lindow. This was no ordinary day.

The captain had sailed over in a small boat with two of his crewmen.

"Time for some lunch!" Mary announced, once they had greeted the captain and exchanged the headlines of their respective news, and she invited the two sailors to join them. A table was prepared outside, and Rosett and Mary attended to the goat stew which had been simmering in the kitchen.

"Where's Sam?" asked Teresa. He was not with them, although even the idea of food, let alone the delicious smell of this stew, usually brought him running to the table.

"He was feeding the chickens", suggested John.

"He's gone to check on the goats", volunteered Ed.

"I thought he was keeping a lookout for the captain", was Edward's recollection.

"Well, I'm sure he'll turn up soon", said Mary. "Get the stew while it's hot, and I'll put some aside for him."

But Sam did not return, and when they had finished their meal, the children were sent off to look for him. Teresa searched the house and the area round about, and went to the slave village to see if he was there or if anyone had seen him. Ed climbed up to Lookout Point and continued to Pirate Hill, using the viewpoints to scour the island for traces of Sam. John took to the southern coastline to Sandy Beach and then crossed the island to check on Rocky Harbour. They all returned to report failure. Not a trace of Sam.

The sailors had already set off back to Tortola to help complete loading the *Abigail* with supplies. The plan was for Lindow to spend the night with the Lettsoms, and for the sailors to return first thing in the morning to take him and John to the ship. It was intended to be a jolly last evening for John and a relaxing break for the captain. But now, everyone was anxious.

"Let's try again", said Edward. "This time Rosett and Teresa will search the house, the surrounding area, and down to the village. I'll go with Ed back up the hills, and Captain Lindow, could you accompany John along the south coast and beaches? Mary should stay here and call out if Sam returns." The searchers were slower and more thorough this time, the adults pressing the children to identify all their favourite haunts and secret hiding places. They called out Sam's name, and looked into ditches and gullies, and down from the steep cliffs of the northern coast. It was evening by the time they returned to share their reports: no trace of Sam. Back at the house, they found another visitor. Accompanied by two of his slaves and two large dogs, Samuel Taine had arrived.

"I heard from 'is sailors you've lost my property!" he started, poking a thumb towards Lindow, whose men he had met at Road Harbour. "Well now I've brought my dogs. Good at catching runaways, they are. You'll pay me good if he doesn't turn up. And I'll take him home and give him a thrashing if he does."

At this, Teresa burst into tears.

"I'll take her back too. You've been spoiling these kids, Lettsom. About time they earned their keep."

*

As it was already getting dark, it was decided to defer the next search until first light. Mary and Rosett prepared another meal, and then a bed was found for Taine: his slaves and dogs slept outside. Before dawn, Edward recruited the help of some of his own workers, led by Cudjoe. Together with Lindow, Taine and his slaves and dogs, and John and Ed, they set off at first light to the far eastern point of the island. Mary, Teresa and Rosett stayed behind, still hoping for Sam to appear from some nearby hiding place. Once at the eastern cape of Little Jost, the searchers turned around and began to work their way westwards, forming a line right across the island and proceeding cautiously and methodically. Once more they called Sam's name as they went. The dogs strained forward on leashes held by Taine's slaves, sometimes barking at snakes or pigeons.

Although the cotton plants were still green and low so that the fields were easy to search, progress through the wilderness areas was slow. Some of the searchers were not following trails this time but using machetes to hack their way through undergrowth or else scrambling over bare rocks. Eventually, the line began to converge as they came within sight of the western shore of the island.

Down by the beach was a small stone structure: a salt tank where a stone wall had been built to augment a natural depression in the rock and form a shallow pool. It would fill at high tide, and then evaporate in the sun to provide salt for cooking. One of the dogs pulled its handler in that direction, and began to growl. The handler was soon running towards the tank, and suddenly a small boy shot out from behind the wall and ran across the sand towards the sea.

Taine called for the dogs to be released, but Lindow authoritatively countermanded that order. Slipping off his boots and shirt, the captain made straight for the waves. By then, Sam was in the water, wading over the sandy causeway that linked the Little island to Jost van Dyke itself. A grown man could easily wade across between the islands at any time of day but for a six-year-old boy, with the tide coming in, this was infeasible. Before long, a large wave knocked him off his feet and away from the shallows.

Now Lindow launched himself into the deeper water and swam with a tidy and powerful stroke to head him off. The watchers held their breath. Sam disappeared below the surface, and the captain dived down too. Seconds turned to minutes, although to the observers on the shore it seemed like an eternity. At last the captain re-emerged on the surface, swimming on his back and holding Sam above the water on his chest. They made it to a beach on the opposite shore, and crawled up to safety above the high water mark. The captain pushed at the boy's chest, forcing water out of his lungs. As Sam recovered, Lindow waved vigorously to the watchers on the opposite shore, who waved and shouted in relief and celebration. This was repeated when they saw Sam himself return a rather feeble wave.

After a short rest, Lindow hoisted the boy onto his shoulders and waded safely across, setting him down carefully on the sand. Edward took a careful look at him. No bones broken. A few shallow scars from brushing against rocks and cacti. A look of fear and exhaustion, but no physical injury.

John ran forward and embraced his friend.

"I'm so scared!" whispered Sam. "You're leaving. Teresa and I will be back with that man. It's over for us. Please, please come back and take me with you to England."

"I will, I promise," pledged John.

Now Taine strode up to the boys and roughly lifted Sam onto his back, hurting him and causing him to cry out.

"I'll take him off your hands, Lettsom," he said, "and I'll be back for the other one shortly."

With that, he was off, accompanied by his slaves and his dogs. They did not stop at the house, but went straight down to the jetty where they had left their boat the night before. The others watched as they pushed off and started to sail back to Tortola. It was a subdued party that returned to the Lettsom house. The captain was praised for his strength and bravery, the slaves were thanked for their help, and Ed and John were complimented for their knowledge of the island's maze of paths. But there was no joy in returning without the one whom they had been seeking.

"Time to go now, young man", said Captain Lindow, almost as soon as they had told their story. His sailors had landed at the jetty just as Taine and his party had been pushing away from it. Edward shook John's hand, depositing in it a golden half-guinea. Mary hugged her son tightly, kissed his forehead, and promised to light her new triton shell lamp every night until he returned. Ed wrestled with him and the brothers pretended to box. Finally, Teresa ran down to the beach and gave John a great big hug and a kiss on his cheek.

"Come back and marry me!" she pleaded.

"I will, I promise," he said, giving his third solemn undertaking in two days.

With that, they were off, waving, waving, waving until the sailors steered the boat around a headland, and John's adventure started in earnest.

CHAPTER 5

It was one of those gloriously sunny, crisp, and bitterly cold January days when the *Abigail* entered the Lune estuary. High up on the main mast, John sat with Captain Lindow, surveying the scene. He was wrapped up snugly in warm clothes Lindow had brought out for his arrival in Lancashire, with a bright red knitted cap on his head and thick woollen gloves protecting his hands. Formerly property of young Abigail Rawlinson, who had long grown out of them.

"Up there to the north are the Furness Fells, and the big hill to the northeast, that's Ingleborough in Yorkshire", explained the captain.

"And the tops are all white! Is that snow?" asked the boy, excitedly.

"It certainly is", came the reply. "Those mountains are over two thousand feet high. There's usually snow up there in winter. But I'm pretty sure you'll be seeing it down in Lancaster soon."

"Ooh! I can't wait!"

"The great stretch of water to the north is Morecambe Bay. The tide's in now, but when it goes out there's vast stretches of sand and mud. Coaches drive straight across but it's treacherous: if you lose the path you can get stuck in quicksand and drown. On the far side of the bay, you can just see the town of Ulverston where I was born. Nearby is Swarthmore, where George Fox met Margaret Fell and they started one of the first Meeting Houses."

"Where's Pendle Hill?" asked John.

"Ah, where Fox had his vision. That's south of Ingleborough, hidden behind the Bowland Fells to the southeast." Lindow pointed to a darker range of hills below the snow line.

John drank in the magnificent scenery, its strangeness softened by its association with familiar stories from his faith.

"Over there", continued the captain, "is Lancaster Castle. George Fox and Margaret Fell were imprisoned there about a hundred years ago."

"What had they done wrong?"

"Nothing! You don't have to do anything wrong to end up in prison. Back then your religion was banned. So they were imprisoned just because they were Quakers."

John surveyed the view one last time, and then descended with the Captain who needed to supervise their landing at St George's Quay.

*

After disembarking, John was sent with one of the sailors to make the short walk into town and to Abraham Rawlinson's imposing house on Church Street. A smart looking footman answered the door, dressed in livery and wearing a wig. In Tortola, only the Lieutenant Governor wore a wig, and so John addressed him as "Mr Rawlinson". He was soon put right, and led into a small, cold room where he could wait. There he sat, with his small bag of belongings by his side and his letters of introduction in his hand. The afternoon wore on, and he fell asleep.

"Who's this strange looking boy, wearing my old hat?" exclaimed a high-pitched voice in his ear, waking him up with a start. "Ugh, he's so dirty!" continued Abigail, "don't you ever wash?"

This was a fair point. Washing facilities had been very limited onboard, and were never the priority of small boys anyway. She was ten-years old, fair, pretty and pampered.

"He'll be the colonial Lindow's brought to be educated", replied her brother Henry. Eighteen months older than John, but no taller, he was a pale, serious looking boy. "Have you brought us some rum?"

Now a servant came in to take the children to the kitchen for their tea. Surprised to see John there with them, she asked whether they would like "their friend" to join them.

"He's not our friend", explained Abigail. "He's waiting to see father."

"Well, I'm sure he'd like some tea."

John introduced himself to the servant, who smiled at him and said that she was called Molly. The kitchen was warm, which prompted John to take off his hat and coat, and the other children to hold their noses and complain of the smell. Although there was plenty to eat and drink, they suggested that there was hardly enough to go round, and only through Molly's kind intervention did John get his fair share.

"So, how many slaves does your father own?" asked Henry.

"Fifty", replied John. Captain Lindow had discussed this answer with him during his voyage. He had explained that Englishmen look down on West Indians because they live out in the colonies, but they are polite to them because they are rich. They imagine that every West Indian settler owns hundreds of slaves and acres of plantation and lives a life of idle pleasure. If they believe that you are both West Indian and poor, then they won't give you a second thought. Lindow felt that saying that his father owned about thirty slaves, that is telling the truth, would do the boy no good. A hundred or so would gain respect. John could exaggerate, and he could even lie when necessary, but he felt unable to invent a complete home life consistent with his father having a hundred slaves. So they settled on fifty. The answer did not impress Henry, but it was enough to avoid scorn.

"How did you enjoy sailing on my ship?" asked Abigail. "And did my Bill sail her well?"

John had never heard the Captain referred to as "Bill" before, but he was able to give answers to both questions that were at once true and pleasing to the questioner.

As soon as the food was consumed, Abigail and Henry shot out of the room to play in other parts of the house. John was left with Molly.

"Shall I go back to the waiting room?" he asked.

"No. Mr Rawlinson won't be home for a while yet. Stay here with me by the fire, and when I've cleared up I'll go and find out where you're to sleep."

Despite Molly's protestations, she could not overcome John's instincts to help with the washing up and tidying away. He told her of his home and his voyage, and listened as she talked about her home in Ireland. Then she took him upstairs to a small bedroom at the back of the house and brought him a washing bowl and a jug of warm water. Later, she returned with a pile of winter clothes that Henry and his cousin Abraham had grown out of.

*

John awoke late the following morning. Drawing his curtains, he saw the garden of the house sloping down towards the River Lune, and a wide green grassy area he was later told was called the Green Ayre. To his right, he could see feverish activity at the shipbuilding yard that occupied part of this plain. To his left was the bridge over the river, leading to open fields and farms beyond.

Mrs Ellin Rawlinson had come home from visiting her sister in town soon after John had had his tea. Molly had taken him in to see her, and she gave him a brief greeting before saying that she was tired and needed to lie down. Afterwards, prompted by John's questions, Molly explained that Mrs Rawlinson was pregnant, and would be having a baby in the spring. It had been agreed that John need not wait up for Mr Rawlinson, who would be late back from his business trip to Liverpool.

So it was mid-morning, after Molly had fed him a hearty breakfast, that he nervously approached the study door of Mr Abraham Rawlinson. On knocking, he heard a loud call for him to enter, which he did to find himself confronted by a large, heavy man with a red face, wearing a brown jacket and a grey wig, seated behind a very large desk. His size and demeanour did nothing to calm John's nerves.

"You must be Master Lettsom", said the man.

"Yes, Sir", replied John, his hands shaking as he handed over the letters from his father and John Pickering. Rawlinson took them, and spent a while reading them. This gave John time to surreptitiously survey the room, the shelves filled with books, ledgers and papers, and the walls covered with charts, maps and lists relating to works in progress. There was a telescope by the window, through which the progress of ships at the docks could be observed. Nothing was there for ornamentation or distraction. Finally, the older man looked up and handed the letters back to John.

"I can see this working very well," he said. "You will attend the Meeting House School here with Henry, Abigail and their cousin Abraham. Abraham lives here during the school term, and you will too. You're lucky to have such excellent schoolmates. It's a fine school. The master is very pious and very strict. Your father has arranged for the payment of the fees for your first term, which starts next week. Any questions?"

John had none: he just wanted to get out of that room.

“Well, I hope you like Lancaster. I lived for some years in Barbados. Too hot, and far too many Africans. You’ll find Lancaster far more agreeable.”

Just then, there was another knock on the door. In strode Captain Lindow.

“And good morning, John,” he said with a smile, after exchanging greetings with his employer. “I trust you slept well. Would you like to see something of Lancaster? I’ve some business to attend to and I could take you round with me. Would that be alright, Sir?”

Rawlinson grunted his assent and so a few minutes later, feeling much calmer, John met Lindow at the front door and off they went to explore.

*

John had never seen a town as big as Lancaster, nor one so solidly built. The huge, tall stone houses of Church Street looked as if they would survive the strongest Caribbean gale, while the castle seemed to be a veritable mountain in itself. He loved watching the carriages speed through the streets, pulled by one, two, or even four sleek, shiny horses. He had never seen such vehicles before: Little Jost was too small for anyone to need one, and Tortola was so mountainous that there was scarcely a quarter of a mile of straight level road to be found.

Lindow gave the boy a running commentary as he called on the merchants and craftsmen he needed to see. He pointed out the house in Church Street, where Bonnie Prince Charlie had stayed just five years earlier on his march south. He paused to let John inspect the vegetable gardens and chicken runs that could still be found on their route, and lamented the replacement of so many of them by houses, offices and workshops due to the town’s rapid expansion. He stopped to assess the progress of the construction work close to the river, including foundations for a new church, and questioned the wisdom of building on part of the river's flood plain.

They called at the Sugar House on St Leonard's Gate to check that the cargo from Little Jost had been delivered from the Quay. The sweet, sickly smell was familiar to John from similar refineries around Road Town. In Pudding Lane, the captain sought out a candle maker whose wares he had sold in Jamaica. Then to Gillows' furniture workshop below the castle walls to settle up for the mahogany he had traded.

Finally, they walked around the Castle, past St Mary's Church, and down a steep path to the Quayside where the captain went to inspect the completion of the unloading of the *Abigail.*

"How do you like the girl after whom our ship was named?"

"Very pretty, very bossy!"

"So you didn't care too much for her then."

On the quay and on the ships, John could see that only a few of the dockers and some of the sailors had dark skins.

"Why are there so few slaves?" he asked.

"There's very few slaves here in England. Even the black people here – many of them will be free men, taken on directly in Africa or else freed in the West Indies and gone to sea to get away from the plantations. There's a few slaves working as domestic servants in the big houses, but none working in the fields like they do where you come from. It's strange. Lancaster's being built on slavery. Many of these ships sail from here out to Africa, taking iron goods from Furness. They exchange them for slaves they take out to your part of the world, and then they come back again with sugar, cotton and mahogany. But very rarely do any slaves get to see the town they're building."

"Do Mr Rawlinson's ships go out to Africa to bring over slaves?"

"Yes. Both Mr Rawlinson and his brother, Mr Thomas Hutton Rawlinson. They both operate from Liverpool."

"Does that make them apostates?"

Lindow was amused that John had remembered that word. "Well, it's tolerated by the Society. More tricky is that their ships carry guns in case of attack. That's against your Quaker teachings on non-violence. Maybe that's why they keep out of sight and don't operate from here."

John spent the rest of the day indoors. The weather had deteriorated, and a cold wind was blowing rain horizontally down the streets and over the fields. A fire was lit in the children's playroom, although the Rawlinson children were not for playing. Abigail was concentrating on some intricate embroidery and Henry was reading about the early Quaker missionaries, known as "The Valiant Sixty", from a book provided by the school for study over the winter break. Henry explained to John, at some length, that his great-grand father Thomas Rawlinson had been one of the Valiant Sixty, spreading the Quaker word with George Fox soon after the Society was founded.

John knew that Mary Fisher and Ann Austin, who had brought the faith to the Caribbean, had also been amongst the Sixty, and so he asked how far old Thomas had taken it. John was unimpressed when Henry looked this up and found that he had got as far as Devon, and had only been imprisoned a couple of times. He was jubilant when Henry found and reluctantly read out the passage relating that, after founding a Meeting House in Barbados, Mary Fisher had sailed on and been imprisoned and almost starved to death in Massachusetts and then some years later had travelled alone to Turkey to spread the faith and been granted an audience with the Sultan. This, of course led to a fight between the boys concerning who had been the greater missionary, in which John (justifiably) prevailed. Abigail got on with her embroidery, oblivious of the argument and the disturbance, and showed no interest in conversation.

*

"Right now, John should be landing in Lancaster", whispered Teresa.

On Tortola, she and Sam huddled together on the bed they shared, talking quietly while listening out for Taine's snoring. Should that sound stop, they would immediately lie down silently hoping not to disturb him nor give him any reason to enter their tiny room.

A week after John's departure, Taine had sent a man over to bring Teresa home. She had found Sam hungry, exhausted and terrorised by his father. He had been put to work in Taine's cotton field, alongside two of his slaves who seemed oblivious that he was just a child and exploited his efforts to give themselves a bit of a break. Teresa's role was to help Grandma in the house, with the vegetable plot, with the chickens and – as she had predicted to John – with the pigs. The dogs were still there, and they seemed even bigger than before.

Teresa felt crushed by her change of fortune. During the early weeks, both she and her brother went to bed exhausted, usually hungry, and cried themselves to sleep. That was if the barking of the dogs, the snoring of their father, or the sounds of him drinking and playing cards with his friends or enjoying the company of one of his female companions did not keep them awake all night. In time, however, they became tougher. They coped better with the physical toil and they learnt how to skive off, which was not so difficult with such a disorganised master. They took advantage of extra food stolen from the garden or scrounged from neighbours when they were sent on errands.

They also discovered their golden hour – the time when, on some nights, Taine would fall deeply asleep and they could snuggle together and whisper to each other. They could even laugh together, provided they did so silently. Much of that time they spent talking about Little Jost, of Edward and Mary Lettsom, of Ed and of John. Mostly of John. Where would he be now? What would he be doing? Climbing the rigging, watching the dolphins, looking out for pirates? And then, according to Teresa's calculations, arriving in that fantastic far-off country called England, in that wonderful, dazzling town known as Lancaster. She was only out by one day. John was now fast asleep after his tour of the port, refreshing his strength for the adventures of his third day in England. He was dreaming of carriages, Mary Fisher, the workshops of Lancaster, Captain Lindow, and of Abigail. He was not dreaming of home, of his parents and brother, nor even of his old friends Sam and Teresa.

CHAPTER 6

Next morning John learnt from Molly that a carriage would be going to Caton after lunch. It was being sent to Thomas Hutton Rawlinson's House to bring his son Abraham to Lancaster to settle in ahead of the re-opening of school the following week. Wanting to ride in a carriage, and to get away from Abigail and Henry, he asked if he could go along. His host couldn't understand why he might want to, but nevertheless gave his permission. John sat up top next to the driver as they swept through the town and along the Lune valley.

Two smart horses kept up a lively speed as ever changing views of woods, fields and the river flashed by. It was another clear day, but very cold – yet John refused any suggestion that he should travel inside. Instead he took tips from the coachman about how to adjust his clothes to keep out the worst of the wind, and shared a blanket with him to cover his knees. The Lune fascinated John. He had never seen a river before. On Tortola and the smaller islands there were gullies, which became torrents after heavy rain, but they were dry for most of the time. This country seemed so big, the views stretching out over wide green valleys to distant snow-topped hills in every direction. Although the coach driver was very aware of dark clouds coming in from the west, John paid them no attention.

On arrival, the driver took John to the forge, so that he could take a look at the works. Thomas Hutton was not there that day, but his older cousin volunteered to act as John's guide. This man was also named Thomas: no wonder Thomas Hutton always used both his names! He was a solid man of over sixty years with a twinkle in his eye and an easy manner. At last, here was a Rawlinson with whom John could feel at ease.

As they toured the forge, they chatted about the Caribbean and about Lancashire. Thomas exchanged pleasantries with each worker they passed, and asked them to demonstrate their skills for the boy. John was impressed by the furnace, and fascinated by the craftsmen using a hammer and anvil to make tools and decorated ironwork from red hot metal. Amongst the spades, shears, pans, railings and other items ready for dispatch, John noticed the shackles.

"Are those for slaves?"

"Aye son, I'm afraid they are. I don't like us selling them for that purpose myself. And I don't think my cousins should be taking slaves across the Atlantic, which I know they do, even though they slip down to Liverpool to arrange it. My grandfather was with George Fox in the Valiant Sixty, you know. He gave up his inheritance and his property to spread the word. He would be appalled by my cousins. They don't let me go to the Meeting House with them, you know, so I won't tell about the guns they put on their ships."

How could a true Quaker carry guns on his ships? wondered John. And how could he organise the transportation of slaves across the ocean, constrained by those shackles? But how else could his parents find the workers they needed to tend their cotton and sugar? John kept these new and disturbing thoughts to himself as he walked with Thomas the short distance from the works to the entrance to Grassyard Hall, Thomas Hutton's palatial country residence.

As they approached the door of the house, it opened and a chubby boy in his early teens emerged, with a servant running behind him carrying a heavy case. The carriage was in front of the house, and the servant threw the case up to the driver who secured it on the roof. The boy was about to get into the carriage, when Thomas addressed him.

"Master Abraham, this young man is John Lettsom, over here from Tortola. He'll be at school with you next term."

"Ugh." muttered the boy, who climbed inside without further delay.

His mother ran out of the house with a small bag, exclaiming that it contained a few more warm clothes she had packed. This was also secured on the roof of the carriage. She too paid scant attention when introduced to John, and rejected Thomas's suggestion that the journey might be delayed until John had had some tea and cake to keep him going that cold afternoon. Apparently, Abraham had already had his tea, and should set off soon before the gathering clouds led to a change in the weather. John's suggestion of riding with the driver was pooh-poohed as far too dangerous. Thomas told him to get in quickly, otherwise they would leave without him.

The two boys passed the journey in silence, the older one consuming a succession of barley sugars, which he did not offer to share. About half way to Lancaster, it started to snow, and John opened the window and leaned out to feel it falling on his face. At once, he was dragged back inside and the window was slammed shut.

*

It was dark and snowing heavily by the time the coach got back to Church Street. Young Abraham shot out of the coach and into the house, while John paused to thank the coachman and discuss snow and its effect on driving. As the latter took the heavy case to carry into the house, John insisted on carrying the small bag of extra warm clothes.

That evening, as Molly cleared away the last of the dishes from the children's tea, a footman entered the kitchen.

"Mrs Rawlinson is entertaining guests in the drawing room", he announced, "and they would like to meet the children."

"Does that include me?" asked John, and Molly assured him that it would.

The four children were led into a front room, where there was a blazing fire, around which sat Ellin Rawlinson with two unfamiliar visitors. Mr Rawlinson, busy with his papers as usual, had yet to join them for the pre-dinner sherry they were sipping. The visitors were introduced as Auntie Bessie and Mr Samuel Fothergill. Bessie, or Mrs Barnes, was the sister of Abraham senior who had left home to marry, but was now widowed. Mr Fothergill was a regular visitor to the Quaker community in Lancaster, there to preach at the Meeting in the morning. They both lived close together in the south of the county and Samuel had offered Bessie a ride in his carriage up to Lancaster so that she could see her brother: a treat that still awaited her. They appeared to be relaxed, jolly and kind people, and were soon making a fuss of the young Rawlinsons whom they knew very well.

"And who is this new boy?" asked Mr Fothergill, looking at John.

"John Coakley Lettsom, sir, from Little Jost van Dyke island in the Caribbean."

"Why, a West Indian! You've come a long way."

John answered the preacher's questions about his voyage, his family, and the Quakers of Tortola, as best he could. He remembered that his father owned *fifty* slaves, and when asked, asserted that they were well treated.

"Are these Africans happy labouring for your father, then?"

"Well, sometimes they seem very happy. When they sing and dance around the fire."

"What are their dances like?" asked Mrs Barnes.

At this, John started to sing the song and perform the dance that Cudjoe had created in his honour. He was unsure in which direction Africa was, so he decided it would lie towards the bay window. Afterwards, he explained what the words and movements meant, and the adults in his audience applauded. The Rawlinson children immediately started to show off things that they had recently learned, crowding round their Aunt's chair. Mr Fothergill beckoned John closer.

"I think that your father's slaves miss their homeland very much."

"Yes, I think they do."

"I enjoyed seeing you dance", said Mr Fothergill, squeezing a ha'penny coin into the boy's hand. John glowed with pleasure.

Now Mr Rawlinson entered the room, and it all went quiet. Ellin suggested that the children might want to go out to play in the snow for half-an-hour, and asked the footman who was hovering in the hallway to fetch them their coats, hats, scarves and gloves. Obediently, they trooped out of the back door, down the garden and onto the Green Ayre. For John, this truly was a winter wonderland. The snow had eased off, but it had settled deeply on the grass, and – which fascinated him most of all – on the trunks, branches, and even the fine twigs of the trees. Every fence post was topped with a little rectangle of snow. John turned to point out this beauty to his companions when – wham! – he experienced his first snowball. Right in the face. This was from Abigail, but Henry and Abraham threw theirs at him immediately afterwards. He ran from them, towards the river and then along its bank, but they pursued him doggedly. Fortunately, they were not quick runners, and soon he was far enough ahead to stop, scoop up a handful of snow, and experiment with how to form it into a ball. He had one in each hand by the time they caught up with him.

All that bird hunting with Ed now paid off. His first missile went straight into the fat face of Abraham, and the second hit the side of Henry's head, and slithered down his neck. Now it was a matter of making snowballs and throwing them as quickly as possible, holding his ground rather than running away. He quickly overcame any reservations about throwing them at a girl, realising that neutralising Abigail was his top priority as she was the Rawlinson team's best shot. But three-to-one are unfavourable odds in any contest, and before long the Rawlinsons closed in on him and pelted him with snow. As he turned to flee, he slipped on the compressed snow and fell on his face. A final volley of freezing missiles covered him over, and they were off. Back to the warm kitchen for a hot drink before bed, leaving him partly buried in the snow.

Samuel Fothergill had spoken of missing one's homeland. Until now, he suddenly realised, he had hardly thought about home at all. His mind had been filled by the excitement of the present and of all the new wonders of this big, cold land. But now, lying abandoned in the snow, the reality of being four thousand miles from home suddenly struck him. He wanted his mother. He wanted his father. He wanted to be with Ed, Sam and Teresa. How they would have enjoyed playing in the snow. How the Little Jost team would have buried the Rawlinsons! How impressed Teresa would have been with the accuracy of his snowballs! His shoulders heaved, his tears flowed and he emitted a cry of anguish.

He felt a hand on his shoulder, and thinking that his tormentors had returned, he pulled away. But he heard a soft Irish voice of reassurance, and looked up to see Molly bending over him. She held him while he wept, comforted him as he sobbed. She knew all about homesickness. Eventually, his emotions subsided.

"Have you ever made a snowman?" she asked.

When he said that he hadn't, she made out to be surprised. As if she expected that little boys in the West Indies would be making them all the time. So, she showed him how rolling a snowball in the fresh snow made it get bigger, and bigger, and bigger. Eventually, her snowball was so big that she could push it no longer, and she announced that it was the body of the snowman. Then she took John's snowball, and with his help hoisted it on top of the body. By now, other children had gathered round – children wearing raggedy clothing and with dirty faces. Children with smiles, and red cheeks, and happy faces. One took off his cap, and placed it on the snowman's head, another contributed a scarf. They gouged out two eyes, and fashioned a nose out of snow.

Some older youths now turned up, carrying burning torches, which they pushed into the soft snow. One had a fiddle, and he started to play. Molly sang tunefully and expressively. Then they danced around the snowman. John was no longer homesick, no longer lonely. He loved being with these people. This was more like home. But soon, Molly told him it was time to go, and he reluctantly walked back with her, excitedly recalling the parts of the evening that had been his favourites.

*

They entered the house quietly, and Molly promised to make him a hot drink before bed. But, as soon as she closed the front door, a voice boomed out from Mr Rawlinson's study, summoning John inside. The Master sent Molly away and stood over the terrified boy, asking him what on earth he thought he had been doing. Rawlinson had used his telescope to watch the revellers in the light of the torches, singing and dancing around the snowman.

"Why did you not come in with the other children? I saw you out there. Do you not know that dancing around a statue is idolatory? Devil worship? Quakers do not dance. They do not sing. They do not cavort with tinkers and common people. This is very bad, John. You are a visitor here, and you have disgraced us."

"Sorry, Sir", replied John, trembling.

"I don't know what sort of faith you've been following out in the West Indies, amongst the savages. It's not our sort of faith. We are modest, God-fearing, humble and plain. Do you understand? It is not allowed to sing and dance."

"And it's not allowed to put guns on ships."

John did not know where that sentence had come from. It had been absorbed into his consciousness during the last couple of days. As soon as he said it, he knew he shouldn't have. For the second time that evening, he received a sudden blow to his face. Not a snowball this time, but Abraham Rawlinson's clenched fist. John crashed to the floor, bringing down a small table with a teapot and two cups and saucers as he fell.

The noise of John's fall echoed round the silent house, and the door opened as the footman peered in to see what had happened. Behind him, Samuel Fothergill appeared. He entered the room and stooped down to look at John. No serious damage. There would be some bruising in the morning, and he had a bump on his head where he had landed. But he was fully conscious, not bleeding, and no bones had been broken. Samuel had the footman call Molly, and instructed her to take the boy to bed. The study door closed, leaving Abraham and Samuel in deep conversation.

*

In the morning, John found that he had a bruise on his left cheek. Mr Rawlinson had pulled back as his Quaker principles wrestled with his anger, resulting in a moderate blow that had left a clear but modest mark. Molly prepared his breakfast in the kitchen:

it being the First Day, the other children were eating with the family. She examined his face, but nothing was said by either of them about the events of the previous evening, neither those out on the Green Ayre nor those following their return. Once he had finished, she told him to wait, as the Master and Mr Fothergill wished to see him immediately after their breakfast.

The meeting took place back in Mr Rawlinson's study, and Mrs Bessie Barnes was also present so that friendly adults were in the majority. His attacker took a close look at his face, and announced slowly and clearly that snowballs were dangerous, and could cause serious injury. John understood: the line was to be that he had been injured in the snowball fight. Then Mr Fothergill took the floor.

"We've been discussing your education here in Lancashire. As well as the school at the Lancaster Meeting House, there is another Quaker school at Penketh in the south of the county near where both Mrs Barnes and I reside. I have supported it for many years, and provide religious instruction there. Mrs Barnes boards some of the boys in her house. It is run by a Mr Gilbert Thompson who has some very progressive approaches to education."

"Not my idea of teaching", said Mr Rawlinson gruffly, "but some people speak very highly of it. What do you say, my boy?"

So, that was the deal. His bruise was due to one of the snowballs, and his schooling would take place at the other end of the county. Under the direction of Samuel Fothergill and Bessie Barnes, rather than Abraham and Ellin Rawlinson. In the company of boys he was yet to meet, but not with Henry and young Abraham, and not with Abigail. No contest.

"I should like to go to Penketh School very much, sir."

So it was arranged. Mr Fothergill and Mrs Barnes would return by road to arrange matters with Gilbert Thompson, and to prepare a bed for the boy. Then, in a few days time, John would sail with Captain Lindow to Liverpool to be met at the dock and taken to his new home. Fothergill would write to John's father to explain the change of plan. The preacher had already decided to secretly make up from his own pocket the increase in fees required for boarding at the more established school.

*

"I wonder if it's snowing in Lancaster now", said Teresa. She and Sam were standing on the dock in Road Town, looking out to sea. They had been sent down to collect letters and parcels from Antigua that Taine was expecting, but they had to wait as the ship bringing them had only just arrived and was still unloading.

"I bet it is!" replied Sam. "Wouldn't it be wonderful to feel cold? It's so hot today!"

"Do you think we'll ever see him again?"

"It'll be a long time, but one day he'll come sailing into this harbour and take us both to England with him."

"Where we can go to school and learn to write and add up."

"Where we can play in the snow and skate on the ice."

"If he still remembers us."

Sister and brother fell silent and stared into the distance. A shared dream of a better future would unite them. Would sustain them.

Then they saw a small rowing boat from the Antigua ship approaching the Harbour Office, and they ran off to collect Taine's mail: already they would be in trouble for taking so long.

In Lancashire it was not snowing. It was cold with a pervasive drizzle blotting out the view as the *Abigail* transported John around the Fylde coast and into the Mersey estuary.

PART II: 1751–67

Education

CHAPTER 7

"Wouldn't it be great to live on a tropical island?" exclaimed one of the local pupils. "No towns, no schools, no preachers!" Many of the other boys expressed enthusiastic support. The class had just emerged onto Penketh Heath following another lesson spent reading *The Life and Adventures of Robinson Crusoe* by Daniel Defoe.

"I used to live on a tropical island with no towns and no schools", said John. "Out in the West Indies where it's hot and sunny, and you can play outside and swim in the sea every day." His fellow-pupils turned to him, impressed.

"Did you have a Man Friday?" asked one.

John thought about that for a moment. Anxious to reinforce the respect he had just gained, he replied: "Yes, my very own black servant, who made boats for me and sailed me over to other islands whenever I wanted." John was now very much the centre of attention, and he was loving it.

"What was his name?"

John paused for a moment, desperately trying to make up a name. His mind went blank. "Sam", he said at last.

More questions were fired at him about his retainer. His answers were all based on the adventures of the Little Jost gang, but edited so that he became the wise and brave leader and Sam the faithful but rather dim-witted follower. His audience lapped this up, wide-eyed when he told them of all his triumphs, in fits of laughter when he recounted all the mishaps of his companion.

Even as he held forth, it dawned on him what he was doing. He was betraying his old friend: using him to gain approval from his current pals. His performance stuttered to a stop, but it was too late for him to retract without losing face.

Fortunately, at that point a younger boy named George Harrison intervened, changing the topic to Crusoe's owning of and trading in slaves. He said that this was abominable behaviour and that no boy should admire a character who could sink so low. Relieved, John encouraged this turn in the conversation, pointing out that such actions rendered Crusoe an apostate. Not many understood what this meant, and the discussion quickly turned to the question of how Quakers should react if chased by cannibals.

That night in his bed, for the first time since joining the school three years previously, John wept. Telling those stories of adventures on Little Jost, even though wilfully misrepresented, brought his old playmates back to mind for the first time in months. At Penketh he was popular and had many friends. But he had no best-friend. No one to share life-threatening adventures with, such as those Sam and he experienced when tossed about by waves on tiny rafts off the dark northern cliffs of Little Jost. No one he could trust quite so much. He cried because he missed his friend. He cried because he had encouraged the boys to laugh at his friend. And he cried because, at this boy's school, there was no one like Teresa – whom he had not mentioned at all. No one to show off to. No one who was pretty. No one to hug. And no one to confide in about his shame for belittling Sam, and to make it right like she used to whenever he and Sam had briefly fallen out before.

*

That night of tears was an exception. John loved his school and thrived there. Indeed, Abraham Rawlinson had done John a great favour by losing his temper on that snowy winter's evening. While the Friends' School in Lancaster had been just as his Uncle John had predicted – boys sat in rows doing sums all day or copying out verses from the Bible – the atmosphere at Penketh was quite different. Some fifty pupils were taught by the master, Mr Gilbert Thompson, assisted by his nephew, also named Gilbert Thompson. The latter was referred to as "the usher". Two of the senior boys were designated as "monitors" and assisted with classes. Although sometimes the class was indeed required to sit in rows paying attention to the master holding forth from the front, for much of the time they participated in small groups led by the usher or by a monitor, arranged by ability in the subject at hand.

On fine afternoons, the master encouraged outdoor pursuits. Some were physical: running, jumping, and swimming in the gravel pits on Penketh Heath which lay just outside the schoolroom. Others involved learning about local animals, birds and plants – recording their positions and habits and making detailed drawings. John had already become fascinated by nature while on Little Jost. On the heath he learnt to formalise and record his observations, to make intricate drawings, and to discuss his findings scientifically with the younger Gilbert Thompson.

John was quick to learn, not only nature studies but also arithmetic, geography, Latin and Quaker history. Presenting the story of Mary Fisher to the class was a high point of his first year. In his second year the set book had been *A True Tale of Robin Hood,* and within a week almost every boy in the school had made a bow and several arrows. John turned out to be an excellent shot in target practice, and was even able to bring down some of the clumsier birds that perched on tree branches near the school.

The day after John's embarrassment, Gilbert Thompson led a nature study class that required every boy to go out on the heath and make sketches. It was a fine day, and John was soon absorbed in the task of drawing butterflies, concentrating on faithfully representing the patterns on their wings. His hurt began to subside, and his self-confidence was restored by the praise for his work offered by the usher. He threw himself back into the life of the school and continued to delight in his popularity amongst the other boys. However, he no longer spoke to them about his life on Little Jost and, thankfully, none of his fellows ever asked him again about his Man Friday.

*

While John had been learning Latin, natural history, and the fundamentals of Quaker faith at Penketh School, Teresa was receiving her own education. It came about by accident. Amongst those who hired out Taine's slaves were Mary and Samuel Nottingham, the Quaker couple with whom the Lettsoms had shared a post-Meeting lunch shortly before John left for school.

The Nottinghams' plantation was called Long Look and was situated about four miles east of Road Town, from which it could be reached along a hilly and winding trail. By the time she was aged ten Taine thought nothing of sending Teresa over to Long Look with messages seeking payment or arranging to send over extra field hands. Teresa enjoyed these expeditions. If she ran part of the way, especially down the hills, she could be at Long Look in little over an hour and spend extra time there. Mrs Nottingham always welcomed her kindly, and asked her housekeeper to bring sugar cane juice to drink and tasty morsels from the kitchen to eat while she counted money into a purse or composed a reply to be taken back.

One day, Mrs Nottingham caught Teresa out. The girl had acquired the habit of pausing at the gate of Long Look, where there was a handy tree stump, and sitting down to try to read Mrs Nottingham's replies. The writer had clear copperplate writing which was much easier to follow than Taine's scrawl. From what Mary Lettsom had taught her, Teresa was able to make out much of the message, although she never let her father know that she could read at all. On this occasion, Mrs Nottingham came along the drive a few minutes after Teresa had left and discovered her reading the message. Teresa quickly returned the paper to her satchel, terrified that she was in trouble. But she was not. Mrs Nottingham was intrigued to find a little slave girl who could read, and paused to help her with some of the words she had been having difficulty with. They agreed that this would be their secret.

From then on, a pattern emerged. Teresa would run even faster with her messages, and stay with Mrs Nottingham for a full half-hour, reading with her. Usually, it was not the reply to Taine that they studied, but another letter or a recipe, and then as the girl began to understand printed words, a book or a pamphlet, and eventually the Bible. Taine's household was so chaotic that no-one noticed that his daughter's errands were taking longer and longer. Except for Grandma, who was eventually confided in. When Taine was away for whole days or weeks, Grandma would invent errands to cover for Teresa to make longer visits to Long Look.

As time went by, Mr Nottingham became involved in Teresa's education too. He took up where Edward Lettsom had left off with her arithmetic. Such an eager learner soon mastered the essentials, and so Mr Nottingham used his account books for examples of sums to test her understanding and set her exercises, and eventually he taught her the rudiments of bookkeeping.

Intellectually, Mr Nottingham was an abolitionist. In practice he was a slave owner, and dependent on captive labour for his income. This contradiction caused him great stress. One day, he asked the ten-year-old slave girl he was teaching, what she thought of being a slave. It was a question that Teresa had never considered before.

"Well", she said, and paused. "Your housekeeper is a slave, and she is clean and neat and tidy and you are kind to her. The only free women I know are those my father brings home, and they are ugly and smell and he is horrible to them. I would rather be like your housekeeper when I grow up." Mr Nottingham had never thought of it like that.

Sam's answer might have been different. He was not as lucky as Teresa. Taine used him for physically exhausting tasks around the house and in his nearby fields. He rented him out with his slave gangs. Eventually, Sam was sent to work for a week at Long Look, and there he discovered his sister's secret. Annoyance at not being told turned to envy of her opportunity to learn, and eventually to pride in his sister's achievements.

*

"That's wonderful news!" gushed John, "I'm so pleased for you."

John and the younger Gilbert Thompson were in the small room at the back of the school where various exhibits and pieces of equipment used for the teaching of science were kept. This was the sixth year of John's education and he was eleven years old. He was there to help with preparations for a lesson the next day, but all thought of that task had been displaced by Gilbert's amazing news. The usher had been accepted for a place to study medicine at Edinburgh University.

Gilbert beamed with pleasure: "I didn't tell anyone I had applied except for Uncle. I was sure I'd be rejected." He went on to describe his visit to the Medical School, the laboratories, the professors, the questions he had been asked. The usually shy and reticent young man was more enthusiastic and animated than John had ever seen him.

"We'll all miss you here", said John, once the torrent of information about Gilbert's new life had subsided. "Me especially. Will a new usher be taken on?"

"No. Uncle can't afford one. The war has knocked the school's finances. Boys can't easily get here from the colonies anymore and local people have less money. Uncle plans to appoint a coadjutor to help the monitors. I shouldn't be telling you this, but he intends to ask you take on the role."

John blushed at this, but as his Latin was not yet sufficiently advanced he had to ask: "What's a coadjutor?"

"A person with equal powers to the monitors, but below them in order of precedence." As both monitors were four years older than John, this seemed reasonable. He promised to express surprise when the master invited him to take on the role, and to ask again what the word meant.

John now turned back to that evening's task of laying out the equipment for the following day's botany lesson, but Gilbert interrupted him again: "What are you going to do when you leave school?"

"Oh, I'm to go home to help father run the plantation."

"Do you still want to do that now? To live way out in the colonies? To devote your life to growing sugar? To be a slave-owner?"

"Mainly cotton actually", corrected John.

Now for the first time it dawned on him, right in the middle of his conversation with this ambitious young man, that perhaps he could choose not to return home. To a slavery system he had learned to despise. To become an apostate. Here before him was a Quaker from a modest background about to go off to enter a distinguished profession. He knew that Samuel Fothergill's brother John was already a leading physician in London, but had always regarded the Fothergills as part of a superior social stratum. Gilbert's success seemed to put similar advancement, one day, within his own reach. As a doctor himself, or maybe as a zoologist or a botanist.

"Do you think my father would allow me to study at university?" he asked.

*

"Wait there!" said Ed, sharply.

Teresa froze. This was the first time she had seen her former playmate since John had left for England. She had wondered whether they might bump into one another as soon as her father told her to deliver a letter to Edward Lettsom's sugar plantation at Cane Garden Bay. By now Teresa could read even her father's hand-writing, and so she had seen that the note explained he had a fever and would be unable to come over to supervise planting until a week later. She knew his excuse was false: it was drink and women that were delaying him. She had enjoyed the switchback walk, relieved to get out of the Taine household for a few hours and excited at the prospect of, just maybe, seeing John's brother.

On arrival at the shack that served as plantation office she had been delighted to find that Ed really was there. He was sitting behind a table talking to another white boy who was slightly older. Although he still looked stunted and thin, there was a look of John in his face that thrilled her.

"My dear Ed! How wonderful to see you again", Teresa had said brightly, smiling at him and giving a little curtsy – playfully pretending that they were both already grown up. She had been shocked and deflated by his reply, but there was no alternative for her but to do as she had been told, and wait. Ed continued to chat to his companion. He had recognized her: that was obvious. Although they spoke in low voices, Ed seemed to be discussing her. They laughed and sniggered and stared, and Teresa could catch something of the older boy's responses which she did not find funny at all. After a while, she sat down on a chair in the corner of the room.

"Don't sit on that chair!" Ed shouted. "Just stand there and wait."

Teresa flushed, but controlled her anger and did as she was told. Eventually, Ed turned to her and, in a formal tone, asked what she wanted. She handed over the letter from Taine, while enquiring how his parents were. She got no reply. Ed read the letter and suggested to his friend some alternative reasons why Taine might not be available to serve as overseer that were even more lurid than the truth. Then he took his time to write a reply, which he sealed with wax before handing it to her. Teresa ran off with it, the tears that she had been fighting to suppress finally flowing as she climbed away from the bay.

Later that day, when she told Sam about the incident, she asked whether he thought John would be like that now. Sam gave her reassurance which she was eager to accept, but privately neither of them could be certain that he would still be their friend. For Teresa, dreams of John's return were now always clouded by the thought that he might snub her. Might expect her to stand while he sat.

*

The master's new leadership structure for Penketh School did not work out well. Once Gilbert left to commence his studies, the two monitors proved unequal to their task. They did not really understand the material they tried to teach and were unable to maintain discipline. They resorted to shouting and violence in their attempts to maintain order. Eventually, they were dismissed from their positions and, despite his age, John was appointed as the sole monitor.

The war with France now hit Edward Lettsom's finances. It became difficult to export cotton and sugar across the Atlantic and he had to sell his Cane Garden Bay plantation. This realised enough to cover his debts, but not enough to pay his son's school fees. John's continued presence at school was now dependent on performing his duties as monitor. This was stressful and lonely, as other boys now kept their distance. He was working in a shrinking school and spending more time teaching others than learning himself.

The real blows of fate were reserved for two years later. First, the master summoned him to his house to explain that the struggle to keep the school solvent had failed. There were too few enrolments for the following year and too many unpaid fees. The school would have to close within a few months. Second, just days later, he was summoned once more. This time the news was more personal. Fever had struck the Virgin Islands. Both his father and his brother had been taken. He was given a letter from John Pickering that explained it all. His mother had escaped illness, but was understandably distraught. The community was doing everything it could to support her.

The third shock came a few weeks before the final school closure in another letter from John Pickering. This described how the two Edward Lettsoms had been laid to rest together in a simple ceremony in graves under the tamarind trees outside their house on Little Jost. This was the spot where his mother loved to sit when her day's chores were done, and where she used to serve sugar cane juice to the children. But that letter then served a body blow. Mary Lettsom had agreed to marry Samuel Taine. The vulgar, violent, blaspheming bully who had had serial disputes with John's father and owned and terrorised Sam and Teresa.

The tone of Pickering's letter became harsher at this point, forecasting that the Quaker community of Tortola would not accept such a match kindly. Finally, it was explained that his father's estate would pass to him on his twenty-first birthday, and until then it would be administered by Mr Pickering. In eight years' time, all of his father's plantations would be in John's possession. And so would all of his slaves.

There had been nothing in the letters from Tortola about John's immediate future and no clue as to how he might be supported until he achieved his majority. Samuel Fothergill stepped in again, undertaking to become the boy's guardian. He arranged for John to take digs in Liverpool and to study mercantile accounting with a view to subsequently joining a merchant's business.

This was the low point for John. He had lost a father and a brother. He had loved them both dearly. He knew how distraught some of his fellow-pupils became on hearing similar news and he understood that that was how he should feel too. The sympathy and concern expressed by people around him reinforced this perception. Yet at this distance in time and in place, he found that he had to work hard on feeling sad. It seemed as if he had already lost his father and his brother seven years before. He was aware that his genuine feelings of desolation were principally due to losing his dreams of a glorious medical career, or of a golden future as a pioneer of zoology or botany.

He considered returning to Little Jost van Dyke and discussed this with Samuel Fothergill. There, he could help his mother and prepare himself to take over the plantation. To support his mother was, of course, his filial duty. To be close to Sam and Teresa again would be wonderful. Or would it? How would they relate to him after all those years? How would Teresa regard him – would his sweet memories of her be erased? Furthermore, his revulsion for the system of slavery had grown throughout his years away from the islands. He had promised to return and free his father's workers. How could he afford to do so? How could he go back and not do so?

And his mother had become Mrs Taine. Back on Little Jost, he would have to live with that man, be controlled by that man. Finally, it was likely that he would have to live outside the Quaker community on the island. That aspect certainly appeared to weigh heavily on his devout guardian. Anyway, there was the war with France – it surely would not be safe to return home yet. A clerical career it would have to be.

*

When Teresa learnt of the deaths of Edward and Ed, she did not mourn the passing of her former playmate, but she was saddened to hear that his father had died. Edward symbolized what a father should be. Caring, amusing, authoritative and wise. More like a father to her than her real father. A model for what John would surely become.

She and Sam were amazed by their own father's reaction to the news. Taine had never got on with Mr Lettsom. They could not remember a conversation between the two of them that was not a rancorous dispute. But now he insisted on making a call to Little Jost to offer his condolences and ask whether there was anything he could do to help – free of charge! He had Grandma repair his children's clothes, he shaved and put on a smart jacket that neither of them had seen before. He refrained from drinking for a whole day. And then the three of them set out to pay their respects.

As they arrived, they saw John Pickering leaving. He had been there to arrange the burial and the funeral service for the next day. Taine spent some time speaking softly and gently to the widow, and then left his children in her company while he busied himself completing various repair jobs that had been left undone during her husband's illness. He returned to Road Town very late in the evening, but left Sam and Teresa to keep Mary company and help her in the house.

On the next day Mr Pickering returned with a couple of dozen Friends and the deceased were laid to rest in a quiet and simple ceremony. Teresa heard Mr Pickering offer to send a couple of his house slaves over to help her, and suggested that Edward's nephews and nieces might be happy to stay and keep her company. Mary declined, saying that Sam and Teresa were with her now and would be staying – the first they knew about it – and as she knew them well already she was not in need of any further help or company.

While the children moved in with Mary Lettsom, Taine came and went, alternating commitments on Tortola with helping to run the plantation on Little Jost. He put the field-hands back to work using persuasion and encouragement, leaving his whip back at Road Town. His visits become longer and longer, all day and then several days at a time, sleeping in the bed that Ed had occupied. He would spend long evenings sitting with Mary outside the house, the children sent to bed, talking about improvements that could be made to the estate. The volume of wine consumed gradually increased. He moved from Ed's bed to Edward's place in the marital bed. Finally, he proposed marriage and was accepted. His deep religious convictions precluded conversion to the Quaker belief and an Anglican ceremony sufficed, witnessed only by Sam, Teresa, the priest and those few parishioners who were in the habit of attending every service.

Soon after the wedding, John Pickering disowned Mary from the Quakers for marrying outside the faith. She had no more visits from her former friends, and Taine discouraged her from leaving the island. Nevertheless, these first months of their marriage were quite happy for all four of them. Taine set to work improving the house, including constructing a veranda on all sides so they could sit outside at any time of day and choose sunshine or shade. Sam's life improved immeasurably, he learnt a lot about carpentry helping his father and he was entrusted to sail the shallop on errands to Tortola and other islands.

Teresa missed her visits to the Nottinghams, but she enjoyed working with Mary and Rosett, learning about cooking, livestock and embroidery. She was also back where she had been happiest. Back where John had lived. She could talk to Mrs Lettsom about him, and learn how he was getting on. Surreptitiously, when the house was quiet and everyone busy outside, she could even seek out and touch the letters that he had sent, read his neat hand-writing and learn of his adventures.

When writing to his mother John never complained of his lot, always finding happy or amusing tales to tell. His readers never appreciated how much he hated his clerical position or his lost opportunities. Teresa would ask to be remembered to him in Mary's letters, and began to find shells, pieces of coral and sweets to be included in Mary's parcels. Out of caution, she refrained from writing her own letters to him – her father still did not know she could read and write. But now she felt considerably closer to John. Surely the friendship of this maturing young man, who always included in his letters a greeting for her, thanks for her gifts and sometimes a little token in return, was not lost to her.

CHAPTER 8

The door to the men's ward swung open and four of the hospital's ambulant patients marched in carrying brooms and pans. Two of them brushed debris from the floor with the brooms, while the other two collected it in the pans. Dust, hair, the rotting remnants of patients' meals, old bandages, rags covered in ugly stains, and unpleasant material of indeterminate origin. In their wake followed the doctor. A thin, pale, ascetic looking man, with a long nose and a tendency to look down it. He wore a fashionable black jacket and bright yellow breeches. Balanced on his head was a huge powdered wig, and at his side he carried an improbably long sword. He walked with a limp, which some of the students walking behind him were from time-to-time inclined to imitate, so long as they thought he could not see them.

This then was Mark Akenside, St Thomas' Hospital's leading physician, the poet and author of the widely admired *The Pleasures of Imagination*, and Queen Charlotte's favourite court doctor. And amongst his entourage of half a dozen apprentices, dressers and pupils that day was John Coakley Lettsom.

"Sister!" exclaimed Akenside to one of the senior nurses present. "Look at the filth in this ward. Can we not expect basic cleanliness in this hospital?"

"Blimey sir, I'm sorry you may 'ave to dirty your shoes. This is an 'ospital for the sick and poor, not the country 'ome of some gentleman," came the spirited reply.

“I do not concern myself with my own convenience, madam. I am concerned with the welfare of my patients. How can they get well in a dung-heap?”

“But sir,” interjected one of the older apprentices, “these people are used to living in filth. That’s not what makes them ill. It’s the miasma.”

“Ah, the miasma, Watkins! The foul air. That is the root cause of all their ills, is it? What does this miasma comprise? Bring me some in a bottle so I can analyse it. I have never seen it myself, but I can see this,” he said pointing to the contents of the pan. “Rotten food that no-one would now eat, bloody bandages, bits of skin, ..., what’s that? Argh, better not to know! Would you have this in the room where you sleep, Watkins? Or in the room where you eat your meals? Who is to say that this mess is not the cause of the patients’ diseases?”

“That’s not what Dr Russell says, nor Dr Grieve,” responded another of the apprentices. “It’s not part of the teachings of Galen.”

“I was waiting for you to mention him, Corbett. Galen, the ancient Greek physician. Have we learnt nothing since his day? Can we not think for ourselves? We must not rely on precedent, on the wisdom of great men, on our belief that it is natural for poor men to live in filth – for it is not! ‘Cleanliness is next to Godliness’, and you will find both in abundance in the poorest of homes, should you ever take the trouble to visit the sick where they live. We must rely on science. On observation and experiment. On arguments based on evidence. And where we have no evidence, we must practice caution and keep an open mind.

“These scraps of people’s bodies and of their food lying on the floor do no-one any good. Do you want this pan-full to take home?” he said, grabbing one of the pans and pushing it in front of his apprentice’s face, his voice rising. “Does this look appealing to you? If it is not going to help the patients' recovery, then it has no place on the ward. Let us observe and record. Let us see whether more patients die in my clean and tidy ward or in the filth and chaos of Dr Russell's or Dr Grieve's. And until then, let us proceed with humility, admitting that we do not know what we do not know."

He walked on, the students following, unconvinced.

Stopping at the bed of a man aged about fifty with a swarthy complexion, he asked the sister: "How's the asthma faring?"

"Very calm, very quiet, sir. He's breathing easily, and not having any convulsions."

Akenside again addressed the students. "So, this case was admitted last week. A great lover of gin, and prone to melancholy. Admitted due to stomach pain and vomiting. Treated with ammoniac, hartshorn and aromatics, his stomach was eased, but then he complained of shortness of breath. Suffered attacks during which he found it so difficult to breathe that he became intensely agitated and in fear of his life. So how, Watkins, would you have treated him?"

"Was he suffering from a fever?" asked Watkins.

"No."

"Did he have chest pain?"

"No."

Silence. No-one was sure what had been wrong with the patient, nor how he might have been helped.

"Anyone else have any ideas?" asked the teacher.

"Was he suffering from dropsy?" asked Corbett.

"No, nor did he have catarrh. It seems that he was suffering from an acute stricture of the bronchia. It is generally known as convulsive, spasmodic or nervous asthma."

"So, how did you treat him?" asked one of the dressers.

"Five grains of ipecacoanha every other morning. He is now recovering, and breathing far more easily."

The senior students were impressed. They knew of the drug ipecacoanha, extracted from the root of a Brazilian flowering plant. They remembered that its name meant "road-side sick-making plant", and that it was commonly used as an emetic. They had never heard of it being used to treat asthma. A discussion ensued. The importance of distinguishing nervous asthma from water in the thorax was stressed, and the measures to be taken to do so were described.

"Might not the convulsions have been due to hysteria?" This question came from John Lettsom.

"So, the pupil is so bold as to venture an opinion?"

John was a pupil, and a surgical pupil at that, the lowest order of student present. His humble aspiration was to prepare for a career as a surgeon-apothecary. He was paying twenty-four guineas a year for the privilege of following distinguished clinicians around the hospital, and sought to get his money's worth.

"Hysteria, you say. Does this patient have a uterus? Is this some raving woman?"

"No sir. But Willis says ... "

"Willis! You have been reading Willis have you? But the good doctor Willis does not just call it hysteria does he? He also refers to it as 'the irregular motions of the animal spirits'. And even he suggests the administration of an emetic, although he attributes its effectiveness to the relocation of these spirits to the stomach to counter this new attack on the body, thus vacating the lungs. Do you believe in animal spirits, Lettsom?"

"Well, Galen describes them. Sydenham, Willis, they all attribute medical conditions to the behaviour of our animal spirits."

"Willis was a great doctor, and a meticulous scientist, but even he was unable to throw off these ancient notions. Have you studied the work of Borelli?"

"No, sir."

"Read about his experiments with dogs, seeking evidence of these animal spirits. He found none! Forget about animal spirits, Lettsom. Let them go the same way as the evil spirits of the witch doctors on whichever sweltering isle it is you come from. Science, Lettsom, science. Experiment and evidence, not the wisdom of the ancients, and definitely not spirits of any sort."

*

John had been as successful at learning mercantile accounting as he had been at Latin and Quaker history, but there was no joy for him in the subject. His course led to a position as junior clerk in a merchants' office near the Liverpool docks. Here he recorded in meticulous detail the cold financial facts of the trade in sugar and cotton, mahogany and logwood, rum and ginger, and most lucrative of all, in slaves.

Nothing could have been less to his taste. Nine hours a day, six days a week, working alone in a small, damp, cold office. The tasks had offered him some challenges during his first week, some satisfaction during his first month, and had then settled down to a tedious, repetitive series of chores. No company, no exercise, no fresh air for the whole of the working day. And on top of the crushing boredom came the inescapable realisation that every day he was making a small contribution to the horrors of the capture and transportation of Africans across the ocean to plantations like those his father had owned. That he was due to inherit.

Then, after two years of clerical toil, his life had suddenly turned around again. All due to the visit to Liverpool of Mr John Pickering of Tortola, the son of the leading island Quaker and one time Lieutenant Governor of the same name. The young colonial was in Liverpool to negotiate new buyers for his father's sugar and cotton, and to arrange for the importation of fresh slaves.

John Pickering Senior had also given his son the task of enquiring about his young countryman's condition and progress. He felt rather guilty about abandoning Mary Lettsom after her second marriage and was concerned that John had been cast adrift from the island's Quaker community as a consequence. Therefore, he had set aside a sum of money to support any worthwhile scheme for betterment that the young man might have. As well as his conversations with John himself, John Pickering Junior spoke with Samuel Fothergill when the latter came to preach at the Meeting House in Liverpool. Between them a plan was hatched. Mr Fothergill had a kinsman by the name of Abraham Sutcliff, a surgeon-apothecary in the Yorkshire town of Settle who was in need of an apprentice. The fee Sutcliff required would be paid for by the Quaker planter. John jumped at the opportunity.

So it was that that John learned about the healing properties of the powders, liquids, syrups, dried leaves and roots that formed the basis of the apothecary's art. He learned how each should be stored and what it was used for. How to make up potions, mould tablets and calculate dosages. In the shop, he would sell these products, and was coached in the dialogue necessary to determine not just what a customer wanted, but more importantly what he or she actually needed. He would also sell the tea and tobacco that was traded to improve the customers' spirits and support the finances of the business. Here, in the shop, he suddenly found the quantitative skills he had absorbed in Liverpool to be worthwhile, spending many evenings making sense of and then improving the accounts of the enterprise.

With Abraham Sutcliffe, John made house calls on the chronically sick and those in need of urgent care, learning when medication was called for, and if so what preparation would be appropriate. He learned the signs and symptoms which would cause him to be sent running as fast as he could to call out the local doctor, and would then watch and later record what combination of sweating, bleeding or application of leeches was applied. Sutcliffe taught him how to set and immobilise broken bones and perform minor acts of surgery such as lancing boils. The apothecary also advertised his services as a "man midwife", and due to his patience and soothing manner was in some demand in this capacity. John's hours spent assisting his master attending childbirths gave him some of his most satisfying experiences, as well as some of his saddest moments.

After dark, by the light of a single candle, John would devour medical textbooks, many of them acquired by Sutcliffe during his days studying in Edinburgh. Some required him to brush up on his Latin, which he had learnt well at Penketh. He would also spend time in the preparation room, carefully dissecting live frogs, mice and rabbits in order to locate, study and sketch their muscles and organs and to observe the beating of their hearts, the circulation of their blood, and the contractions of their muscles.

Abraham Sutcliffe was a committed Quaker, and John joined him in his religious observances. Besides his circle of Friends based on the Meeting House, he also became a popular figure in an overlapping circle of young friends who met regularly to dispute religion and politics, frequent local taverns, bathe in the Ribble during the summer months, and take long walks through the dales and over the hills whenever time permitted. John was not slow to exploit the exoticism of his birthplace, the romance associated with wild colonial boys, and the respect accorded to the young heir to a plantation with fifty slaves. He dropped hints about the young, beautiful, dusky maiden he had had to leave behind on his island, without ever being clear about just how young he had been when he crossed the ocean. He was soon a favourite with the young women of the town.

So passed the years of John Lettsom's apprenticeship, by the end of which he was making many straightforward house calls by himself, and he felt he had mastered all that was to be known about the practice of medicine. Then he progressed to study in London and quickly discovered that he had barely scratched the surface. This had always been the plan: complete his initial training in the north and then proceed to London to develop further by attending ward rounds at St Thomas' and assist in the practice of Samuel Fothergill's brother, Dr John Fothergill, by then one of the leading physicians in the capital. Then he would be ready to establish himself in some country town as a surgeon-apothecary in his own right.

*

"He's outrageous!" said John, "rude, supercilious, arrogant!"

"He" was Dr Mark Akenside, and this was John's wind down after his ward round with St Thomas' finest physician. John's audience in the cosy tavern near Billingsgate comprised James Beesley and Gilbert Thompson. James was a fellow native of Tortola and an aspiring writer and poet, whom John had met at London Quaker meetings. Gilbert was the usher from Penketh who had been such a vital part of John's early education. He had excelled in the scientific aspects of medicine during his studies in Edinburgh, but was far less confident in dealing with patients and was now working in the back room of one of London's largest pharmacies.

"John's education so far has been very old fashioned", explained Gilbert to James. "The Greeks believed that the body's functions are controlled by three spirits, vegetative, vital and animal, and that all diseases are caused by imbalances between them. The animal spirits come down the nerves from the brain to control the body, but if too much comes down they cause uncontrollable spasms like the attacks that affected the breathing of John's poor patient."

"But, John," Gilbert continued, now turning attention to the medical student, "your learning has come from Sutcliffe's old books. They teach very different things in Edinburgh nowadays. The Greeks are definitely out and theories based on observation and experiment are in. Harvey's circulation of the blood, Willis's brilliant exploration of nerves – but not his outdated clinging to animal spirits. We repeated Borelli's experiments: there were no bubbles of animal spirits coming down through the nerves!"

"Well, there's no reason for Akenside to be so rude when explaining this to me. I'm only a student. And he's so inconsiderate to patients. He never spoke to the man, nor told us his name. He was just 'the asthma patient'. "

"Medicine without actual patients. Just bodies to observe and cure. Bliss! I could work with him," claimed Gilbert.

"Why did you choose to study with this brute?" asked James. "Aren't there other physicians at the hospital?"

"Yes, there are. But, I have to admit, none of them understand physiology and disease as clearly as Akenside."

"Well, his poetry is pretty good too. If only I could write like he does. And be as recognised for it as he is. He seems to encompass in one person what we both are striving to become."

"I suppose I must stick with him, take his ridicule, and learn whatever I can from him. Pick his brains and combine his understanding with Abraham Sutcliffe's kindly bedside manner. Then I'll be unstoppable!"

*

John worked hard throughout his time at St Thomas'. He followed both surgeons and physicians, learning how to cut out disease, repair injury, coax sickness to leave the body, or train the body to adapt to loss of function. He noted down the physicians' prescriptions and took them to the apothecary and observed how they were made up. He kept records of everything: how the patient first appeared to him, his initial diagnosis of their affliction and how it should be treated, followed by what his tutor had concluded and the course of treatment that was actually prescribed. He then noted down the progress of the patient and the eventual outcome.

Soon John knew more about the effectiveness of most of the clinicians than they did themselves, and was more aware of their relative skills than the hospital management. If he had ever needed surgery himself, he would have submitted himself to Thomas Baker, whom he had regularly observed. For medical treatment, he would certainly have put himself under the care of Akenside and adhered strictly to the regimen prescribed, provided he did not have to talk to the man.

When not working, Quaker meetings and polite and proper tea parties and discussion evenings with the Friends would take his time. With his personal friends, Gilbert, James and others, evenings at the tavern would be more relaxed, the conversation less guarded, and the refreshment more stimulating. Amongst the more colourful characters of the city – the fashionable gents, the fops and the dandies – their long, dark coats, plain bobbed wigs and flat brimmed Quaker hats marked them out as serious and sober young men. Nevertheless, their curiosity did lead them to explore some of the more refined attractions of the capital.

The British Museum was a favourite haunt of John and his companions, and recitals of his own recent compositions by Johann Christian Bach on the newly invented pianoforte provided a suitably intellectual form of musical appreciation. More risqué ventures, such as visits to the Pleasure Gardens at Marylebone and Vauxhall were not reported to John's fastidious patron, Dr Fothergill, and certainly not to his prim sister, Ann. They kept away from the theatre entirely: it was considered altogether too licentious.

For John, suitable female company was hard to find. In Settle, a lively, mixed group of young unmarried people had found it easy to strike up conversations in the street, to get to know one another and to enjoy long country walks, picnics, parties and gossip together. He had become close to a few of these girls, and formed short-lived romantic attachments with some of them. Although many of his elders shared Abraham Rawlinson's conviction that a Quaker should not dance, he could not resist the local tunes and the intricate moves, and with practice he soon found his sense of rhythm.

In London, meeting with young women informally and developing friendship was more difficult. Professional young gentlemen would be introduced to unmarried ladies through their families, and after some chaperoned coffee mornings and genteel afternoon walks in the park, and following much study of the family tree, financial holdings, and future prospects, a marriage proposal might be made. Otherwise, "women" might be encountered in the tavern or in the dark lanes behind the Pleasure Gardens, but that was not an option for pious young Friends.

Dr Fothergill never invited young women to his domestic gatherings, and striking up a friendship across the silence of formal Meetings, at the end of which all participants would speed off to different parts of the city, would have been a challenge. As the women sat to the right of the aisle, and the men to the left, it was difficult even to assess what opportunities there might be. Somehow, James Beesley had managed to overcome the barriers, and was sometimes joined in the group's visits to museums and concerts by a rather plain and dumpy young woman named Nancy Miers, together with her plainer and dumpier unmarried Aunt Mary. This aroused no envy on the part of James's friends.

During his time in London, John became a better correspondent with his mother. His anger over her hasty marriage to Samuel Taine had subsided, but to be on the safe side both correspondents avoided direct mention of him in their letters. Instead, John was updated on the local gossip, although Mary's knowledge of the goings-on amongst the Quaker community was limited since her estrangement from them. She knew mainly about deaths. His Uncle John had died following a riding accident not long after Mary's remarriage, and Aunt Margery and his cousins had had little to do with her since. The younger John Pickering, who had visited him in Liverpool had died, although Mary did not know the cause.

Most of Mary's news was about Sam and Teresa. The former now sailed the shallop around the islands, taking supplies and labourers to and from wherever his master was working. He had acquired many useful skills which he applied to keeping the house in order and maintaining the plantation and its tools. Teresa helped Mary in the kitchen and with the garden and animals, and her needlework was highly valued by her mistress and appreciated by their occasional visitors.

Whenever John read of Sam's progress in mastering the shallop, it brought back warm memories of his trusty friend and fearless companion in so many hazardous adventures. And whenever he received the little presents that Teresa added to the packages from home – the shells, preserved sweets or embroidered handkerchiefs – he was reminded of their happy and intimate childhood days roaming Little Jost. What would she look like now? How would that bubbly and affectionate child have transformed into a young woman? He spent a lot of time seeking out suitable trinkets in local markets to send to her in return.

CHAPTER 9

"Ouch! That hurts!" cried Mary, pulling her face back from Teresa. "What's in that water?"

"Just some vinegar and a tiny pinch of cayenne pepper" replied Teresa. "Hold still Mary, please. It'll bring down the swelling and stop it going purple. My Grandma swears by this remedy."

"She used it when he hit me", added Sam. "It does help."

Mary reluctantly submitted to the treatment, wincing now and then as Teresa continued bathing her inflamed cheek.

Taine had hit her hard this time. Only Sam and Teresa's early return from the cotton fields had saved her from worse. While four thousand miles away in England, John was complaining about his modern medical education, on Little Jost van Dyke Teresa was administering more traditional remedies.

"What made him so angry this time?" asked Sam, still furious at his father's behaviour.

"I stopped them whipping Issabel. He said she'd been idling, but that's not like her. More likely he tried to get his way with her and she resisted. I've seen how he looks at her. I never let him beat the slaves anyway. Edward left Issabel to me! She's not his to beat – nor to do anything else with. And he got poor Bentorah to do it too. Bentorah who never hurts anyone! I told him to stop, and he did. Eagerly. He knows he belongs to John and should do as I say. That man followed me back to the house, shouting and swearing, and then he hit me to the floor. And then, thank the Lord, you both came in and he stormed off."

Mary had now had enough of Teresa's treatment and gently pushed her away. Gingerly, she felt at the swelling on her face.

"Has he taken the shallop?" she asked.

Sam went to take a look, returning to confirm that he had.

"He'll have gone to Road Town. To be with that latest girl of his. What's her name?"

"Polly", answered Sam.

"Yes, Polly. A free woman of colour. Very free, like they all are."

Mary left them to go to her room, and they heard her sobbing there. Later, Teresa prepared a small meal, persuading Mary to join them at the table. She was a little more composed now. When they had finished eating, she told them more about her relationship with Taine than she had ever revealed before.

"To begin with it was quite joyful, and a bit of relief to get away from all those Quaker restrictions. He didn't drink too much in those days – mainly wine, and we enjoyed that together. But after three or four months, the real man began to emerge. He started to go away a lot, working on his little dodgy schemes, wheeling and dealing and making money out of the war with France. Always came back drunk, smelling of his other women, often furious that it was he who'd been swindled." Mary paused, staring beyond her listeners as if looking in vain for traces of the happier parts of her second marriage.

"But life was still tolerable." She reached out across the table and took hold of one of Sam's hands and one of Teresa's. "The best part was having you two around the house again." For a while she just sat there looking at them intently, squeezing their hands. Then she released them and looked away.

"I expected some marital chastisement from him anyway. That's the lot of married women unless they're lucky enough to marry a Quaker." At that she laughed, mirthlessly. "At first I just put up with it. After all, my father used to cane me when I behaved badly. It's been these last three years that have been unbearable. For everyone else the end of the war brought relief, but it put an end to his little schemes and he really began to lose money seriously – as you know. It's made him more angry. More violent. Not just beating me when I did something wrong – in his eyes at least – but for no reason at all."

Mary stopped, evidently having said all she intended to say on the subject. Teresa and Sam said nothing. They did not need to: their sympathy and their love were in their faces.

"So now we're marooned here", observed Mary, in control of her emotions once more and attempting to take control of the situation.

"I guess so", said Sam. "If he doesn't come back in a couple of days, I'll try to patch up Edward's old boat."

"Do you think we should write to John and tell him what's happening?" asked Teresa.

"Oh no!" replied John's mother. "He'll be very busy. We can cope. I won't mention any of this in my letters." With that, she wished them goodnight and retired to her bed.

On this occasion Sam had no need to repair the old boat. A few days after his angry departure, Taine returned. He was looking quite smart and expressing repentance. He was sober, and promised to stay that way. He promised not to beat the slaves. He claimed to have kicked Polly out of his house in Road Town, and said she would not be coming back. He brought Mary a new bonnet and some colourful fabric from which she could make a new frock. Mary was surprised at his tasteful choice of gifts, but well aware that he could not really afford them. Nevertheless, she forgave him. Life appeared to return to normal. Mary's next letter to John was the same mix of bright and cheery news as previous ones and Teresa inserted a colourful pair of stockings she had knitted – far too thick and warm to wear on Little Jost!

*

"You know, Gilbert's come into a lot of money."

This was Dr John Fothergill talking to John Lettsom over the breakfast table one First Day morning at the former's elegant house in Whitehart Court, just off Gracechurch Street, prior to them going together to the nearby Meeting House.

"His uncle left him £4,000 when he died last year, but he still hasn't decided what to do with it. He talks of buying an apothecary's or setting up a school but, with that sort of money and his experience and qualifications, he could purchase a lucrative medical practice right here in the centre of London and be set up for life."

"But he's frightened of treating patients," replied the younger man. "He gets extremely nervous every time he has to make a clinical decision. Was it the right diagnosis? Did he prescribe the right treatment? He lacks all confidence in his own abilities."

"Well, he shouldn't. He has outstanding abilities. His teachers in Edinburgh were very impressed. You're right though, if he makes a mistake – the kind we all make from time to time – he takes it very hard. But surely he could learn, gain experience, become more confident in his abilities. Perhaps a nice practice in the new suburbs where the patients are rich and idle, and they take your time and pay you well to attend to minor ailments and imaginary conditions. His voice can be very soothing."

"That's as may be, but it's what he says that's the problem, not how he says it. He always tells patients exactly what's wrong with them, and exactly what's likely to happen to them. No sugar coating, no compassionate white lies. Just: 'There's nothing at all wrong with you – snap out of it!', or 'This disease will probably kill you within six months'. "

"You must talk to him, John, persuade him to become more tactful. Get him to see reason and encourage him to invest in a practice. He'd soon earn enough to marry his sweetheart Mary

Edmundson who's still waiting patiently for him in Lancashire. Perhaps he could establish himself as a country doctor up there."

The two Johns were alone in the dining room, passing the time until their departure for the Meeting House after eating their fill of bread, porridge and kedgeree. Ann Fothergill, John's sister who kept house for him, had quickly consumed her usual Spartan breakfast and was already supervising its clearing away and the preparations for lunch. Young John refilled their tea cups, and the older man turned to a different subject.

"I've received a document from Pennsylvania that might interest you. It was written by Anthony Benezet who used to teach at our school in Philadelphia. It concerns the Society's approach to slavery."

"I've heard of him. He was one of young John Pickering's teachers when he was at that school, and he was very highly thought of. He conducted evening classes for black children, and John assisted him whenever he could. John was constantly amazed how eager those children were to learn, and how quickly they mastered writing and arithmetic. 'Close your eyes', he said, 'and you wouldn't know these children were being raised for slavery'."

"Well, in his pamphlet, Benezet argues that slavery is inconsistent with the Gospel, with reason and with 'every common sentiment of humanity'. He uses sound theological reasoning, questions the legal basis of the system, and urges Quakers in particular to withdraw from the trade, free their own slaves, and campaign for the end of this injustice."

"To end the trade in new slaves is one thing, and it could easily be achieved. It would make plantation owners care for the slaves they have, rather than working them to death and then buying new. But plantations depend on labour. My mother's living, old John Pickering's living, they all depend on labour. Perhaps granting freedom needs to be done gradually. Perhaps

Quakers need to welcome their labourers into the Society first, to acquaint them with God and their Saviour, and then gradually ease their harsh conditions. Some owners treat their workers with great consideration, and some slaves would quickly descend into licentiousness if released without due preparation."

John said all this, as he had heard these arguments from West Indian planters all his life, but in truth their persuasiveness was beginning to wear thin. When talking to slave-owners and defenders of the practice, he found himself arguing for immediate abolition on the grounds of humanity and to end cruelty, and he would quickly dismiss the attitudes that he had just expressed. When debating with abolitionists, he became stuck on the practicalities. He was a slave-owner now. How would his mother survive without their labour? What would the slaves do if suddenly freed?

Slaves were not abstract people to him: they were Sam and Teresa, Cudjoe and Rosett. How would they live? As for cruelty, there was little of that in his memories as a young child growing up on a tiny plantation governed by Quaker principles of compassion and non-violence. Nor could he really imagine the hard-working and conscientious Little Jost slaves whom he had known falling prey to licentiousness. He looked down at his bright new stockings, cosy and warm against the lingering nip in the spring air. The product of forced slave labour or a thoughtful gift from a treasured friend?

"Well, said Dr Fothergill. I'm going to encourage him to publish his pamphlet, and offer to help arrange for it to be done here in London. So please read it carefully, and let me know of any comments to be passed back to him first. And now, it's time to call for Ann and set off for the Meeting."

*

"Who just spat?" cried Akenside. Another ward round. Another mixture of profound medical enlightenment and condescending ridicule and scorn.

"It was I," volunteered Watkins. "Just rather congested this morning, probably a cold coming on."

"Yes, here is the evidence", proclaimed the physician. "Disgusting! Clean it up immediately."

"Clean this up for me," requested Watkins of a passing nurse.

"No – you clean it up! This young woman has far more important tasks to complete than to attend to your revolting habits." As Watkins bullied a younger student to lend him a handkerchief and reluctantly and inexpertly wiped up his deposit, the teacher continued his lecture. "Cleanliness is everything in a hospital ward. Wipe your boots before you enter the ward. Wash your hands before you attend to patients. Refrain from spitting, catch your sneezes in a handkerchief, do not breath or cough into patients' faces. All of these things can spread disease."

"But all of that's surely unnecessary," responded one of the better-bred followers. "They're the stinking poor, the foul and sick, and we're the gentlemen. It's ludicrous to suggest that *we* might pass disease to *them*."

"We're not all gentlemen. Butcher's boys should certainly scrub before entering the ward." That comment was whispered, its source unclear. The reference to Akenside's humble origins was meant to hurt, and it did. As it was unclear whom to upbraid, and to avoid prolonging any discussion on his upbringing, Akenside just continued.

"The sources of disease are poorly understood. Some conditions clearly spread from one person to another. Any of us can transmit disease, from ourselves to the patient, or from one patient to another. The nurses know this, and they practice strict hygiene and change the patients' bedsheets regularly. We must learn from this and refrain from rushing from dissecting corpses of fever victims, straight to the bedsides of the living, without cleansing ourselves of the fluids we have been touching."

"No-one else tells us this," ventured John, who was sceptical about the whole matter, and unwilling to spend his time on the wards attending to his own body. "The surgeons never waste time washing their hands."

"Then they are not serving their patients well. Following a post-mortem, a fatal disease from a cadaver might be transferred to yourselves and thence to your patients. We must study and observe. Note how well those patients operated on by the cleanest surgeons survive, and how well those who are dealt with by fellows carrying the blood of their last victim on their coats and the remains of his innards on their hands and under their filthy finger nails. We need to answer the question by scientific study, and until then practice a safe and cautious approach." He feigned not to have heard the comment: "Just like a butcher" that had followed his reference to blood-stained coats.

Akenside moved his coterie on through the ward to surround the bed of a tall, thin man. "What do we observe about this patient?" he asked. His sweating was mentioned. John pointed out that he was shivering, despite the day being warm. The ward sister was asked about his progress, and mentioned that he had been vomiting continually and was unable to keep his food down. He complained of headaches and pain in his joints. Corbett asked where the patient came from, and on being told that he was from Essex, suggested that the affliction was the ague, which was prevalent in marshy areas.

"Quite right!" affirmed Akenside. "And what should be his treatment?"

"Purging and bloodletting", suggested Watkins.

"How out-of-date you are."

"Peruvian bark", was John's suggestion, recalling a case he had discussed with Dr Fothergill the previous week.

"Ah, cinchona bark. Yes, an excellent suggestion from our surgical pupil. You will have an excellent career in future treating the wealthy of London. But in the meantime, who is going to pay for such an extravagant treatment?"

John blushed. Wrong again!

"A couple of years ago, Captain Stone spoke at the Royal Society of his experiments with the use of willow bark for the treatment of ague. An impressive record of success over a period of five years, every bit as effective as Peruvian bark and freely available here at home by any river bank. Read his paper in *Philosophical Transactions*, Lettsom. Study the evidence, don't just take my word for it."

"So, if willow bark is so effective, why does the patient look so sick?" This was Watkins again, clearly gunning for Akenside now. The teacher paused and looked more closely at "the ague patient". He was not satisfied by what he saw.

"Sister, has the patient been taking his medicine regularly?"

"Sir, you specified a large bolus of bark three times a day, with food. But he can't swallow it, and if he does, he can't keep it down."

"Well, that is the cure. He must swallow it."

A thin, reedy voice then entered the discussion. "I try sir, but I can't swallow anything. Can you give it me in a drink?"

"This is a private discussion between medical experts!" barked Akenside. Then, turning to his students again, he resumed his tutorial: "What should we do when a patient is unable or unwilling to take the medicine that will cure his ailment?"

"Could the willow bark be formulated in liquid form?" asked John, thinking of similar preparations he had made in Settle.

"No. Only the solid form shows any efficacy."

"Then there's no point allowing this man to take up space in the ward", suggested one of the gentlemen apprentices.

"Quite right!" responded Akenside enthusiastically. "Sister, discharge this patient. His presence here serves no further purpose."

Without waiting to be asked, or for any help, the man rose slowly from his bed and pulled a small sack of personal effects from underneath. He glared at Akenside. "Some hospital this! I'll go and take my chances at home. I said to my Dorothy that nothing in the world would cure me as quick as her rich broth." With that, he stormed off. Or at least he tried. Before he reached the door, he stumbled and fell. John was the first to reach him. After a brief examination, he looked up and announced that the patient was dead.

"Ward round ended," announced Akenside, and he turned on his good heel and walked out, leaving John and two other pupils helping the ward sister remove the body to the morgue.

*

"The man's intolerable," John informed his friends over a mug of ale. "He'd rather a patient die than admit his treatment doesn't work."

"Surely, if a patient doesn't take his medicine, he's wasting the hospital's time," ventured James.

"Maybe," responded John, "but this man was incapable of swallowing it. Some alternative could have been tried instead of instant discharge."

"Anyway, you'll get a break from Akenside next week," Gilbert reminded him. "Aren't you following Baker to observe surgery?"

"Urgh. I wouldn't be able to stomach that," said James. "A small cut makes me dizzy. Watching a man's leg being sawn off would quickly make me throw up."

"It's my favourite part of medicine," confessed Gilbert. "No need to talk to the patient while treating them."

"Now, Baker is a man I do respect," observed John. Then he smiled as he recollected: "A few weeks ago, he really put Akenside in his place. The mighty physician asked Baker what plans he had for his son Tom. You know, the one who's rather dim. 'I fear he's not bright enough to become a surgeon like me,' replied Baker, 'so I'll send him to Edinburgh to study to be a physician.' That sent old Akenside scurrying off in a huff. He's not spoken to Baker since."

"I think," said James, "that you all look down on Akenside because his father was a butcher. Have you no charity?"

"Well, it's hard to forget his start in life. They say his limp arose because his father got angry and threw a meat cleaver at him, chopping off his heel."

"Now, you're putting me off my ale. The man's probably lonely."

" 'Too much my heart of Beauty's power hath known, And three rich years of youth consumed in vain.' That's his *Love, an Elegy*. I used to like his poetry, but now whenever I try to read it I just see his ridiculous wig and bows and hear his snarling contempt. Better never to meet your favourite writers. They say that the Beauty of that poem consistently rejected his advances, and he's given up on women ever since."

"But he does have a very intimate friend in Mr Dyson," observed Gilbert. Anticipating James's obvious question, he expanded: "Mr Jeremiah Dyson, MP. A very rich man. They met as students in Edinburgh, and then went on to study together at Leiden. Dyson set his pet doctor up in a property in Bloomsbury and arranged for him to become physician to the Queen. He keeps him on three hundred pounds a year so he's time to write his poems and spend intimate time with his benefactor when he's not curing the sick."

"You're both impossibly prejudiced," was James's conclusion on the matter.

CHAPTER 10

"Why on earth did you buy these?" Mary's furious question was hurled at Taine, standing there surrounded by the pieces from an eight-person china tea service. He had just completed emptying them from their packing case and arranging them in a display on the table when his wife walked in from feeding the chickens. Her shriek was loud enough to bring Sam and Teresa running in from their tasks outside.

"It was a bargain. This is real blue Delft pottery, you know. Very much in demand by gentlefolk in London. This set was ordered by the old Lieutenant Governor but he died before he could use them. Aren't they beautiful!"

"But we can't afford them! Don't I keep telling you?"

This row was taking place six months after Taine's reconciliation with Mary following the whipping of Issabel, and Mary was right: he couldn't afford the tea service. She knew for sure because a year or two earlier, while tidying up the house, Teresa had come across the Little Jost plantation accounts. She found that, although they were never as neat and correct as Mr Nottingham's books for Long Look, the pages maintained by Edward Lettsom were legible and marred only by a few omissions and arithmetical errors. However, once the hand-writing changed to Taine's abominable scrawl, all sense of order, accuracy and completeness broke down.

Having spent several afternoons trying to understand them, Teresa began to compile her own records. Since Edward had died, the estate had been losing money. Once Taine had begun to try to win back his wife's affections through the purchase of bonnets, dress material, slippers and other expensive gifts, the decline accelerated. Eventually, Teresa had felt obliged to share her concerns, and her evidence, with her mistress. That was the start of regular marital rows about money. This one was the biggest yet.

"Why do you hate it when I buy you nice things? Do you only want to have the things Edward bought you?"

"We can't afford them!" Even louder this time. Then Mary disappeared into their bedroom and a couple of minutes later returned with the account book and waved it in his face.

Taine was furious. He refused to look at the book.

"What do you know about it? What makes you think you understand finances anyway? We've plenty of money! That isn't my account book anyway!"

Mary just stood her ground, staring at him in fury and holding up the pages for him to see. So he hit her. And then again, so she fell to the floor bringing one of the piles of plates crashing down beside her. He moved in to kick her, but Sam intervened.

"Careful! You touch me, and I'll have you whipped. I'll have you hanged!"

Nevertheless, Taine turned around and strode down to the jetty to sail back to Road Town.

Again, Teresa attended to her mistress's injuries. Again she pleaded with Mary to write to John to tell him what was happening.

"No, I don't want to worry him, he's got such important studies to concentrate on."

This time, after discussion with Sam, Teresa resolved to slip her own note into the next package bound for London.

*

A few weeks later, in London, John was having an unsettling day. In the morning, an unprecedented thing happened: he survived a complete ward round with Mark Akenside without any verbal sparring between them. Even more remarkable, after the round the physician invited him for a drink at a new coffee house close by the hospital.

"You've now completed almost a year observing our practices at St Thomas' ", his tutor observed. "What do you intend to do next?"

"Oh, I don't think I'm ready to make a move yet; I'm still learning so much. Another year here perhaps. And then practice as a surgeon-apothecary somewhere, like my old mentor Abraham Sutcliff."

"I thought as much. But that would be such a waste. You and I have had our arguments, and I've pressed you very hard. That's because you're one of the brightest young apprentices I've encountered. Your fellows are mostly from rich families. Some of them are stupid and some are lazy. Some are both. None of them pay such close attention during ward rounds as you, and none of them work as hard between rounds to understand what has taken place. This morning, all of your diagnoses were correct, and most of your suggestions for treatment were well thought out and would have been effective. You should aim to fulfil your potential. Leave London this summer, and enrol at a medical school. I know your faith closes some doors to you, but Edinburgh and Leiden where I studied would both be open to you. I can provide recommendations."

"But I don't have the money for that!"

"Then get it. Find a rich sponsor. Sell some of those slaves I hear you own. I'm not prepared to have you follow my rounds for much longer if it's only to prepare you to be some provincial saw-bones."

With that, Akenside left. Leaving John to pay for the coffee was not a constructive contribution to his finances, but he had answered one of John's nagging questions. "Was he good enough to go further?" Self-doubt had reconciled him to his more modest ambition. Now he suddenly resolved to do everything he possibly could to realise a more glorious medical future for himself.

*

It had been John's idea to go to the Greenwich May Fair. He had always enjoyed visiting the annual autumn fair in Settle with his lively gang of young companions. They would inspect the fruit and vegetables on show and make their own private (and very low value) wagers on which would win first prize. They marvelled at the sheep and cattle, so immaculately turned out: washed, brushed and combed as carefully as any high society beau or belle. The girls in particular loved to pluck up the courage to approach and even stroke the huge bulls that stood complacently awaiting the judges – although they would have given a very wide berth to the same creatures had they spied them out on their country hikes. They were impressed by displays of horse riding, acrobatics and juggling, and a few of them went into the dark tent where their happy fortune would be foretold. Towards the end of the day, they would repair to the plentiful food and drinks stalls, and then stay for the first hour of the dancing, leaving before events turned more boisterous. Now, he persuaded Gilbert and James to accompany him to Greenwich, as well as their other friends from the Meeting House, Richard and Samuel. Richard's sisters Lucy and Hester came along too, and James brought Nancy and her ever-present aunt.

The fair at Greenwich was not like that at Settle. It was a funfair, and it catered for all manner of fun, provided that you were neither sensitive nor squeamish. In Settle, John had been expert in throwing stones at clay pots, thereby winning prizes – usually spoons – to award to his current favourite amongst the girls. Here instead, you could throw stones at live cocks tethered to posts. Although John's throwing skills had been honed through attempting to hit birds on Little Jost, they had had the advantage of being able to fly away and usually did so unharmed. He saw no sport in "Throwing at Cocks", although Lucy had to be dissuaded from trying her hand. They moved on to the archery stand where, thanks to his Robin Hood phase at Penketh, John was able to hit the straw targets and claim his prize.

The site was thronged with visitors of all types and stations, amongst whom entertainers wandered, trying to lure them into their tents. Fire eaters disgorged flames towards their faces, jugglers caught their clubs just in time to avoid the heads of fine gentlemen and ladies, entertainers whose only accomplishments were their short stature or their enormous height, their wrinkled face (signifying over one hundred years of age!) or their impressive beard (considering that they were female), promised much more astounding sights for those who paid to enter their lair. A cacophony of music filled their ears. Some performers would have been worth pausing to listen to, but their more refined and delicate sounds were drowned out by loud drumming and trumpet fanfares as well as the calls of the sellers of gaudy clothes, flimsy mementos, and cheap food and drink.

Their progress across the muddy site was slow. Although they did stop occasionally to admire some exhibition of magic or rebound-tumbling, most of the time they moved on, repelled by the sights of bloodied prize-fighters, fighting dogs or people attempting to catch greased piglets.

"I'm sure there must be some show animals here somewhere," called out John to his companions, feeling guilty at bringing them to this place.

"If it's animals you want to see, come to our tent," interrupted a large black man wearing a long robe and a circular cap. "All the animals of Africa are in there."

"Is it quiet?" asked Nancy.

"Oh yes, perfectly tranquil and peaceful."

"Let's go in."

So they paid, and took their seats. It was quiet while more customers filed in and preparations were made on the stage. A quartet of African musicians took their places on the stage – with a large drum, a fiddle, an instrument that resembled a lute, and a form of harp. Then it was no longer quiet, as the drum beat out a rhythm around which the other instruments weaved their tunes. A commentator, hidden behind the stage, urged the audience to forget where they were, and to travel with him to the jungles of darkest Africa, to witness the strangest of animals. At this, three zebra were led across the stage, pausing in the centre for their stripes to be admired by the crowd. Next came a monkey and a pair of baboons, guided by boys bearing bright green parrots on their shoulders. Finally came an elephant, small for its species and topped off with a boy wearing a jewelled turban and colourful silk robes.

"Indian, both of them, surely," whispered Gilbert.

With a somersault, the boy leapt off his mount, and landed in an area of the stage where some rocks and vegetation had been placed. After the applause, the animal walked off slowly. The boy made to follow him, but appeared unable to get to his feet. The commentator explained that his leg was caught in the weeds, and that this was a dangerous thing to happen in the jungle at night. At the word "night", the lights inside the tent were dimmed. The drumming continued, but quieter and at the pace of a racing heart. From the other side of the stage, a creature appeared, stalking slowly towards the boy. He struggled and writhed, but was unable to free himself.

Now the lights gradually brightened, and some in the audience gasped and screamed as they could clearly see the huge male lion approaching the boy. Nancy's scream was the most piercing, and she grabbed hold of James's arm. Gilbert later claimed that he was pretty sure he had seen thin black ropes restraining the animal, but for now he too held his breath. The commentator underlined the boy's plight, asking whether anyone in the audience would like to take his place on the elephant for the next show, as he was surely doomed. There were some volunteers.

Eventually, the lion reached the boy who put out his arms to fend him off. At that, the lion licked the outstretched hands, the lights went fully up, and the audience gasped a huge sigh of relief, followed by applause and cheers. The boy sprang up, took a bow, ruffled the lion's mane, bowed again and ran off, only to reappear at the back of the tent with a cap in his hand working his way forward collecting tips. The lion returned the way he had come.

"And now for the most valuable and dangerous creatures on the whole continent of Africa", proclaimed the commentator.

At this, the music began again, at the pace of a slow march. Onto the stage trooped half a dozen Africans, three men and three women. All wore grass skirts, and were otherwise naked except for brilliant bead necklaces and bells attached to leather bands on their wrists and ankles. They were secured together by chains, with braces around their necks and ankles. The commentator explained how they had been purchased on the Windward coast of Africa. He apologised for their chains, but explained that these creatures would be far more dangerous than lions were they to be released.

The sight of chained Africans transported John back to Road Town and to a day long ago when he and Sam had watched newly arrived slaves, secured just like those on the stage, being led from the dock to the market place for sale. It had upset him deeply then, and it did so now, even though he knew that this time it was just an act.

Now the drum beat quickened, the Africans began to jump up and down in time to the music. The chains and braces shattered and were flung to the back of the stage. More gasps from the audience, as the performers began to dance. The men grabbed spears that had appeared to be stage ornaments, and shook these at the crowd; the women took gourds filled with dried seeds to rattle with the drum beat. All of the performers put on headdresses made from huge feathers, white for the men and crimson for the women. Having braved the elephant and the lion, the sight of prancing half-naked bodies proved too much for Nancy.

"Can we leave now?" she asked James.

"I think we should," added her aunt.

They stood and, with James in tow, began to move along the row of seats to extricate themselves from this horrific spectacle. To let them out, John stood up and moved into the aisle between the seats and the tent wall. The whole thing took some time, checking with Lucy and Hester whether they wished to go too – they didn't, reassuring James that he could stay if he wanted – he insisted on accompanying them, responding to the calls for them to sit down and to keep quiet from those on the seats behind them, and carefully checking whether they had all of the belongings they had come in with.

Standing in the aisle, patiently waiting for his friends to make their exit, John did not realise that the dancers had reached the part of the show where they went into the audience to look for partners. The African girl whom he had identified as the prettiest of the three appeared at his side, speaking to him with a broad Cockney accent, and complimenting him on his pluck for volunteering to join the dance. Something about her, and something about the music, made it impossible for him to refuse, so hand-in-hand with his new partner, John allowed himself to be led onto the stage.

The six guest dancers were welcomed by the Africans, given a sweet cake to eat and a powerful punch to drink, and received a round of applause from the audience. Then the music began, and they did their best to imitate the swaying, stamping and leaping of their hosts. It was not as easy as it looked, but from somewhere – a long time ago – John's body found the movements familiar and the steps natural. All too soon it was over, and the cheers of the crowd expressed appreciation. Four of the guest dancers were thanked and left the stage, but John and one of the female guests were asked to stay. More cake was provided, and a larger, even stronger drink was served.

Then the music started again, louder, faster and more insistent. This time there was singing too, with the audience quickly being taught to join in with the sounds of the African words of the chorus. The movements of the dancers became more frenzied, and John managed to keep up with the changing rhythms and to leap and shriek at the right moments. Round and round they whirled, sweat breaking out on John's forehead despite him having already taken off his jacket. His African partner danced closer and closer to him, encouraging him to hold her, swing her and lift her, in imitation of the other couples.

Not a moment too soon, the music came to a dead stop. John let go of his partner, staggered to keep his balance, grabbed on to her again to avoid falling over, and then finally regained his composure and bowed formally and thanked her as if it had all been a Yorkshire barn dance. The cheering and whooping was now ecstatic, coins clanged into the buckets being passed around, and people slapped him on his back and congratulated him on his courage and his performance as he passed to rejoin his party.

"Wow!" said Gilbert. "What was in that drink?"

"Memories", came the reply.

*

By now it was becoming clear to John what he must do next. Akenside had made him realise that there was a successful medical career for the taking if he had the confidence to pursue further training and if he could secure funds to pay for it. Anthony Benezet's pamphlet had deepened the revulsion he felt for being a slave owner, and the sight of chained Africans on stage and the memories that provoked pressed the feeling home. The dancing had reawakened his nostalgia for Little Jost, and he felt an urgent need to be there again with his mother and his friend Sam, and to meet the young woman that Teresa had become.

Finally, a week after the trip to the fair he received another package from his mother. A fairly routine letter accompanied it, the main part relating to a huge fish that Sam had caught for them, and how she and Teresa had prepared a special meal from it. But within the wrapping of Teresa's parcel of sweets was a small piece of paper she had inserted when Mary was not looking. On it she had clearly written the cryptic message: "Please come home soon. Your mother needs you."

PART III: 1767–68

Reunion

CHAPTER 11

"Is it really you?" his mother asked again, releasing him from yet another tight embrace.

"Yes, it really is. Your John. Here to look after you again."

"Oh, that's so wonderful. And you look so well. So well. It's been marvellous to hear all your news, but I'll have to go to bed now. I'm so tired. Is John's bed ready, Teresa?"

"Yes, Mary. We made it up for him this morning."

"Yes we did. You stay up and talk some more to Sam and Teresa. I must go to bed. We can talk some more in the morning. Good night."

Another hug, then a wave, then Mary Coakley closed the door to her bedroom. Then opened it again: "Teresa, is there some more stew in the pan for John? I'm sure he'll be hungry." Then, finally, the door closed again, and it went silent.

The three old friends sat quietly together for a while, and then Teresa asked whether John did want more stew.

"Yes, please," he replied.

"Me too," said Sam, as Teresa caught his eye.

As she divided the remaining goat stew between the two young men, Sam refilled all three glasses with the wine that John had bought when his ship had paused in Madeira.

"She's exhausted," explained Teresa. "Two weeks ago we heard you'd been seen in Madeira, and we told her you were on your way. She didn't believe us at first. Then she became more and more excited. Yesterday, we got news that the *Alice* had passed

Barbados and would soon be here. Sam worked out that you were most likely to arrive today, so we were all up before dawn. Mary personally cleaned the whole house, again, ready for your arrival, and had Rosett and me tidying the yard and sweeping the veranda. That stew went on at midday!"

"I took the shallop over to Road Harbour, prepared to wait a few days if necessary."

"It was wonderful to see you there when I landed. I wasn't expecting a reception."

"You didn't recognise me!"

"Well, seventeen years is a long time. And you had the advantage. Just one passenger coming off a ship that you knew I was on. You've certainly grown!"

That much was true. Sam had grown into a powerful and confident young man. Teresa was – obviously – no longer the pretty little girl of John's memory, but now a fine young woman. Handsome rather than pretty. Her long, straight hair was sensibly tied back, and she glowed with authority and competence. John had quickly noticed that his mother was now "Mary" to both Teresa and Sam, not "Mrs Taine" or "Ma'am". Over dinner, they had interacted more like mother and children than mistress and slaves. Concerned children at that, and as they left the table and sat back in the easy wicker chairs on the veranda, Sam having opened the second wine bottle from John's case, Teresa began to explain why.

She told John of life in Road Town with Taine, making it clear that she and Sam had hated it, but leaving out the most painful and humiliating details. She quickly progressed to the time when they had heard the news of the deaths of John's father and brother, and – endorsed by Sam – told him how heartbroken they had been.

"Taine had become dependent on the business your father was putting his way, and anxious that it didn't stop", continued

Teresa. "He started visiting. His masterstroke was to arrange for Sam and me to move in to keep Mary company and help her with the plantation. She was very keen on this arrangement, as she knew us from the old days."

"We were very keen too," said Sam. "We were freer, away from heavy and dangerous work, and away from him. In fact, we had to insist on working. Mary would've been quite content for us to laze around and play all day, like when we were children."

"That's what she missed, those days of you and Ed, me and Sam."

Brother and sister described Taine's campaign of wooing the new widow, and his ruthless and successful efforts to cut her off from John Pickering and the Quaker community. Despite Taine's actions, Teresa apportioned most of the blame for Mary's isolation on her former friends. She could not understand how such close bonds could be severed so utterly and so quickly, how the dictates of religious faith could count more than long-standing ties of family and friendship.

Since their Anglican wedding, neither of the Taines had been inside a church, and so there was no new religious community for Mary to take the place of the old. As for Teresa and Sam, with all due respect for John's convictions, they confessed to him that they had never been persuaded of any form of faith.

Sam refilled the glasses, and declared the second bottle empty. John and Teresa both resisted the suggestion of opening a third.

*

Sam continued the account, explaining how Taine had appeared to be a reformed character in the first few months after marrying Mary.

"Of course, he was never like your father. Your parents, Ed and you: that was the only experience of real, happy family life we've ever seen. No, it was certainly never like that. Then the war ended, which was good for most of the planters, but not for Taine. He'd taken advantage of shortages and there'd been little competition for mending and fixing things. We're pretty sure he was involved in smuggling too. After the war, he started to have money problems."

"He really did. Your mother and I started keeping accounts!"

"You understand accounts?" asked John, realising too late how patronising that sounded.

Teresa let it go: it was indeed an unusual thing for an enslaved person to be able to do. She described her visits to Long Look, her efforts to improve her reading and writing, and how practicing her arithmetic had led to Mr Nottingham teaching her bookkeeping.

"Mary started having rows with Taine about money," continued Sam, "and about his resumption of drinking."

"And about his women in Road Town and his over-familiarity with her slaves here," added Teresa.

"Eventually, he started hitting her – especially when we were both out of the house."

Details of life on Little Jost van Dyke now began to pour out, Teresa tearful as she described Mary's suffering, Sam apologetic and ashamed that he had been unable to prevent it. John was aghast. He had accepted the bright and cheerful letters from home without question. It had suited him to do so, even though he had known what Taine was like.

"Taine is more away than here nowadays", Sam was saying. "He was so desperate for money that he sold two of your slaves last year, Tom and Damon. Got a hundred and thirty-five pounds for them. Made up a story to tell Mary about Tom being a drunkard and Damon being in the habit of running away, which was nonsense."

"I've kept the record of that transaction and an inventory of the rest of your slaves he had drawn up – there's not many of them, I'm afraid. He was going to send the list to you with the money, but just needed to 'borrow' it in the meantime. We've not seen that hundred and thirty-five pounds yet."

"We've been struggling to cope here. I've supervised the slaves myself – and worked with them in the fields. Even Mary came out to help with the picking. We managed to harvest a little cotton last season and that's brought some money in."

"Since that last big bust up, Mary's been very withdrawn. She hasn't left the island and there's been no visitors. Until she heard you were coming, she'd not done any housework or cooking. I'm not complaining mind, I'd do anything for her. It's just a sign of how down she's been. She gets very frightened whenever Taine comes over, especially if Sam is away. Sometimes he's trying to charm her, bringing presents and doing repairs. Sometimes he's trying to persuade her to give her money, and when she explains that she has none, to sell things. She passed over your father's property on Green Cay and Sandy Cay to him, which he sold, and even gave him some of her family jewellery to sell. There's very little left."

"Except us", said Sam.

"Except us", echoed Teresa.

*

On that note, the conversation petered out. Teresa did ask for John's news, and he told them of the awful storms through which he had sailed to reach Tortola and of how sick he had been most of the way. He told them little of his life in London: to describe his successes and achievements after learning of the hardships at home seemed inappropriate. He expressed his deep gratitude to his friends for the care they had taken of his mother and of his plantation. Before turning in, he asked whether Sam could take him over to Fat Hog Bay the next afternoon to meet with John Pickering and discuss how to earn some money. With that, they retired, it having been a long day for all three of them.

Teresa did not sleep well that night. She felt a strange sense of excitement mixed with relief. Relief because the problems of Little Jost were now shared and because she believed that John would be able to sort them out. Relief because John was clearly still their friend and had spoken to them as equals. As for excitement: where had that come in? From the moment John had entered the room she had felt an unfamiliar frisson. A larger-than-life feeling. When he spoke, when he came close to her, when they touched – squeezing past one another around the table or handing plates to one another – somehow the contact seemed to linger. She had determinedly pulled away, and intentionally averted her gaze from him while she spoke. But her physical reactions did not always respond to her mental intentions, and she caught herself pressing against him when they were close and staring at him across the dinner table. She had better be careful. She wanted to spend more time with him and his help was needed for keeping the plantation going and for protecting Mary. She must do nothing that might scare him away.

For most of the night, it was the plight in which he found his mother that kept John awake. She seemed so tired and frail. Why he had remained so unaware of what was going on and how on earth could he intervene to help her? What of his desire to free his slaves? Could he afford to just write off their value? How, on top of these things, could he also raise funding for his medical ambitions? And, just as he managed to banish financial worries from his mind and began to drift to sleep, another image entered his mind. Teresa. Not the half-remembered face of his former playmate and connoisseur of shells, but the fully shaped young woman looking at him intently, openly, trustingly. These feelings were not the same as after a day's hiking or an evening's dancing with the belles of Settle. They were deeper and stronger. Whatever happened, he wanted them to continue.

CHAPTER 12

"That's where we're heading," explained Jim, pointing due north towards a promontory reaching out into the blue Atlantic waters. "Rogue Bay Point, they call it. All the land sticking out to sea, and up the mountain towards here, is Pickering land. There'll be sixty or seventy people down there for you to see."

John and Jim were looking down nearly a thousand feet to the sea from a spot aptly named "Belle Vue" on the narrow trail following the high ridge that formed the mountainous spine of Tortola. John was mounted on a sturdy brown mare named "Mary Fisher", as her owner – John Pickering – recognised in her the same fearless characteristics as the Quaker heroine. Jim was also owned by Pickering, and he was on foot.

John had arrived at the Pickering plantation house at Fat Hog Bay a couple of days earlier to discuss his plans. They were as simple as they were vague. He sought to make enough money in Tortola both to secure his mother's financial position and to establish a medical career back in London.

The older man reacted calmly to John's apparently impossible position. "You've arrived at a good time," he had said. "Peter Douglas, the only doctor on the island, has become increasingly frail. He last made a medical examination of my workers five years ago. Nowadays he only comes out for medical emergencies amongst the settlers."

Pickering lent him the use of Mary Fisher and the services of Jim and sent him off to talk to the aging Scottish doctor.

Douglas confessed to being unable to fulfil his former duties, and encouraged John to take them up himself. He was able to provide equipment, medication from his own dispensary and herb garden, and most important of all an annotated list of all of his patients and all of the planters who had previously arranged medical check-ups for their workforce. He listed the most common complaints and the most effective remedies. He advised on what fees to charge, brushing aside John's protestations that he was as yet only partially trained and had no formal qualifications. John, he said, should have no qualms about charging full fees. It would be sufficient for him to tell clients that he "had trained at St Thomas' Hospital in London, and was recommended by Dr Douglas".

So, John had started first thing next day with a thorough examination of over a hundred of Pickering's workers and their families on his Fat Hog Bay plantation. For the most part, they were fit and healthy. He performed some tooth extractions, identified children who needed to be wormed, advised that some workers be given lighter duties or retired, distributed ointments for skin complaints and drops for eye infections, suggested some changes of diet and an increase in the provision of citrus fruits and fresh vegetables.

After three hours, he was done, and ready to make house calls on some of the settlers whom Douglas or Pickering knew were in need of treatment. He examined expectant mothers, reset a couple of broken limbs, and treated "Fevers" – the local name for the ague. Here Peruvian bark was not a luxury medicine: Douglas's dispensary had abundant supplies obtained from the cinchona shrubs that grew in profusion in his medicinal garden. By the late afternoon of the same day he was at the Nottingham's property at Long Look, examining their two dozen slaves and making similar recommendations as at the Pickering plantation. He took tea with Mary, her husband being away on one his many preaching tours of the Caribbean. She could still see in him the small boy she had last seen at the Meeting House, and she asked to be remembered to his mother and to "that clever little girl": Teresa.

*

Jim now pointed to the coastline west of Rogue Bay Point. "All along the north coast there are the plantations of Bezaliel Hodge. He's the richest man on Tortola and owns more land elsewhere on the island."

"He's on my list of people to see," responded John. "Probably on my next visit."

"You'll not find his slaves in as good a state as Pickering's or Nottingham's. The Quaker owners are the best to work for. Hodge runs a productive estate, but he squeezes his people to get the most out of them."

"How do you mean?"

"He works them long hours and has them beaten if they don't produce enough. He keeps expectant women working in the fields almost till they give birth. He reckons on getting as much as he can from each body until they die, then he stocks up afresh with new blood straight from Africa. You didn't find whiplash wounds on the workers yesterday, but you will on the Hodge plantation, and it'll be no use suggesting days off or light duties either." Jim had helped John make his examinations, bringing slaves to him when called and sometimes repeating to them, at greater length and in terms that they could more easily understand, what the doctor had just recommended.

"So is the Hodge plantation the worst to work on here?"

"Yes, but not that Hodge. Bezaliel is about typical, I'd think. All masters want to force everything they can out of a slave. Except during the war, when prices shot up, it was cheaper to buy new than to look after what you had. Thank God for the Quakers, and your Mr Fox and his ideas of peace and non-violence. Mr Pickering is loved by his slaves, as they realise what they've been spared. And worst of all is Mr Arthur Hodge, who owns that land there." Jim had turned around and was pointing down towards the south coast. "You see Road Town. Well Arthur Hodge's place is to the left, over on the other side of the Bay. You won't get asked to go there. Most owners are strict because they want to make a profit. Arthur Hodge is cruel because he enjoys it. He beats his slaves personally, and often he kills them. He seems to forget he's damaging and destroying his own property."

John shuddered at these words. During rounds with Abraham Sutcliffe and Dr Fothergill, John had helped treat injuries incurred by masters beating their servants and husbands beating their wives, but the cruelty he was hearing about on this island was on a different scale.

"You seem to know about all the owners on the island", he remarked.

"Word spreads. You run errands, you get told things. Not that you can do anything to alter your fate." Jim looked John in the eyes. "Now you'd be a good owner, I guess."

"Well, Jim, I do own a few slaves over on Little Jost, but I intend to free them."

Jim looked amazed at this idea. "Free them! What will they do?"

"I guess they'll work the land as free men and women. What would you do if you were free?"

"Well, that's it – what could I do? Do you think I could be a doctor like you? I'd like that."

But Jim was being cheeky, as both knew it to be impossible.

"Alright then, I'll set myself up on a little plantation, buy myself half a dozen slaves, including some nice young women, sleep in till noon every day and stay up all night drinking and feasting."

"You would buy slaves!" exclaimed John.

"I sure would. If I were a free man, I certainly wouldn't work on the sugar myself. And what else is there to do on this island?"

Now Jim stopped grinning and lowered his voice to confide in John. "Seriously, on days like these, I am free. I just run after you and the horse. My mind is free. I enjoy the vast views of the sea and the islands. I know you won't beat me if I'm slow, nor suddenly stop and pick flowers and tell me to run all the way back to Mrs Nottingham to give them to her and then catch you up before you reach Rogue Bay. That's what other white men do here. Days like this are all I can hope for. Mr Pickering doesn't beat us, but when times were hard during the war he sold off my woman and our children to a planter in Antigua. Freedom now would be too late for me."

*

By the time he returned to Little Jost, John was feeling happier and clearer about his plans. He had with him two purses of money. One contained his earnings from medical consultations and examinations of enslaved workers. From the efforts of a couple of long days of hard work he had already made almost thirty pounds. He had been asking for the sort of fees that qualified doctors in England earned, and the planters had paid up without demur! Still, considering that a fresh healthy African would cost about a hundred pounds on the dock in Road Town, it no doubt made good business sense.

The other purse contained two hundred pounds that John Pickering had given him to provide for his mother, confessing to guilt about the way the island's Quaker community had treated her, both as a Friend and as an old friend regardless of her persuasion. He had told John to convey his best regards and to let her know she was welcome to visit his plantation house next time she was on Tortola. He also warned John not to let her know the source of the money. "Just combine it with your earnings and give it to her as your own contribution to running Little Jost when you leave. She'd be too proud to accept it as charity from me."

Entering the house, he found his mother sorting through a pile of clothes stacked onto the dining table, choosing which to mend and which to discard. She warned him to leave her to it until she had finished and promised to alter some of his father's shirts for him to wear while on the islands. Taine had not been around while he had been away. He gave her all of his news, showed her his earnings purse, and passed on Pickering's message.

"It's all very well for him to say that now. Anyway, I don't go to Tortola these days. If he's keen to see me, tell him to come over here some time."

Mary brought him a mug of coffee as he sat on the veranda and got back to her work, leaving him to gaze at the half-familiar, half-forgotten features of the island of his happy childhood. Which brought him back to thoughts of his old friends. He had had a little time to reminisce with Sam during their crossings from and back to Tortola on the shallop. They had resumed their friendship almost where they had left off, recalling little private jokes and making the sort of friendly digs at each other that had amused them so many years before.

So far with Teresa, there had been no chance for intimate conversation. He felt deep gratitude to her for the care she was giving to his mother and respect for her calm and confidence. He had also already glimpsed in her smile and noticed in her gestures reminders of the sweet, cheeky little girl he had said goodbye to. But as for his contemplation of how the shape of her hips and thighs could be discerned through her thin skirt, and the contours apparent around the low neckline of her bodice: these were not childhood memories.

His reverie was interrupted by the arrival of the woman in question, very much in business mode. Teresa reported to Mary on the condition of the chickens and the goats, gathered up some papers from a side table, collected her own mug of coffee, and came to sit with John outside.

"Here's the inventory of your slaves Taine compiled a couple of years ago", she said, passing him a paper. "Just eight of them. Rosett and Cudjoe were valued at forty and twenty pounds, but they've not got any younger since. I don't think you'd get much for Cudjoe since his fall last year. Bentorah and Cassia are both in their prime, but the other four are still children. Toney is growing fast and will soon be worth something, but you'd have to wait some time to get much for the others. Your father left Tracy, Issabel and young Rosett and her two daughters directly to Mary."

"I used to tell people in England that I had fifty slaves", sighed John.

"I can remember your father owning thirty or so, but it was never fifty. Still you always did exaggerate!"

"I'm not going to sell them. I'm going to free them."

"Then you'll have nothing. Your father's land here has been neglected and it's now worth very little. Here, read the accounts." Teresa passed him a sheaf of documents. "Besides, what would they do? Who would support Cudjoe and Rosett? You say that you'll free your slaves as if it's so easy, but what does it really mean? Bentorah and Cassia could go off and live a free life in Road Town, I guess. So could Tracy, although her talents are not those approved by God or even your George Fox. But where would that leave the rest of them? This needs careful consideration."

*

John and Teresa had been so intent on studying the accounts, and each other, and Mary so busy sorting clothes, that none of them had noticed a small boat that had crossed from Tortola and was reaching the landing place below them. However Sam, who was supervising work in the cotton fields above the house, saw it. He also recognised the people on it as Samuel Taine and two of his slaves from Tortola. So it was Sam who first interrupted the peace at the house, arriving panting from his run down the hill to warn of the approaching visitors. Mary immediately scooped up the clothes and disappeared with them into her bedroom while Teresa and John quickly went inside to hide the papers they had been discussing. A few moments later, Taine made his entry.

"I heard you were back!" he shouted at John, peppering his language with profanities. "Have you brought money to pay me for looking after your father's estate all this time?"

John calmly replied that he had not, and that Taine had had access to all of the profits of the estate since he had married Mary.

"So you're no help to me. Where's my wife? I need to see her now!" By the slurring of his speech and the stench of rum on his breath, it was clear that Taine was drunk.

"Mrs Taine has not been well", answered Teresa. "She's resting at the moment."

Taine lurched towards the bedroom door, but John and Sam moved to block his way. The confrontation was defused when Mary opened the door and ventured out.

"What's all this noise?" she asked. "I was having such a pleasant, quiet time, with the children all here again."

"I've got papers for you to sign", replied Taine, banging a document down onto the table and then pulling a pen and ink from his pocket. "There and there, at the bottom. Just sign, then I'll go and leave you alone."

Sensing that Teresa did not wish to reveal her business knowledge to her owner, John picked up the document.

"This will lease out the cotton fields of Little Jost for five years. This is my land!"

"Yes, and I've been managing it for you."

"I shall not approve of this lease, and my mother has no legal power to do so. I suggest you return to Tortola, and leave us in peace."

Taine grabbed his papers back and turned to go, but he paused on the step as a new idea occurred to him and he turned back to face them all. "Then I'll do what I should've done years ago. I'll sell those two lazy wretches", he said, waving towards Sam and Teresa. Then pointing at John: "Now you're back, you can look after your mother, so they're not needed here." He leered, dribbling as he spoke. "How much do think I'll get for them on the market at Road Town?"

"You can't sell Sam and Teresa", pleaded Mary. "I need them with me. John has a career in London to get back to, and medical duties to perform while he's over here."

"Well, he can forget all that. He's neglected you all these years – what sort of a son is he? I've made my mind up. I'll take them now. What do you think John, would I get more selling them as a pair, or disposing of them separately?"

It was clear that Taine was deadly serious this time. Teresa stood there shaking, a look of horror on her face, while Sam struggled to control his fury.

"Yes, you're right", said Taine, as if John had answered him. "Selling them separately would bring in more cash." He went to the door to whistle his two slaves up from the dock to help him take his children away, but before he could do so, John intervened.

"If you are to sell them," he said, with all the self-control he could muster, "then I shall buy both of them from you".

"You! You can't afford them. What'll you pay with?"

"I think you'll find that this is enough," John replied, slamming his second purse down on the table.

Taine hesitated for a moment, and then sat down at the table to extract and count the banknotes.

"Two hundred pounds! That's a pretty penny. Where did you get this from? But with my fine girl here, you'll have a dozen more workers out of her by the time she's done."

"Well, maybe. But all her descendants are to belong to me as well. That's the deal."

Taine relented, rather overwhelmed by John's spontaneous offer. He knew he would not get a better deal elsewhere. "All right, offer accepted. I'll get papers drawn up and you can come and sign them at Road Town. I'll let you know when." With that, he pocketed the purse and almost ran down to the landing. John, his mother, and his two new possessions sank down onto the dining chairs and looked at one another, speechless. The relief was palpable.

CHAPTER 13

John was dancing again. Not the wild, uninhibited leaps and swirls of the African troupe, nor the organised chaos of a Yorkshire barn dance, but the elegant, courtly moves of the gavotte and the minuet. Or at least, the West Indian planters' rather boisterous interpretation of those dance steps, accompanied by a distinctly African take on the music from the black fiddlers and flautists of the little plantation orchestra.

"It's wonderful to be back in Cane Garden Bay, Letitia", he said, when the music paused. "You know my father used to own land here. I often visited as a boy."

"Call me Lettice", responded his partner, having already progressed from being Miss Martin to her formal Christian name after just two days' acquaintance. "You dance really well." She had had plenty of time to judge, as he had danced with no-one else all evening.

John's second medical round of Tortola had focussed on Bezaliel Hodges' plantations on the north coast. Five contiguous sugar plantations, each with about eighty workers to examine. More teeth to extract, worms to eradicate, rashes to salve, and as Jim had predicted, whiplash wounds to soothe. It was Jim who first noticed that the punishments appeared to be systematically timed for just a few hours before their arrival at each estate. "Brutal but efficient", he called it. Arranged first to inflict maximum pain, but then to ensure minimum loss of value. John made no comment to the overseers, but took all the time needed to clean and dress the man-made wounds, and silently raised his fees for each man or woman so abused.

At a small cotton plantation north of Cane Garden Bay, he had first met Miss Martin on the estate her father had gifted her. She was a young woman one could never forget, for her vivacious spirit and for the luxuriant, long, wavy, flame-red hair that framed her attractive face. As a businesswoman, she had created an alternative way to work with enslaved people. He had never before encountered such a healthy group, not even on the estates of his Quaker Friends.

Letitia knew each of her thirty or so workers by name, and their children too. She was genuinely concerned about their welfare, and John was, for once, confident that his long-term prescriptions would be assiduously followed. He overheard her discussing the work to be done that day with the gang leaders, in a patient and constructive tone. She explained to him that those who do the work often know best how to overcome the day's difficulties. Her yields were amongst the highest for the island: her cotton certainly looked stronger and more luxuriant than his mother's. The resulting profits were, in part, invested in the cleanest, smartest and roomiest slave village that he had seen on the island, and her workers had time to tend their kitchen gardens and mind their goats and chickens. Some were given time to practice their contributions to the little estate orchestra, and that itself earned additional income as it was in great demand for parties throughout the island.

"My neighbours tell me I'm too soft, that slaves are lazy and must be beaten in order to get a full day's work from them. But my people often work longer and harder than they would on other plantations because they help decide what needs doing, and because they share the benefits when there's a good harvest."

She led John onto the balcony, and they looked out to where her workers were also dancing, to the sound of the orchestra inside augmented by the beat of their own drums. No trace of gavotte or minuet steps here, but something altogether more passionate. They had lit fires, and prepared tables for when the remains of the generous buffet that had been served inside would be brought out for them. When they saw Letitia, a cheer went up. The drumming and dancing paused, while a middle-aged man stepped forward and gave a small speech of thanks to their mistress. The object of his praise raised her arms to acknowledge his compliments. When the revels recommenced, John asked her if they should join the dancers outside – the drumming had entered his soul and he felt his own need to leap and swirl.

"Oh no!" said Letitia, laughing. "A mistress should be kind, but she does need to maintain distance between herself and those who serve her".

On returning inside, Letitia went off to check if her guests had yet had their fill from the buffet, and seeing that they had, began to make arrangements for the rest to be taken outside. John turned to the serious business of the evening: locating the wealthiest of the planters present and offering to conduct medical examinations of their workers. Luckily, Bezaliel Hodge was there, and able to provide testimony to his thoroughness and the value that he had added to his workforce. John's diary quickly filled.

*

"Are you the doctor?" asked the breathless slave as he intercepted John and Jim on the mountain trail.

"Yes. Is there an emergency?"

"Follow me to the plantation house as quickly as you can", and he set off at a run along a side trail descending steeply from the ridge.

"That's the way to Arthur Hodge's place", Jim informed him. "No good will come of a visit there."

John was en route between two of Bezaliel Hodge's properties, having spent a morning examining and treating workers by the blue waters of Banger's Bay, followed by a hearty breakfast with Bezaliel himself at his smart new house across the harbour from Road Town. His afternoon was intended to be a repeat performance with a smaller enslaved group working additional sugar fields some distance away.

John was led to a cluster of shabby wooden buildings surrounding a dusty yard where a crowd of enslaved people were standing in a semi-circle. In the centre, two large black men were holding another smaller black man who was clearly terrified. A red-faced and furious looking white man stood with them.

"Arthur Hodge", whispered Jim, who had soon caught up as it had not been possible to entice Mary Fisher to proceed quickly along the uneven, stony track. "And over there by the house are his overseers, his wife and his son." The last was a thin and sickly looking boy aged about five, who was watching proceedings with great interest.

The master approached John. "You the doctor?"

"Yes. I'm Dr John Lettsom. How can I help?"

"Cut a leg off this man!" instructed Hodge, pointing to the slave being held.

"Which leg is it? Let me examine it – see what's wrong. I may be able to save it."

"Oh, there's nothing wrong with his legs! That's the problem. He keeps on running away. Only way to fix it is to cut off one of his legs. I don't care which one."

"I can't do that, sir", replied John, visibly outraged. "I can't butcher a perfectly healthy man."

"Oh, I'll pay you. Don't worry about that. What's a fair price? Three guineas do you? Make a good job of it mind, then he can hop around and still earn his keep."

"It's not the money, sir. It's the principle. 'First do no harm' – that's what we're taught."

The argument continued but was getting nowhere. Hodge was becoming abusive: towards his would-be runaway, towards the rest of his slaves and finally towards John himself. At that point John bid him "Good day" and he and Jim turned round to return to the ridge. They had not got very far when they heard a loud crash and a piercing scream. Looking back, they saw Arthur Hodge holding a bloodstained axe: the rest was obvious. As they rushed back, Hodge called out: "He's not perfectly healthy now. Do what you wish, but you'll get no payment from me."

The crowd were sent back to work, herded off by the whips of the overseers, and John and Jim were left with the shocked and wounded man. John got to work at once, stopping the profuse bleeding, tying off blood vessels and cleaning the stump. The leg had been taken off just below the knee in a single clean blow. Jim held the victim from behind and offered him sympathy and encouragement. He was faint and giddy and in enormous pain, but he remained conscious. All the time, they were observed by the master's son, who jeered at the idea of them trying to help and offered a constant stream of deeply unhelpful and cruel advice. Finally, when they were done, the two men who had earlier been roughly holding the victim reappeared from behind some bushes where they had been hiding, and gently and kindly carried him to one of the dirty huts. A woman appeared behind them and carefully picked up the severed leg and took that away too.

*

"So, Miss Martin has acquired one more devoted slave!" exclaimed Teresa, with a laugh.

John blushed. "I just enjoyed dancing with her. She knows all of the latest steps, and moves with such grace."

"Show me! What's this gavotte that's so fashionable in Europe?"

John resisted, and it took a great deal of persuasion and teasing – and a careful look around to establish that the house was empty – before he plucked up the courage to start to sing a simple tune and demonstrate the steps. Teresa doubled up in laughter.

"Is that it? That's what the crowned heads of Europe spend their time doing!"

"Well, it makes a lot more sense to dance it with a partner."

Now they were committed. John bowed, Teresa curtsied, and they began to dance. She mirrored all of John's steps and the flourishes of his arms. At first, almost every move ended in disaster for her, moving the wrong way, advancing towards John when she should have been retreating, but before too long she was clearly getting the hang of it. Even beginning to understand why it might be fun. Her giggles were replaced by long haughty looks at her partner, in keeping with the spirit of the dance. Neither of them knew that the version of the dance practiced in the West Indies owed more to its French peasant origins than to the polished realisations in the ballrooms of London. So there was much handholding, and John suddenly recalled that the dance culminated in a polite kiss for one's partner. His resolve to omit that final flourish crumbled, and for the first time since his return he kissed a very surprised Teresa.

Involuntarily, Teresa stepped backwards. John blushed again, protesting that this was all part of the dance. Both of them were secretly thrilled. Wanted more contact. Both of them backed off, she excusing his move as it was all part of the dance, he assuring that it certainly was, and was considerably more formal and restrained when his partner was Letitia. Did that mean he thought her forward? Did that make him sound as if he had not really wanted to conclude the dance that way?

"Have you time to look at the plantation papers now?" she asked, after an embarrassed pause.

"Certainly. Let's go out on the veranda."

Once seated outside, Teresa put the sheaves of papers she had brought into some sort of order. To move the conversation on from dancing she remarked on what John had told her about the condition of the workers on Tortola.

"Obviously Miss Martin's slaves are in a far better position than those on Hodge's plantation. But they're still slaves. They still dance to the drums outside, while the white people dance to the fiddles inside. The sin of slavery is injustice, inequity. Cruelty can occur between white people, between black people, and especially between men and women. That's a different sin."

"It is. I haven't been cruel to my slaves, but I am resolved to free them."

Teresa now pulled out the inventory of John's human possessions.

"I've been talking to them about that. Bentorah and Cassia would be very keen to be free. They would both like to stay on at Little Jost to begin with, if the pay was right. Bentorah would like to do more sailing of the shallop for us: Sam has taught him and occasionally sends him out alone on errands. Cassia would like to help more in the house. She says that their children, Myal and Cotto, are happy here. But you have to work out how they would be paid. The plantation finances are pretty dire. Young Toncy says he'd be off like a shot. To the excitement of Road Town, I think! We'd have to think about the future of Nanny. Being an orphan, there's no-one else to look after her, and she's still too young to fend for herself."

"It's not many, is it? Seems like a tiny gesture set against all of those poor captive people I've been examining."

"Well, it's a good gesture, as long as you can afford to do it properly. From what you've been making on Tortola, I think you can. There's Rosett and Cudjoe too. Rosett is terrified of the idea. Thinks she'll be thrown off the island as soon as she's freed. I've assured her that it'll make little difference and that she and Cudjoe will keep their cabin. You won't charge them rent will you?"

"No. I hadn't thought of that, but no. Nor Bentorah and Cassia. At least not at first."

"That'll help persuade them to stay. I had a long talk with Cudjoe. You know, he was a slave in Africa before he was brought here. I never realised. When he was young, just old enough to have been initiated to manhood, he became a warrior. On the wrong side in a local war. He was captured and enslaved by a powerful kingdom and taken away to a village at the opposite end of their territory, near the coast. He was put to work, labouring in the fields.

"He said the worst thing about it was the shame. He'd failed as a warrior, and he'd not had the courage to fight to the death. In the end, he'd surrendered and begged for mercy. The work he had to do was not excessive, and his captors often worked alongside him doing the same tasks. He told me that, in Africa, the opposite of slavery is not freedom, it's belonging. He didn't belong in the village where they held him, he wasn't part of those people. And they saw him as an outsider, a failed warrior, someone contemptible. And the slaves – there were a few of them – despised one another too. They knew they were all failures as men. Then he was sold to African slaving merchants who took him to a fort on the coast and sold him on to white traders.

"Your father bought him directly off the boat in Road Town, and he's been on Little Jost ever since. He says that he slowly recovered his spirit. He became respected within the slave village, and his opinions and advice were sought. Edward and Mary treated him fairly, and he felt secure that they wouldn't sell him.

He'll be proud to be free, but in his own mind he ceased to be a slave once he retrieved his sense of belonging."

John listened in silence to this story, amazed at how complex Cudjoe's life had been, and how none of his family had been aware of any of it before. While he listened, he studied Teresa's face intently. One minute he was dancing with and kissing this handsome young woman, the next she was demonstrating her business sense and her empathy. What was it he was feeling for her now? But all he said was: "I'm happy that my parents are well thought of. I know father would have been pleased to know this."

"But your mother doesn't understand what you're doing at all. She'll not free her slaves. She thinks it would amount to abandoning them. She feels very protective towards them, maternal even. For free black single women, she thinks the world is too dangerous."

"It all gets so complicated when you move on from 'free the slaves', to 'what's best for Bentorah, Cudjoe and Issabel?' ", reflected John.

"That leaves you with two slaves", concluded Teresa.

"I thought you'd covered them all."

"Sam and me", she said gently. After a pause she asked him quietly: "What have you in mind for me?"

This direct question was a risk for Teresa. She waited anxiously while John hesitated, all the time managing to appear cool and detached – it was just a matter of business after all. John did have something in mind, but it was a half-formed, ill-thought-out idea. As the silence lengthened, he said it anyway.

"Perhaps, I should take you to England with me."

Teresa's heart leapt. But what did that mean?

"As what? Slave, servant, mistress, sister, ... wife? You did promise to come back and marry me." John blushed yet again, as Teresa laughed. "You remember!"

"Yes, I remember. We were very little."

"And now you've met Lettice, and it's too late for me!" She was still smiling, but tears were forming in the corners of her eyes.

"It would be very difficult."

"All the best things are."

They sat, staring at one another, the conversation exhausted. Closer now even than when they had been dancing. Then, at almost the same time, his mother emerged from the yard where she had been feeding the chickens and collecting their eggs and Sam appeared from the landing stage with three goats he had just bought from a settler on the main Jost van Dyke Island. The spell was broken.

CHAPTER 14

"Your people are mostly healthy", reported John. "There's no fever here, and very few are suffering from worms." He knew, by now, to start with the good news. "But they don't appear to be adequately nourished, they suffer too many accidents due to exhaustion, and the punishments inflicted on them drain their strength and productivity."

"So, you think I should run my plantation along the lines of our beautiful red-headed friend, pampering the poor blacks and letting them laze around all day playing the fiddle", responded Harald Pedersen.

John had been introduced to the tall Norwegian planter at another of Letitia's parties. He had anticipated finding harsh conditions in his sugar fields, just from the way he had spoken. He used the foulest words to refer to his African workforce, and cursed them for what he claimed to be stupidity, laziness and insolence. Although John had danced with his hostess for half the night, she seemed cooler than before the novelty of entertaining a man of science and of religious rigour was beginning to fade. Nor did he appreciate her willingness to echo Harald's language and opinions about enslaved people, and to share jokes that demeaned them. He was beginning to suspect that her softer treatment of her workers was but a clever and effective means of increasing their output, rather than indicating any true empathy.

At one stage during that evening Harald remarked that John seemed to be reluctant to adopt the words commonly used to specify, and simultaneously denigrate, Africans. "How do you refer to your slaves then?" he had asked. "Oh, as Bentorah, Cudjoe, Rosett and so on." This answer led to laughter from Harald, and worse, to irrepressible giggles from Letitia. She whispered something to Harald, which led to further sniggering. As they recovered, both appeared to conclude that the only way to avoid giving irrevocable offence would be for Harald to arrange for John to conduct a medical audit on his plantation.

So, here he was, on the island of St Thomas, under the flag of the Kingdom of Denmark and Norway. This small Scandinavian possession lay just ten miles to the southwest of Tortola, and the landscape and agriculture was similar to its British neighbour – beaches, mountains, and sugar, sugar, sugar. Although Harald mocked his guest's sensitivities, he respected his right to his own opinion as well as valuing his medical skills. John had started with a check up of the family, and his advice on Harald's daughter's eczema and his son's attacks of asthma had been carefully noted. John was more confident of the settler's commitment to act on those parts of his advice than on his exhortations to improve rations for the workers and reduce their beatings.

While John reported back on the condition of the workforce, Harald's wife could be heard in the kitchen, busily preparing a lavish supper for their guest. Kirsten was a thin and pale young woman, about twenty years younger than her husband. John had examined her, and found her to be rather frail and shy, but not suffering from any ailments requiring treatment. Now, in the kitchen, she sounded like a different woman – in her element coaxing local ingredients into some semblance of Scandinavian cuisine. She chatted and laughed with her white servant, Sofia, and shared jokes with the children as they were given their tea. They spoke in Danish, so John was unable to appreciate the jokes, but the warm atmosphere of happiness and love was unmistakable.

With some effort, John concentrated on his more serious conversation about the state of the planter's human property.

Sadly, it was the anxious and shy Kirsten who joined the men for the meal. Sofia served the courses, and she too was now reserved and formal. Harald explained that Kirsten had been born on the neighbouring island of St Jan soon after her parents had emigrated from Denmark. John asked her a few questions about her parents and her children, receiving polite but cryptic answers: both of her parents were now dead, both of her children were fluent in Danish, Norwegian and English. He complimented her on the food, which was indeed delicious and novel, but failed to initiate a discussion of Nordic cooking. Now Harald turned the conversation to his personal approach to running the plantation.

"Letitia cultivates her slaves as she does her crops. She wants them all to grow tall and healthy, to survive until they bear fruit, and to accumulate value. My predecessor on this plantation thought the same, though without developing an in-house orchestra! But too much prime sugar land was tied up in food production, and too much of their time was devoted to tending it. It's much more efficient to buy in grain, give them a simple, basic diet and concentrate on growing sugar. And on these islands, we're painfully aware of the need to discipline slaves, and not to allow them time to think, to organise, to rebel."

Harald paused and slowly refilled his and John's wine glasses, and took a long and hard look at his wife before he continued in a more sombre tone.

"Thirty years ago, while I was away exploring the world, the slaves over on St Jan rose up. They massacred the garrison and murdered planters in their beds along with their wives and children. They didn't spare owners who'd been considerate or caring – they slaughtered all the whites they could find. Kirsten was among the few who escaped here to St Thomas, but her parents and her brothers were all killed. The rebels took control of a large part of the island."

"It was terrifying", interrupted Kirsten, who now found her voice. "In the middle of the night they burst into our house. They attacked my parents in bed where they lay. My brothers and I heard the commotion and ran into their room. They'd already killed father. Two of them were struggling with mother. She screamed out for us to run, but my older brother tried to rescue her, only to be cut down by a third slave with a machete. They weren't our people – they'd all fled. They killed my mor right there in front of me!

"Then I ran. My younger brother followed me, but he tripped in the dark. I just kept running as fast as I could, all the way to Cruz Bay. Behind me, our house was on fire, and all around there were settlers running, buildings burning and slaves looting and killing. Some of our militia were organising resistance and running towards the rebels with muskets. At the bay there were boats leaving. A family helped me down to the beach and onto a small boat which landed me at Redhook on this island. I just sat on the quay, trembling and weeping. I was only seven.

"Eventually, I was found by Harald's elder brother, Magnus, who had come down to see how he could help. He knew my father, and he brought me here to live on this plantation. Eventually he became my guardian. Twenty years later, he died. Then Harald came home from his travels to inherit the estate and I was rescued again: this time by a husband."

This vivid account had brought back her terror, its narrator now shaking, her face even paler than before. She looked up at her husband for support, and he took her hand in his while he completed the historical details.

"They were well organised and understood that together they had the strength to overcome us. What they did not know – how could they? – was the strength we could muster from other European powers in the region. They held out for nearly eight months until they were eventually defeated with the help of a French force. Many of the rebels then killed themselves and others were brutally executed. It all left a deep mark on my dear wife. To this day she is frightened of black men. All of our house servants are white – which is pretty expensive – and she won't go out of the house without a white man to escort her."

"I hate them! I loathe them! I'm terrified whenever I see them, or hear them, or worst of all smell them! I'm immediately back in my parent's bedroom with them butchering my family all over again. I never found out what happened to my dear little brother after he fell. I wish we could get rid of all of them!" After this outburst, Kirsten fell silent again.

"Since then it's been abundantly clear that in order to survive, we must crush the very concept of resistance. Squeeze out the humanity and the imagination of the slaves and ensure they have no time and no intellect for plotting rebellion. They outnumber us on this island ten to one. Short, harsh, productive lives are all we can allow. Then, when they drop dead, buy new ones."

John had been shocked by Kirsten's story, and expressed his deep sympathy for her loss and the trauma she had suffered. But he was even more horrified by the cold and heartless conclusion that Harald had drawn. His host had not finished.

"I used to work on the Danish forts on the Gold Coast of Africa, and I travelled inland extensively. Met the chiefs and the kings in their villages and their cities. They do have cities, you know. Clean and well maintained, beautifully laid out, and decorated with subtle craftsmanship – woodcarvings, metalwork, beautiful colourful textiles. Despite what I say at parties and to humour fellow-owners, I know they're not actually stupid either. Quite the contrary. They know good business deals when they hear them; how to eliminate their rivals and make a profit out of it at the same time. So, we worked with them when we could.

Much better to use the local powers to deliver the merchandise than to try to take it yourself. They have few guns, no modern weapons, so we can always destroy their power if need be. It's precisely because they are intelligent and cultured people that we have to crush their spirit completely in order to reduce them to the beasts of burden that we need."

For John, this was far worse than imagining that Africans were stupid. Such a belief could be demonstrated to be false, and once that was done a European might begin to question how enslaved workers were treated. Harald had gone one further. He had accepted the African as his intellectual equal, and yet still wished to enslave him. John had no rejoinder to make. Kirsten, having recovered her composure, offered him another helping of the meal. To be polite and to show appreciation, he accepted a little more, but he no longer felt hungry nor desirous of prolonging the conversation. Harald could see his discomfort, but pressed on regardless.

"You should come and work here, John. There's great need for medical provision amongst the planters. And you will find we're a remarkably free and tolerant society. Apart from administrative and military people, there are in fact very few Danes and Norwegians here. The planters are mostly German, English, Irish and Dutch. Every religion is allowed: Catholics, Lutherans, non-conformists, and new sects that no-one has even heard of. We're short of Quakers though, so you'd be most welcome to put that right. We've plenty of Jewish merchants. They find greater acceptance of their faith here than anywhere else in the Caribbean. So, you see, we're a very inclusive and equitable society. But some people have to do the hard work, and we're all agreed that it's to be the black people."

*

"Not many of them are Danish, as it happens. They take great pride on being open to settlers from any country and tolerant to all religions, but they treat their slaves just the same as settlers here – abominably! All the same, they pay pretty well to have them checked over."

John was giving an account of his three weeks on St Thomas and St Jan to his medical colleague Peter Douglas. By this time, John was lodging with his cousin Edward Lettsom during visits to Road Town. He had never met any of this Anglican side of his father's family until he had been called upon to treat Edward's wife. Meeting another Lettsom led to a conversation about mutual relatives, and eventually to an invitation to move out of the small rented rooms he was occupying into Edward's substantial house. The two medics were seated in Edward's front room, and the older man went on to discuss his recent bout of yellow fever and John's successful treatment of it.

"I felt so wretched when you came to examine me. I've suffered fevers before, but I've never vomited so much, nor brought forth such disgusting green fluids. I thought I'd die, and wished only to be through with it quickly. I've never administered Peruvian bark for yellow fever myself. I would have bled the patient, and then given calx of antimony or valerian as an emetic."

"Oh, I'm a great believer in cinchona", replied John, using the botanical name for the successful remedy. "It's already aided the recovery of another patient during my time here. A young woman suffering from intermittent fever, having too quickly left her bed following childbirth. After a week she was on the brink of death. I gave her laxatives, applied water and wine to her mouth using a feather as she couldn't swallow, and had warm bricks applied to her feet and legs. This took off the fever. After one night, I was astonished by her improvement. As she could swallow again, I started her on a course of Peruvian bark to strengthen her system and prevent any recurrence. She made a quick and complete recovery. It was similar to what I did for you. I'll write a paper about these case studies when I return to England."

"Have all of your experiences with cinchona been so successful?" asked Douglas.

"Well, one patient was too far gone when I started treatment and even the bark was unable to save him. For another, I administered too low a dose, and so that was unsuccessful. I won't mention those in my paper though: it's clear to me now why it didn't work for them."

"You should surely mention all of the patients in your account, and not just select the ones for whom the treatment was successful."

"But that might confuse my readers. My recommendation will stand or fall by virtue of the persuasiveness and clarity of my writing. Mentioning those who failed to thrive for other reasons would just muddy the waters."

The medical seminar was interrupted by Edward Lettsom who emerged from his study with a reminder that it was time to attend Henry Beaverhood's legal office to sign the Deed of Sale of Sam and Teresa from Taine to John. Leaving Douglas to enjoy a second cup of coffee while he waited for a downpour of rain to stop before setting off home, John and Edward hurried to the office where the lawyer and Taine were already waiting. It was the first time John had seen his step-father without at least a week's stubble on his chin, and he was dressed in his best jacket and breeches. For this occasion, he cleaned up his language just as thoroughly as he had cleaned his face and clothes.

"I'm sad to do this, Mr Beaverhood. They're my children, you know. My own flesh. But I can't provide for them as I should. This rich young man will take them to England where they'll prosper." John almost expected him to burst into tears. "It's just like a wedding", his cousin whispered. "Taine is giving his daughter away – and his son for good measure".

John and Edward read through the Deed of Sale, a long and rambling document, drawn up to Taine's instructions. It acknowledged the receipt of two hundred pounds and granted ownership of Sam, and Teresa and her "Issue and Increace", to John and his heirs forever. It referred to those sold as a "boy" and a "girl", but when John pointed out that they were both well into their twenties, Taine looked sorrowful, and responded: "They'll always be my boy and my girl".

Satisfied with the document, John signed, and Edward added his name as witness.

The deed was done. On emerging from the office, John found one half of his new property waiting. Sam had sailed the shallop over to take him home to dine with his mother.

"I just made the harbour in time", exclaimed Sam, shouting to be heard over the fury of the wind, which was now stronger than when they had gone into the office. "I'm afraid you'll miss dinner, but I'll take you across to Little Jost just as soon as this storm abates." They ran through the now torrential rain along the muddy street to the shelter of Edward's house, where the host ordered lunch to be prepared for himself and John, and for Peter Douglas who was still stranded there. Sam disappeared into the slave quarters to be fed. However, a doctor's time is not his own. Before he was even able to sit down, a hammering on the door revealed Jim, panting, sweating and covered in mud from the mountain trail.

"The master's taken bad. Please, can the doctor come and see him at once!"

So John took Edward's horse and set off along the five mile mountain trail that led to John Pickering's plantation. Without stopping for food or drink, Jim followed on foot, never falling far behind.

CHAPTER 15

It took three hours for John and Jim to traverse the treacherous trail to John Pickering's plantation, climbing steeply for eight hundred feet above Road Town before descending at a slightly less precipitous gradient to Fat Hog Bay. Underfoot, the way alternated between sharp rocks and oozing mud. In places, usually dry stream beds had become torrents, washing away the surface of the track. John's horse stumbled several times, and he repeatedly lost the track where it was blocked by fallen trees, submerged or covered with gravel loosened and carried down by the flood water. At these times, John had to wait for Jim to catch up to give him direction: not usually for long as the advantage of horse over man was almost wiped out in the conditions.

As they approached the Pickering plantation house they began to hear African drumming beating out the news of Pickering's collapse, and then to pass workers converging on his home from his other plantations. A great crowd of them surrounded the house. Inside, John found the master of the house lying fully clothed on his bed, attended by his wife Rebecca, his daughter Rebecca, his sister Mary Nottingham, and half a dozen house servants. John Pickering had gained a great deal of weight in recent years, and indeed he had collapsed suddenly while in the kitchen seeking a sweet snack to tide himself over to breakfast. With great difficulty, and perhaps unwisely given the delicacy of his condition, his servants had carried him up the narrow stairs to his chamber. John sent away the servants, examined his patient, and asked the elder Rebecca a few pertinent questions.

"Apoplexy", thought John, who was familiar with sudden collapses like this. Although he could give the condition a name, he – in common with all his medical colleagues – knew very little about either cause or mechanism.

A servant hovered in the doorway, relaying a commentary on John's actions and questions to another at the foot of the stairs who passed it on to the crowd outside. They were respectful and concerned, earnestly praying for their master and reciting their praise for his benevolent treatment of them in hushed tones. The drums relayed the bulletins farther, and the crowd continued to grow despite there being no let up in the storm.

John Pickering drifted in and out of consciousness. His doctor could do little to help him, having checked that his airways were clear, and ensured that the doors and windows were open – despite the weather – to provide plentiful ventilation. Gradually, the older man worked out who was attending him, and gave a beatific smile.

"So John, you have come to me. I am so pleased." He raised his right hand slightly, and John grasped it in both of his.

"So few Friends now. So few family. All our children who were taken from us. My daughter Dorcas, named after my dear first wife. My son, Zachariah. Then Dorcas herself died."

He stared into the distance, as if trying to visualise his lost wife and children. Tears rolled down his cheeks, but he made himself go on.

"And then I married my dear, dear Rebecca. And her daughter Dorcas died. Only young Rebecca is still here – such a great comfort to me." Young Rebecca, about fifteen years of age and sobbing uncontrollably, stepped up and kissed her father's face gently.

"John, I hope you have many fine children, and they all outlive you. My John grew up to be a man, you know. But he died in New York."

"I know. I was very saddened. We got on well when he came to Liverpool."

"Yes, but he turned his back on our faith."

"Relax, my friend. Don't waste your energy."

"It's been a great disappointment to me. And Josiah died in England this spring from a fever." This was news to John, and although he had never met John's youngest son, he sympathised with this further loss.

"Couldn't get him into your old school. It closed, you know. Gilbert Thompson would've looked after him. Nine years old. Very clever. Cleverer than Isaac. And kinder too. Isaac has a hard edge to him, you know. And no love for this island. Couldn't wait to leave for school. But Isaac is the only son I have now. I wish he was here." The planter's voice was becoming weaker, and his eyes shut. Then suddenly he was awake again, and trying to sit up.

"Don't stir yourself", said John. "Just lie there quietly and let your strength recover."

"Rebecca, go and get that purse from my desk drawer." As his wife went off to undertake the errand, Pickering continued. "You know, I wish you'd been my son, John. Or that my sons had been like you. I'll leave my estate to Isaac, though I fear for the future of my plantations and the future of my people. They do love me, you know. Here, take this purse", and Rebecca passed it to him. It was fat. "This is for you to further your career, and to look after your dear mother. Don't tell her where it came from."

Having completed that task, Pickering's eyes closed again, and he began to snore softly. His wife knelt down and cradled his head and his sister held his other hand. His daughter stood at his feet, reaching out to touch them. The commentary paused and the crowd outside went completely silent. For quarter of an hour, time stood still. Then suddenly, John Pickering awoke, and forgetful of what had happened to him made a sudden lurch to stand up. He almost succeeded, but his heart gave out completely, his legs buckled, and he dropped back onto the bed. For five more minutes he lingered on the boundary between life and death, and then, accompanied by an echoing gasp, death won. John closed the deceased's eyelids, and announced the end of his life.

*

As soon as death was confirmed, a dismal and mournful yell went up from the people crushed outside the door, and spread in a wave throughout the wider crowd beyond. It was now dark, but the wind had abated and the rain had stopped. The drums took up a heavy and slow beat, and their tolling was echoed on one neighbouring plantation after another. Now the Africans closest to the front door began to press to enter the house in order to view the body and pay their last respects. A large man named Oswald, who acted as the headman amongst the slaves, barred their way, but he was finding it hard to maintain control.

"They mustn't come in!" exclaimed Mary Nottingham. "There's too many of them. People will be injured in the crush and they'll break through the floors and bring the house down."

John now hastened to the bedroom window to address the crowd. "For the sake of the memory of your noble master, please step back. He has died peacefully, with his family around him. He expressed his great hopes for the future of the people, you people, who have served him so well. Please go back to your homes now, and mourn him with respect within your own families." John deliberately spoke quietly, so that the slaves, anxious to hear what he had to say, had to stop pushing and talking in order to hear. He then explained that, as a Quaker, their master believed that his spirit would live on in his son and his daughter. He asked for the crowd to remain silent or if possible join him as he led them in a brief prayer.

The crush having eased, Oswald now moved to the front of the house, where he could look up and respond to John. In a loud and clear voice he made his address.

"We, the master's loyal servants express our sorrow at the loss of a blessed man, and convey our sympathies to his wife, his daughter and his sister. We thank you, doctor, for your ministrations to him at the end. You have taken what comfort you can from the prayer of the religion that he and you share. We have our own beliefs and our own rituals. For us to ensure that our beloved master has the safest passage into the realms of the dead, we implore you to let us see his body and pay our last respects." On this there was a surge towards the now unguarded door.

"Stop!" cried John. "Oswald, please stop them! Arrange for them to file through in groups of just twelve. One group at a time. Allow us to arrange his body with dignity, and then I shall give the signal for the first group to come in."

And so began John Pickering's lying in state. His wife and daughter were too distressed to help, and they retired to another room while his sister washed his face and arranged him so that he looked dignified. Then, for several hours, John supervised sorrowful groups of African workers as they filed up the stairs and through the temporary mausoleum, some reciting prayers in various languages to various gods, some in tears, some looking shaken and fearful. Eventually, the last melancholy party filed out as the new day was about to dawn. Emotion and exhaustion finally claimed John, who collapsed onto the guest bed that Mary Nottingham had prepared for him, weeping copiously and uninhibitedly until sleep overtook him.

*

The following morning was bright and warm, with exceptionally clear visibility as the heavy rain had settled all of the dust. By contrast, the mood was subdued as John took his breakfast with the female relatives of the deceased. Recollections of the virtue of the great man were shared, and funeral arrangements discussed.

The heir to the estate, Isaac, was at Shelborne School in England. He was just thirteen, the same age and in the same situation as John had been when he had received the news of the death of his own father. His mother was adamant that he would remain where he was and complete his education, and took comfort in John's support and precedent for this decision. John Pickering's nephew, also named Isaac, would be asked to oversee management of the estate until the boy's return, and indeed he arrived before they had completed their meal having set off early from his own small estate near Road Town. He warned John that the track had deteriorated considerably during the storm, and advised him not to travel alone.

"The distress and grief of the workers last night was profound and very moving", remarked John to Jim as they climbed up the track from Fat Hog Bay. Following Isaac's advice, he had requested a companion for the journey, and Jim had once more volunteered. Wanting to find out more about why the slaves had reacted as they did, and also conscious of the state of the trail, John was leading his horse and walking beside Jim.

"Many loved the master. They found him fair and accepted him as they would an African chief. He sometimes made hard decisions and inflicted punishments, but they understood that as the role of a leader. He wasn't cruel, and didn't give beatings. Others just knew that anyone else would be much worse. I'll never forget that he sold my family, and never forgive. But I'm afraid for what'll come next. Isaac was not a kind boy. Not as nasty as young Arthur Hodge, but he never showed the compassion of his father. And his cousin, the older Mr Isaac, is no Quaker. He's strict and hard in running his own estate and can inflict beatings as savagely as any owner."

A change of ownership had the power to transform the lives of the enslaved fundamentally. John could understand how the grief expressed the previous night had been tinged with fear for the future.

The steep descent into Road Town was especially treacherous, and John had to lead the reluctant mare down gently and slowly. Aware that those waiting for him had seen the power of the storm and would have received reports of the crowds surrounding the Pickering home, he was anxious to let them know that he was alright. He gave his cane to Jim and instructed him to run ahead and announce his imminent arrival, the cane serving as his calling card. Jim covered the distance quickly, but the occasion not being as urgent as on the previous day he went round to the servants' entrance. Seeing his approach, Sam went out to meet him just as Edward emerged from the front door, concerned at what the news might be. Sam reached Jim first, saw his smile, and grasped the cane from his hand. In great relief, he kissed the cane, proclaiming, "I am glad my master is returned safe!"

Edward later told John of Sam's reaction. John was deeply touched by the genuine joy expressed by his old friend on hearing that he was safe. Knowing Sam, he also suspected a note of sarcasm in Sam's reference to him as "my master". At least, he hoped that it had been sarcasm.

CHAPTER 16

"Here's my copy of the document: you and Sam now belong to me." John and Teresa were once more sitting on the veranda at the house on Little Jost van Dyke, discussing business. He showed her the bill of her sale. Teresa studied it carefully.

"Can I make my own copy?" she asked.

"Certainly."

"What does M.D. after your name mean?"

"It signifies the degree of Doctor of Medicine. In Latin, so it comes out backwards."

Teresa rolled her eyes at such pomposity.

"But I thought you hadn't got your medical degree yet. Surely, that's what you're going back to study for."

"Well, yes. But the islanders prefer to be treated by a real M.D."

Teresa gasped at this admission of deception. She took the pen and lightly scratched out the offending letters. John looked on, amazed and ashamed. He took back the document, but made no attempt to undo Teresa's correction.

"I shall earn it in time."

Now he handed her further papers.

"These are letters documenting the freeing of my slaves. One each for Cudjoe, Rosett, Bentorah, Cassia and her children, Toney and Nanny. A copy for them to show to anyone who needs to know, and a copy for the estate files."

Teresa examined the letters with some difficulty as the evening light was beginning to fade. "There's no confirmation from Beaverhood. Are these arrangements legal?"

"I have my own copies too. I'll take them over to his office and ask him to make the necessary arrangements."

"Don't forget!" warned Teresa. "Bentorah and Cassia will stay on. Mary and I have agreed suitable arrangements with them. They'll also take responsibility for Nanny, which they've already been doing anyway. Toney will be off: he now hopes to go to sea. Cudjoe and Rosett will live out their retirement here. They've been loyal and hard working over the years, and they say they'll still help out informally when they can – as neighbours, I guess."

"And here are the letters of freedom for you and Sam", continued John.

"And what am I to do?"

"You'll be free to choose! That's how it works."

"Will you take me to England?"

"If you want."

"As what?"

This was the question John was still unable to resolve. Having found Teresa again, he did not want to let her go. He did not know any other woman with whom he would prefer to share his life. There had been no further close physical contact between them since they had danced the gavotte, but that had been enough for him to realise that he had never wanted to touch anyone else quite so much. Dancing with Letitia had held no magic the second time round.

Teresa had pondered this question a great deal. Almost constantly since their last discussion of the matter, in fact. She now conveyed her thoughts to John.

"I cannot accompany you as your wife, obviously. You plan to devote yourself to your career, your medicine, your patients. A black wife! An ex-slave! A heathen! How would that go down in

London society? How would your Quaker Friends respond? It can be done out here, just about, though there's still loss of status. But you're not going to stay here, are you? You love your work. You need your M.D. You're dead set on a career in London. The island's slaves are now so healthy you won't be needed to examine them again for years."

John nodded, tearfully, accepting this analysis.

"Not as your mistress, either. It has some attractions." Here Teresa grinned and giggled, reaching out to squeeze John's hand. "But no, I couldn't do that. And nor could you. Of course, an ordinary M.D. could get away with it, but not a Quaker M.D., I think."

Right again, thought John.

"And not as your 'sister'. I couldn't live that role and I'd have no security."

Both of them were now in tears, and it took some time for them to regain their composure. Then Teresa released John's hand and announced her conclusion.

"I shall stay here to help Mary run the estate. Taine is useless, and hasn't been here since he sold us to you. He seems to have settled down with Polly in Road Town and hopefully he'll stay away. Mary's been so good to me and Sam since we were children. I love her as a mother, and I can't let her down. And I love living here on Little Jost, working with the little community we have here.

"Don't free me. Mary has a low opinion of free black women, based mainly on Taine's mistresses. I have told her about respectable free black housekeepers, seamstresses, businesswomen I know in Road Town. And those who live as faithful wives and loving mothers. It's no use, her mind is closed. If I were free, she wouldn't want me to stay, wouldn't want to pay me. She wouldn't understand such a relationship. On the other hand, if I remain your slave – her dear John's gift to her – then she'll accept my company and my support. And frankly, I too am scared about how I might get on as a free woman on Tortola, on my own."

John sighed, and then nodded. He put one of his letters in his pocket.

"What about Sam?"

"What have you told him?"

"Nothing."

"Take him to England with you. Don't free him yet, then he can't argue. Take him to England, give him some opportunities to develop. One of us should have the chance of real freedom, and it'll be easier for him as a man. If he isn't your slave, at least for the time being, he'll insist on staying here to help me and Mary. That would be a waste. The task here doesn't need both of us. Let him find his own way in England, and when you see that he's ready to make the most of his own life, then let him go."

There was no arguing with her wisdom, and he nodded his assent. He rose and put the one remaining letter back in his pocket. Teresa stood up too, kissed him gently on the cheek, and for a while they embraced tightly. Then they reluctantly released one another, and walked together into the house where Mary was supervising Issabel in laying the table for their dinner, and bringing in the roast chicken ready for serving. Everything being in place, Issabel was dismissed and left for the slave village, just as Sam rushed in to announce that Taine had arrived at the landing and was fast approaching the house.

*

Taine was alone, having sailed across from Tortola single-handed. He did not come straight into the house. Instead, they heard him rummaging around in a small storage room accessed from its own external door below the veranda and muttering to himself as he did so. Peeping out, Sam saw him throwing unwanted items onto the ground, and making a small pile of the things that he did want. He pushed these into a sack, ready to carry away, and then barged his way into the house. John, Sam and Teresa stood firm in the centre of the dining room, Mary having disappeared into her bedroom at the first news of the unwelcome arrival.

"Where is she?" yelled Taine. He was unshaven, dishevelled and very drunk. Quite a contrast to how John had found him in Beaverhood's office just a few days before. To John he said: "Tell your new slaves to fetch her out to me. They do do whatever you command, don't they?"

There was no response from his audience, who continued to stare him out.

"I've come for my tools. I won't be coming back. Me and Polly are settled down nicely. We've got a new baby girl! A sister for you two – you should come over and see her. But I need to talk to my wife. I need my money off her. I spent months improving this house and building that veranda. I could have been earning money elsewhere on the island, but I did it all for my dear wife. Now she's thrown me out in favour of her precious little son and his slaves. Well, give me the money for the work and I'll stay away! She's still my wife, and she must come out when I demand it."

With that, he strode two paces towards the bedroom door, but John and Sam barred his way, physically pushing him so that he fell backwards against the wall. Slowly he raised himself.

"Think you can stop me, do you?"

Taine grabbed the large knife that had been placed on the dinner table ready for carving the chicken. He lunged at Sam who was closest to him. Sam was unprepared, and received a wound in his hand as he sought to fend off his attacker, falling over due to the shock and the pain. Now Taine approached John and Teresa, waving the bloody knife.

"Of course, you won't fight back, will you? Quaker coward! So just let me through."

At that point, the door to Mary's room swung open and she emerged, carrying a long musket in her hands pointed straight at Taine.

"I'm no longer a Quaker!" she said. "You made sure of that. This gun is primed and loaded, and I know how to use it. Go!"

Everyone in the room stared at the furious woman, and Taine went white as a sheet. He hesitated, then as he looked into Mary's eyes he saw that her fear had gone. Her fear of him, and her fear of the consequences of what she might do. He turned around and scuttled out of the door, grabbing his sack as he did so. He bounded down the steps and into the gathering darkness, along the rocky path leading to the landing. He must have got about half way when they heard an almighty crash and a piercing scream as he fell and his tools scattered around him. John immediately made for the door to go to his aid, with Teresa following him.

"Stop!" commanded Mary. "There's no hurry to help that blackguard. Our dinner's getting cold. John, take a look at Sam's hand and apply your medicine to that. Teresa, there's one more bottle left of the Madeira that John brought. Go and find it and pour it out for us. Let's enjoy our meal in peace and harmony. Then you can go and see what's left of my husband."

John hesitated, but Teresa busied herself locating the bottle of wine and finding a corkscrew and a clean carving knife. Sam groaned, got up and offered John his hand to inspect. John relented, and turned his attention to cleaning and binding the wound, which was not very serious.

"Won't the slaves have heard the scream?" asked John.

"They never heard when he made me scream", responded Mary.

"Slaves don't get involved in white people's quarrels if they can avoid it", commented Teresa.

When the chicken was carved, the wine poured and the wound dressed, they sat down. Mary slipped back into her bedroom, and came out with an oil lamp made from a triton shell, which she proceeded to light. It had a very smart and well-constructed wooden stand.

"I always use this lamp in particularly dark times", she said. "Two of my favourite people made it for me", she continued, stooping to kiss Teresa and John on their heads. "And a third repaired the stand for me", and she kissed Sam on his head. The lamp provided a bright, warm glow, lighting the faces of the diners.

*

"The gun was my father's", explained Mary as they tucked into their meal. "He taught me how to load and fire it, and how to clean and look after it. I was a good shot when I was a girl. Then we went Quaker, and Edward wanted rid of it. We buried it in the mortar of the house foundations when we did the renovations, before you were born. I made sure it would stay dry, and put its ramrod and cartridge case with it. There's still about twenty cartridges left, each with powder and shot, wrapped up carefully. After Taine first hit me, I dug it out and hid it under the bedroom floorboards. Recently, I've been taking it out and loading it whenever he comes by."

Mary told them more of Taine's mistreatment of her than any of them had heard before. Of initial comfort and companionship followed by escalating arguments and rows. Of times he had hit her without Sam or Teresa knowing or finding out. Of little acts of meanness, deliberately damaging some of her favourite things, burning some of the clothes that Edward or her sons had worn that she kept as mementos.

Aware that her talk was upsetting her companions, she changed the topic to how wonderful it was to have them together in her house again, and proposed a toast to her "beloved family". This evening, Mary was in charge, and alive in a way that she had not been since John's return; since her rows with Taine had begun. At last, the chicken having been reduced to a pile of bones, the wine bottle having been emptied, and each member of the company having been praised and honoured by the others, Mary said: "I suppose you'd better go and see if he's still there."

John and Sam set off down towards the landing, accompanied by Teresa holding a lantern. They found him about half way down. He had slipped on a dusty, sloping rock and his tight hold on his sack of tools had prevented him from breaking his fall with his arms. His head had hit another rock, and he had suffered profuse bleeding. John examined him carefully, and pronounced him dead.

"How long would he have survived after the fall?" asked Teresa.

"Probably up to an hour", replied John.

They each shuddered as the implications of that judgement sank in. When they related it to Mary, having carried Taine's body up to the house, she merely shrugged and said: "But didn't we have a lovely meal together?"

Mary now instructed them to dig a grave under the tamarind trees alongside those of her first husband and her son, and bury him there. They complied, although it took several hours to complete the task, all three taking turns with the digging, Sam being hampered by his wounded hand. They dragged stones over the grave to mark the place, but following the Quaker practice that had been observed with the other two graves, no indication was given of who was buried there.

"No-one comes here anyway", said Mary, "and they don't come counting graves." She paused, and then continued: "It's such a beautiful place. Promise you'll bury me here too, when the time comes."

At first light, Sam sailed Taine's boat round to the north of Little Jost and sank it, while Teresa put Taine's tools back into the storeroom along with the items he had tossed onto the ground. John took the musket up the hill from the house and aimed it at a large tree and pulled the trigger. To his surprise it went off as if it were new. His shoulder was nearly dislocated by the recoil that he had not been expecting – Quakers do not often fire guns – and a three-quarter inch diameter lead ball was deeply embedded in the tree trunk.

"No trace of his visit now", said Mary once they all got back. "We won't mention it to a soul. He's unlikely to have told anyone where he was off to, least of all Polly. He never told me of his movements. For a man like Samuel to simply go off and disappear is not unusual at all." Despite her sleepless night, she seemed more alert and confident than at any time since John's return.

CHAPTER 17

"There's no woman in the world whom I could be as comfortable with, nor as thrilled by, as you, Teresa." It was the afternoon following the dramatic events on Little Jost van Dyke. John was not actually talking to the object of his affections, but imagining doing so as the boatman he had arranged to collect him took him back to Road Harbour.

"Mother is now physically safe and financially secure. I did suggest she come to live with me in London, but she'd have none of it. 'How could I leave the islands I've lived on all my life?' she said. 'What would happen to our workers if I went away? Who would look after Teresa?' Yes, she was particularly worried about you." John's imaginary companion made no response.

Mary had been adamant that the Caribbean was dangerous for a young black woman on her own. When John had told her that Sam was to go to England with him, she became even more insistent that she must stay to protect his sister. So, he had signed over ownership of the estate on Little Jost to her. The total of his earnings and the gifts he had received exceeded two thousand pounds and he had given her half of this sum.

"I've loved practicing medicine more than ever these last six months", his fantasy speech continued. "It's involved working long, hard hours, but it's not just been the money that got me up every morning before dawn and kept me going until well after sunset. It's been the satisfaction of relieving pain and suffering, and fascination at the way medication can transform lives. There are so many novel approaches to medicine these days, and I want to be amongst those discovering new treatments, demonstrating their efficacy, and eliminating disease."

He watched the plantations, forests and mountains of Tortola passing by. They gave no hint of Teresa's reaction to his words.

"I now have enough money from my portion of my earnings to complete my medical education. It's time for me to return to England to do so.

"You would be my perfect companion, friend – and lover." Even in his private rumination, he hesitated in adding the last word. "There'll be no other woman in my life, I can assure you. But for me, medicine has to come first." He stared towards the beach where the pelicans were diving into the shallow water for fish, wiping away his tears. "After I've qualified," he concluded out loud, "who knows?"

*

A couple of weeks later, having made arrangements to leave his practice, John walked over to Peter Douglas's house to return his equipment and unused drug supply.

"I'll be sorry to see you go, and so will your patients", said the older doctor as John took his leave. "They've never been healthier, and nor have their slaves."

"Well, it wouldn't have been possible without your support. Now, I must be off to make my final visits in town and collect the fees still owed to me."

John's departure was, however, interrupted by Douglas's housekeeper coming in to announce that a lady had called with her two children and requested a consultation. Douglas asked John if he could attend to her. The use of the term 'lady' had led John to expect a white woman, but he was surprised and discomfited when he recognised her as Mrs Arthur Hodge, the woman whose husband had asked him to amputate a slave's leg. He also recognised her young son, also named Arthur, whose right arm was clearly the reason for their visit.

"Oh, it's you! I was expecting Dr Douglas", she said.

"Dr Douglas is no longer receiving patients, but he asked me to see whether I could help."

"Well, take a look at my son's arm then. He broke it a couple of days ago, and my husband splinted it for him. I don't think he's done it right. It's at an odd angle, and it's very painful for young Arthur."

John examined the arm. The humerus had been broken. It was held in place by a roughly made splint.

"How did this happen?"

"A slave tried to kill me!" replied the boy.

"Served you right!" commented his older sister.

"Keep quiet, Anne", scolded their mother. "The doctor doesn't need to know how it happened, he just needs to put it right."

"He was trying to brand his slave", explained Anne, regardless.

"Father gave him to me for my birthday", added the boy. "Said he was mine, and I could do whatever I liked with him. I called him 'Prosper' ". At this the boy laughed, repeating it several times to emphasise the clever irony in the name that he had chosen. "I decided to brand him so everyone would know he was mine."

"He pressed the brand on for far too long – almost set fire to the boy. He was in agony. He's only the same age as Arthur. Then Prosper's brother Joseph came over and pushed Arthur away. It was just a little shove, but the little brat fell over."

"It wasn't! Joseph tried to kill me. He deliberately broke my arm."

John had by now removed the home-made splint and completed his examination of the arm.

"The bone is misaligned. If it's left, it'll set like that. It will always be painful, and never regain its full strength. I shall have to pull the two ends apart, and then push them together in the right position. It will hurt, I'm afraid."

"It won't hurt me", said the boy, unwisely. John let him prattle on, as that distracted him, although his story distressed him.

"So, father had Joseph hanged yesterday. It was great! My first hanging. It's now my favourite thing. It was so funny. He looked so surprised when they pulled the stool from under his feet, and twitched his legs about – ouch!!"

John had not been too scrupulous about avoiding pain, although his realignment was accurate enough. The boy had screamed very loudly, and was then reduced to floods of tears. His sister Anne laughed, and said what John could not say: "You don't enjoy pain when it's you that suffers, eh!"

His mother gave her daughter a slap and scowled at John, suspecting that he could have been gentler. She tried to soothe her bawling child. Once he had calmed down a little, John applied a more professional looking splint and a sling, and explained the aftercare required from his mother. He mentioned a rather extortionate fee, but Mrs Hodge, knowing no better, paid in full.

*

It was John and Sam's last day on Little Jost van Dyke. Their ship would leave Road Harbour for Liverpool the following day, and the free man, Bentorah, would take them over on the shallop first thing in the morning. Well, almost free. John had found that Beaverhood was away in Anguilla for a family wedding when he called to file the necessary papers. He now resolved to formalise the freeing of his workers on his arrival in London.

It being a perfect Caribbean day, bright and sunny (of course) with a gentle but cooling breeze off the sea, John, Sam and Teresa decided to revisit some of their childhood haunts. It was the first complete day of leisure for John since his arrival.

At Sandy Beach, which was much smaller and narrower than John had remembered, Sam immediately stripped off and ran into the water. Teresa walked further along, looked back to check that John had not followed, and then slipped off her dress and quickly submerged herself. John followed Sam, but unable to catch him, swam slowly and contentedly in the warm water of the shallows. Later, clothed again, he walked over to where Teresa was digging in the sand. Triumphantly, she leapt up grasping a magnificent conch shell.

"Remember when we used to come here and do this?" she asked. "This is the biggest yet: must be a whole foot long! And look," she paused, counting: "eleven whorls on its spire. We can take this one home to show Mary, just as we used to."

Now Sam emerged from the sea and joined them, carefully carrying an armful of sea eggs. He suddenly remembered that he was both fully grown and naked, so he quickly put them down on the sand and ran back to find his breeches.

"These taste disgusting!" exclaimed John, spitting out the soft flesh from the sea egg. "And I used to love them."

"Give them to me then", replied Teresa. "Your London tastes are obviously far too refined for the colonies. I don't suppose that you want the conch meat either."

"Yes I do! That was my favourite." John went over and had to wrestle a portion out of her hand. In truth he found it no better than the sea egg, but he did swallow it without complaint, having fought for it.

"Now let's see if you can still run up to Lookout Point", challenged Sam, and they were off up the steep rocky trail to the top of the island. Up through the dense trees where John and Ed had hunted for a racer snake: on this day he must have seen half a dozen of the creatures. Arriving last at the cluster of huge rocks by the summit, he had to endure more teasing.

"You've got too used to riding around on your horse and letting Jim do the running", suggested Teresa.

"I was watching the racer snakes", was John's poor excuse. "Do you remember the one that Ed and I caught?"

His companions nodded, and they went quiet as they remembered their childhood escapades with the absent twin.

"What was Ed like after I left?"

"Well, we moved away to live with Taine and we only saw him occasionally", answered Sam, carefully. "He became more formal with us when we did see him."

"He became a white West Indian", explained Teresa. She hesitated, but then decided not to spoil the day by telling John the whole truth about his brother. "He learned his place, and he learned what ours was. We couldn't possibly have had a day like this with him once we'd been apart for a couple of years."

"So, I'm strange, am I?"

"Yes", answered Sam. "Very strange. You went away still a child, and you took your innocent notions of us and of Tortola with you. Then you came back and took up with us as you'd left off. We've loved having you back with us – a grown up version of that little boy. It couldn't have happened if you'd stayed. You'd have changed. You'd have learned to establish a distance."

"Thank God, you didn't!" added Teresa.

They spent a little longer gazing out at the view. Teresa reminded John of the names of the features they could see: their private names and the official ones too. John had intended to tell Teresa the things that had been on his mind. There were moments when Sam left them alone together when he could have. But on this day the mood was light-hearted and innocent. John found he did not want to spoil it with heavy topics such as money, career or even love. So, eventually they sauntered down to the house together, chatting, reminiscing and gently mocking one another as they went, not really wanting their walk to come to an end. When it did, it was in the perfect way. With Mary greeting them with a huge jug of freshly squeezed sugar cane juice, and admiring the conch shell they had found with a poignant mixture of smiles and tears.

In later years, John would look back on this day as the happiest of his life.

*

On the voyage to Liverpool, John was given a small bunk in a tiny cabin, and his manservant – Sam – slept in an even smaller cot in the corner. Except when bad weather struck, at which time they changed places as John was more resilient than on the way out while Sam suffered terribly. John worked his passage as ship's doctor, boarding with several sacks full of oranges and lemons for the crew to guard against scurvy. Once Sam had found his sea-legs he began to revel in the life at sea he had dreamt of for so long. He helped in the galley and assisted when John had surgery to perform.

When neither of them was working, under the dim light of an oil lamp, John resumed the task of teaching Sam to read, write and add up that his parents had started. Sam was an eager and competent pupil, but not as quick to learn as his sister. The close quarters of the ship and the shared medical duties helped to blur the difference in status between them. They continued to chat and joke and reminisce as they had on Little Jost. They both missed the company of Teresa, but only Sam admitted it.

On the second day, while John was watching dolphins playing in the wake of the ship, he heard a familiar voice behind him: "Mister Lettsom, sir, thank you so much for granting me freedom."

It was Toney, who was a member of the ship's crew.

"Please sir, don't tell them that you know me. I told them I've already done three voyages – otherwise they wouldn't 'ave taken me on. This was the fourth ship I tried."

John Lettsom 'M.D.', understood the importance of qualifications, and undertook to keep their secret and ensure that Sam did too. That did not stop them chatting when they bumped into one another on board, nor prevent John from watching Toney with some trepidation as he inexpertly climbed the ship's rigging and attended to the sails.

As the ship passed due south of Newfoundland, they encountered the most violent storm of the voyage. Sam was confined to the cabin. John was on deck attending to a sailor who had fallen down the companionway, when he heard a scream and saw something fall from the foremast into the ocean. Later, he discovered that it had been Toney, and that he was lost. Toney's experience of freedom had proved to be fleeting.

PART IV: 1769–70

Courtship

CHAPTER 18

"This one's a triton", said John, reaching into the cabinet and pulling out the shell to show her. "When I was a child, I made an oil lamp out of one like this for my mother. She was still lighting it in the evenings when I saw her last year."

"It's beautiful", said Betty, putting her face close to his as she examined the shell. "You must have been a very clever child."

A busy year had elapsed since John's return from the Caribbean. Dr John Fothergill had arranged for him to spend the winter studying clinical medicine in Edinburgh, followed by a medical tour of France. He then spent some months of study at the University of Leiden where he was awarded the degree of Doctor of Medicine, finally justifying those letters "M.D." written on Sam and Teresa's Deed of Sale.

Now, he had returned to London, renting a couple of rooms in Gracechurch Street and spending much of his time assisting Dr Fothergill. The distinguished doctor had moved with his sister Ann to establish a home and surgery in Harpur Street in Bloomsbury, closer to his growing list of wealthy patients in the West End. But John was not on duty this day. Indeed this autumn, for the first time in many years, he was not working round the clock. And to complement and enhance his increased leisure time, it coincided with a visit to the capital of Betty and Molly from Warrington, daughters of Dr Fothergill's late brother Joseph. Their mother had remained at home to look after their younger sisters, but they were accompanied by their Uncle Samuel, and all were staying in the Bloomsbury house.

John had met the sisters at Mr Samuel Fothergill's house several times while a schoolboy at Penketh. To the responsible school monitor these girls, several years younger than himself, had been a source of irritation – always playing tricks on him and seeking ways to puncture what they saw as his pompous self-regard. Now, the pesky, undisciplined children had grown into attractive and considerate young women, and the conceited, inflexible scholar into an upwardly-mobile and self-assured junior professional.

John had already taken Betty and Molly for a tour of St Thomas' and Guy's Hospitals, and joined them again with their uncle to visit the Queen's zoo near Buckingham House. There they saw elephants and zebra, which greatly impressed the girls. John had the benefit of having seen such creatures before, and was able to avoid any impression of surprise at their size or their stripes. Instead, he could explain where they came from, how an elephant never forgot, how a zebra could not be ridden, and suggest that they were not quite as impressive as the specimens he had seen in London a few years earlier. He made up for the lack of any lions in the zoo with his story of the last lion he had seen and its miraculous taming by a young boy.

They all commented on how small and shabby the new royal residence at Buckingham House was, and then they wandered through St James' Park back to Harpur Street for tea. John's doctoral thesis had concerned the botany of tea and the physiological effects of drinking it, and he was able to warn his audience at length of the dangers he had discovered about the beverage. During his lecture, Mr Fothergill had nodded off due to the walk and all the fresh air and Molly began to fidget, but Betty remained alert and attentive and joined John in drinking only milk with hot water, sweetened with a little sugar.

So here they were a few days later, together again. John had come over for breakfast, as he was doing with increasing frequency these days, and he stayed on to show her the shells Dr Fothergill had collected over the years which were displayed in a fine glass cabinet. Ann Fothergill was in the room too, staying for propriety's sake but not really following the conversation. Molly was nineteen, two years older than her sister, and she was already smitten with one of the young men her uncles had introduced her to at the Gracechurch Meeting House. She had politely taken her leave after breakfast and gone off to work on decorating her bonnet. Both sisters knew how to look their best even in subdued Quaker garb. They were excited to be in London for the first time, and one of them appeared fascinated by all of the subjects in which John was such an expert.

*

The discourse on sea shells was interrupted by a soft knock on the door just as John was carefully replacing the triton. Ann called "Come in", and Sam appeared carrying a full coal scuttle and a box of other fire-lighting necessities.

"I've come to lay the fire for tonight, Miss Ann, he said. "I thought this room would be empty, but I can come back later."

"Oh, don't worry Sam, you can do it now. It's getting cold these days and we may need it soon after lunch."

Sam glanced over at John and Betty hunched together over the shell cabinet, and then got on with cleaning out the remains of the previous night's fire prior to laying a new one. John and Sam had landed in Liverpool as two good friends, their easy relationship on Little Jost having been extended for a few additional weeks while they shared a cabin on the ship. However, as soon as they set foot on dry land, things changed. It was not so much that Sam was John's slave – people could not tell that from looking at them.

It was the more self-evident fact that Sam was John's manservant. What else could he be, after all?

On their first night they stayed at Mr Samuel Fothergill's house in Warrington. John was taken to a large bedroom with a view overlooking the garden, while Sam was shown the way to the servant's quarters and to a cramped, shared attic bedroom. That evening, John joined his host and other fashionable Quaker guests in the dining room, while Sam ate with the staff in the kitchen downstairs. For the short duration of their stay, John accompanied Mr Fothergill on tours of the district, to lunch or tea with various Quaker Friends, and on the First Day to observe their faith at the local Meeting House. Sam, not needed by his master as a personal servant, helped with regular cleaning chores in Mr Fothergill's house. In truth, both of them had known that this was the way it would be. Nevertheless, for Sam it was a shock when it actually happened.

In London, accommodating a servant in John's two-room apartment proved crowded. There was also a lack of things for Sam to do: plain Quaker clothes needed very little attention and the cleaning could be completed within an hour, even to Sam's exacting standards. With John due to travel, another solution was urgently needed, and so John arranged for Sam to act as servant to Dr Fothergill and his sister. Another attic room was available for him, but he had this one to himself as the only live-in servant.

Ann Fothergill acted as housekeeper herself, and was not above performing many of the chores that others of her class kept servants for. A middle-aged woman came in to wash and clean, and her daughter Becky helped out in the kitchen where Ann would supervise and often take the lead in cooking and baking. Sam regularly got roped into kitchen duties which he came to enjoy, but he was soon at a loose end and so he obtained permission to do odd repair jobs around the neighbourhood. Ann arranged the first couple with her friends, and then Sam's fame spread around Bloomsbury. In order to placate rival odd-job men, it was agreed that he should charge for his services at standard rates, and he first used the proceeds to build up an impressive array of tools, and then began to save.

Each time John returned to London, the relationship between the two old friends became more distant. On his return from Edinburgh, John took Sam to a local tavern for a meal, a drink, and a catch up on the news. That had gone very well until they were joined by John's friends Gilbert Thompson, who had eventually succumbed to pressure from Dr Fothergill to take up a practice in London, and James Beesley, who was still persevering as a writer. Conversation turned to the pressures of practicing medicine and to the success of James's new book about George Fox, and Sam shrank into his corner, drank his ale too quickly and became morose and inebriated. They helped him home, but even John's liberal-minded friends felt that walking through London guiding a staggering and singing African servant was not something to be seen doing.

After John's later travels in Europe, there were no more social occasions with Sam. Just awkward conversations on the stairs or in the hallway, between the reception rooms and in the servant's quarters. The main topic was news from Little Jost. Sam felt his writing was not up to composing a whole letter and, as Teresa did not know he would have been able to read one, she did not send him any. Mary and Teresa did write to John, although not frequently. Their news was generally good. Bentorah and Cassia had stayed on the plantation and were working harder as paid labourers than they ever did when they were enslaved. Cudjoe was less mobile than previously, but still mentally alert. However, old Rosett had sadly succumbed to a fever. Each letter included congratulations on John's latest success.

"What's this shell?" chimed Betty's voice. "It's huge, ..., and very heavy!"

Sam glanced round to see Betty almost drop a fine specimen of a conch shell. John quickly intervened grasping the shell, and momentarily the arms that were trying to hold it.

"This is a conch."

"Did you find many of these in the West Indies?"

"A few", replied John flatly, as he reached over to replace it. "Now your uncle tells me that this shell comes all the way from China", he continued, taking out a smaller and rather drab specimen. John and Sam were unable to suppress a quick exchange of glances.

*

A Tuesday morning, early in November. Overnight rain had settled the smoke and soot, the sky was bright blue, the sun shining, and the architectural grandeur of the city could be appreciated. John was in his small living room in Gracechurch Street, drinking hot milk and water and heating up some porridge over his open fire. His breakfast preparations were interrupted by a knock at his door, which he opened to admit Sam.

"Miss Ann offers you her kindest wishes," said Sam between taking deep breaths as he recovered from running all the way from Bloomsbury. "She asked me to let you know that the Fothergills will be receiving a family party this evening, unexpectedly in town from Northampton. Instead of you coming by for tea as arranged, would you like to join them for lunch?"

"Well, yes. That'll be splendid", replied John. "Before you rush back, do let me show you the latest parcel just arrived from Little Jost."

"There's no rush. Miss Ann told me they'd assume you'd be coming. I'm to accompany you back to Bloomsbury."

"Don't they trust me to find the way?"

"Well, I think Miss Ann was happy to let me spend some time with you. She's asked me all about life on Little Jost, and about you as a child!"

"I hope you were complimentary."

"I told her you'd been the best friend a boy could have."

At this, John smiled: although he noticed the past tense and was rather upset by it. "So sit down, and join me in some porridge."

Master and slave sat down to eat together for the first time in over a year. John put the parcel down on the table between them, and pulled out a couple of letters.

"This one is from my mother, and this from your sister." Both were in tidy handwriting, Teresa's plain and easy to read, Mary's more elaborate but strangely difficult to decipher. "They both say the same things. Issabel has had a baby, and she's a healthy young girl. No mention of whom the father might be. The cotton crop is growing very well this year – they should have harvested by now, this letter's two months old. The chickens have been multiplying. Bentorah encountered a sudden storm on his way back from Road Town and almost lost the shallop, but he's learning to master the craft now and brought it safely home in the end. Both mother and Teresa have visited my Aunt Margery in Road Town."

"Let me see the letters", said Sam. Poring over them carefully, he put Mary's to one side on account of her writing, but proclaimed that he could follow much of Teresa's, reading out some passages and then passing the pages back to John for confirmation and correction. "I'd like to reply to Teresa, but I really need to learn to write better. You say a letter takes two months to be delivered."

"Yes. A bit quicker on the way out. But you have to catch a ship. There's one leaving in about ten days, and I'm putting together a package for them. You could add a present."

“I will”, said Sam eagerly, “and I’ll try to write a letter too. Perhaps you can help me.”

“Of course”, replied John rather offhandedly, as he proceeded to take from the package some pieces of coral and a few pretty shells.

“From Teresa”, said Sam, his face breaking into a smile. “I remember those shells. She loved the colours – I loved the meat inside! None of that, I suppose.”

“No, but some sugary sweets.” John divided the contents of a small carton between them. The porridge was finished now, and they unwrapped the sweets and popped them into their mouths. They tasted like – childhood.

“Will you give the shells to Dr John for his display cabinet?” asked Sam. “To add to his conch – which you can hardly recognise these days!”

“That was strange. Seeing you by the fire. Having the conch thrust into my hands. Suddenly, I felt as if she was in the room with us.”

“But she wasn’t”, responded Sam. “Just a silly, giddy, flirty girl.” John made no attempt to defend Betty. Sam was feeling more at ease with his old friend than for many months. “Do you miss her?”

“Yes.”

“So do I”, Sam responded reflectively.

*

Fortified by their breakfast and reconnected through the contents of the parcel from home, the John and Sam set off to walk to Bloomsbury.

“I need to stop off at the Guildhall on the way”, explained John. “I’ll be going there with Mr Fothergill and Betty and Molly on Thursday, and I want to arrange a surprise.”

"Are you going to watch them draw the lottery?" asked Sam, and when John nodded he added, "I thought Quakers didn't gamble."

"Well, there's nothing to say we can't watch. And my surprise is to arrange for us to go to see the exhibits and the paintings in the gallery. All very proper, I assure you. Last month I delivered a fine young son to the wife of an official who works there, and he said he could arrange for us to go up."

The splendour of the Guildhall was on full display in the bright autumn sunshine as they approached. As they entered the main hallway, a loud voice boomed out: "Dr Lettsom, isn't it?" This was not the man John was seeking, but John Miers whom he knew only vaguely and had not seen since returning from Tortola. He was the father of Nancy Miers, the one-time companion of John's friend James Beesley. James was no longer courting the young Quakeress, and John had not seen her since she had stormed out of the Africa pageant during their visit to Greenwich Fair. John recognised Mr Miers from Quaker gatherings and from the odd occasion when he had met his daughter after the young people's cultural outings.

"How nice to see you again after all this time", continued Miers. "I hope your return to the West Indies was a success". John provided the briefest of summaries of his visit home, and of his more recent travels.

"Now here comes a man I'm meeting with this morning", said Miers, as a clerical gentlemen joined their group. "This is the Reverend James Townley, Headmaster of Merchant Taylors' School. We're here for a meeting about educational provision by the London Livery Companies. I represent the Worshipful Company of Tin Plate Workers, you know." Then he introduced John to the Headmaster.

"And who is this fine young man?" asked the cleric, looking at Sam. Ashamed at having fallen into the conventional habit of ignoring retainers, John responded: "This is Sam, my servant". An incomplete reply, but better than nothing. Sam smiled and bowed.

"I must go and find the person I have business with here", explained John, leaving Miers and Townley awaiting other advocates of education, and his servant waiting with them. Townley, a man who was always keen to talk to anyone and always knew the right questions to ask was soon deep in conversation with Sam. By the time John returned from his mission, the conversation had borne fruit.

"Mr Townley has told me the boys of his school run a class to teach local working men how to read, write and reckon. They meet every Wednesday afternoon. He says I'd be able to go if you were willing to let me."

"I'll need to ask Miss Fothergill", said John. "But it sounds like a very good idea."

"The boys do most of the teaching themselves", explained Townley. "I go along whenever I can just to supervise and encourage. Everyone seems to learn a lot. But Sam, are you a church-goer? It's intended for those of the Anglican faith. Or are you a Quaker, like these gentlemen?"

"No", replied Sam. "And I should like to come to the church too, and learn more about our Lord."

"Aha. You Quakers are very keen to abolish slavery, but I'm yet to meet any black Friends. You'll find a warm welcome in the Anglican church. Come along tomorrow at the time and place I told you. We'll soon have you writing letters you can be proud of."

By now all the members of the education committee had arrived, and the group said their farewells and went off to their meeting room. John and Sam continued their walk to Harpur Street.

"Actually, you don't need to ask Miss Ann", Sam pointed out. "You do own me."

This stung John, but he answered calmly. “It’s only polite to ask Miss Fothergill, but I promise to recommend that you go. Both to the class and the church service.”

CHAPTER 19

"Our Friends in Philadelphia are enjoying the boycott", volunteered Mr Fothergill. "They tell me that since the colonists stopped importing clothes from England, everyone in the city is looking just as plain and dowdy as the Quakers."

This report was delivered over the lunch to which John had been summoned.

"There's no such thing as dowdy clothes", ventured Betty with a grin, "just dowdy people."

"Well, you and Molly are never dowdy", observed John, gallantly. "You could both contrive to look alluring dressed in coal sacks." To their uncle, he continued: "The situation in the American colonies is becoming critical, and neither side seems willing to back down. In Boston there's now one British soldier for every eight residents."

"If there's conflict between Britain and the colonies, where will our West Indian settlers stand?" asked Dr Fothergill.

"With Britain, I'm sure", was John's reply. "On the mainland, white settlers greatly outnumber African slaves. On the islands, it's the other way round. Without the protection of the crown and the navy, the settlers would feel desperately insecure."

"Are there really so many slaves in the West Indies?" asked Molly, sounding surprised.

"Certainly. On Tortola there's ten slaves for every European", answered John.

Both sisters appeared amazed at this ratio.

"Do you own slaves?" asked Betty, the thought suddenly entering her head.

"My father left me his whole estate when he died, and that included the fifty slaves working for him. When I returned a couple of years ago, I freed them all. It left me penniless! Some of them now work happily for my mother as free people."

"That was so noble of you", commented Betty.

"But John still owns two slaves, don't you?" Ann always valued accuracy – although even she did not know to question the count of fifty. "One is serving us here at table." Betty's jaw dropped. She had not realised she had actually met an enslaved person.

Sam had been back in the kitchen during this exchange, but now he re-entered with a bowl full of preserved fruit. All eyes turned to him.

"Are you not ready for dessert?" he asked, unnerved.

When Sam had gone again, John tried to explain. "Sam's sister works for my mother. She thought she would be safer under my protection, as it were. And that I could keep better track of Sam's progress here this way. I don't beat him or anything!"

"But the point is that you could, or you could sell him to someone who might. You know my views on the matter", said John's guardian, disapprovingly. Nevertheless, John's account had placated Betty. To burnish his image as a thoughtful master further, John now took the opportunity to tell Ann of Sam's intention to attend classes at Merchant Taylors'. He informed her, rather than asking her permission. Ann was very supportive: she had a soft spot for Sam and, like her brothers, she deplored his enslaved status. However, she did express regret at losing his assistance in the kitchen while he was away at school. He was now able to prepare some of the simplest family dishes himself, and was beginning to get the hang of baking.

After lunch was finished and once the conversation abated, John rose to leave so that his hosts could prepare for the arrival of their family visitors. Ann caught him at the door, just as Sam was helping him into his overcoat.

"And do you find my niece Betty alluring?" she asked.

John laughed at this, although he was surprised by the question. "She's always very attractive and well turned-out", he replied.

"My brothers are both pleased to see that the two of you get on so well. They would be delighted if their protégé were to become family too."

"And you Miss Ann, would you also be delighted?"

"Betty's a lively girl. She needs excitement and company and entertainment. At the moment you've got plenty of time to spend with her, and she's enjoying your attentions. But you're also ambitious for your career. Were you to become as committed to medicine as my brother, you'd have very little time left for a wife and family. That's my only concern. I should not like her to become lonely or neglected in the future. The girls are staying here until the spring, so there's plenty of time. But I wouldn't want her to return to Warrington without knowing your intentions."

Sam disappeared down the stairs just as Ann turned back into the house. John walked back to his rooms, pondering what she had said.

*

"The first thing I'd do would be to buy a phaeton." This was the ambition of James Freeman, the husband of another niece of the Fothergill brothers. It was the answer to Mr Fothergill's question: "What would you do if you won the top prize of twenty thousand pounds?" – a relevant question as Mr Fothergill, Betty, Molly and John were on their way with James to the Guildhall to watch the lottery being drawn. That Thursday morning was fine and sunny again, warming up after an early frost, and so the party was walking along Holborn on the mile-and-a-half route from Harpur Street. For clarification, James added: "An English, four-wheeled, two-seat, high-flyer".

"You'd certainly cut a dash on one of those!" remarked Mr Fothergill, "but there'd only be room for you and your driver."

"I'd drive myself, of course, so there'd be plenty of room for Ann too. I'd go very fast!" He mimed the act of steering the horse. By "Ann" he meant his wife, niece and cousin to the Fothergills, who had claimed illness this morning but actually had been none too keen on going to witness gambling.

"Oh, I'm not sure Ann would wish to join you for such a reckless drive", suggested Betty.

"Then I shall ride with my sweetheart instead!"

This provoked general mirth. "But you don't have a sweetheart", pointed out Molly, who then suddenly wondered whether he might.

"He soon would have, if he had a phaeton", observed John.

No-one mentioned that James' excessive girth would probably leave no room for anyone but the slimmest young lady, nor that his substantial weight would be likely to topple such a tall carriage at the first sharp turn.

"What about you, John?" asked Betty. "How would you spend twenty-thousand pounds?"

"I would found a new hospital", came the earnest reply – clearly John had been considering this dilemma already. "I've been reading Russell's book on the curative properties of sea-water. I'd found a sea-bathing hospital down on the coast."

"And charge people a fortune for indulging in your cure", suggested James.

"Yes certainly, and then use the profits to fund provision of the therapy for the poor of London", was the righteous riposte.

"And you, uncle?" asked Molly.

"Invest it prudently, of course, and live very comfortably on interest of a thousand pounds a year. But as I told you, I've bought just one ten pound ticket, to be shared equally with John, Betty and yourself. James has his own ticket: only he could be transported out of his struggle for existence to a life of unceasing leisure."

Mr Fothergill had told his siblings over breakfast of the plan to go to watch the lottery draw, but only announced to the girls that he and John had already bought a ticket after leaving the house. His brother and sister would have been shocked to learn of such disregard for Quaker views on gambling, let alone contributing to a government fund that – amongst other things – helped pay for soldiers, canon and warships. They would have been less surprised to hear that their nephew-in-law had purchased a whole ticket for himself, or that their niece was unaware of this gamble. James was well known to be choosey about which of many of the doctrines of the Society to uphold, and which of various other standards of society too.

*

There was no time to elicit feminine plans for spending a fortune, for now they were there, pushing their way through the crush to enter the Guildhall and its Great Medieval Hall where the numbers were to be drawn. Fifty thousand ten pound tickets had been issued, and every one had been sold. One thousand tickets were drawn each day – Sundays excepted – over the two months between early November and Christmas. Mr Fothergill and James Freeman had bought their tickets together, and they knew that both would be drawn that day.

The hall had quite a small floor area, and so the spectators were crowded in, standing room only. What it lacked in length and breadth, it made up for in height, and from a prominent position towards the top of the back wall, likenesses of the king and queen looked down at the audience who were funding their regime. High on a platform at the back of the hall were the two great wooden "wheels of fortune", each six foot tall and containing one hundred small boxes around its rim. One was already loaded with the lottery tickets to be drawn that day, ten in each box. Each box of the other wheel contained ten chits specifying the amount won, chosen randomly from those prepared for the whole season. Most prizes were valued at twenty pounds, but some were for fifty, one hundred, and so on, right up to that top prize of twenty thousand pounds. A substantial proportion of the chits were blank, signifying that nothing had been won (except by the government).

The Master of Ceremonies ascended the stage and made a speech expressing gratitude to the investors for their contribution to the Government's expenditure on vital public services. He welcomed those who had come to see their tickets drawn, and reminded the audience that most of the winners would be informed by letter as they lived all around the country. He then signalled to two attendants who began to turn large handles that set the wheels spinning. After whirling at alarming speed for a short time, they were allowed to decelerate and gradually come to rest, each with one box accessible at the lowest point. At that point, two boys from the Blue Coats Charity School arose from where they had been sitting on the stage. One selected a raffle ticket from the box on the Ticket Wheel and brought it to the Master of Ceremonies, who announced that "Ticket number four thousand, six hundred and ninety-one has won ..." the sentence left hanging in the air, while the second Blue Coat brought him a chit selected at random from the box in the Prize Wheel. The sentence could then be completed: "... a prize of twenty pounds". A cheer went up from the audience, although it was announced that the lucky winner was somewhere in Hertfordshire rather than amongst them in the hall. A clerk noted down the result. The first Blue Coat then selected each of the other nine lottery tickets in turn, each paired with a prize selected by his partner from the Prize Wheel. After ten tickets and ten prizes had been drawn, those boxes were turned back to front and the wheels spun again.

Each set of ten tickets took three and a half minutes to pair with prize chits. The wheels would spin one hundred times that day, from nine o'clock in the morning until three o'clock in the afternoon. At some stage the Fothergill-Lettsom ticket would be drawn, and so would the Freeman ticket, but there was no way of knowing when. Fortunately, tea, coffee and pastries could be purchased, and later in the day there would be small beer and wine. On request, John could get milk mixed with hot water made up, although Betty had already reverted to drinking proper tea.

For the first hour, great excitement accompanied every draw, and when a chit for one thousand pounds was drawn, there was uproar. The winners were a couple from Winchester, who had travelled to London for this moment: the lady whooped for joy, but her husband was quite overcome and fainted on the spot. John was able to step forward to raise the man to a sit on a chair with his head between his knees, loosen his collar, and send Betty to bring over some sweetened milk with warm water.

After an hour, people began to tire. A queue for refreshments formed, and some took a walk outside the hall, anxiously checking the lists of winners posted at the door as soon as they returned to be sure they had not missed their draw. John went off to look for the official who was to show them round the gallery to check that the arrangements were in place, but as soon as he left the Great Hall, he was accosted by the Reverend Townley.

"Dr Lettsom, how splendid to see you again! Here for the lottery, I see. I'm back for yet another meeting on provision of education for the masses. Talking of which, your man Sam did very well in his class yesterday. Like so many men without a formal education, the main barrier to him writing is lack of confidence. He thinks he should be able to write a perfect letter straight off, with no spelling errors, no smudges or blotches and no mistakes.

"I didn't put him with one of our boys who writes well, but with one who struggles himself. Sam was able to see that a proper school boy at a top establishment (if I may say so) also makes mistakes – but that this is all right. As long as the reader gets the message, then the letter has served its purpose – yes? He needs some help with forming his words clearly, some practice with spelling and a little basic grammar, but he'll soon be able to write that letter to his sister. He says you need it to send off next week. One more lesson, and he'll finish it. Nice boy, he is. Clean and polite. A shame he never went to school earlier."

After that monologue, John had the opportunity to thank the headmaster for organising Sam's tuition, and turned to continue with his original errand. But he made his move too soon.

"By the way, would you like to join me for an evening at the theatre in a couple of weeks' time? I'm making up a party to see David Garrick play King Lear. He's a wonderful actor, you know. John Miers will be coming, and his daughter Nancy and his sister too. You could bring a companion if you wish. I want to book a box close to the stage: we'll almost be there amongst the action! What do you say?"

John said "Yes" to the invitation, but "No" to the suggestion of bringing a companion. Theatre was another activity generally avoided by Quakers, and indeed he had never been to see a play himself. Mr Fothergill could get away with defying the expectations of his brother and sister, but that was the privilege of family. The Reverend supplied details for the forthcoming evening, and then continued: "John Miers is a fine man you know. From a distinguished family that pioneered tinplating, and he now owns a huge works in Glamorgan. He has a substantial fortune, a fine house in Cannon Street, a country mansion near Swansea. He plays a major role in the Worshipful Company of Tin-platers. Sadly, his wife died some years ago. You'll enjoy his company when we visit the theatre, I'm sure. Now, I must dash. My meeting started five minutes ago. It was such good fortune to bump into you." And with that, he was off.

*

A week later, John was at home in Gracechurch Street, making up the parcel to be sent to Little Jost van Dyke.

Eventually, their lottery ticket had been drawn, and paired with a prize of fifty pounds. They were all delighted. The splendid morning was topped off with the visit to the gallery that John had so carefully arranged, but which he passed off as a spontaneous whim based on a chance meeting with his former patient's grateful husband. Betty and Molly were awed by the huge statues of Gog and Magog flanking the staircase as they ascended to the art collection above. This encouraged John to launch into such a detailed account of the biblical stories and myths behind those names – were they men, tribes or locations? – that even Betty turned to her uncle to ask about the paintings instead.

Later, they deposited their winnings at the bank, with Betty and Molly solemnly instructed to describe the money as a gift from their uncle when they got home, and to keep it invested for their future needs. Finally, they dropped in on James and Ann Freeman, to find him returned from the Guildhall looking forlorn and holding a blank prize ticket, and Ann resting upstairs in bed but looking quite well and refusing to answer John's enquiries about her health or to let him examine her.

A busy week had followed, with John assisting his mentor on his rounds and deputising for him at the Harpur Street surgery.

He was learning a great deal about the ailments of the wealthy, particularly those associated with over-indulgence and excessive anxiety. Dr Fothergill also made regular visits to the poorer areas of the city where ill health was mostly the result of deprivation, bad diet and stress. John was able to witness the gulf between the medical care available to the rich and that which could be spared for the poor.

Earlier that day he had seen Betty for the first time since their lottery win. He had gone over to Harpur Street to report to Dr Fothergill on his rounds, and to collect items from Sam to include in the parcel for home. Betty intercepted him in the hallway, expressing surprise at seeing him and accusing him of having abandoned her and her sister. John replied with an account of his busy workload, and the duties imposed by her uncle. "But", she said, "you still have time to arrange a visit to the theatre." There was no use trying to keep secrets in the Quaker community. Through the Meeting House, Betty had made friends with a local young lady, Polly Plumstead. Visiting to take tea, she had met Polly's cousin – Nancy Miers.

"She was so excited about her forthcoming trip to see King Lear and the opportunity to meet the dashing Dr Lettsom again! You could have taken us rather than go with that boring little dormouse."

John had promised to be more attentive in future, and had soon elicited an invitation to tea on the day after the theatre visit, so that Betty could "learn of all of the best parts of Shakespeare's play without having to sit through the whole thing, struggling to understand Elizabethan verse."

Now in the privacy of his lodgings, John looked at the items to be packed into the parcel. His letter was quite fat: he had written over a dozen pages about life in London – focussing on his medical activities rather than the social life which was actually taking up almost as much time. Sam's letter was considerably thinner, and securely sealed. John could only judge by the outside, where the single word "Teresa" was beautifully inscribed. He did wonder what lay within.

There was also a parcel from brother to sister. This had got wet as John walked home through a heavy downpour. Opening it in order to repackage it in dry brown paper, he saw that it comprised a collection of ribbons in a variety of brilliant colours. Cheap, yes – but very pretty. He could imagine Teresa using them to brighten up her hair or her bonnet. His present was a collection of intricate lace handkerchiefs he had purchased in Leiden. They had been expensive, and the work that had gone into them was outstanding, but they were too dainty and impractical for a woman with little leisure. Beside the ribbons they looked uninteresting, worthy and colourless. He knew which present Teresa would make most use of.

*

"Our drooping country now erects her head, Peace spreads her balmy wings, and Plenty blooms. Divine Cordelia, all the gods can witness, How much thy love to empire I prefer! Thy bright example shall convince the world, (Whatever storms of fortune are decreed), That truth and virtue shall at last succeed." With these words, Edgar brought the play to a glorious close. The audience applauded wildly, and the curtain rose again for the cast to receive their acclaim. Cheers and whoops were added to the clapping as David Garrick appeared to take his final bow.

"Lear rescued. Cordelia declared Queen and happily married to Edgar. What a wonderful and joyous ending!" exclaimed Nancy in a rare fit of enthusiasm as the party stood together in Drury Lane waiting for John Mier's carriage to collect them.

"Yes, it's a wonderful play", agreed the Reverend Townley. "Garrick prepared this splendid adaptation himself, and he chose to use Nahum Tate's ending rather than Shakespeare's. In that dismal original version, Lear goes mad and Cordelia is hanged. It ends with Lear carrying Cordelia's dead body onto the stage and then dying from grief himself."

"Oh! I wish you hadn't told us that", responded Nancy. "It'll spoil my memory of such an uplifting story. Who would want to make it so gloomy?"

"Perhaps people who want to remind us that truth and virtue will never succeed through war", was her father's Quaker explanation.

Her Aunt Mary suggested that: "The moral of the tale is never to lie about your love. Regan and Goneril lied to their father and received their just deserts in the end."

"And you, John. What was your favourite part?" asked Nancy.

"Oh, definitely when Albany rescued Cordelia and Lear in the final scene", he replied. Actually, the line that was lingering in his memory was: "Fairest Cordelia, that art most rich, being poor; most choice, forsaken; and most loved, despised!"

Reflections on the play continued during the carriage ride to the Miers' home in Cannon Street, after which the driver proceeded to take the clergyman and the doctor directly to their doors.

"Young Sam continues to make excellent progress with his lessons", observed Townley. "He now wants to learn more arithmetic and to study how to keep accounts. He tells me that his sister does the books on your estate in the West Indies. They must be two very talented young people. His latest ambition is to become baptised into the Church of England. He has also mentioned that he is not just your servant, but actually your slave. I must say that I find that to be a remarkable arrangement here in England, but it does mean that I have to ask you whether you will permit his baptism."

John was taken aback at this request. He was not surprised at Sam's quick progress with reading and writing, nor with his desire to improve his arithmetic. But the idea of baptism was a surprise. Like Teresa, Sam had shunned any form of religion before coming to England. Perhaps the widely-held (but legally dubious) belief that in England baptism implied freedom for a slave had influenced him. It was clear to John that Sam's baptism would mark a change in their relationship, and the fact that Sam had not discussed it with him first showed that the change was already under way. The carriage had now stopped at the headmaster's residence, but the Reverend waited for John's reply. Divining the cause of the younger man's hesitancy, he added: "Of course, if I do baptise him, he will not be content to stay with you as a servant for much longer."

"Please go ahead. I have no choice in the matter," replied John, recalling his promise to Teresa.

It was now mid-December, and light snow had begun to fall in the London streets. In Madeira, it was hot and humid with dark clouds threatening thunder, and a parcel wrapped up in brown paper had arrived, in transit to Little Jost van Dyke.

CHAPTER 20

The Fothergills, being strict and traditional Quakers, felt that Christmas Day was special. Just as special in fact as all the other three hundred and sixty-four days of the year. In the morning Dr Fothergill had consultations with some of the equally pious members of the Gracechurch Meeting, and then took on the Christmas afternoon hospital round that was so unpopular with most of his colleagues. His brother Samuel had returned to Warrington the previous month – he might have been up for a bit of fun. Ann roped Sam in to help with a thorough cleaning of the kitchen.

Betty and Molly were used to treating Christmas as somewhat more special than other days, but they had concluded that protestations would be futile and contented themselves with catching up on some reading and needlework. Then they accompanied Ann and Sam on their regular weekly visit to the poorer streets of the capital to distribute unconsumed food that had been collected at the Meeting House. There at least, they had the opportunity to wish and be wished a Happy Christmas.

John had memories of various lively Christmases, as a child in Tortola where both enslaved workers and their Quaker masters had celebrated together with abandon, and as a schoolboy in Penketh where special treats were provided for those unable to return home for the season. Two years ago he had been run off his feet with medical emergencies – mostly due to the overindulgence of planters on that day – and one year ago he had celebrated both Christmas and Hogmanay with gusto in Edinburgh. This year he decided to avoid the temptation to go over and incite the Fothergill girls to some mischief, and instead obediently accompanied his mentor on his rounds all day.

Following a dutiful and sober Christmas, John was determined to mark New Year's Eve. It being a First Day, the full round of Quaker observance took place and John spent a restrained and reverent day with the Fothergills. But that evening he had dined at his favourite local tavern with James Beesley and Gilbert Thompson and now the three friends were back in his room, following up the landlord's ale with John's best red Madeira wine.

"A toast to 1770 then!" proposed James. "A year during which I shall return to the West Indies, develop my writing career with my magisterial work on the culture and climate of Tortola, and also find a wife."

"So, no luck with Sally, then?" asked Gilbert.

"She was willing. Very willing! But her father was not. And now she's engaged to another. I'm seen as an impoverished colonial over here, but I'll appear a rich and cultured man at home. Sally was an improvement on Nancy: a smaller fortune, but a lovelier girl." James sighed wistfully, thinking of what might have been.

"I hear you've been seeing Nancy Miers of late, John," continued James. "Has she forgiven you for the outing to see the wild animals? Are you now seeking a fortune? With Sally's father it was all about my money and prospects, but John Miers has money to burn. With him, it's all about class. A professional doctor certainly beats a writer in his eyes. You'll be alright there my friend."

"I've no interest in courting Nancy."

"But you endured the whole of King Lear just to sit next to her for three hours – that must be love!"

"Not at all. I happen to enjoy Shakespeare. No, I'm not interested in Nancy Miers."

"So come back to Tortola with me. My brother's letters tell me there's need for a doctor on the island again. And you can be reunited with your lost love. Who was that again? I keep asking my brother, but he's been unable to work it out. He thought it might be Letitia Martin, but she's married a soldier and moved away to South Carolina. We know you're still corresponding with some dark lady over there."

John's cheeks had started to colour as soon as James had mentioned a "lost love", and they reddened further at the mention of a "dark lady", even though he knew it was meant as an allusion to the mysterious female of Shakespeare's sonnets. He had often unwisely offered sweets and shown off shells to his friends that he passed off as presents from a secret admirer in the Caribbean.

"It's Betty Fothergill he's after", suggested Gilbert. "Now she is pretty and vivacious, and could tie him even closer to the Fothergills. They're all keen on the match, especially Dr John. She's a country girl like my Mary. Now my ambition for 1770 is to marry Mary and move up to Lancaster and practice there. How about you, John? A future as a country doctor in Warrington with your lovely little Betty and your ten children?"

"Shall we go and join the throng on the streets?" asked John, deflecting the question. "It must be getting close to midnight, and I can hear music. There'll surely be dancing."

*

"So, merchants who regularly process, inspect and pack large volumes of tea leaves can suffer from giddiness, headaches, universal spasms, and loss of speech and memory as a result, and those who drink large amounts of tea can suffer from loss of energy, weakness and effeminacy." So ended John's lecture on the physiological effects of drinking tea, delivered to a small audience of medical practitioners invited that cold January afternoon to an informal meeting at Dr Fothergill's home. A lively discussion followed, with advocates of the "cup that cheers but does not inebriate" citing evidence in support of their contrary views.

Gilbert Thompson asked whether those handling great volumes of tea might be suffering due to the inhalation of fine particles, in the same way that coal miners, carpenters and flour millers do – the botanical nature of the particles being irrelevant. Perhaps it could be recommended that better ventilation be provided in such settings. Richard Watkins, who had studied with Akenside alongside John and now was in practice nearby, suggested that the ailments of tea-drinkers might be due to taking the beverage too hot rather than any intrinsic dangers of tea. Maybe they should be advised to let their beverage cool a little before consumption.

Ann Fothergill had entered the back of the room to gauge when the gathering would be ready for refreshments. She asked – with all of the directness of a woman well used to speaking up in Quaker meetings – what was wrong with developing effeminacy anyway. Perhaps more tea drinking could lead to a gentler society and the end of violence and warfare. That observation was greeted with some applause, and her announcement that tea would now be served, with general laughter – and cheers from at least part of the company.

The medics crowded around the table, and chose between tea, small beer and sweetened milk with hot water, although John was the only taker for the last option. Sam entered and laid down a large tray of freshly baked scones in the centre of the table. These were eagerly taken and consumed: John's summary of his medical thesis had taken more than an hour and everyone was hungry. The scones were so good – warm, moist, fruity and sweet – that several of the participants complimented Ann. "Even better than your own usual high standard", was Gilbert's opinion.

"Don't thank me", replied Ann. "Thank my pupil. Sam here baked them all himself." More applause, and Sam shyly took a bow before disappearing back into the kitchen.

As the company thinned out, John Fothergill gathered John and Gilbert together.

"Are you yet aware that from next year, it'll be necessary to have a licence from the Royal College of Physicians to practice in the City of London?" he asked. "There'll be an examination in June, and you'll be required to answer detailed questions, in both English and in Latin."

"In Latin!" exclaimed John. "Does my knowledge of Latin really determine my ability to heal?"

"No, but it does keep out the riff-raff", suggested Gilbert, cynically. He knew that he would have to work harder than John to brush up his acquaintance with the language.

As he walked back to Gracechurch Street, John reflected on this new requirement. It applied only to practicing in London. Was that where he wanted to be in the long-term? At the centre of things, like Dr Fothergill? Or would a country practice and a life devoted to a sweet Quaker wife and innumerable children suit him better? Or did he want to travel again, and perhaps return to his Caribbean roots? To his "dark lady"? So far, he had been drifting towards a medical future on the model of Dr John Fothergill, but in truth he had options. Soon he would have to choose one of them.

*

"Thank you for such a wonderful expedition this afternoon", said Betty to John. "St Paul's is a truly majestic building. I was quite overwhelmed. And I loved the Whispering Gallery: a magical place. Thank you for persuading me to climb all those steps, it was worth it in the end. For the views within the church, the panorama of the city way above the smoke down in the streets – and for your intimate whispers!"

"Well, I wanted to see it again myself. I was so disappointed that Molly and the others didn't want to join us."

"Oh, I wasn't. Anyway, Cousin Freeman would have got stuck on all those narrow stairways!"

Dr Fothergill and his sister were currently reciprocating their Northampton relatives' visit, and had taken Sam with them to help with luggage and other personal needs. Betty and Molly had declined the invitation to accompany them, so now the girls were staying for a few days with James and Ann Freeman, who just happened to live on Gracechurch Street a few doors down from John. In truth, the senior Fothergills were hoping that Betty's spending more time so close to Dr Lettsom might move things forward between them.

The Freemans were friendly and generous, but they prized their leisure which they usually enjoyed separately, and they were rather careless about the state of their establishment and the normal proprieties within. As James was in his forties, it was imagined that he was a responsible adult who would be sure to safeguard the reputations of his young cousins, but that trust was somewhat misplaced. So now, following the strenuous exertions of a day's sightseeing and a lengthy evening of chat over a hearty dinner washed down by a generous supply of wine, Betty found herself left in the drawing room, unchaperoned, still talking to John after other guests had returned home and the rest of the household had retired to bed.

"There are so many wonderful things to do and to see here in London, and I'm so grateful to you for being such an attentive guide. I thought I'd be missing home by now, but I'm not. I thought I'd be missing my Alec too, but I'm not."

"Who's Alec?"

"Oh, surely you know of Alec. Mr Alexander Chorley of Warrington. My beau. Warrington used to seem like a fine town to me before I came to London, and Alec was my idea of the perfect, modern young gentleman. But now I see that he's rather a country bumpkin. He just doesn't have the manners, the panache, the finish of young men down here. And his dress sense is so dated."

"Is he not a Quaker? You know, we can't dress like dandies."

"No, but even the most sober clothes can be worn with style – like you do! I wrote to him last month suggesting a few of his habits that he could easily modify or correct in order to become more fashionable, and I sent him one of those stylish neckties you wear. I do love him and I was only trying to help, but I got a very curt reply. I don't know what to do now, as I fear I've offended him." She paused for a while as if unsure whether to say what had come into her mind next. Then she went on and said it anyway: "I also fear that I don't fear it enough! Do you understand what I mean?"

John nodded, as he did understand. Actually, he had heard about Alec Chorley from Ann, but had not heard his name mentioned by Betty until now. Perhaps his northern rival was beginning to fade out. Betty continued: "And what of your West Indian sweetheart? I've heard the rumours. Who is she?"

"Oh, don't believe rumours!" cautioned John, caught off-guard. "Although the young women of the West Indies are indeed very beautiful and very accomplished."

"Isn't there a particular woman who writes to you?"

"Ah yes, a childhood friend. A close friend and companion of my mother since my father died. It was lovely to see her again when I returned to Tortola, and see how she's turned into a fine young woman since we used to play as children. I went to several of her parties, which are considered the peak of Tortola's social life. How she can dance! She's one of the most beautiful Tortola belles, with long, fine, straight hair. Very dark – her hair that is. She's clever too, and runs a whole plantation herself. She keeps all the accounts as she's good with figures, adopts all the latest agricultural innovations, and she's very kind and considerate to her slaves who love her in return."

John was already falling in love with the composite of Teresa and Letitia he was creating. Perhaps a young woman with all of the talents and good sense of Teresa with whom he could be perfectly at ease, combined with the advantages of being a rich heiress like Letitia who was also – let's face it – white, would indeed be his ideal. But it was Betty he was wooing now, and so he went on: "Sadly she's found another, a fine young colonial man with whom she plans to share her future. So I just get the letters giving me local gossip and an honest report of my mother's health – which is currently very good – and the presents of shells and corals that we both used to collect as children."

That account seemed to work. Betty was impressed with the talents of this former lover, and complimented to think that she might compare with her. John would not reveal a name, and so Betty admired his discretion too. They edged closer together on the sofa, using the fading heat as the fire began to burn out as an excuse. They made comparisons of London and provincial life. Betty admitted that, although she was finding her stay in London exciting and was not yet ready to go home, she saw her future as a country wife, somewhere amongst hills and fields and small villages and market towns. John extolled the life of the city, and the opportunity for being in the vanguard of medical practice that it offered, but then softened and suggested that in the longer term it could be satisfying to apply lessons learnt in the capital to the wellbeing of the people of some traditional country town. Reminiscences of childhood were shared, guarded frustrations with some of the constraints of following the Quaker faith were confessed, and mutual friends were appraised and constructively criticised.

The clock striking one genuinely surprised both of them, making them jump in the silence of the house. They noticed, not only that it had got late, but also that the fire was now completely out and it was cold. Their innocent intimacy ended abruptly, and their recent avowal of the wisdom of at least some Quaker observances left only one option. John rose to go. They agreed to meet again the following day, and visit the Tower together. Custom dictated that this would once more be a group outing. They stood close as John put on his long coat and wide-brimmed hat, and their hands touched as Betty passed him his cane. Their faces were close, their gazes focussed on one another's eyes, their breath felt warm in the freezing hallway. Then, with a soft "Goodnight, my dear", John turned abruptly to the door, opened it, and was gone.

CHAPTER 21

Through the cold and frost and snow of January, John continued to work hard in the Harpur Street surgery, in the homes of the rich and the poor of the city, and in the hospitals where his mentor made rounds. He also continued a hectic social life, often breakfasting with the Fothergills and then arranging trips to the capital's various wonders. The visit to the Tower was a great success, and they came away intoxicated with stories of Traitors' Gate and the consequences should the ravens ever leave. Inevitably, he and Betty were joined in their expeditions by Molly, and often by George Wheeler – a young man with obvious designs on her. James Freeman would come along too, but not usually his wife. There would be other young friends, and sometimes if the trip was not too arduous and there was no-one else to join the party, Ann Fothergill would act as chaperone. There was little opportunity for John and Betty to resume their intimate late-night conversation.

John also accepted invitations to tea (where he drank milk and hot water) and to dinner (where he drank a modest amount of good wine) at John Miers' palatial town house in Cannon Street. There he was always placed next to Nancy. He got to know a great deal about her brother John, who was loquacious on the subject of tin plating and on the operation of the family rolling mill near Swansea that he and his brother Henry managed together. He learnt how to say "Ynyspenllwch", which was the location of the works, and "Ynysygerwen" which was the site of the family's nearby country estate, although at that stage he had no idea how either might be spelt.

Nancy's older sister – another Molly – proved to be an expert on fashion, expressing a critical but disinterested opinion on the latest trends in both men's and women's attire. She did this without the slightest hint of envy, judgement or disapproval, and clearly had a finely developed aesthetic sense despite her own garb being the plainest and most modest of Quaker dress. She was quite complementary on John's choices, but had a few useful suggestions in the hat department. Aunt Mary, the sister of Nancy's late mother, was always present and had plenty to say about the Quaker issues of the day, mostly urging caution on matters such as agitating for the abolition of slavery and criticising those who called for Friends to mount an embargo on the supply of tin plates and mugs for the military.

Nancy's father's conversation consisted mostly of questions to John. How much property did he own in the Virgin Islands? How profitable was the cultivation of cotton? Was he now fully qualified to practice medicine? Would he soon be looking for a practice in a fashionable part of the city? As a result, most of John's contribution to the conversation comprised answers. As for Nancy; she asked for the mustard once, replied affirmatively when asked whether she would like more pudding, and expressed concern about John choosing to walk home when it was so icy outside. She was indeed a reserved young woman.

*

In the middle of the month, another parcel arrived from Little Jost van Dyke. This was not in response to the parcel John and Sam had made up in November, but to the one before. There were some new sweets flavoured with cinnamon and ginger, which did not work very well together. There were two handkerchiefs, embroidered with his initials by his mother, and there was a drawing of a girl playing the violin surrounded by people dancing, executed by Teresa. He had not seen any artwork by her before, and this attempt was naive but charming, and two of the dancers looked familiar. And there was news. One letter from each of Mary and Teresa.

Both letters announced the sad death of Cudjoe who had epitomised for John the dignified face of Africa, unbroken by enslavement and respected by both his owner and the community he led. John could see again the tall man, built like a warrior, singing the song composed for him against the background of the campfire on the night shortly before his first voyage to England. He had already seemed old, with his hair beginning to turn grey. He had died a free man, cared for in his last days by Cassia, Teresa and Mary. John wanted to know the cause of death, but insufficient detail was included.

His mother's letter told him that the cotton harvest on Little Jost had been excellent, although on Tortola it had been a bad year for sugar. Nevertheless, their relatives on the main island continued to get by. And so on. Also many questions about London, his medical activities and how he was dealing with the cold.

Teresa devoted a lot of her letter to explaining the picture she had drawn. An itinerant free black worker helping with the cotton harvest had brought with him a fiddle and he had spent every evening teaching Nanny how to play. The young girl was a natural, and soon had mastered a small repertoire of jigs, reels and waltzes. Bentorah bought her a third-hand instrument in Road Town and made a drum covered in goatskin for himself. Now there was dancing every week for the free blacks, Mary's remaining slaves, and any visitors who happened to be on the island. Teresa and Mary went out to watch the first time, Teresa joined in the dancing in the second week, and in the third and ever since the ex-Quaker, Mary, joined in too.

The second part of Teresa' letter was far less uplifting. On a visit with Mary to Road Town she had met Jim – John Pickering's former slave who had run from plantation to plantation accompanying John on his medical rounds. He was now working for the Lieutenant Governor, running the length and breadth of the island with official communications.

After John Pickering's death, his plantation had passed to his son Isaac. However, after a short visit, Isaac had returned to England and passed the management to an overseer. Whereas John Pickering had managed the estate with fairness and some compassion – notwithstanding his cruel separation of Jim's family – the new administration sought total control. The slightest shortcomings were severely punished, regardless of blame. There was no longer any give and take, and the workers and their families lived in fear. The new, stringent regime proved inefficient, with slaves no longer motivated to work hard unless they were being closely watched, and becoming increasingly careless with their master's produce and tools if they thought they could get away with it. This led to more punishments, less cooperation and less production.

Jim was no longer lent out to other masters to run errands, and spent more time in the field gangs, falling foul of the overseer's whip on numerous occasions – first for offences that were outside his control and later for acts of sabotage that were deliberate but insufficiently concealed. He was lucky, because when the Lieutenant Governor asked to hire him out to run errands for a few days and was refused, he made a good offer to buy him outright and was accepted. Now Jim was content with his new life and the freedom he enjoyed while out alone on the trail. The worst part, however, was delivering death warrants for slaves who had committed capital offences such as stealing livestock, running away for long periods of time or striking owners, overseers or their families. These offenders would be tried in absentia and then handed over to the Lieutenant Governor for punishment.

The Hodge plantation was an exception to this rule. Arthur Hodge, as John already knew, was keen to dispense justice, even lethal justice, himself. Eventually, he had agreed to the Lieutenant Governor's insistence that evidence of the most serious crimes be heard in the island's slave court, and that only those found guilty be executed, but he had secured permission to exact the punishment himself. Just prior to meeting Teresa, Jim had delivered warrants for the deaths of three of Hodge's slaves, who were dispatched even before the messenger had left the plantation. Unsurprisingly, their supposed attack on Hodge's family had involved young Arthur, now aged about seven, who had been attempting to learn about female anatomy by exploring the body of a slave girl of about his age. Her father and two brothers had intervened, and it was they who were hanged. Teresa expressed concern that the lot of slaves on Tortola, always harsh and unjust, was deteriorating further.

At about the same time as John was reading the news from Little Jost, the ship carrying his latest parcel was docking at Road Town. The next day, Teresa was up early, already composing a reply, sitting in the sunshine with brightly coloured ribbons woven into her hair.

*

It was rather late when Ann joined John and her brother for breakfast as she had been busy in the kitchen receiving her butcher's order and supervising its storage. John was at Harpur Street for his first meal of the day prior to assisting his mentor with his surgery.

"Molly and Betty have finished already?" asked Ann.

"They've gone off to visit Polly Plumstead", replied her brother. "They said something about sewing and swapping fabrics and silks."

"Well, that's as may be, but I think their main purpose will be to talk about letters they've just received. Molly got one from George Wheeler yesterday, and a letter from Alec Chorley arrived this morning for Betty. Our nieces will have some big decisions to make soon. And perhaps John here will have to make his mind up soon as well."

John said nothing, but he looked uncomfortable and avoided Ann's gaze.

"You know that my brother and I would be very happy to cement our ties with you further", said the older medic. "Betty is a fine girl, and we have seen how well the two of you get on."

"Not just your brother, John, but your sister too", added Ann, irritated at being left out. "Betty's been here since November, and it's now the middle of January: she won't wait forever. Personally, I just want to see both girls make a good match. Betty needs a husband to provide security and stability, but also companionship and joy. My brother's success and fame is down to hard work that takes up most of his waking hours. If you follow that road you'll not have time for a wife like Betty and she won't be happy. All my brother needs is a housekeeper, and he's got me for that."

"And very grateful I am too", commented Dr Fothergill in an attempt to placate her.

"If you want a wife to provide a home and family for you, while you throw yourself into your work and your meetings, then choose Nancy Miers", continued Ann. "She's such a quiet girl. I've never heard her say a single thing at Meetings. Her brothers always have plenty to say, during and after, and her sister Molly makes some good observations, but Nancy – nothing – ever. She helps with the charity work conscientiously enough, and she's kind and patient when she comes on visits to young mothers with children. She'd be a very good mother and a very undemanding wife. The latter can't be said about Betty!"

Distracted, John poured himself a cup of tea, forgetting that he had long given up the beverage. He still could not think of a response, and so he just sat there awkwardly, sipping – at least the liquid had cooled down.

Ann broke the silence, opening a new topic: "By the way, I attended Sam's baptism yesterday. First time I've been in an Anglican church for years. I think the vicar was worried I was going to shout out something disruptive, but I told him afterwards that we Quakers don't do that anymore. It was a nice service. Sam was scrubbed up clean and tidy in his best clothes. He'd even made some of his tastiest cakes to pass round afterwards! He seemed to be proud and serious about the commitment. A couple of other lads from his English class were there and one of the senior Merchant Taylors' boys who teaches them. Becky from our kitchen too. Sam asked why you weren't there."

"Oh, we were busy with our rounds – ministering to the poor", answered John, almost choking on his tea in his haste to respond.

"I could have spared you. We weren't that busy. You should have said."

"Anyway, he's called 'Sam Coakley' now," explained Ann.

"Not Lettsom then", observed the senior doctor. "Strange that he should take your middle name."

"Taken my mother's maiden name, I suspect. He's always looked up to her." John was still struggling to speak after his tea had gone down the wrong way.

"I think you should free him now: it really doesn't seem right to own a fellow-Christian", said Ann. "He says the two of you were such close friends when you were little boys, and it seemed to be like again that when you went back to the Virgin Islands. Now he doesn't know where he is with you."

"It's hard for a professional man like John to be a close friend to a handyman", observed the elder John.

"Well, I'll encourage him to spend more time doing odd jobs around the neighbourhood so he can earn more money, and he can help more with the food distribution which he finds worthwhile. He says he never expected to find poverty and children going hungry in England."

John had been uncomfortable enough while the conversation had been about Betty, but he found this discussion of Sam even more difficult. Teresa had told him to let Sam find his own way in England, and to let him go when he was ready to make the most of his own life. Was Sam ready now? Of course, he did want Sam to be free. But he had always imagined a free Sam, of his own volition, wishing to remain close to him. Even wanting to serve him in some way. He had not envisaged a free Sam doing just what Sam wanted. Doing things he did not approve of. Although, intellectually, he did realise that that's what freedom is all about.

From somewhere came irritation whenever he was asked to approve of Sam establishing his independence: taking English classes, attending Anglican services, being baptised. He never refused such requests, but every one of them seemed to be a slight on himself. To represent a desire to move further away from him. And why not? He was confused by the inconsistency between his logic and his emotions. And what applied to Sam would also, later, apply to Teresa.

"We move in different worlds now", said John, at last. "It's true that I'm losing him as a friend. Losing him as a slave too would cut our ties altogether. This way, I retain some responsibility for him, and that's what I want. I'm quite happy for him to be set whatever tasks you think appropriate." John was unable to put much conviction into this answer.

"And if he wants to leave us?" asked Ann.

"Then he will."

*

One evening in late January, James Freeman hosted a very special performance for his young friends and relatives. Betty and Molly were there of course, staying overnight as proceedings were due to last until late. Their friend Polly Plumstead was also in the company, as well as John and James Beesley. After the sort of leisurely dinner that had contributed to Cousin Freeman's stout figure, accompanied by generous provision of red Madeira wine, a knock at the front door was heard and James's servant, Rachel, announced the mystery guest for the evening. Although Ann Freeman retired early, the rest of the company relocated to the drawing room where a fire was blazing leaving Rachel to clear the remains of their meal, and the nature of their entertainment was revealed.

"I am pleased to welcome to my home tonight, Andrew Curtis, who has brought along with him his electrical machine with which he will demonstrate the wonders of this amazing force of nature," announced the host. He also encouraged his guests to help themselves, and one another, to port or to tea or coffee while Andrew set up his apparatus. Most, including John, chose the port so as to prolong their cheery mood. Andrew declined all refreshment and focussed on his task.

The equipment comprised three principal elements. The large wooden horizontal wheel was the most familiar looking part; a handle placed towards the edge allowed the operator to turn it easily. A cord around the rim of the wheel transferred the motion to another, smaller wheel on which the second component stood. This was a large glass jar, against which a leather pad rested. Close to it, a serrated piece of metal was supported by a broad metal rod, looking rather like a clenched fist on the end of a man's arm.

This was resting on the top of the third item situated between the other two – another glass jar partially covered in metal foil.

"Would someone like to feel the foil here?" asked Andrew. "Check that it's smooth and taut?"

James Freeman eagerly volunteered, and reported that it was fine.

Andrew then grasped the handle and turned the wooden wheel a few times. As he did so, the first of the glass jars turned more quickly than the wheel, rubbing against the leather pad. Soon a gasp went up from his rapt audience as brilliant sparks began to fly from the rotating glass jar to the metal fist.

"James: could you check for us that the foil is still smooth and taut?"

This time, as soon as James touched the foil his arm was knocked back, and he uttered a quiet yelp as he felt the electric shock.

This set the stage for Andrew to begin his account of static electricity, of the Franklin generator which created the "electrical fire" as he called the sparks, and of the Leyden jar which had stored it until dramatically discharged by James. As he was a man of science, everyone expected John to be familiar with all of this, and he tried to give that impression despite never having seen such a thing before. Andrew went on to talk of lightening and lightening conductors, of the folly of flying kites in thunder clouds, of John Wesley's observations on electricity, and of potential medical applications of his apparatus. The last topic led to a lengthy discussion between the demonstrator and the doctor in the audience of the benefits and dangers of electrical therapy, and of the conditions that might be alleviated. Sensing a fall-off in the attention of the rest of the audience, Andrew changed the subject, and asked whether they would like to see further demonstrations of the power and utility of this force.

There followed a series of experiments in which volunteers held a brass rod connected to the Leyden jar while seated on a stool that Andrew had brought with him, resulting in tingling sensations and shocks. The stool was then placed on a rosin mat and volunteers felt nothing, although their friends were intrigued to see their hair standing on end. Molly untied her long locks to give a particularly striking demonstration of this phenomenon. Andrew explained that rosin was a pine tree resin with strong insulating properties so that the volunteers were themselves storing some of the Leyden jar's charge.

The mat was then removed, and the company held hands with the volunteer on the stool to demonstrate their own conductivity, after which they pulled on cotton gloves and held hands again to show how this material would insulate them from the electrical fire. Finally, stressing that this exercise was taken directly from John Wesley's own impeccably Christian book on electricity, Andrew called for two volunteers, one male and one female, for his last demonstration.

Betty was first up, after which the rest of the company immediately called on John to be the second guinea pig. Betty was asked to stand on the rosin mat, and was given the live rod to hold. John stood on the floor, and was asked to kiss her lips without touching any other part of her body. Both turned a deep red, but could not disappoint their audience. Except that they did. Every time John leaned forward to place his lips on Betty's he received, not a warm sweet kiss, but a nasty shock from which he involuntarily recoiled. At the urging of the onlookers, Betty finally dropped the rod and John was safely rewarded with a lovely wet kiss.

*

As glasses were refilled and Andrew dealt with questions from all sides, James Freeman's voice cut through the chatter asking, "What about the other use of your machine you mentioned: to determine whether people are telling the truth?"

"Oh, that's not very reliable, and it's got quite late."

"Well, I'd like to try it. There's lots of questions I'd like a truthful answer to!"

Others of the company, especially the young ladies began to plead for Andrew to demonstrate this application, and at last he relented.

"In that case, I shall accept your offer of a large glass of port", he said and went over to the table to pour himself a good measure, sneaking a whispered exchange with Betty as he did do.

Naturally, the host of the evening was the first victim. He was instructed to take off his jacket and roll his right shirt sleeve up. He then sat on the stool, on the rosin mat, and Andrew fastened a brass ring to his right arm, just above his elbow, with a chain that fell onto the floor. He gave him a cotton glove to put on that hand and the brass rod to hold in it. Some gentle questions followed, about his name, address and religious persuasion. Enquiries about how often his house was cleaned and his clothes were washed led to some visible embarrassment and evasion, but he felt nothing more than a tingle in his arm and began to feel in the clear.

Then Andrew came to the big one: "Have you ever kissed your servant, Rachel?" This had been a subject of speculation amongst his friends for some time now, but he had never realised that they suspected anything. He began to perspire. He tried to deflect his interrogator with statements about how hard working she was, how honourable he was, and how happily married he and Ann were. His arm began to tingle. Challenged to provide a simple "yes" or "no" answer, he bellowed out "CERTAINLY NOT!", and then shot upright as the current connected through his sweaty glove.

This got the final session off to a good start. Molly was up next. A paragon of truth and honesty, she never felt a thing. Asked whether she loved George Wheeler, she answered "No", and appeared to be relieved to have settled that in her own mind. Others took their turn, and revealed secrets, or by careful control of their own emotions and emissions managed to continue to hide them. Soon, only Betty and John were left, and being a gentleman, John allowed Betty to go first. Polly asked her whether she loved Alec Chorley. After a pause, perhaps to ask herself the same question, Betty replied in the negative without ill-effect. Cousin Freeman then asked her whether she was in love with anyone in the room. Another pause. The shyly: "Yes". No sign of any discomfort.

"Is it John that you're in love with?" The question came from Molly. The answer, eventually, was "Yes". Again, both parties turned a deep crimson, but no shock, electric or otherwise, was felt.

Finally, John could avoid the hot seat no longer. Various questions about his childhood home and his schooling followed. Eventually, Betty asked whether he still had hopes of winning back his West Indian sweetheart. John focused on a mental image of Letitia, and answered, as calmly as he could: "No". Not a tingle. He was ready for the direct question about Betty now. He did not know the answer himself, but he would say "Yes", and keep his options open. On evenings like this, when she was so close, so lively and so lovely, surely it was coming true. He felt under control, able to pass this test. However, the machine operator sensed what he was thinking and cut in with his own question: "Do you still think about your West Indian sweetheart every day?" He knew that he did. Not Letitia, but that trick was no longer working. He began to sweat. "No", he answered. His arm jerked straight and the brass rod clattered onto the floor.

CHAPTER 22

The weather that February and early March was awful and this curtailed the young people's socialising and sightseeing. Storms and high winds were followed by a cold snap accompanied by snow and then hard frosts and ice. Food availability was always limited at this time of year, and difficulties of transport and distribution due to the bad weather exacerbated the shortages. The wealthy cut back and lived on plain fare, while the poor just went hungry. Smallpox saw its opportunity, coming first for the children of the overcrowded slums. Inexorably, it moved on to their parents and then to the richer districts.

The doctors of Harpur Street were kept very busy. Their wealthy patients suffered injury from falls, overturning carriages and toppling trees during the gales, and from further falls and colds and chilblains in the snow and ice. Their poor patients suffered from hypothermia, frostbite and malnutrition. They lavished care on unlucky gentlefolk stricken with smallpox, treating them with bloodletting and purging, dosing them with spirit of vitriol mixed into bottles of beer, and ensuring that their fever was brought down by leaving their bedroom windows open and allowing no fires in their rooms. For the poor patients, only the last element of this cure was available, and not through choice. Despite this, the younger doctor could not help but notice that survival and recovery amongst the poor was somewhat better than amongst the rich.

Ann's activities of visiting the sick and distributing food in deprived neighbourhoods intensified during this season. She formed an effective partnership with Sam. Out collecting food from the wealthier residents, Ann would take the front door, while Sam went round the back to find the kitchen staff who would really know what their employers could do without. In time, their collaboration became less mistress-and-servant, and more of a joint effort. Decisions on which streets to make a priority for their charity, which patients to refer to the doctors, and how best to relieve the various sorts of suffering they encountered became easier when they pooled their experience. The sort of true companionship that comes from sharing a worthwhile task developed, in which success of the venture is the sole consideration.

Betty and Molly remained indoors for much of this time. First Betty suffered from a severe cold and was nursed by Molly, and then Molly became the patient and Betty the nurse. Finally, they both attended to Polly, who suffered worst of all. For some time after the game of truth, Betty was cool towards John. When Alec Chorley braved the elements to travel down from Warrington to visit her at Harpur Street – after her own cold had subsided – somehow his awkwardness and lack of fashion sense no longer seemed to matter.

Throughout Alec's brief stay, Betty became certain that he was the one. Only when he had returned to the north did she begin to notice the dedication of the young doctor who was working so hard in support of her uncle. Watching him fully engaged as a professional serving his patients, rather than as a tour guide and a suitor, made him seem all the more desirable. Alec would always have time for her, as his inherited wealth made him a member of the leisured classes. Having less time for her was actually working in John's favour.

All this time, battling against the winter gales of the north Atlantic, a ship was proceeding towards England bearing another parcel from Little Jost van Dyke.

*

"Soon all your northern colonial compatriots will be drinking that", observed Dr Fothergill, watching John prepare himself his favoured hot water, milk and sugar concoction. "It looks like the Townsend Acts are to be repealed, and duties on imports to the colonies abolished – except for the one on tea. I don't think the people of Massachusetts will be impressed, and I certainly don't think they'll be drinking tea again for a long time. Things are getting critical over there."

"Samuel told me they call it 'Cambric tea' in Virginia," added Ann, "and they prepare it for infants and old people. It's named after a very fine French fabric – so fine that there seems to be nothing of it!" John sipped his drink, unperturbed by this banter.

He and Gilbert were taking "tea" at Harpur Street with the Fothergills, following a couple of hours' practice of being examined on medical knowledge in Latin by their mentor. The College of Physicians examination was due in three month's time. Becky was serving, as Sam was attending his class at Merchant Taylors'.

"How did your practice go?" asked Molly.

"John was perfect. He could answer all of the medical questions, and he's completely fluent in Latin. He could dispute with the Pope himself!" was Gilbert's answer.

"Well, not totally perfect," interjected their inquisitor, "but good enough at this stage. And you, Gilbert, you have an excellent grasp of physiology but perhaps your ideas of ideal treatments are different from mine. Sometimes bleeding and purging can be therapeutic, you know. Of course, the real examiners will have their own personal approaches, so it's not a matter of learning what I would do, but being able to defend your own treatment plans. As for the Latin, that'll come with practice. That's why we've started in good time."

They were interrupted by Becky, coming in to clear away. "All of Sam's currant cakes have gone already," exclaimed Ann. "Could you fetch us some more?" The range and quality of Sam's baking was improving all the time.

"I've been reading about Count Bernstorff", remarked the senior doctor. John knew he was referring to the long-serving foreign minister of Denmark. "Three years ago, he freed all the serfs on his estate near Copenhagen. They pleaded with him not to, as they thought they'd not survive without his guidance. But he persevered, allotting a parcel of land to each family, granting a set of tools to each man, and providing agricultural instruction for them all. He also agreed that, if in five years time they wished to revert to serfdom, then he'd take them back. The article I read suggested that they're very unlikely to choose to revert to bondage. They're now happy and their productivity has increased. It's expected they'll be paying rent to the Count this year for the first time, and their prosperity will increase substantially in the future. Isn't this a model for freeing slaves on British plantations?"

"It's a wonderful example," agreed Gilbert. "Trading in slaves is evil, and no true Quaker – no true Christian – should imagine that God has given them a right to own other people."

"Surely most slave owners are very considerate", volunteered Betty. "You can't expect Africans to be as honest or resourceful as Danish peasants who are surely more like us. Alec says Africans are like children and need their owners to guide them and to bring them to God."

"On the contrary, many slave owners are very cruel", replied John. "They cut off men's legs for running away and hang men for protecting their children against attacks from settlers. Even the better owners will sell a man's wife and children to another estate, miles away where he'll never see them again."

"Your Alec's father is in business with Thomas Hutton Rawlinson up in Lancaster, trading slaves and sugar from his plantation in Grenada", said Ann. "So Alec would claim the system is benevolent."

"But that's nothing to do with Alec. He's a merchant and a gentleman. He doesn't own a single slave", shot back Betty, looking directly at John as she delivered her last sentence.

"Well, his brother now works with Thomas Hutton's nephew, Henry Rawlinson" continued Ann, relentlessly. "They're seeking to finance a slaving voyage to Africa. I still have my spies in Warrington you know, from when I lived at your father's house before you were born. What I don't understand is where your Alec fits in with all this. Is he active in these trades, or does he just live off the proceeds?"

Seeing that Betty was increasingly uncomfortable with this conversation and finding it difficult to defend Alec due to ignorance of his business affairs, John gallantly turned the focus of the conversation to the Rawlinsons.

"I stayed with Abraham Rawlinson when I first arrived in England. I must admit I didn't get on with him. Nor with his son Henry, who looked down on a poor colonial lad like me. I was so relieved when your brother rescued me and arranged for me to go to school in Penketh rather than Lancaster."

"And what about your slaves, John?" asked Ann, refusing to be distracted.

"You know I freed them when I went back to the West Indies – despite the cost to myself. Perhaps I should have followed the example of Count Bernstorff and provided an education for them first, but they seem to be getting along fine now, working on my mother's estate."

"Maybe, but you seem determined to remain Sam's legal owner. Well, I have some news for you. Sam wishes to join the navy."

Suddenly, everyone paid attention. Sam was very popular within the household, but it was clear to all of them that he wanted more out of life than being a domestic servant.

"Good for him!" said Molly. "He'll see the world."

"The navy is a fighting force. You can't approve of him taking a role in warfare", warned Dr Fothergill.

"Well, he'll be feeding people, not killing them", responded Ann. "He wishes to become a cook onboard ship. When they heard he was a slave, they requested a letter of permission from his owner. He asked me to ask you, John."

"So, it's his baking, not his shooting, that's got him in", commented Molly. "Congratulations, Aunt Ann! It's your training that swung it for him."

"Why didn't he ask me directly?" asked John, angrily. Again Sam wanted to move away from him. Perhaps finally, this time. John felt hurt.

"I think he's scared of you these days", Ann went on. "It's a shame. He's told me of your childhood adventures, out on that island. You and your brother and him and his sister. It sounds like it was idyllic. But here, he's constantly aware of the difference in status between you, and he's very nervous about what you'll say."

"What happened to your brother?" asked Gilbert.

"He died of a fever at the same time as my father, about ten years ago", replied John, curtly.

"What happened to Sam's sister?" asked Betty.

"She remains on Little Jost, serving my mother."

"Is she your secret West Indian sweetheart?" asked Molly.

"This was all years ago, before I was six!" said John. As ever, his rapidly colouring face gave him away.

"But you saw them again when you returned and brought Sam back?" pressed Betty.

"Oh, there was very little time then. I saw Teresa a bit, but I was mostly practicing on Tortola."

"So, Teresa! Now we have a name", remarked Molly, triumphantly.

"And what of Sam?" asked Ann, coming back to the point. "Will you let him go to sea?"

"Yes. Yes, I must." No hesitation here. Although John would have loved Sam not to go, his agreement with Teresa took precedence.

"And will you free him?"

"I shall have to give that some thought."

Compared with that exchange, the earlier inquisition about his medical knowledge had been straightforward, even if it had been in Latin. As he was leaving the house, Ann intercepted him.

"You have two important decisions to make, John. One is about Sam and his freedom, the other is about Betty. Alec is pressing her for an answer now. She's attracted by his wealth and position, and she's too naive to understand where it all comes from. She's also attracted by your vigour, ambition and idealism. If you intend to make a proposal to her, you should do so within the next week, otherwise you may find it's too late. If you do ask her, it's most likely that she'll accept."

"Thank you. I promise to resolve both matters soon."

*

The parcel was bigger than usual. It had arrived early on a Tuesday morning in late March, just as John was about to rush off to help Dr Fothergill in his surgery. That evening, when he finally got the opportunity to open it, he discovered why it was so large. Inside, carefully boxed and wrapped, was a huge conch shell. A foot long, with eleven whorls on its spire – he recognised it as the shell Teresa had found on their last day together on Little Jost. He placed it on one side with great care, somewhat concerned about what might have led her to part with the prize of her collection. He took out the bag of sweets and his mother's letter, and then reached into the bottom of the parcel to retrieve Teresa's letter. Placing his candle on his table, he sat down to read.

She started with thanks for the lace handkerchiefs and an update on Nanny's improving fiddle playing. This had led to an increase in Mary's enthusiasm for dancing jigs, culminating in a sprained ankle and an enforced period of rest while she recovered and Teresa and Cassia shared out her work. Further cruelties on the Pickering and Hodge plantations had come to light, and were causing a wave of resentment and anxiety amongst the enslaved population. The Little Jost community had reacted by working even harder to ensure that they could remain where they were.

"I was delighted that my brother wrote to me", continued the letter. "I had not realised that he had learnt so much already. A separate letter for him is included in the package." John broke off reading to feel around in the parcel, and located it.

"He has told me of your friendship with Betty, your employer's niece." Well, not strictly his "employer", but never mind. "Sam still has illusions that you and I might be married one day, just as you promised when you left the island for the first time. He urges me to find a way to come to London to make sure you honour your promise, or to persuade you to come to Little Jost again to settle as a planter, a doctor, and a husband and family man. My brother is such a romantic! You and I had this conversation before you left. Island life could never satisfy your ambitions, nor provide enough people for you to help with your medical skills. I would never be accepted in London, being too dark and insufficiently genteel for polite society.

"You did want love, and I think you need it. If you have found it, seize it! Marry Betty, with my blessing, and raise brilliant and beautiful children. I have no doubt that she is everything you need, and that she will be able to support you in your career. I wish you both the greatest happiness. But don't forget me. I am sending you my finest shell, the one we found on your last day here, to make sure you don't. And remember, I still belong to you." John's tears stained the paper, causing some of the ink to run, as he folded it to put it away. And again, as he re-opened it to read once more.

*

The next day, John found Sam alone in the washroom at Harpur Street, rinsing a batch of the doctor's shirts in a large tub.

"I have two letters for you", he said. "One is from Teresa: it came yesterday in a parcel from home. The other is from me, recommending you for the Royal Navy and granting my permission for you to join."

"I won't actually be enlisted in the Navy", pointed out Sam as he swirled the shirts around in the water. "I'll be a steward: personal servant to Captain William Locker on board *HMS Thames*. I met him last month at my class. He used to help with it when he was studying at Merchant Taylors'. He'd come back to visit Reverend Townley."

Now Sam began to wring out each shirt in turn while continuing his account. "When he heard that I was learning bookkeeping and that I could cook and bake and do repair jobs, he immediately asked whether I wanted to go to sea with him! He's an impulsive man the headmaster told me, but he thinks he'll be good to work for. He's very busy preparing his ship for sea as well as being about to get married, so he probably didn't want to spend a lot of time looking around for a steward. I'll cook for the Captain's table, buy his supplies, clean and maintain his quarters and generally look after him. Keep his chickens too. The trick in this job is for him not to notice that I'm there, just for him to find that everything he needs is."

John watched this self-assured young man working, as he listened to his excited talk. It suddenly dawned on him what a transformation had taken place since they had come over to England together. How he had acquired so many skills. Why could they not have remained close? What was it about society that dictated that they move in separate circles?

"I think my letter covers everything. It's mainly about you and your honesty. And my permission for you to keep everything you earn while in his service." Then he took Sam's wet hands in both of his and held them tight for a moment. "You'll do very well in this new role and it'll be a great adventure for you. Captain Locker will be well looked after. Sam, I do wish you every success."

"I'm very grateful", replied Sam, pleased by John's warm words. For that moment, they were simply two old friends once more.

"I've also decided I must free you. I'm so sorry not to have done so sooner."

"Oh, that hardly matters now", replied Sam with a smile. "At sea, I shall be as free as any man can be. But, should anything happen to me, then as your slave they'll be obliged to seek you out and let you know of your loss of property. Then you'll be able to inform Teresa, Mary and Miss Ann. You and those three women would probably be the only people who might care."

"I'm sure it won't come to that", said John, heavily, aware that there was a substantial risk that it might. "I understand your logic. We'll leave things the way they are then. If you ever feel it would be advantageous for you to be free, write to me and I'll get the papers sorted out."

John paused, as Sam had taken the shirts from the draining board to the box mangle, which had to be pulled out into the centre of the room to operate. John helped him move the heavy piece of equipment, and then observed as he put the first shirt under the roller.

"I am truly sorry to have neglected our friendship since we came to England", said John. "I do value it, you know."

Sam took the shirt from the mangle, shook it, and checked that it was dry enough. Then he looked John in the eye. "I know. You have pursued your career, and you are committed to it and you're making a great success out of it. Now, I must follow a career of my own. I should probably have discussed it with you sooner – as a friend!" Sam grinned at his master as he said this. The conversation continued as Sam attended to each of the other shirts in turn.

"I might even get to sail to the West Indies one day, and see my sister and your mother again. Wouldn't that be wonderful!"

John nodded and expressed his hope that that would happen. They speculated on what Sam might find there. Once Sam had finished the last shirt, John handed him the letters. Sam wiped his hands and sat down to read the one from his sister.

"So, she won't come here", he said when he had finished, looking disappointed.

"No. She's realistic: it could never work."

"So, now you'll marry Betty."

"No. I intend to ask for the hand of Nancy Miers."

"What! Why?" Sam was amazed.

"I like Betty a lot. She's pretty and she's fun. But Teresa still has my heart. It would be unfair to pretend any different to Betty. Nancy has a fortune and a docile personality. She'll support me, while not demanding too much of my time or attention in return. As I can't choose for love, I shall go for money and for the interests of my career."

Sam said nothing to this, but took the shirts out into the yard and hung them up on the line. By the time he returned, he had worked out how to express what was on his mind.

"You made three promises when you first left Little Jost. You promised to come back and take me to England with you. You've kept that promise, and it's provided this wonderful opportunity for me. You promised to take all your slaves back to Africa. Well, you freed them – and I suppose that taking them back to Africa is harder than you could have understood back then. And you promised to marry my sister. I'm truly sorry that that's the one you've been unable to keep."

*

A few days later, John spoke first to John Miers and then to Nancy. Both responded favourably to his proposal of marriage, and so the matter was settled. Betty was furious when she heard the news. Her uncle John was disappointed, but rose to John's defence giving Betty the impression that he supported this union and depressing her further. Molly was passing through a phase of distrusting all men, and shrugged the whole episode off as being typical. Only Ann understood what had happened. She was relieved that Betty would not spend her life playing second fiddle to a great man's career, but at the same time annoyed with John for not having proposed to her and given her the choice.

Following John's announcement, a coolness descended on Lettsom-Fothergill relationships. The doctors still worked together in a professional and cooperative manner, and preparation for the forthcoming Licentiate examination continued. A few more outings took place in which John served as guide and Betty and Molly were amongst his audience, but the magical tension of unspoken feelings, the electricity of close physical proximity, and the excitement of unknown future possibilities had all been discharged.

In June, both John and Gilbert Thompson successfully gained their licences of the College of Physicians. Almost immediately, John began to collaborate with his network of medical colleagues to establish a general dispensary in Aldersgate Street which opened later that year to provide advice and medication for the poor of the area.

The summer and autumn of 1770 saw a spate of weddings. John and Nancy married on 31 July at the Friends Meeting House in Devonshire Square. The couple were surrounded by nearly a hundred Quaker well-wishers, although not a single Fothergill attended.

On 18 October, Betty Fothergill married Alec Chorley in Warrington. Her adventures in London were over, and while they provided a rich vein of memories for many years to come, no change to her destiny had resulted. Two days later, in Addington, Kent, Captain William Locker married Lucy Parry, an admiral's daughter. After a week's honeymoon, he joined *HMS Thames* on its home river, where his new steward had prepared everything for his comfort and health during his first voyage in command.

It was not until the following year that Gilbert Thompson married Mary Edmundson in the village of Wray near Lancaster. Contrary to what he had forecast the year before, Mary came to London to live with him and he never became a country doctor. James Beesley did not return to Tortola, nor did he find a wife. He continued to write essays about the natural beauty of the West Indies, the iniquity of slavery, and on religious and philosophical topics of the time, but without the success that had greeted his first book on George Fox.

PART V: 1778–95

Careers

CHAPTER 23

On a bright sunny morning in February 1778 Teresa was feeding the chickens outside the house when she noticed a small boat sailing over from Tortola towards the jetty on Little Jost. She did not recognise it, and it did not look like any of the rather old and battered vessels that usually plied these waters. It looked clean and new and was approaching fast. As the British Empire was at that time at war with the American colonies, she was alarmed. She ran back into the house, taking the small child who was strapped to her back with her. There she roused Mary and Nanny, and together they locked and barred the door and shuttered the windows.

Her concern, although prudent, was misplaced. The boat was a Royal Navy pinnace, and when it docked just one man alighted before it pulled away again. He was in his mid-thirties, of mixed race, wearing a smart green jacket and a black three-cornered hat. On reaching the closed up house, he was not fooled for a moment as he had seen Teresa run inside. He stood there and called her name. On getting no reply, he called instead for Mary. Inside a whispered conversation took place about the likelihood of an American rebel knowing both of their names. Tentatively, Nanny opened the door.

"A strange man out here", she reported.

"Me, strange!" said the man. "Tell them to come out and see how strange I have become."

There was something familiar about the voice, although the accent sounded all wrong.

Cautiously, leaving the child inside, Teresa emerged. She looked at him. He smiled. She studied his face. Then suddenly she gave a great whoop of joy. "Is it really you?" she asked, almost as if she still expected that it wasn't.

"Yes it certainly is."

Brother and sister then enclosed one another in a tight embrace, which neither wanted to release. Nanny peeped out again to see what was going on. Realisation slowly dawned on her.

"It's Sam!" she cried, jumping up and down. "Sam, it really is!" Mary was then at her side. She passed the child in her arms to Nanny, and then prised Sam away from his sister to give him her own hug. Never was anyone more welcome than Sam on returning home that day.

*

Sam explained that his ship was in Road Harbour for a few days being repaired, and that his captain had granted him leave when he heard he had family close by. He handed out scones from his latest batch, to their evident delight.

Despite his present, Mary appeared to think that Sam would need feeding up. She was obviously unaware that, with the possible exception of his captain, Sam was the best fed person onboard his ship. So the meal that evening was substantial and it lasted until well after darkness had fallen.

"Last year, Captain Locker was moved from *HMS Thames* to *HMS Lowestoffe*, and he took me with him", explained the visitor.

"He must be very impressed with you", said Mary.

"He's always appreciative. Good to work for." Sam pushed his empty plate aside, strenuously resisting Mary's attempts to offer him a third helping. Instead, he poured himself another glass of wine. Teresa's and Mary's glasses were still quite full. In the corner of the room sat Nanny, having asked to stay on after serving the meal to hear the traveller's stories. Next to her, the baby girl slept oblivious.

"We sailed out here last year and we patrol the Leeward Islands; all the way from Antigua to here. We've already seen action and captured a couple of rebel ships."

"Was that dangerous?" asked Teresa, betraying her anxiety.

"Not really. The first was just a cargo ship carrying rice. We completely outgunned her and her master was wise enough to surrender without a fight. The second was more of a match. A privateer, quite well armed. Our guns soon overwhelmed her though. The main enemy was – as always – the sea itself."

His listeners gazed at him with rapt attention. A man whom they knew so well, now so full of exotic and swashbuckling tales.

"We were in the middle of a gale, and the sea was very heavy. To seal our victory, the enemy had to be boarded. The First Lieutenant led an attempt, but he was beaten back by the waves and his boat almost capsized. Locker was ready to give up after that, but we had a new young lieutenant onboard, and he volunteered to lead a second attempt. He was just amazing, calmly guiding the boat through mountainous waves and being the first to leap across to the ladder on the privateer. He and the men he took across with him took control of our prize and sailed her back to port with us."

At this, Sam raised his glass to drink a toast to: "Horatio Nelson – the hero of the hour!"

Sam continued his account, of life at sea, of ports he had visited, of banquets he had prepared, and of cakes he had baked. They laughed when he spoke of his rivalry with the ship's cook and the lengths to which each of them would go to secure the best supplies, Sam to cater for the captain and the cook to feed the crew. A little bit of thieving and chicken rustling during the long watches of the night was not beneath either of them.

On a more sombre note, he did admit that he sometimes felt lonely – being neither an officer nor one of the crew. He had made friends with the ship's doctor and got on quite well with some of the young lieutenants, but there was a small clique amongst the crew of whom he was wary. They seemed to resent the privileges he enjoyed and had tried to swindle him out of money.

*

Eventually, Mary tired and went to bed. Teresa told Nanny to go home to her shack in the worker's village. Then Sam insisted on showing her how efficiently and quickly one could clean and tidy up after a big meal. As they worked together, just the two of them now, each had a burning question to ask the other. Sam went first.

"So just who is that little child?"

"Little Mary", replied Teresa. She paused, but realised that she would have to say more. "I found her under a bush at the market in Road Town."

For half a second, Sam believed her. Then he smiled. "No. I reckon that there's some man involved. There usually is!"

"Alright", said Teresa, steeling herself to tell the tale. "He was a local planter and he came to stay here for a few weeks about eighteen months ago. I'd spent ages trying to persuade him to come over to supervise some extensive land improvements that really needed to be made, and that was after spending ages persuading Mary that they had to be done and were worth paying for. She even made me write to John to seek his advice and approval, although she owns Little Jost now and I really didn't need the opinion of someone in London! Finally, she agreed and he agreed and he came over. Once he was here, I must say he gave it his all, working long hours, organising our workers and bringing people over from Tortola and even further afield to complete specialist tasks. He was very capable, and I liked him. He became a great favourite of Mary."

At this point, the child whose existence was being explained awoke and her mother picked her up and sat down to feed her. Sam broke off from washing up to contemplate the loving scene between mother and daughter, and then he sat down to focus on hearing the crux of the story.

"One evening, when the work was almost done, Mary made a special meal for the three of us. She opened the best of our wine, and then the best of our rum. Just like tonight, she went off to bed early, leaving us to talk. Actually, I think she wanted us to get together. Unlike you, he certainly didn't want to wash dishes." Teresa paused, gently rocking the infant who had now sucked her fill. "I should have gone to bed too. He would have let me at that stage. But I was enjoying the evening, enjoying being close to a fine and handsome man. I felt excited, and thought that I could just stay a little longer, perhaps allow him to touch me and hug me a little. He started to kiss me, and I enjoyed that too, but then I said, 'Goodnight, now I must go to bed.'"

"So, you can guess what happened. He pressed himself on me and I resisted. I fought him off, but he overpowered me. I said 'No', but he ignored me. I could have shouted for Mary to help me. I could have screamed. But you know what I'm like. I was thinking, if I do that, he'll go away and this job will never be finished. If I do that, Mary will think I led him on – maybe she'll throw me out. And of course, I was curious – just what is it like! So I found out. And the result is Little Mary here." Little Mary was now fast asleep again.

"Mary turned out to be very understanding and helpful once it was no longer possible to hide what had happened. She didn't scold me at all, although she believes he seduced me rather than forcing himself on me. She loves Little Mary, loves being

'Granny'. She has three real grandchildren in London whom she's never seen, but this little one is definitely her favourite!"

"Did you ever tell the father?"

"No. He became engaged to a young woman in Jamaica and moved away. Actually, Mary and I didn't want anyone else involved in raising her. She's ours!"

"Even so, can her uncle hold her?"

Teresa passed her over, warning Sam to continue the gentle swaying that kept her asleep. Then she took over completion of tidying away of the dishes, and turned the conversation to her burning question.

*

"How was John when you last saw him?"

"That was nearly eight years ago! I tried to call on him when I was on leave in London, but he was away working. All I can say is that he was very well eight years ago. He got his M.D. in Leyden and he was working with Dr Fothergill who is just about the top doctor in London. When I was there, he was always very busy, always very successful. He spent a lot of time with patients from the poor areas of London as well as with the rich."

"Yes, I get all that from his letters", said Teresa impatiently. "He's obviously doing very well for himself. But how was he with you? Why didn't he marry that Betty girl?"

Sam thought about how best to answer her questions, while concentrating on maintaining his gentle rocking motion.

"We grew apart. Almost as soon as we arrived in England. There were very few things that we could do together, places where we could go together. I was the servant, he was the master. That's what everyone else saw, and eventually, that was what he saw. I should have realised that would happen all along. He wasn't ever nasty, like Ed was with you. I think he regretted it too. It was really amazing to see how single-minded he was about developing his career."

"And Betty?"

"He said he loved you."

"Loved me?" Teresa sounded surprised.

"His actual words were 'Teresa still has my heart'. He said he couldn't marry Betty because she wanted love and he didn't have any more to give. So he married Nancy, because she was set to inherit money, and he needed that for his career. He seemed to think Nancy wouldn't be hurt by his lack of love. I hardly met her, but I don't think that any woman wouldn't be hurt by that. Everyone needs love."

Teresa stared at him, trying to take this all in. Then suddenly she took in his last sentence, and realised that she knew nothing about her brother's own romantic interests. It was something they had hardly ever discussed.

"And what about you?" she asked. "Have you found love?"

Sam must have stopped rocking at this point, because Little Mary woke up and started to cry. He handed her to her mother who pacified her, but the conversation had been killed and soon after the child was asleep again, both adults retired to bed.

Sam managed to avoid that question for the rest of his stay. After he had gone Teresa and Mary speculated on whether he had a secret love, or a girl in every port, or whether he had no love at all.

For three days, Teresa and Mary treated him like a king. On the third day, two sailors landed at the dock to take him back to *HMS Lowestoffe*. There had been news of rebel naval activity off Puerto Rico, and Captain Locker had been given orders to set sail.

CHAPTER 24

A few days after Teresa and Mary had joyfully celebrated the visit of Sam to Little Jost, over in London John had apparently disappeared. Early in the morning, messengers had been sent to find him and bring him home urgently, but he was not to be found in Dr Fothergill's surgery, nor on the wards at St Thomas' Hospital, nor even in any of the meeting rooms at the Gracechurch Meeting House. Eventually, towards the end of the afternoon, they tracked him down in prison: the Wood Street Comptor. There he had been examining the incarcerated felons and debtors, and inspecting the cells in which they were confined to determine whether any of the capital's endemic infections were lurking and whether all due care was being exercised to keep them away.

As soon as the messenger burst into the superintendent's office where he was praising the improvements to hygiene that he had seen and detailing the further measures that he wished to see in six month's time, he knew what the message would be. His little daughter Harriet had died. Muttering apologies, he hastened to follow the messenger to the coach waiting outside which took him as fast as was possible through the busy evening traffic to his home in Great Eastcheap.

Gilbert Thompson, who had been attending, met him at the door. He described the child's final, painful hours. How her sore throat – the Boulogne sore throat as he called it – had progressed.

The grey membrane coating her pharynx had continued to enlarge, until finally it had closed up and choked her.

John went to view the little body. He examined her throat, as a professional. Then he clasped her hand and gently kissed her cheek, as a father, and he allowed his tears to flow. She was at peace now, her desperate attempts to continue breathing having ultimately failed. John had spent many hours at her bedside, and tried every remedy that he was aware of. But he had also had other very sick patients to care for, important committees to attend and urgent reports to complete. He had called Gilbert in to administer his treatment regimens in his absence, and now he thanked his colleague for his efforts and bade him goodnight. Nancy had taken to her bed, devastated by her loss. He went in to see her, and she accepted a consoling embrace from her husband. She had little to say – there was nothing that words could add. By her side, as she had been throughout her child's illness, was Nancy's Aunt Mary.

As there was no consolation he could offer, John retreated to his study, ringing for a servant to bring him a cup of "cambric tea", and then taking out of his bag the papers relating to his prison visit. He had hardly put them in order when Aunt Mary appeared. These two had never got on well, their mutual mistrust dating from the time when Aunt Mary had acted as chaperone during John's courtship of Nancy.

"Where on earth have you been all day?" she started. Then, "Prison! Is it any wonder that all of the diseases of London come into this house!" Next, it was, "Your place was here, looking after your little girl, comforting your wife and helping your colleague. He's so cold and uncaring that one, why couldn't you have brought in Dr Fothergill himself?"

Next came the great-aunt's lament for the departed. "She was so lovely. Just nine months old! How could God want to take her so soon? She was so good natured." Then the retrospective:

"It was the same when Mary Ann died. She was desperately ill and you were away at your Medical Society giving some talk, with no regard for your first-born, or for your poor, poor wife! You neglect Nancy, you know. You always have. She should have stuck with your friend James Beesley – he would have known how to care for her."

John should have learnt by now to say nothing, but this last observation got him started. "James had no prospects", he told her angrily, "never had and never will. Sure, his book on George Fox was quite successful, but since then there's been nothing. Now he relies on the generosity of his friends – I myself pay him to transcribe notes for my books. It's not that I need the help, it's just a way to help him out. Anyway, Nancy is very well provided for. She never complains. She understands the importance of my work. I'm looking for a country residence, so she'll have plenty of space and fresh air for ... ." Here he stopped, choking on his words.

"For the children", completed Aunt Mary, and she turned on her heels and left him to return upstairs and minister to her bereaved niece.

*

John returned to his prison papers, and began to write some notes about his visit. He finished his "tea", and then sought out his oldest brandy and poured himself a measure. No use, he still could not concentrate, so he went up to the nursery. He found the children's nanny weeping quietly while she watched over his son, John Miers, aged five and his surviving daughter, Mary Ann, aged two. Both were asleep. He kissed each of them on the cheek, very softly so as not to wake them. Mark Akenside would have frowned: John had washed neither his hands nor his face since touching Harriet's body. Mercifully, on this occasion no contagion occurred.

Well he would build a magnificent country house for them. For his wonderful children. John Miers, who would take his name, combined with his mother's maiden name, forward into the world. Who would build on his achievements and take them further. And Mary Ann, named for both of her grandmothers, who would perpetuate the memory of both of them – although one of them he had never met. Yes, their first daughter Mary Ann had died at the age of two years and nine months, almost exactly the age that his sleeping daughter was now. It would not happen again! This Mary Ann would surely thrive!

John returned to his study, but did not sit down at his desk. Instead, he sat in the armchair, by the fire that a servant had lit for him while he had been upstairs. Of course, he knew that Aunt Mary was right. He did neglect his wife. And although he loved his children, he did not spend enough time with them. He should have been there with Harriet at the end, even though there was nothing he could have done medically.

But Dr Lettsom had to keep going. Tending to his practice, maintaining the Aldersgate Street dispensary, supporting the Humane Society, building up the Medical Society of London which he had founded, working to improve hygiene in prisons, exposing the quacks, taking inoculation against smallpox to the poor. So much to do. How could he turn down requests for his help? Ignore opportunities to serve? He knew that he could achieve these objectives so much better than anyone else. He still loved his work, but these days he found it difficult to give any single task the time required for it to fully satisfy him. Every job seemed to present itself as a nuisance, standing in the way of other worthwhile jobs, and so to be completed as quickly as possible. And, alas, imperfectly. On and on, relentlessly.

Even though John gave much of his time freely, and supported charitable causes generously, his fortune continued to increase. Due in great part to the continued demand for tin-plated goods from South Wales. Thankfully, Aunt Mary had not worked that one out yet.

He had not married for love. He knew that. And his true love still wrote to him, still sent him mementoes of the Caribbean. But he had been shocked when she wrote to tell him of the birth of Little Mary. He had been given no details of how she came about, and his imaginings of what might have happened gave him no comfort. According to Taine's Deed of Sale, Little Mary belonged to him. From his mother's letters he could see that Little Mary had conquered her. Besides the mystery of her origins, there was also envy. His first born had also been named after his mother. She had died, and had had to be replaced. Now he had just lost another daughter. Teresa had had only one opportunity, and even from this distance he could appreciate how well it was turning out.

And Teresa had become more demanding of late. She had sought to involve him in the agricultural improvements she planned for Little Jost. What did he think of this idea, of that innovation, of the other change of practice? Not one for providing off-hand advice, he had looked into the issues and consulted with fellow Quakers who had connections with cotton plantations. It seemed that Teresa's plans were very sound. He responded to tell her so. But his mother owned the plantation and Teresa obviously knew what she was doing. Why bother him when he was so busy?

Loss, loss, loss. That was what life seemed to hold for him now. Loss of his true love. Loss of his children. He must keep working, keep succeeding. That gave him satisfaction. That helped to blot out his loneliness.

CHAPTER 25

As the wind strengthened, the three women began to prepare for the worst. Little Mary had been told to remain in the bedroom she shared with her mother, and under no circumstance to leave it. Teresa went out to round up the chickens and bring them inside, shutting them in the far bedroom. Considerations of hygiene would have to wait. Catching the first half dozen birds was easy, but after that the silly creatures either ran off or were blown away as Teresa approached. Eventually she did manage to trap four more, although one of those already in the bedroom escaped as she brought in the second batch.

"Quick, catch it!" yelled Teresa, as Nanny opened the door. Nanny did try, but it shot out to freedom before she had a chance.

"I couldn't find any more of the goats", she reported, once safely inside. Already three goats were tethered inside the living room, beginning to give the house the whiff of a stable.

"I did see the little brown and white kid perched on top of one of the cliffs, but a huge gust swept it over into the sea before I could reach it. Then I was lifted right up in the air and went sprawling. It's getting impossible to move out there."

"Have you seen Mary?" asked Teresa.

"No."

Mary had gone off in search of Tracy, Issabel, Rosett and their children. They had been working in the fields and Mary had intended to bring them to the house as it was substantially stronger than the wooden cabins of the workers' village.

Teresa and Nanny ventured out into the gale in search of her, linking arms and fighting the wind side by side as they made slow progress along the path towards the cotton fields. There they found Mary, blown several yards off the track, unconscious and with a large crimson gash on her forehead. Somehow, they managed to lift her and stagger back to the house, stopping to brace themselves each time a particularly fierce blast of wind hit them. Back in the house, they slammed the door shut, secured it with ropes and furniture, and lifted Mary onto her bed. She was still breathing and no longer bleeding, but she remained unconscious.

*

This was just the opening salvo of "Hurricane San Calixto", later known simply as "The Great Hurricane": the strongest to hit the region since European settlement had begun. It struck in October 1780, sweeping across the eastern Caribbean leaving enormous destruction in its wake, and smashing into Tortola and the surrounding islands far quicker than any warning of its approach could travel.

One person about whom Teresa did not have to worry, as she sat watching over Mary, reassuring Nanny and holding her daughter close, was her brother Sam. He was certainly not out at sea in this. Six months earlier, she had received a letter from John informing her that Sam had been washed overboard in heavy seas and had drowned. Both she and Mary had been devastated, the more so because of their recent, brief reunion. The current storm and Mary's accident brought memories of her brother, and imaginings of the circumstances of his death, flooding back.

Just as Sam had predicted, because he was still legally enslaved when he died the navy had informed John. They also mentioned that Sam had written a will leaving all of his money to some of his shipmates. Suspecting this to be a forgery, John had contested it. As Sam's owner, all of the deceased's savings legally belonged to him. Eventually he had to settle for half of Sam's money, but even this was a surprisingly large amount.

"I am sure that Sam would have wanted you to have it, Teresa, and so here it is enclosed with this letter." John expressed his profound sadness at hearing of Sam's death, his regret at not being a better friend of his while he was in London, and his sympathy for the loss that Teresa was bound to feel. This was the first letter that Teresa had received from John for quite some time and despite its sad message, one of the warmest. As well as the money, John's package contained presents for her and his mother, and a wooden doll wearing a pretty dress for Little Mary. A doll which her daughter was now clutching tightly in order to protect it from the wind.

*

For three days the women, Little Mary, and assorted goats and chickens, sheltered from the storm as its severity increased. During the first two of those days, Mary remained unconscious, awakening on the third asking for Edward and furious to find goats inside the house. She insisted on taking them outside, but found herself unable to rise from her bed. On working out who Teresa was, she immediately demanded to see John and would not accept that he was away in England, accusing Teresa of having locked him away somewhere. She declared that the storm was just a bit of a breeze and would not acknowledge the danger they were all in. She refused any food or drink. After a few hours she was exhausted and lost consciousness again.

On the fourth day, the wind began to subside. Teresa cautiously emerged, leaving Nanny in charge of the two Marys. The workers' village was flattened, and the inhabitants nowhere to be seen. The jetty had been swept away and there was no sign of the shallop. The bodies of three recently drowned goats had been washed up, well above the normal high-water level. Teresa sat down on a rock amidst the scene of devastation. For the first time since the storm began she was not in immediate danger of her life. She began to weep, the tears seeming to come from deep inside of her, inexhaustible and uncontrollable. Then as suddenly as her despair had started, it abated, as she saw Bentorah striding across the beach towards her.

"Everyone's alright", he told her. "We found the women and children in the fields and then we all took shelter amongst the boulders. Everyone's hungry, and some have cuts and bruises due to falls, but we've all survived."

Now there was no more time for grieving. Things had to be done. Teresa the organiser snapped back into action, gathering all of the workers together. They looked to her for instructions, and she gave them. One of the dead goats was to be brought up from the beach and butchered, vegetables were to be collected from the kitchen gardens and a great stew prepared. Some of the least damaged cabins were to be repaired. Bentorah and a couple of newly-hired workers were to wade across to Jost van Dyke and find out how other people were coping and if possible find an undamaged boat to bring back with them. On the next day someone would have to cross to Tortola in search of medical help for Mary.

*

Gradually, in the days that followed, the recovery began. The weather reverted to normal: sunshine and gentle breezes. The cotton crop was ruined, except for the small plots on the Cays. Teresa decided to abandon the rest of it for a year and to tide things over using the money Sam had left her. The kitchen gardens had sustained limited damage, and some of the goats and chickens that had been left outside had survived.

However, Mary's condition was unchanged. Occasionally she would wake, confused and complaining that her head was bursting. She still would not eat and she drank very little. After a few hours of consciousness she would be gone again. Bentorah had come back from Jost van Dyke with an old boat exchanged for the carcass of one of the drowned goats. After spending time repairing it he went off with one of the plantation's temporary workers to Tortola, only to return with news of death, destruction and chaos on the bigger island, and no likelihood of medical help for several days.

By the time a surgeon from one of the naval ships taking refuge in Road Harbour made it to Little Jost, all he could do was confirm what Teresa already knew: that Mary was dead. Following her wishes, she was buried under the tamarind trees alongside her first husband and her late son, and – as only Teresa knew – with her second husband too. Although not a religious person, Teresa made a short and eloquent speech expressing the affection and gratitude that all present felt for the woman who had kept their community going for the previous twelve years.

Now Teresa opened the envelope that she knew contained Mary's will. As she had been told, the plantation had been left to her. There was just one complication: as a slave she could not take possession. Formal control of the estate was to rest with the lawyer Mr Beaverhood in Road Town until Teresa could secure her freedom. Mary's slaves Tracy, Issabel, Rosett and their children were bequeathed to John.

There followed the most difficult letter Teresa had ever written. First she had to inform John of the death and burial of his mother, and to convey the distress that she herself felt as a result. Then she had to tell him of the hurricane and its consequences for the plantation. She skipped over how terrifying the ordeal had been and how serious the damage inflicted – she was now on the other side of the disaster and no longer wished to dwell on it. She reported on John's new human property and asked whether he intended to free them. Finally, and with great trepidation, she raised the matter of her own freedom and the need for it to be arranged quickly in order for her to fulfil Mary's wish of assuming ownership of the island.

Once the letter was dispatched, the urgent and most harrowing consequences of the hurricane were complete. What was left was the long-haul. In the twelve years that had passed since John had left Little Jost for the second time, and since his mother had been widowed for the second time, Mary and Teresa had put the plantation onto a sound commercial footing. Together, they had worked methodically to improve the island's cotton yields and stabilise its finances. They had even been able to buy back the tiny islands of Green Cay and Sandy Cay and cultivate a small crop on each of them. Some of the people freed by John were still on the island, proud of their new status and anxious to make a success of the plantation. They had been joined by several newly hired workers.

Now restoration of the fabric of the settlement and preparation for the resumption of cotton cultivation would have to begin. Work that would proceed day by day, week by week, month by month. Work that Teresa would have to take responsibility for alone. And once the plantation was restored, it would have to be maintained. Indefinitely.

Teresa had never felt so alone. As a child she had always had Sam to rely on, to keep her company, to give her courage. Then she had had Mary for support. Mary, who respected her, who loved her almost as a daughter, and yet was quite happy – insistent even – that she remain a slave. Mary, who would roll up her sleeves and work side-by-side with her and with her own slaves, who never inflicted physical punishment and rarely uttered a harsh word of criticism, but who just accepted that in the great scheme of things some people were owned by other people. Mary, who was always quick to point out the shortcomings of freed slaves, especially free black women, and unable to recognise the successes achieved by them. Mary, from whom Teresa had learnt so much and whom she, in her turn, had loved. Mary, who was now dead, and who had left her this sweet little plot of land to cultivate and care for.

Teresa knew that Mary would have expected her to devote her life to the island and to the wellbeing of the people on it, just as she had done. And in reality, she had no choice. How else to keep Little Mary safe and to ensure that she grew up strong, healthy and secure?

There was no-one on Tortola to whom Teresa could turn for help. Mary had restored relations with her first husband's relatives, but they were unlikely to offer support now that Mary was dead. Besides, they would be facing their own challenges of reconstruction. Teresa's mentor Mary Nottingham and her husband had moved to New York the previous year, freeing their slaves and passing Long Look over to them before they went.

So the responsibility for restoring Little Jost fell upon the shoulders of Teresa, and her alone. She could trust Nanny, Bentorah and the others to fulfil their tasks, but she would need to make the decisions, negotiate the sale of the crop, hire and sometimes fire the temporary labourers. It was not that she wanted to hoard power; just that she knew the people she had worked with for years, the things that they could do so well, and their limitations.

So there was just her now. John was far away, married, the head of a growing family of whom she knew very little, absorbed by his work, and rather neglectful of his correspondence of late. What was he to her now? Soon he would no longer even be her owner. Would that be the final end to their relationship? One thing she knew for sure. She would not be seeking to find a husband on

Tortola or from anywhere else in the islands. There was no-one with whom she was prepared to share this task. No-one who understood Little Jost and what it meant to her. No-one who would not be tempted to say: "Let's sell this lump of barren rock and buy a decent plantation somewhere else". No-one apart from, one day, her own Little Mary.

CHAPTER 26

In January 1781, John was in mourning. Not for his mother, as the news of her death had not yet reached him. No, John was marking the death on the day after Christmas of Dr John Fothergill, who had succumbed suddenly to the effects of a prostatic obstruction. John had not attended his former mentor during his final illness. In fact the close relationship they had enjoyed during the years of John's training had never recovered from John's spurning of his niece Betty. Since then, they had worked together effectively enough on various medical committees and Quaker bodies, and their social contacts had been cordial, although they had consisted exclusively of large occasions to which they were both invited rather than events organised by one of them in order to spend time with the other.

There was no doubt that at the time of his death, and for many years before that, Dr Fothergill had been the leading physician in London. The capital's Quaker community had been quick to embrace him and he had successfully broadened his appeal to encompass many more of the wealthy and professional segment of the population. Over the years Lettsom had carved out a rival practice, and those who could not get onto Fothergill's list or afford his fees would often feel fortunate to receive the attentions of the man widely regarded as his protégé. Both doctors were generous with their time and their money, devoting much of the former to treating the poor and a substantial proportion of the latter to funding dispensaries and clinics in the poorer areas of the city. This too became part of their rivalry, as did founding medical societies and promoting such good causes as better hygiene in prisons and improved interventions for victims of drowning.

Now there was a vacancy for "top doctor in London". Not a formal post of course, but an accolade that might be granted by patients and medical practitioners to the person who could earn the highest fees, attract patients from the highest social strata, and be regarded as pioneering the most advanced medical treatments available. John was in no doubt that Fothergill's mantle should fall upon his own shoulders, and he was determined to ensure that it did. He had of course attended the great man's funeral, and taken care to be seen talking to his relatives, colleagues and principal patients. Next, he identified two further strategies to secure success: to move into the late doctor's consulting rooms and to write his biography. The key to both of them was Ann Fothergill, who had inherited the property in Harpur Street and was also in possession of all of the professional papers needed to prepare an account of her brother's life and achievements.

*

"My brother's death came as a great shock to me. So sudden. At the pinnacle of his career. He never had what you might call a robust constitution, but right up until a couple of years ago he somehow managed to avoid serious illness. And that's despite plunging himself into the midst of any disease outbreak that was occurring. Serving him was my whole life. A widow always attracts sympathy, but a bereaved sister's another matter. An independent party in most people's eyes. But my world has collapsed, just as it would for any bereaved wife. I really don't know what I should do next."

Ann Fothergill had agreed to meet with John at Harpur Street a few weeks after the funeral. She knew what he had come for, but she was trying to delay discussion of the subjects that most interested him. To be honest, she was laying her distress on a bit thick. John again expressed his sympathy for her loss, and commented on what a stalwart supporter of her brother she had been for so many years. He recalled some of the occasions when Ann's self-sacrifice had been invaluable to her brother, and hinted that perhaps it had not been appreciated as much as it should. Then he started to broach the matter he had come about.

"Do you intend to continue living here at Harpur Street?"

"Oh, I doubt it. It's too big for me. But I've inherited sufficient money from John to buy somewhere smaller and cosier nearby. Speaking of John's bequests to me, I had a shock when his will was read. He left me a share in Jory's estate on the island of Nevis. A sugar plantation, that is actually called 'Fothergill's'! He's made me a slave-owner. Our brother Samuel would turn in his grave. All that time when John was talking of the need to end the slave trade and grow sugar in Africa instead of the West Indies so the poor wretches could go home. All that time, a substantial part of his income – of *our* income – was coming from the labour of slaves. I've been living on their subjugation all these years! Unlike you, I can't free *my* slaves – I own only a share of the estate. I'll sell it as soon as I can, no doubt at a hefty loss. It makes me feel so dirty."

John was indeed surprised and shocked to hear this of a man he had always thought of as enlightened and compassionate, and he sympathised with Ann. Then he tried again to steer the conversation towards the matters that interested him.

"If you move into a smaller house, will you sell Harpur Street?"

"No. I intend to pass it to my nephew, William Hird."

John went pale. This was terrible news. He knew Dr Hird, who had a successful practice in Leeds. Well regarded as a provincial doctor, but surely he would be out of his depth in the capital. Ann noticed John's reaction, but carried on.

"William is such a fine doctor: it's the practice that he really wants of course, not just the house and surgery. He'll be a great success, and it'll be most satisfying to keep it in the family. It's his wife, Sally, who's the Fothergill of course. Sister to Betty and Molly. Such a shame you didn't marry Betty all those years ago. Then you'd be family too. But you would have neglected her wouldn't you, so busy with your work? How are Nancy and your family?"

John provided news of his wife and family. He dwelt particularly on the good health and sweet nature of his youngest son, born the year before, taking care to remind Ann that he was named Samuel Fothergill Lettsom in honour of her younger brother. But he was then pressed into revealing that he hadn't actually been home to his new country house at Grove Hill in Camberwell to see any of them since Christmas. "So busy in London", he confessed. Now he changed tack.

"I am very keen to write a biography of your brother", he said. "Its publication will ensure his fame endures and his work is celebrated by future generations. It will also furnish material for an address on his legacy to the Medical Society of London."

"Ah yes. That society you founded. You know, John was never a member. Well, I think it would be good for you to write a biography and help perpetuate my brother's name. But at this moment, all of his papers are in the hands of your good friend Gilbert Thompson. He's also writing a biography and will read it to the Medical Society in London when it's ready. That's the society that my brother founded some years before your new outfit. You're not a member, I think."

John acknowledged that he wasn't. In fact there were very few members of Fothergill's Medical Society *in* London left, while his own Medical Society *of* London was thriving. John felt crushed.

"When Gilbert has finished with them, I shall ask him to pass the documents to you. Incidentally, my nephew-in-law William has also been looking at them. He's writing a short eulogy to be published next month."

John could hardly hold his temper any longer. He concluded the meeting as quickly as was consistent with politeness, thanked his hostess for the permission to use her brother's papers when Gilbert had finished with them, and left crestfallen and angry.

*

It took less than a week for John's self-confidence to return. A couple of Dr Fothergill's most aristocratic patients had contacted him seeking to join his practice. They explained that they were none too keen on the Yorkshireman to whom they had been summarily assigned. Perhaps John would be able to inherit his former mentor's patients after all. Not by a direct takeover of the Harpur Street premises, but by picking them off one by one over the next year or two. He started to look for a new property where he could establish a fashionable and spacious suite of consulting rooms with all of the latest equipment. It needed to be bigger and more stylish that his current clinic in Great Eastcheap, and definitely more impressive than the rather dated and dingy surgery in Harpur Street. He also began to sketch out his ideas for his biography of Dr John Fothergill, in anticipation of receiving the detailed records he would need to complete it.

John was still too busy to get over to Camberwell to see how Nancy and the children were settling into their new house, so he wrote her an encouraging letter instead. His servant took it off to the penny-post house, and returned with a letter addressed to John. At first he put it on one side as he was making such good progress writing of those medical achievements of Dr Fothergill that he had witnessed at first hand. However, he could not help noticing that it was from Little Jost, and that it had been written early in the previous November. Teresa's writing of his address looked rather rough compared with her usual tidy hand and, strangely, there was no accompanying parcel. "What does the woman want now?" he thought, anticipating another request for urgent advice on agricultural practice. Well he certainly had no time to look into that sort of thing right now. He reluctantly moved away from his desk to sit in his armchair to read the letter.

"Oh no!" Then "No, no, no! My God no!"

His servant reappeared and asked what was wrong, and receiving no reply asked if there was anything his master wanted.

"Nothing." And then, as his servant turned to go, "Actually, bring me a large brandy."

Suitably fortified, he read the letter again.

"Was there a swelling associated with the cut on the head?" he asked out loud, although not loud enough to bring the servant back. "Did you carefully feel to determine whether the skull was fractured? Couldn't you have got a surgeon to see her sooner? He could have operated and perhaps saved her if he'd arrived in time." Then: "If only I'd been there." Then tears.

The brandy was finished, and his initial shock had subsided. He still couldn't understand why the letter had taken eleven weeks to reach him: Teresa had devoted few words to the violence of the hurricane and its effects on the islands. But he did take in her demand that he grant freedom to her and to Little Mary. So that she could take over the plantation. His mother was hardly in her grave, and all that concerned Teresa was her status and securing her property. How ungrateful! How could anyone be so grasping?

Yes, he would do it. He would free her. That would be the end of their links. As for his mother's slaves, he was now their owner, and he would remain so.

He called out for his servant to bring him another large brandy, and then went over to his desk to resume his work on the achievements of Dr Fothergill.

*

Eight weeks later, Teresa received John's reply. It was rather curt. He did thank her for caring for his mother during her final hours, and for arranging her burial in the place where she had wanted to rest, but he was not effusive. He did not ask about the damage to the estate, nor how rebuilding was progressing. He did enclose papers granting freedom to her and to Little Mary and also to any "future issue and increase" that she might bear. "No chance!" she thought when she read that part. A witness whose name she did not recognise was specified. However, when she took the papers to Beaverhood, he pointed out that neither John nor his witness had signed the document. He passed the papers over to the Register's Office on Tortola, and told Teresa that she would have to inform John of his omission and John would then need to request the return of the papers for their proper completion.

There was no mention in John's hastily written letter of Tracy, Issabel, Rosett and their children. Beaverhood confirmed that that meant they now belonged to John. "But," thought Teresa, "they do say that possession is nine tenths of the law". She was now their effective mistress. She spoke to them at some length to determine what they wished to do. All three wished to stay and work on Little Jost. Every other property in the Virgin Islands had been damaged by Hurricane San Calixto, and they were confident of Teresa's ability to restore their island more quickly than most. They felt it was a secure place for their children. Teresa felt gratified, and promised to treat them in just the same way as she treated her free workers.

Teresa's isolation was now total. She chose not to care. She chose to devote the rest of her life to her plantation. *Her* plantation! To her daughter, whose welfare depended on the prosperity of the island. And to the people who worked on the plantation, especially those whom she had known for so many years.

John's irritation only grew when he received Teresa's letter pointing out that his papers had been incomplete. He did not rush to rectify his error. Nevertheless, eighteen months later valid papers freeing Teresa and her daughter were received in Road Town. John sent no covering letter to the beneficiary, although she did send a thank you letter accompanied by a large pot of his favourite sweets.

CHAPTER 27

The first guests to arrive were Ann Fothergill and her niece Molly.

"Are we early?" asked Ann as John helped her out of her hired carriage.

"Just a bit," answered John, "but all the better for you to make the most of your visit."

As one of John's servants helped Molly alight, Nancy joined the welcoming party.

"I see you're expecting too!" exclaimed Nancy. The two pregnant ladies compared the size of their bumps: Molly just beginning to show and Nancy a little further advanced.

"Molly has left her husband behind in Ireland and come to stay with me until this little one is born", explained Ann. "Here in London we have all the care they can possibly need. Everything will go well this time."

Knowing of the succession of tragic miscarriages that had befallen Molly, John endorsed her aunt's prediction.

"And how is Betty?" asked John.

"Run off her feet by all her children", replied Molly. "Eight of them now, and they're all bursting with good health", she added, unable to suppress a note of envy.

Perhaps a little tactlessly, Nancy now took Molly up to the nursery to meet her own children. John Miers, the second Mary Ann and Samuel Fothergill had been joined by baby Edward just a year before.

John steered Ann through the house to show off the ornamental gardens at the back.

"Such a lovely estate, John", commented his guest. "And you have arranged perfect weather. Shall we be dining outside?"

"Of course."

"Now, I know these trees!" exclaimed Ann, having arrived at John's new American arboretum. "That's John's hornbeam tree, and those are his maples. You've moved Upton to Camberwell!"

Upton had been Dr Fothergill's country estate in Essex where the late doctor had acquired a magnificent collection of exotic plants, said by some to rival Kew.

"I was lucky enough to purchase a number of his plants at the auction", replied John, modestly.

"A number! Just how many was it?"

"A little over two thousand, all told. And the glasshouses to keep the more delicate ones in. They've been re-built at the other side of the house, should you wish to see them."

"I think I've seen them all before."

*

Ann and Molly had arrived at Grove Hill, John's new country residence in Camberwell, for a garden party. This was August 1782, and the weather was indeed glorious – at long last as the year until then had been cold, wet and stormy. This gathering was John's first opportunity to show off his new residence. He had replaced the original modest house by a splendid three-storey country mansion topped off with a small observatory. For his guests that day there were bowls to play on the lawn, the greenhouses and the arboretum to inspect, and distant views of London to admire.

Ann's name had been one of the first on the guest-list. It was in John's interests to maintain good relations with the "medical dowager of London" despite her recent coolness towards him. Her plans for the succession to her brother's practice had started to come unstuck when Dr William Hird died soon after moving down to London. She had then persuaded a reluctant Gilbert Thompson to take over at Harpur Street, but his cold and precise manner had turned the trickle of desertions from the Harpur Street practice to Lettsom's smart new premises at Sambrook Court into a flood. She was now trying to persuade Gilbert to relinquish the practice, and install a distant relative from Northampton to make a go of it. Nevertheless, she was beginning to realise that the eventual victor in this tussle might well turn out to be John. Wishing to avoid being cut off from the medical circles in which she had moved for so long, she had accepted John's invitation.

About fifty guests were expected, and they now began to arrive in a flurry. John welcomed each of them as they arrived in front of the house, and his servant Agnes offered them a drink and a savoury snack to keep them going until lunch. Medical guests included John's old friend Gilbert Thompson, accompanied by his wife Mary. Captain William Lindow and his wife Abigail were there, down from Lancaster on a summer tour of the south of England. Abigail's cousin Lydia Rawlinson was with them, the sister of Abraham whom John remembered hitting with snowballs. John's top "trophy guests" that day were Dr Samuel Johnson and his companions James Boswell and Francis Barber. The last had started life enslaved in the West Indies, but was sent to school when his owner moved to Yorkshire. Later, he was freed, served in the Royal Navy, and started to work with Dr Johnson as a valet before his own literary talents were finally recognised.

Also in the company was John's neighbour, Henry Smith, whose older property had become completely encircled by John's expanding estate. Henry was a military man: a captain of artillery who had served with distinction for four years fighting colonial rebels in Massachusetts, New York and Virginia before taking an administrative role in London. Despite their different outlooks, the former soldier and the committed Quaker had formed a respectful friendship.

The last guests to arrive emerged from a coupé that sped down the drive and came to an abrupt halt in front of John, just as he was about to leave the front of his house to mingle with the company. As there were only two seats inside, James Beesley had ridden alongside the driver. He now jumped down grinning: "Not one, but two surprise guests from Tortola! Bill Thornton is following in your footsteps and studying medicine at Edinburgh". The young man in question emerged from the vehicle and shook John's hand.

"I'm down in London arranging to continue my studies at Bart's and I bumped into James at the Gracechurch Street Meeting", explained Bill. "So pleased to meet you. My aunt told me a lot about you. Rebecca Pickering: she was extremely grateful for what you did when my uncle died."

As they spoke, a second young man joined them. He looked vaguely familiar. James introduced him: "And this is Arthur Hodge, another native of our island. I met him yesterday at the home of a mutual acquaintance and he said he'd met you before."

Arthur Hodge! The sadistic little brute who liked to watch hangings.

"Remember me? You set my arm after it broke – not very gentle I recall. Father sent me to study at Oxford, but Oriel College is such a bore that I'm joining the army next month."

Arthur surveyed the grounds. "Didn't a famous murder take place round here?"

"Yes, it's said that George Barnwell murdered his uncle in a cottage just to the north of my land. I hope to buy that plot eventually and incorporate it into my estate."

"You'll then be able to show guests round the murder cottage. People love a grisly tale like that. There's a play about it all isn't there? Ends with a good hanging, I seem to recall."

*

With all of his guests now present, John mingled, as a good host should. Around one of his garden tables, he found most of the Quaker guests engaged in spirited conversation.

"Please do join us, John. You're just the man we need to talk to." This was from George Harrison. John had known him as a boy at Penketh School, and always remembered his disgust on reading that everyone's fictional hero, Robinson Crusoe, had been a slave trader. Many years later, they had become reacquainted at a Friends' function in London.

"George is trying to organise a petition", explained James Beesley. "I've promised to support it, and I've told him that you certainly will."

"It's a petition against the slave trade", added George. "We want to persuade the Yearly Meeting to present it to parliament as a statement from the Quaker movement. I'm taking soundings to see how many Friends would support us."

John promised his support.

"I'd like to sign it", said Ann Fothergill, "but George says it's only for men. That's not the Quaker way!"

"It's because parliament is only men. It's them we have to persuade. Women's signatures would be discounted."

"You wouldn't have said that to Margaret Fell", snapped back Ann.

"Nor to Mary Fisher", added John. "But I suppose that MPs answer to their voters, and only men can vote, more's the pity. I'll sign as soon as you have it ready."

"I doubt whether parliament will be impressed." This intervention was from Lydia Rawlinson, who up to then had been sitting sour-faced at the far end of the table, looking increasingly annoyed as the conversation progressed. "My brother Abraham and my cousin Henry are both MPs now, and they would certainly vote against any limitation to the trade. The Society shouldn't interfere in proper legal business activities. Our family would incur substantial losses if the trade were abolished. It's unfair to make Friends like me and my sister Mary suffer so."

"Suffer!" barked Ann. "You don't know the meaning of the word. Your great-grandfather, Thomas Rawlinson, was one of the Valiant Sixty. He suffered for his faith. He gave up his wealth and his comfortable life to preach the gospel and spread George Fox's vision around the country. Many of the Sixty went to prison! And now Friends are unprepared for a little loss of business and the lack of a few sweet luxuries to pursue what's clearly God's will. I'm absolutely committed to this cause – and to my right to sign the petition!"

*

John managed to snatch conversations with most of his guests that day.

"You know, you're quite famous back home", Bill Thornton told him. "John Coakley Lettsom, the native of Tortola who went to England and made his fortune."

"That's how they see me? Someone who got rich?"

"It's said in admiration. You're seen as a humble Quaker, a man of letters, and someone with the gift of healing."

John smiled at this tactful assessment. "Who just happened to make some money along the way. Not a bad combination you know."

"Well, I've been emulating you for some time now, and intend to continue. I was born on Jost van Dyke, came over to England for schooling, served as an apothecary's assistant, and now I'm at Edinburgh where my medical studies are going well. Next year I'll come to London to gain more practical experience."

John liked this open, amiable young man, and recognised some of his own youthful enthusiasm in him. They swapped stories of Edinburgh professors, confessed to their own early medical disasters, and discussed what most satisfied them about attending their patients. John told of his own fascination with botany while Bill disclosed his growing interest in architecture. On that note, the guest mentioned a desire to walk around the grounds and make a sketch of the elegant new house.

William Lindow explained to John that he was no longer going to sea, but was instead working in partnership with Abraham Rawlinson organising transatlantic trade from a desk in Lancaster. Abigail told him of their lovely new house in the recently developed Queen Square, built for them by Robert Gillow. He met their servant John Chance, whom Lindow had bought in Antigua. Abigail volunteered him to help the servants in the kitchen.

"Lunch *al fresco*!" said William, approvingly, when told of the plan. "Just like that wonderful Quaker lunch on Tortola when I came to arrange your voyage to England all those years ago."

Dr Johnson told John about his essay on the poems of Mark Akenside, and asked what he had been like as a medical teacher. James Boswell praised the beauty and grace of John's home and gardens. He suggested that it was only possible to live like this and appreciate modern science and high culture because there were others do the labouring. Slavery abroad was necessary to support this lifestyle, and a return to a benevolent form of feudalism at home would benefit the aesthetic life further. Dr Johnson disagreed with every word.

Gilbert Thompson complained of the difficulties he was experiencing with the Harpur Street patients and his suspicions that Ann Fothergill was trying to ease him out. John's conversation with James Beesley was more practical. His old friend's writing career was still stuck, and to help tide him over John agreed to pay him to catalogue the vast collection of books he had bought from Dr Fothergill's estate.

John watched Henry Smith and James Beesley defeat Bill Thornton and Arthur Hodge at bowls. Arthur was an aggressive but inaccurate player, and a bad loser too. He questioned the legitimacy of some of James's rolls and then claimed that Abigail Lindow, who had been umpiring, did not understand the rules of the game nor how to judge the distance between the bowls and the jack. As his protests fell on deaf ears, he suggested a re-match, but Henry – who was by far the most talented of the four players – would have none of it and surrendered the green to a waiting party of players.

*

Inside one of the greenhouses, John came upon Dr Johnson's colleague, Francis Barber. He was in conversation with John Chance, whom he had detained when he came round offering fruit punch and savouries.

"Dr Johnson has been very kind and helpful to me", the writer was explaining. "Most people are surprised that he puts up with me as I am not just a man of no consequence, but an ex-slave as well."

The astonished servant had never met a black gentleman before, and although he knew he should get back to distributing refreshments, he wanted to hear more of the man's story. John's joining them, without giving the slightest indication that the servant should move on, encouraged him to stay.

"Are you a free man?" asked Barber.

"I don't really know", answered Chance, hesitantly. Then, aware that both of his listeners wanted more, he continued: "Since the ruling on James Somerset, it seems that I couldn't actually be sent back to Antigua as a slave."

John was surprised by the servant's knowledge of the law, although Francis was aware that most black people in the country paid close attention to legal developments concerning their own status. Ten years before, the case in question had led to a legal ruling that the status of slavery had no basis in English law.

"So, why don't you leave service and make your own way as a free man?" asked Francis.

"Oh, I don't think I have your talents. Your education and wit."

"Before taking up writing, I joined the navy as a landsman and learnt enough to become an able-seaman. You don't have to be an intellectual to live as a free man."

"My master's stories about life at sea are enough to put me off such a career. I'm a servant, and I try to be a good servant. I'm not a plantation slave, and I don't get whipped, although I know some white servants in Lancaster who are beaten regularly. My master is fair with me: sometimes the mistress can be rather sharp and exacting. My life in Lancaster is alright for me."

*

Later, at the highest point of the grounds, surveying the view over to the city, John found Arthur Hodge in conversation with Molly and Lydia Rawlinson.

"This had better be a good occasion today, Lettsom", said Hodge as John joined them. "I passed up the chance to watch a particularly juicy execution today."

"My goodness!" responded Lydia. "Is that your hobby then?"

"I love a good execution, and today's will be a corker! The traitor David Tyrie who sold us out to the French is to be hung, drawn and quartered on Southsea Common. There'll be a huge crowd there. Not often you get the full works these days. He'll be hanged by the neck for a while, then eviscerated while still alive and conscious, and finally beheaded and his body chopped into four pieces."

Molly went pale and quietly left the group, but Arthur continued unabashed. "I've not seen an execution for a while. We used to have them all the time on our estate on Tortola. It's the only way to keep [them] under control. My father used to let me watch, and sometimes to pull the stool from under ..."

"That's enough!" interrupted John, appalled at this account and at the foul words that Arthur was using to refer to his father's enslaved workers.

"Oh, I'm fascinated", said Lydia. "It must be hard to keep so many strong, healthy men under control. Of course, the Society disapproves of violence, but our world depends on maintaining discipline. People look down on my family's business – we have land in the West Indies and we help keep the plantations supplied with workers – but we all enjoy the produce of the islands, so it's rather hypocritical, don't you think?"

John hurriedly moved on, leaving Lydia and Hodge deep in conversation about the unfortunate necessity of physical chastisement and the ultimate sanction for disobedience, and the naivety of those who thought that persuasion and encouragement were enough to bend people to one's will.

*

Having allowed everyone plenty of time to admire his house and grounds, John signalled for lunch to be served. The servants helped the guests find their places. Dr Johnson was seated between his companions, and Arthur Hodge – not included in the original seating plan – was shown to the place opposite Francis Barber. He muttered an introduction before sitting down and then sat silently for a while, looking troubled. Once everyone was settled, John saw him stand up and heard him shout: "I'm not sitting down to dine with a black man! This is more than I can take, a calculated insult to my person!"

"Calm down", said Boswell. "Dr Johnson needs help these days with his meals. He can't always see clearly what's on his plate. Francis usually has to help him."

"Oh, I see. He's here as a servant then." Hodge gestured towards Francis as he said "he", not wishing to dignify him with a name. He sat down again to think this through. Then he smiled, and gestured to Agnes, who had just brought out the first plates of food. "Remove the plates and cutlery from this servant. He's not actually dining with us."

Agnes hesitated, unsure. Boswell nodded, and Francis remained silent and motionless. Dr Johnson had not heard what had been said. Agnes started to pick up the place setting to take it back to the kitchen.

"What's this?" bellowed Dr Johnson. "Mr Barber needs those to eat. He does not use his fingers you know!" Agnes began to replace the utensils.

"He's here as a servant, not a guest", insisted Hodge. "He'll be too busy helping you with your meal to eat himself. He can eat later with the other servants." Agnes looked towards John who had been following the dispute, disgusted by the behaviour of his uninvited guest.

"Please sir, is this gentleman 'ere as a servant or a guest?" she asked.

"As an honoured guest, of course", came back the ruling.

"Sir, you disrespect me!" shouted Hodge, standing. "If you were a man and not a Quaking coward, I would call you out to a duel for this insult. I am, of course, an excellent shot."

"Is it a duel you want?" asked Captain Henry Smith, also standing. "Then I shall be happy to oblige. What is it to be? Swords, pistols, ..., bowls!" The laughter that followed the last remark struck at Arthur Hodge's heart. Kicking over his chair, he made to leave, calling out that he would accept no substitutes and that he felt totally dishonoured by his host. His dramatic exit was unfortunately impeded by four more servants, hands and arms full of plates of food. He had to stand aside, advance a few paces and then stand aside again, fuming and sweating as he did so. At last he managed to extricate himself from the dining area. Seeing another servant walking back to the kitchen, he demanded to know the way to London. John Chance smiled at him, and pointed down the road leading away from the city, all the way to the south coast.

"It's that way, sir", he advised.

*

Eventually, all of John's guests departed. Last to go were Ann Fothergill and Molly, having spent time in the kitchen with Nancy organising the packing of surplus food into boxes for distribution to London's poor the following day. Now John was able to take advantage of the warm evening and sit outside on his terrace, looking over to the lights of London and contemplating the day's events.

Apart from the presence of the appalling Arthur Hodge, the occasion had gone well. It really did look as if he was on his way to becoming the undisputed successor to Dr Fothergill. Putting his name to the anti-slave trade petition allowed him to lend support to a cause he had long been passionate about, and it also reinforced his reputation as a leading opponent of the foul practice.

He suddenly realised that, apart from making a short tour after lunch to introduce the ten-year-old John Miers to some of his closest friends, he had not seen his children all day. He must make a fuss of them in the morning. Otherwise, Nancy's Aunt Mary would be on at him again.

He had found the conversation with Francis Barber unsettling. Born into slavery, brought to England, educated, and served at sea. Just like Sam. But, with the support of Dr Johnson, Barber had settled in London and achieved success as a writer. Could Sam have achieved more? Should he have been more supportive? Why had he never even considered that a professional future might have been possible for his friend?

Thinking of Sam brought Teresa back into John's mind. She seldom left it for long. Even though he was no longer writing to her. He had made a similar mistake with her as he had with Sam, hadn't he? He had wanted to think of her as his lost love back home, never changing, never establishing her own life. So news of her having a baby daughter, letters demonstrating her intelligent and independent approach to growing cotton, and her thoroughly reasonable request to be set free, had all rankled. After a few unanswered letters she had stopped writing to him too. Now he missed that link with home, but was too proud to try to start it up again. Too proud, and too afraid of an angry reply. Or no reply at all.

CHAPTER 28

Teresa had been in Road Town when the first reports of the 1790 uprising emerged. It was Jim who told her. He was still running the length and breadth of Tortola on behalf of the government leader on the island, now termed the President of the Island Council rather than Lieutenant Governor. These days he was paid to do it, the leader before last having granted him freedom in recognition of loyal service. Teresa had been meeting with representatives of cotton merchants in a new coffee house that had recently opened on Main Street and had just negotiated a good price for her next crop. The buyers had left her repacking papers and samples into her bag, when Jim entered, breathless and desperate for refreshment.

"It's not like you to be so exhausted", she observed, after they exchanged greetings.

"I've just run all the way from Fat Hog Bay to the President's office", he replied, struggling to get the words out. Looking around to assure himself that they could not be overheard, he continued: "There's trouble on the Pickering plantation. Bad trouble. Please don't tell anyone else yet, but this is going to be really serious. They've imprisoned the overseer and his family and set fire to the big house. The other white people on the estate and some of the loyal slaves have been driven out. Now they're arming themselves and demanding that they be freed."

Teresa was amazed. Uprisings happened on other islands, but not on Tortola. She was also worried. Worried for those whose desperation had driven them to rebel. Worried for those facing the brunt of their anger. Worried for what this might mean for her business – for her daughter.

"What happened to bring this on?"

"They believe that the British Government has abolished slavery. That their overseer has not told them, but they are already free men. They demand their freedom be recognised. They're sure that if Isaac Pickering hears they're still being treated as slaves he'll sack the overseer and come over from England to supervise their transition to freedom himself."

"It's not true is it? The British haven't abolished slavery?"

"A man in the President's office assured me that it isn't. In January, somebody called William Wilberforce persuaded the British parliament to set up a committee to consider the future of the slave trade. That's all. Just a committee to talk about it, and just the trade rather than slavery itself. But this rumour will spread further. In a couple of hours I've to go back to the President's office and collect letters to take round the plantations to spread the truth. But the lies will probably get there first. And it'll take more than letters to pacify the rebels on the Pickering plantation – they've already passed the point of ever being pardoned."

*

During the ten years since the Great Hurricane, Teresa had rebuilt and prospered. She had worked with a single-minded determination, and inspired the rest of the Little Jost community to give of their best. In Road Town, she had established a reputation for the quality of her produce and the fairness of her dealing. Other Virgin Island planters had eventually accepted her as one of them, professionally if not socially, and were impressed at her readiness to adopt agricultural innovation and her ability to use encouragement and reward to maximise the productivity of her workers.

On Little Jost, Bentora and Cassia had now slowed down and taken the place of Cudjoe and Rosett as the village elders. Their children Myal and Cotto and their respective spouses had become the backbone of the workforce. Nanny helped Teresa around the house. Fever and an accident had taken two of John's slaves: Issabel and Rosett (once known as young Rosett). Tracy had gone into Road Town one day and never come back. Issabel's daughter Issabella and Rosett's daughters Margaret and Jane were now grown up and working on the island. They and their own children still belonged to John.

And Mary was now thirteen, her mother's pride and joy and as bright as a button. Teresa had managed to arrange some schooling for her on Tortola, and had taught her a great deal herself, both academic and practical. Teresa was no longer alone.

*

The Pickering revolt did not spread. Slaves on other plantations were sceptical about the rumours of emancipation, and their owners put on a show of strength. The President of the Island Council ordered the militia to advance on the rebels, and Royal Navy warships visiting the island were deployed to Fat Hog Bay.

The rebel leaders were not intimidated. When they heard their demands were not to be met, they carried out their threat to murder the overseer and his family and went on a rampage of destruction, setting fire to the sugar crop and destroying everything associated with the back-breaking work of cultivating it. As the militia advanced on their positions, they resisted fiercely and many of those not killed in the fighting chose to leap to their death in the sea rather than face the bloody alternative of torture and execution. Indeed, the remainder of the men and several of the women were slowly and painfully put to death in the public space behind the prison in Road Town, in front of a crowd of angry white planters and of enslaved workers brought in chains and forced to watch.

For most of the colony's residents, that was that. Rebuilding the fabric of the Pickering plantation and restocking the workforce took time, but neighbouring planters were generous with their support. The remaining women and children of the rebellious slaves were sold separately, mostly to buyers on nearby islands. For some years to come, trust between masters and slaves declined throughout the island, workloads were increased, rations reduced and punishments became harsher. Little matters of give and take, the occasional treats, the friendly banter, were all casualties of the deterioration in relationships. News of the incendiary and successful slave revolt that engulfed the whole of the French colony of Saint-Domingue the following year increased the fear of insurrection across the Caribbean and further hardened attitudes on Tortola.

So what of the mixed-race ex-slave whose cotton was highly valued whenever she brought it to market in Road Town and whose business and agricultural prowess was universally respected? Who now wanted to do business with a woman of colour? No-one. Within three months of the insurrection, Teresa found she could not sell her cotton, and she could not even buy the supplies needed to grow it.

After two more months, Teresa faced up to the inevitable and sold her whole estate to a planter on Jost van Dyke at a price that was a fraction of what it was worth and hardly enough to cover the debts she had recently incurred. The buyer, a Mr Tomlinson, was sensible enough to realise that much of the value of his purchase lay in the workforce, and he kept them all on.

John's slaves were in an ambiguous position, but they were retained and paid as if they were free. One of the motivations for purchase was to give Tomlinson's son experience in running a plantation, and what better start than a small property that was already being excellently run? Thus there was no room for Teresa in the new arrangements, nor for Mary. They were forced to leave and seek what they could in Road Town. It was made clear that they would not be welcome if they tried to return.

Because of the consequences for John's slaves, Teresa felt obliged to inform him of what had happened. As was her wont, she underplayed the difficulties that she and her daughter were facing. To John, this was just another nuisance to deal with, coming as it did when he was extremely busy (when wasn't he?). He prepared the papers for the release of his slaves, and this time he and the witness made sure to sign them. He was, for the first time since reaching his majority, no longer the owner of any human property at all.

*

Somehow, Teresa avoided total despair during her exile in Road Town. Conditions were appalling. She was forced to throw herself on the charity of the free black people whom she used to meet when on business in the town. She and Mary were taken in, found a place to live in a crowded shared room, and given some of the limited supplies of food available to the community. Hers had not been the only black business to be shunned. Every one of them was affected in some way, losing much or all of their livelihoods. Teresa became acquainted with hunger for the first time in her life, although she endeavoured to protect Mary as best she could. She lost a great deal of weight and began to look drawn. Worry and the crowded conditions robbed her of her sleep.

Periodically, mobs of angry white people came into their part of town, shouting insults, attacking and beating anyone they found on the street, and threatening to burn the whole area down. For protection, the free black community concentrated themselves into just half a dozen buildings adjacent to one another. They put up defensive walls and armed themselves with knives, clubs and iron bars, aware that should they ever have to use them, the law would not take their side.

The angry crowds that tormented them were sustained by the myth that they had supported the rebellious slaves of the Pickering Plantation, helping plan their revolt and supplying them with weapons. Some even claimed that certain of the free black men had been seen on the plantation, fighting alongside the rebels. None of this was true.

Gradually, the situation stabilised. The frequency of the demonstrations lessened, and their character became perfunctory. Some of the white population of the island declared support for the besieged community and organised the distribution of food and other essentials to them. Some commissioned work from them, or took them into employment away from the town. For quite different reasons, some of the white men who had previously prevailed upon more intimate professional services of free black women began to find ways of resuming their habits.

After three months of total dependence on the generosity of others, and with great trepidation, Teresa agreed to Mary taking up paid duties as a live-in maid with a family on a plantation three miles from Road Town. Then she herself began to take in clothes for mending and embroidering from sympathetic members of the white community. Acute anguish evolved into chronic hardship.

*

Eighteen months after abandoning Little Jost, Teresa was sitting in the yard by the cabin she shared, doing some darning for the woman who employed Mary. She was surprised when one of her neighbours told her that there was a white man wanting to speak to her. Her clients never came to deliver or collect work directly, always sending their slaves or servants, so it was a mystery who her visitor could be. She went to find him outside the community's defensive enclosure.

"Teresa Coakley, I presume", said the stranger by way of greeting, and when Teresa nervously nodded, he continued. "My name is Dr William Thornton, a colleague and friend of Dr John Lettsom."

Teresa suddenly felt weak. Her body sagged and she slumped down heavily in the dust and leaned her back against the enclosure.

"I'm sorry", she muttered breathlessly. "I'm just so surprised to meet someone who knows John – Dr Lettsom."

Thornton gave her some time to recover and then led her to a bench beneath a tree where they could both sit under its shade. He avoided helping her physically as he knew that could be seen as inappropriate by passers-by. Indeed, the sight of a free woman of colour sitting with a European in the middle of Road Town might have provoked wrath a few months earlier, but it was a sign of the gradual recovery of relations that they were not molested. Thornton had come prepared with a bottle of weak beer and some food, which Teresa consumed eagerly. She then began to regret her guzzling and her appearance, and wiped her mouth and sat up smartly, ready to hear what the stranger had to say.

Rather than speaking, Thornton reached into a bag he was carrying and took out a sketch pad. He removed the top page and passed it to Teresa. She burst into tears. It was a beautifully executed and faithfully accurate drawing of the house on Little Jost van Dyke. Her home.

"Is it still standing?" she asked in a whisper.

"Yes, and mostly in good repair. It had obviously been well-maintained for many years."

"And the surrounding estate?"

"Abandoned, I'm afraid. Overgrown and neglected."

Teresa had already heard that it had taken a year for Tomlinson's son to bring the plantation to ruin. With no interest in agriculture, he had spent his time there drinking and gambling with friends. The workers soon realised they would get no guidance from him, and strove to continue cultivating the cotton themselves. However, they needed him to organise the purchase of supplies and the sale of the harvest. This he was incapable of doing. Eventually his father intervened, sending his errant son off to work for a cousin in a merchant's office in Antigua where he could be closely supervised, redeploying the workers to his own land on Jost van Dyke and leaving the smaller island to revert to nature.

"Dr Lettsom asked me to take a look at Little Jost for him after I told him I was about to visit Jost van Dyke. I found most of your people on the bigger island, working for Mr Tomlinson. They told me where I might find you."

Teresa took this all in, struggling to comprehend what it meant and where it was leading. Eventually she responded: "Now you've found me, what will you do?"

"Let Dr Lettsom know how you are."

"And how am I?"

Thornton looked straight at Teresa. It was clear that she wanted the truth.

"Not very well, I'm afraid. You look exhausted, undernourished and anxious."

"Tell him so. Tell him how poor we are, and how I have to take in mending from the kind white families round here. When I can get it, that is. Tell him my daughter has to work so very hard as a maidservant just so we can scrape enough together to get by. I only see her on Sundays. I made sure she got an education, but now she's forgetting everything she learned. She's learning to be coarse and mean instead, and not to trust anyone."

Teresa broke off and wept again. Her pain was so great. She had accepted that for her, life would always be like this. Just get through one more day, she would think. But she had never accepted it for Mary. Every day she still yearned for a miracle that would release her daughter from this grind and give her an opportunity for something much, much better. And now this man, whom she had never met before but who knew John, might bring just such a miracle. He was going to tell John how she was. Maybe John would help her – maybe he could help Mary.

Thornton was now preparing to leave her. Saying that he was so pleased to have found her, so sorry about the circumstances she was now in. He hoped that the situation on the island would soon improve, and that her daughter would be able to find a better position. He was standing up now, about to walk off. Had she made it clear how much she needed help? How much Mary needed help? This opportunity might not come around again.

Thornton was turning to go. Suddenly, this proud woman snapped. She had never begged for anything in her life, had hardly ever even asked. Now she found herself on her knees holding the hand of a shocked stranger, crying out: "Write to John. Ask him to help me. Not for my sake but the sake of my daughter Mary. My daughter whom his mother loved. My daughter who is named after his mother. Please, please, please ask him to help us."

Then she recovered. Stood up to face him.

"I'm sorry", she said.

"No, no, I quite understand", replied Thornton, obviously moved. "I'll do whatever I can."

He reached out his hand for the drawing of the house on Little Jost, to which Teresa was still clinging. Instead of handing it to him, she held it close to her heart.

"You can keep it," he said gently, "I did a few of them while I was there."

"No, no. Take it. I've nowhere to keep it safe." She pressed her lips to the picture, and then handed it to him. He took it back, and put some money into her hand in its place. Teresa hesitated, made to protest, and then – thinking of Mary – pushed it into a pocket in her skirt. She watched Thornton walk off, wondering if anything would come of their meeting. Hoping that it just might.

*

Receipt of Thornton's letter brought John up sharp. It arrived in the same mail as letters concerning his latest pet project: his sea-bathing hospital in Margate. This had long been one of John's keenest ambitions, and now he had been able to form an organising committee and raise funding for its building and for the support of people from the poor districts of London to benefit from the health-giving effects of immersion in sea water. Indeed, three months earlier he had laid the foundation stone for the main building in a lavish and well-attended ceremony. Now he had letters to study concerning progress of the building works and further contributions to its financing. These letters he opened first, spreading them on his desk in order to preview their contents. The news looked good, and he was impatient to read more.

But before doing so, he opened the letter from the Virgin Islands and pulled out a drawing that immediately put all thoughts of Margate and the poor of London out of his mind. He was instead transported back to Little Jost. He was running up to that house in the picture, to the place under those two tamarind trees where his mother was pouring sugar cane juice for Ed and Sam. Behind him ran a pretty little girl called Teresa. She had wept when she first saw this picture, and now he did. To Teresa the picture represented lost safety, security and happiness. To him it spoke of lost simplicity, friendship – and happiness.

In the accompanying letter, Thornton explained how the house was in remarkably good condition even though the surrounding plantation was ruined. He described how he had found most of the former estate workers still together on Tomlinson's plantation. When it came to his account of his meeting with Teresa, he avoided mention of her pleading with him. Instead he described her desperate circumstances in his own words. He wrote about how saddened he was to see such a fine and noble woman reduced to such impoverished circumstances. He expressed serious concern over what might become of her daughter, and slipped in a reminder that she had been named after John's mother and had been a favourite of hers. All in all, it was a powerful statement of the need to provide some help.

One reason for asking Thornton to visit Little Jost had been John's guilt about neglect of his parents, particularly his mother in her later years. He was toying with the idea of exhuming their remains, and those of his brother, and transporting them to England for reburial in a newly purchased extension to his grounds. Close by the murder cottage in fact. There, using the hard purple amarat wood that formed the framework of the house on Little Jost – and was probably responsible for its preservation – he could have a mausoleum constructed in memory of his beloved parents and of Ed. He would just have to take care that the other body at the site was not brought over too, nor even discovered. Now the nature of his project changed. Surely it was more important to support the living survivors of Little Jost, rather than memorialising those who had already passed on.

It took three years to achieve, but eventually Teresa and Mary were able to move back to Little Jost. John contacted Mr Tomlinson and arranged to buy the island. He also wrote to Thornton and asked him to persuade the former Little Jost workers to move back and Tomlinson to let them. Finally, Thornton revealed the plan to Teresa. "My miracle has happened!" she said. With the aid of a loan from Thornton and some material help from Tomlinson, she was able to begin to rebuild for a second time.

That was the physical outcome of Thorton's intervention. The psychological effects ran even deeper. Teresa no longer felt abandoned. Once more she had a friend to call on, albeit seven weeks away by letter. She resolved to ensure that she did not need to do so again. But it comforted her to know that he was still there, thinking of her.

And he was thinking of her. "Do you still think about your West Indian sweetheart every day?" Andrew Curtis had asked during the electricity demonstration, so long ago. John had thought about her less and less in recent years. After receiving Thornton's letter, the honest answer was once more: "Yes". It unsettled him. Why was he in London, setting himself ever more challenging professional goals, in a cold and formal marriage, and not in the Caribbean with the love of his life? He needed to work harder on finding the answer. Although he considered himself to be a medical scientist, he had never really grasped the fundamentals of the scientific method. He knew the question – had he been right to choose medicine and Nancy rather than Tortola and Teresa? He knew the answer: of course he had been right. All he had to do now was find the evidence to justify that answer.

PART VI: 1808–13

The next generation

CHAPTER 29

"There's a man coming up from the jetty", called Mary.

"What sort of man?" asked Teresa.

"White, young – oh – very good looking!"

"Then go and welcome him and bring him in here so I can take a look at him."

Teresa stood up ready to greet the stranger, but as soon as he entered the room she fell back into her chair, looking as pale as her dark skin would permit. Mary rushed over to her: "Are you all right, mother? You look like you've seen a ghost."

"John Coakley Lettsom. Have you come home after all these years?"

"Pickering Lettsom", replied the visitor. "His son. Very much alive."

Pickering Lettsom was indeed a handsome young man, confident and of athletic build. Aged twenty-five, just two years older than his father had been when he last set foot in this house. And his father was there in his manner, in his eyes, and especially in his nose. His clothes were more expensive and more flamboyant than the simple Quaker trainee doctor had worn, and his accent more cultivated, but Teresa had to concentrate to keep in mind the reality that this was the son, not the father.

Recovering her poise, she moved to sit at the table, beckoning Pickering to join her and instructing Mary to bring out what was left of a toto cake they had baked together the previous day and to open a bottle of their best Madeira wine. Mary seemed as flustered as her mother had been. She had to call out to ask where the cake had been put. Then she made a bit of a mess slicing it: a piece too big, a piece too small, and a piece that crumbled and fell apart. Her attempts to open the wine bottle were no better: half of the cork came out, half stayed in. The visitor had to go over and finish the job. As he did so, he found himself standing very close to Mary, reciprocating her intense glances.

"So, I am Teresa Coakley, and this is my beloved daughter, Mary", said the hostess bringing the young people's attention back to the moment in hand. Cake shared out and wine poured, they both sat down while Teresa continued: "Welcome to Little Jost van Dyke. Our little paradise. We will do our best to make it feel like home to you, just as it was for your father. A toast to your father!"

They raised their glasses, and began to talk. Pickering first had to assure Teresa that his father was well, that he was always pleased to receive her letters and presents, that he always shared the sweets she sent amongst his children and grandchildren and passed on the exotic news from across the ocean. He reached into his bag and brought out the gifts for the two women his father had entrusted to him. A large, intricately embroidered shawl for the mother, a dainty pair of bright pink indoor shoes for the daughter. Both were received with delight and gratitude, Mary being especially effusive with her thanks. Then he talked about his mother and his brothers and sisters, starting with his eldest brother John Miers who had died eight years earlier.

"John Miers was the apple of father's eye. He was the one chosen to follow in his footsteps and study medicine in Edinburgh and Leiden. He married a lovely girl, and she bore him three beautiful children. He'd just started out on a brilliant career when he suddenly caught the putrid fever and died within a fortnight. He was only twenty-nine. Father was devastated. Still is. His other sons are no substitute! My brother Fothergill is in business, working in grandfather's tin-plate factory, and sadly my brother Edward suffers from a brain disease. He can be very sweet and affectionate but he has now totally lost his memory and needs to be cared for night and day. Three of my sisters have died, two before I was born, and Mary Ann six years ago. That leaves my little sister Eliza, who is already married with children of her own, and me. I was sent to study law, so it's too late now to turn me into a doctor to continue father's tradition."

Teresa already knew much of what Pickering told her. Following his purchase of Little Jost, she and John had resumed their correspondence and their long-distance friendship had been restored. Their letters were now more regular, and more personal – although their intimate exchanges concerned her daughter and community of workers and his detailed the births, achievements, and sadly deaths of his children, rather than dwelling on their own concerns. Even four thousand miles away, Teresa was conscious of the enormity of the blow losing his eldest son had been to his father.

"Your father took John Mier's death very hard", she said. "But he must surely be proud of you."

Pickering did not look convinced.

Changing the subject, she continued: "Now you must tell us what brings you here."

Despite their regular correspondence, the arrival of Pickering on the island had come as a complete surprise. The letter warning Teresa to make ready for his visit and explaining its purpose actually arrived a couple of weeks later.

"I am appointed a judge to the Virgin Islands."

"You're too young to be a judge!" exclaimed Mary, almost shrieking.

"I thought so too", agreed Pickering, modestly. "I've been serving as a barrister at the Inner Temple in London, and when this opportunity came up I grabbed it. I've always wanted to see where father was born. He told us so much about these beautiful islands and the wonderful people who live on them."

Teresa smiled. His father's charm had been inherited.

"How long are you able to stay with us? Tonight we are set to dine on goat stew, prepared according to the tradition of these islands – well of this island anyway! You would be most welcome to join us, and to stay with us until morning."

Pickering stole a quick glance at Mary, and seeing her broad smile, he eagerly accepted. As he made to go down to the jetty to ask the boatman who had brought him to return in the morning, Teresa insisted that Mary go with him and take him on a tour of the island while she started to make preparations for the meal.

*

After taking Pickering down to the boat, Mary led him along a narrow undulating track to a small beach nestled at the head of a bay. From here, the islands of Jost van Dyke and Tortola appeared to enclose the water completely, making it look like an inland lake. Calmer now, Mary named all of the hills and bays that were in view and then kicked off her shoes and paddled in the shallow water.

Pickering was not yet ready to do the same. With some persuasion he had left his heavy coat at the house, but removing his boots seemed too big a step for this Englishman to take on his first day of leisure in the Caribbean. He had left a freezing cold England covered in snow from the first fall of the winter, and he still could not quite believe that he was now feeling the full warmth of the sun in January.

Pickering's voyage out had been long and tedious. On arrival, he had reported to the Road Town residence of the President of the Island Council to receive his instructions, only to find that he was away on business. A secretary had found him lodgings and advised him that, as it might be a few days before a meeting could be arranged, he should take the opportunity to see something of the island. The next day he had risen early, gone straight down to the harbour, and arranged to be brought to Little Jost. So now, he was observing the unfamiliar Caribbean scenery properly for the first time. And he loved it.

"It's so hot, he exclaimed", sitting down on a washed up log.

"You'll get used to that. It's cooler here in the sea."

"Oh no. I'll just sit here for a while and take it all in." There was a lot to take in. First, the warmth. Then the realisation that it was tempered by a gentle breeze coming off the sea. The waves rolling in towards him. Then the spectacle of black-capped petrels gliding low over the water, their wings almost touching the surface, and then ascending sharply before plunging vertically downwards onto unsuspecting fish. The surrounding islands rose steeply out of the sea, thickly covered by sugar cane and higher up by virgin forest – so unlike any land he had seen at home. Finally, and most remarkable of all, there was Mary – now knee-deep in the water, her skirt gathered in her hands, still staring at him.

"Let me take you up to Lookout Point", she said, emerging from the sea. In her childhood, she had got to know all the island haunts her mother had explored with John, Ed and Sam, and the names that original gang had coined had been passed on. Mary's companions had been the children of freed slaves who had stayed on, and the games and expeditions they invented had been similar to those her mother and her friends had enjoyed.

Pickering was sweating and out of breath by the time he caught up with his guide, who was sitting on a huge rock on the highest point on the island grinning at him. The view was much more extensive than from the beach and Mary once more recited all of the landmarks. They took a different way down, passing groups of black workers attending to the cotton crop. "Our free workers", emphasised Mary, greeting them as they passed. Pickering told her how proud of his father he had been when he first learned that he had freed his fifty slaves on Little Jost.

The trail ended on Sandy Beach at the far end of the island, where his father had swum with Teresa and Sam on their last day together all those years ago. This time, Pickering was unable to resist exhortations to take off his boots and bathe his hot feet in the cool sea. The wet sand felt marvellous! Mary took his hand and pulled him further into the waves until, with his breeches now soaked beyond the knees, he pulled free and retreated to shallower water. He paddled along the shoreline, watching her intently as she hitched up her skirt and waded in deeper, waving back at him and calling out to tell him what he was missing.

Their way back took them past the place under the tamarind trees where Pickering's grandparents and uncle were buried. Mary pointed out the graves, and they stopped and silently contemplated these West Indian pioneers. Even Mary did not know about the fourth body buried with them.

That evening, Pickering enjoyed his first taste of West Indian cooking. The addition of several slices of ginger and a generous splash of rum transformed the taste of the goat stew from anything he had experienced before. Like everything else on the island so far, he was hoping he would experience it again. Teresa proudly told him that her estate was thriving. She mentioned the difficult times following the slave insurrection but, typically, she understated just how desperate they had been. She expressed her heartfelt gratitude to his father for buying Little Jost and inviting her and Mary to return there. She told him how generous his father had been in freeing his slaves all those years before, and pointed out that some of those people were still on the island. His father would remember Nanny, who was serving them at the table, as a young girl. There were also Myal, Cotto and their mother, Cassia, although Cassia's husband, Bentorah, had passed away a few years earlier. Just one of Pickering's grandmother's former slaves, Margaret, was still on the island with some of her children.

Mary said little during that meal, and Pickering addressed most of his remarks to her mother. But if meaningful looks count as conversation, they never stopped chatting all evening. Teresa did notice. She felt excited for her daughter, but was much better at concealing it. She was also too well aware of potential pitfalls, should this relationship develop.

*

A week later, Pickering finally got his meeting with President Thomas Thomasson at his residence in Road Town. After welcoming the new judge and explaining a little about the islands and their white residents, Thomasson got down to business. Could Pickering chair a series of forthcoming hearings for people accused of minor offences? Could he attend various government meetings discussing policies likely to have legal implications? Could he assist with drafting an appeal to the Crown objecting to the designation of Tortola as reception centre for Africans rescued from foreign slave ships?

"Since the abolition of the slave trade throughout the Empire last year," explained Thomasson, "the navy has been disrupting the operations of our rivals. Africans taken from European ships entering the Caribbean are to be landed at British ports here and either settled as free men or recruited into the army. Our island is too small to hold these people, and there is too great a risk of unrest or of them being illegally traded to other islands or to our own planters."

Pickering agreed to all of the duties offered to him, taking careful notes of the details he was being given.

"Do you think you'll be able to cope with all that?" asked Thomasson.

“Certainly. In fact, it doesn’t sound too much at all. Are there any other tasks you’d like me to take on? I do feel I should be doing more to earn my keep.”

“Don’t worry about that. Explore the island, enjoy the sunshine, sample the rum.”

Sensing that the younger man was not satisfied by this answer, Thomasson went on: “If you really want more work, there’s plenty of little private legal jobs to be picked up here. The islanders are a litigious lot. In a small, tight-knit community like this, resentments fester and enmities flare up suddenly. Then they either call each other out for a duel, or if they haven’t the stomach for that, they sue. There’s lucrative business to be had, if you want it.”

“It would certainly be useful to widen my experience.”

The President duly wrote down the names of a couple of lawyers on the island whom he knew were unable to keep up with the requests for advice they received, and Pickering undertook to visit both of them that same afternoon.

Thus it was that on the next day Pickering approached the substantial plantation house at Banger’s Bay, the home of Ruth Georges. She had become the richest planter on Tortola on inheriting, first the estates of her grandfather Bezaliel Hodge, and then those of her late husband William Payne Georges. She greeted him wearing a long, plain, grey, high-collared dress that wouldn’t have looked out of place on a servant or a housekeeper. Her hair was swept back and tied in a neat and practical bun. Behind the plainness of her attire, Pickering discerned a strong-willed, attractive and intelligent woman. At forty-two years of age, her figure was still trim, and her deportment poised.

“I’m so pleased to meet you”, said Ruth when Pickering had introduced himself. “I knew your father when I was living in London. He is a very compassionate man.”

She led him into her study, where on a table piles of documents were laid out.

"The case I should like your advice on concerns a land dispute with my neighbour. Eight years ago he conveyed his entire plantation in trust to my husband to secure an income of five hundred pounds a year for his wife in the event of his untimely death. I think it must have been a condition imposed by her family, for as soon as he was married he began to negotiate to repossess the property. Everything was squared apart from the status of one parcel of sugar-growing land to the north of his estate, bordering my own land. He believes he now owns it again, while I believe it remains mine."

Ruth was sitting close to Pickering as she sorted through the papers and took a map out to point at the position of the land in question. He could feel the warmth of her body, and she betrayed no reticence in reaching across him to pull out another paper that laid out the agreement between her husband and her neighbour. This was not like his consultations with clients in London.

And there on the agreement was the name of the neighbour: Arthur Hodge. A name that made him start. His father had recited to him a list of people he should look up when he got to Tortola. And just one person whom he should avoid at all costs: Arthur Hodge. Sixteen years before, the older Arthur Hodge had died and his son had inherited the Belle Vue estate and sailed out to take up residence there.

"Arthur Hodge!" said Pickering.

"Do you know him?"

"My father did."

"I see. He's not a nice man, but I hadn't realised his reputation had spread so far. He still expects that, should he die, his widow would receive some income from his arrangement with my late husband. Although the payments would be much smaller than originally intended, this suggests recognition that I remain the owner of the disputed land. Sometimes he takes things from there like materials from abandoned buildings, or he uses the cattle that graze there – which he also claims to own – as beasts of burden to transport his sugar to the coast. He's not yet taken any of my sugar or stolen any of the cows. Just minor intrusions to annoy me, intended to make me think it's not worth hanging on to the property."

She put together a pile of papers relevant to the dispute, which Pickering put into a satchel to take away.

"You'll need to visit Mr Hodge, I'm afraid. He has papers which he says prove his claims. Please come back to me just as soon as you make some progress."

Then, with a look of concern on her face she added: "Do take care when you visit him. He's the most notorious duellist in the West Indies. The story goes that he was once humiliated in England when he ran from a call out by a military man. After that he strove to become supreme with both the sword and the pistol. They say that many of his opponents have been badly wounded or even killed but no one really knows who they were."

"Humiliated in England", thought Pickering, recalling his father's account of Henry Smith calling out the young sadist on his behalf during a garden party at Grove Hill just before he was born.

*

"When was this veranda built round the house?" asked Pickering.

Since his arrival in the Caribbean he had become a frequent visitor to Little Jost van Dyke, and he was back there, relaxing for a few days between legal meetings.

"Taine did that: your grandmother's second husband", replied Teresa. "He was a good handyman. Handy with his fists too, more's the pity."

"But it's not shown on the painting of the house that William Thornton gave to father."

"So observant! In fact it was in the original drawing, as that's how it was when Thornton saw it. But your father asked him to leave it out of the painting he made from the drawing, so the house would look like it was when he'd been a boy. He didn't want to be reminded of any part of Taine's handiwork."

The three of them were sitting on that veranda as they spoke. Teresa was perched on a stool peeling and cutting sweet potatoes, and Pickering and Mary were squeezed together on a bench shelling peas. Helping to prepare a meal was something he had never done at home, but here it seemed perfectly natural and pleasantly intimate. Very intimate in fact: he could feel Mary's thigh pressed close against his. Just because the bench was rather short of course!

On each visit, Pickering and Mary managed to find tasks that involved working in close proximity. They roamed across the island together further away from the house, and spent hours alone deep in conversation. This island, Pickering discovered, was a world without chaperones. It was the consequently the first time he had spent any appreciable amount of time alone with a young woman. Teresa certainly appeared unconcerned about them being together so much.

Given how different their upbringings and experiences had been, it was amazing how much they agreed on, how many of the same wrongs in the world they had identified as needing to be put right, and how many of the same things they found irresistibly funny. So uproariously funny, in fact, that sometimes they laughed so hard that they had to cling onto one another to avoid falling over.

That afternoon, Mary took him to Sandy Beach again. Swimming was in Mary's mind. As soon as they arrived on the sand, she slipped off her dress and ran into the water. Far out, she turned and waved, shouting for him to join her. This time, Pickering did not hesitate, although he was not wearing the sort of clothes that you can just slip out off. After a gargantuan struggle to detach his left boot, he eagerly but clumsily shed the rest of his attire and dashed into the waves, finding them warm and welcoming. He swam with the purposeful strokes that he had learnt at school; Mary had her own self-taught but highly effective style. Before long, they were wrestling and trying to submerge one another, but in reality merely seeking a playful excuse to touch and hold one another.

Later, they emerged from the water, and found a shady spot under a few low fruit trees to lie. The urge to hold onto one another had not gone away. They kissed, caressed, and soon they were making love: gently, tenderly and yet urgently. Later, they roamed around the beach together, finding sea eggs to open and eat and a ripe mango to pluck and share. Then they dressed and returned, hand in hand.

Teresa saw them walking up the path to the house, and knew immediately what had happened. How had her daughter learned to be so forward? She certainly didn't get that from her mother. She was pleased, although nervous about what might become of their happiness.

She let them spend a lazy evening on the deck, drinking wine and chatting about silly things that amused them disproportionally. She helped Nanny prepare fish for their meal, and sat with them while they ate, contributing little to their conversation. She retired early, and heard them both making for Mary's room for the night. She lay awake, thinking of herself and John when he had visited, feeling regret for what had not happened then, taking new hope from what was happening now.

CHAPTER 30

After all he had heard about Arthur Hodge, Pickering approached the Belle Vue plantation house with some trepidation. At the house, a big, muscular slave reluctantly rose from a wooden seat where he had been slouching and greeted him with a scowl. He took his horse and pointed at the front entrance. There, a white maidservant, heavily pregnant and rather timid, explained that the master was out supervising the sugar harvest and would be back soon. She took him to a lounge where he could sit and wait.

The room had been elegantly decorated and richly furnished many years ago, but was now in a state of untidiness and disrepair. Unwashed empty glasses littered a table in the centre of the room, the planks of the flooring creaked and some were loose, the settee and armchairs were stained and their upholstery torn. Curtains covered the windows to keep out the sun, but in places they hung ineffectively off their rails allowing shafts of light to reveal the decay inside. There was a damp, musty smell, with hints of dog and incontinent children. Pickering carefully chose the least dirty looking of the chairs and sat down.

When he had been waiting for about twenty minutes, a woman wandered into the room. Like the lounge itself, she was a picture of faded elegance. She was wearing a long evening gown, which had once been striking but now was grubby and ragged. An attempt at combing and styling her hair had been made, but it looked as though she had lost interest half way through the task. When Pickering rose to introduce himself, she jumped in surprise and became even paler, reaching out for the table to steady herself and knocking a couple of the empty glasses onto the floor in the process. As Pickering stooped to pick them up, she spoke in a thin, reedy voice.

"Don't concern yourself with those. They'll come to no further harm down there."

"I'm sorry to have startled you. Allow me to introduce myself. I am Pickering Lettsom, here to meet your husband on some legal business."

"Yes, very good. I'm Ann, Mrs Arthur Hodge. So pleased to meet you." Ann reached out a cold, clammy hand which Pickering clasped in greeting and then quickly let go. As she turned to him, the light caught her face and he could see bruises on it, some old and fading, others new and raw.

Now a girl of about seven ran in, calling for "Mummy" and throwing her arms around her mummy's legs when she found her. Ann patted her on the head, without actually looking down at her. The maidservant entered again, cradling a baby in one arm and grasping the hand of a little boy in the other.

"All my children", said Ann. "Here is Jane", she said indicating the girl trying to climb up her legs, "and here is Henry Cecil and little Justina. Aren't they lovely?"

"Oh yes. They're perfect", lied Pickering, thinking how malnourished and sickly they all looked.

The two women now coaxed, carried and dragged the children back to some nursery towards the rear of the house. Later the maid reappeared with a cup of tea for the waiting visitor.

"He shouldn't be long now", she said reassuringly.

"And you are Mrs Hodge's maid?"

"Yes sir. I'm Beverley."

*

Beverley paused, wondering whether to say more. Something in Pickering's sympathetic face encouraged her to continue.

"I grew up with Ann and her sister on her father's farm in Shropshire", she said, her face brightening as she remembered. "It was lovely, and we were all such good friends! When Ann got married, she asked me to come out here with her as her maid. Of course I said 'yes': it seemed like such a lark."

"And has it turned out as you expected?"

Now Beverley's face darkened. She dropped her gaze from Pickering's face and stared down at the floor. She hesitated, but then she continued, in a whisper.

"It all seemed very nice when we first arrived. I'd never thought much about slaves, and I was scared of them at first. Mr Hodge seemed very firm with them, and that was reassuring. But gradually, I got to realise that other plantations run just fine without Mr Hodge's form of 'chastisements'. He's so very cruel."

"What does he do?" From all he had heard about Hodge, Pickering was not surprised to hear that he was cruel, but as a lawyer he felt the need to know details from a first-hand witness. Beverley needed further coaxing before she would say more, and she went to the window to check that they were not about to be disturbed before going on.

"You ask for an example. Well, just this morning he was punishing some of the mulatto children. Some of them are his, some are McKeough's – that's his overseer. He had Bernardo, the slave you saw outside, pick them up by the ankles and dip their heads into a tub of water. He kept them under until the master said to pull them out – only just in time to stop them drowning. Then, after they coughed and spluttered a bit, he had Bernardo dip them again. He did that again and again, one child at a time, with the others watching. Then he hung them from a tree by their hands and whipped them."

Beverley shuddered as she relived the horror of what she had seen. Pickering himself went pale: he had expected to hear about mistreatment of grown men, but not of children.

"I don't know what they'd done. Something trivial, I'm sure. They're punished just for being born. For spoiling his pleasure with their mothers. Ann watched the whole thing. She was rooted to the spot and I couldn't get her to come inside, even though he told me to."

Beverley broke off and wept. Then she wiped her eyes on her sleeve and regained some of her composure.

"He's like that all the time. Something awful every day. It's sending Ann mad. She was such a happy girl, and so joyful when she got married to her dashing, handsome soldier. Now she's a complete wreck. The children are suffering too."

"Does he hit her?"

"You can see it on her face, can't you? It used to be because she complained about his cruelty. Now it's just because she goes around looking so miserable. And he beats the children. That hurts her even more."

"Does he hurt you?"

"He doesn't hit me. He hasn't yet. But he does force me to do what I don't want to do", she said, stroking her bump. "I'm wretchedly unhappy here. A white servant! Who's heard of one of those out here? The other servants shun me because I'm white, the other white people 'cause I'm a servant." The tears started again. She reached out for Pickering, who held her close to comfort her.

"Keep your hands off my servants!" boomed a loud voice. Beverley detached herself and scampered away, while Arthur Hodge strode over to Pickering, a big grin on his face, and shook his hand. "I can find you better than that pale pregnant mouse, if you're interested."

*

"Made you some tea, did she?" said Hodge, looking askance at the innocent beverage. "Joshua!" he bellowed, repeating the call a second time when there was no immediate response. A small middle-aged black man scurried in wearing an outsize livery coat that had once been brightly coloured, with a grey wig perched skew-whiff on his head. "Take this thing away", he said pointing to the tea. "Bring my visitor a proper drink." Then to Pickering: "Port all right?" Pickering nodded, although he would have preferred to have the chance to drink the tea instead.

"You're here to sort out this silly dispute with Mrs Georges, aren't you? It was all very clear between me and her husband. Decent chap was Bill Georges. We shook hands on it and it was all done with. Silly woman starts looking at the papers and gets it all wrong. Let me find you the documents."

Hodge disappeared towards the back of the house, and the servant arrived back with Pickering's port. A very generous glass-full, which he sipped slowly. He sat down, just as a large, black potcake dog bounded into the room and jumped onto his knee, almost knocking the drink from his hand. As this Belle Vue resident was neither angry nor sad, Pickering allowed him to stay, and to lick his hand. Eventually, Hodge reappeared, carrying some papers.

"I met your father a couple of times, you know. Worst bloody doctor on Tortola! He insisted on fixing my broken arm, even though my father had done it perfectly well already. No gentle touch from him – it hurt like hell! Then I saw him again in Camberwell. Are you a man of honour, or a Quaker sissy like your father?"

"I was brought up a Quaker, but lately, I must admit I've lapsed."

"Good. No excuses should we fall out. Here's the papers. You can read them here, but don't take anything away with you."

With that, Hodge was gone. He called his dog away too, leaving Pickering alone with the papers. He neglected his glass of port, and instead moved a hard chair to a spot where the damaged curtain allowed the light to enter, and there began to pore over the documents. He took a pad and a Keswick pencil from his bag and began to take notes. For an hour Pickering was undisturbed by dogs, children or servants. Having completed his task, he left silently, and finding his horse tethered in the yard, he rode off back to Road Town. He had learned a lot, and not only from the papers.

*

As the weeks went by, Pickering's life on Tortola took on a regular pattern. He spent time in court, presiding over trials of men accused of theft, fraud and violent disturbance, and assisting the Chief Justice with more serious cases. He visited the home of President Thomasson to advise on the legal aspects of government documents, and joined committee meetings concerning policies likely to have legal implications.

In his heart, Pickering was an abolitionist. From his Quaker upbringing he had absorbed George Fox's teaching that Africans and Englishmen are of one blood. He admired his father's dedication to treating the poor in the most squalid streets of London – even in the prisons. Pickering wanted society to go further – it was not sufficient to manage slaves considerately or to treat the poor when they fell sick. There should be no slaves. There should be no poor.

So much suffering was due to the laws that governed the Empire, and laws could be changed. So he had become a lawyer. But now his job was to uphold the law as it was written, not to change it. And here out in the colonies he was also expected to find ways around the law as it was written, for the benefit of those rich enough and powerful enough to put pressure on the President. He became frustrated with his official work, and sometimes ashamed of the compromises he found himself making.

The most satisfying part of his legal work was that that he did for Ruth Georges. His conscience was quite untroubled by going after Arthur Hodge. He was delighted deploy his legal training in support of his client, and he enjoyed his regular visits to her house at Banger's Bay to discuss the case. He was sure that Hodge's paperwork was insufficient to support his claims, and suspected that at least one document was forged and that dates or signatures on others had been tampered with. Nevertheless to make Ruth's case watertight, he encouraged her to assemble more documents, some of which had to be sent for as they were in the possession of her lawyer in England.

When not talking about her land dispute, he and Ruth also discussed the Leeward Islands Amelioration Act of 1798. This legislation outlawed the imposition of "cruel and unusual punishments" on slaves. The treatment of children described by Ann Hodge's servant Beverly certainly fitted that description. They agreed that it would be gratifying to prosecute Hodge for this abomination, but were not sure that Beverley could be persuaded to testify, nor that the island's courts would be prepared to convict. The legislation had been introduced locally to head off the imposition of stricter limitations by the Colonial Office. There had been some intent to avoid cruelties that might fuel slave rebellions, but punishment of a planter's own illegitimate children was unlikely to fan the flames of resistance. Pickering agreed to keep an eye out for more persuasive evidence.

Following their initial meeting, Ruth used his visits as an excuse to show off her London wardrobe, and to display the various items of jewellery her late husband had bought for her. She spent a considerable time attending to her hair and fingernails in anticipation of his visits. For his part, he at least turned out in the best and the cleanest of his jackets and pairs of breeches.

Conversations diverged from legal and business matters to encompass more personal matters. He learnt much about her life on the island before her marriage and about the cultural life of London during her years living in Manchester Square. Music, painting and poetry had been her passions then. She was able to dabble in each of these forms herself, although musically she was restricted to the violin now, having had to leave her piano behind. She had been distraught when Mozart died, and was now an avid follower of Beethoven. In art, she favoured landscape painting, especially Gainsborough and the new man Constable, while her favourite poets were the romantics: Wordsworth and Coleridge. Pickering began to wonder how he could have lived in London for so many years, and yet be ignorant of all these trends.

Pickering never saw any other white people at her house, and their evenings were always spent alone. Ruth's son, William Payne Georges III (both his grandfather and his father had borne that name), was away at school in England. Her two younger daughters had remained in England after the death of their father. Her eldest daughter, Frances, was married and living on one of Ruth's properties elsewhere on Tortola.

*

The best part of each week was, without a doubt, the time he was able to spend on Little Jost van Dyke. Here he felt relaxed and at home in a way he had never experienced before. Not since he had been sent away to school anyway. Everywhere else, the people he mixed with were gentlefolk, professionals, merchants, craftsmen, servants, or here in the Caribbean, slaves. He had always been acutely conscious of which type everyone was. On Little Jost, there were just people: Teresa, Nanny, Cassia, Myal, Cotto, Margaret – and of course, and very special, Mary. They all talked together freely, worked together and shared whatever they had.

One day when he arrived, Mary solemnly shook her head and told him that he had arrived at a bad time. Cotton harvest. Everyone, and that included him, was to be up at first light for a long and painful day picking cotton and lacerating their hands in the process. No overseer's whip could have spurred the pickers to greater efforts than Teresa's encouragements and humour. Nevertheless, his bag refused to swell as quickly as everyone else's did: even the children seemed to collect more.

After dark a great quantity of goat stew was prepared, which everyone ate together, accompanied by beer, wine and rum. Nanny was persuaded to get out her fiddle, and the dancing began. Teresa had hired three men from Road Town to help with the harvest, and one of them produced a flute, while another improvised drums from a couple of empty barrels. The third was a gifted singer with a rich bass voice and a repertoire of unfamiliar songs that everyone was eager to learn. The festivities continued until midnight.

The following day was a copy, but now the work was accompanied by song. Pickering got used to being addressed as "Cotton", a nickname that evolved from "Pickering", to "Picker", to "Cotton-Picker", to "Cotton" in the course of a single morning. By the end of the second day, he felt more exhausted than ever before in his life. Still, he did summon the energy from somewhere to dance with Mary for another couple of hours. When he returned to his legal work the next day, he was relieved to have stopped the physical labour but was already missing the camaraderie.

*

Faraway, at Grove Hill in Camberwell, John Coakley Lettsom was worried. During the last few days he had received three letters and now, following a typically hectic week in London, he had the leisure to study them properly. None of them was encouraging: in fact all of them were deeply troubling.

First was the letter his son Fothergill had sent from Wales. He was now running the late John Miers' tinplating factory near Swansea. The letter was accompanied by plans, drawings and specifications for a large extension which Fothergill sought to have built close to the existing works. In fact, the proposed development would more than double the size of the enterprise. Enormous steam engines would power the whole plant, and output would increase by a factor of four. Pages and pages of tables concerning the costs and supply of raw materials, the quantities and value of finished products, the available markets and consequent profits were included. What Fothergill wanted was money: specifically, for John to underwrite a large portion of the costs of the venture. All morning, John pored over the documents trying to understand them. They just didn't add up.

The second letter was from Pickering. He had received one letter already, just to say that his son had arrived safely and had found comfortable lodgings. This second letter was more expansive and covered the first month of his stay. John received it in late April, about seven weeks after it had been written. The (selective) accounts of his son's legal work pleased him: Pickering appeared to be acting diligently and wisely in adjudicating the minor offences brought to him, while showing no hint of considering them beneath his well-educated capabilities. He was pleased that Pickering was working for Ruth Georges, whom he remembered from her time in London as a sensitive and cultured woman keen to discuss abolition and to hear of his own experience of freeing slaves.

So, it was a very favourable letter. Nancy certainly thought so, commenting on how well Pickering seemed to be settling in. However, one passage concerned John. A long passage about Pickering's visits to Little Jost van Dyke. How gracious and welcoming Teresa had been. How lovely Mary was, and how well they got on with one another. They had visited Lookout Point together, swum from Sandy Beach, danced together. John read it, imagined it, filled in the blanks, and was horrified. Where would this lead? A mixed-race mistress? That would be the usual Virgin Islands outcome, but out of character for his serious, romantic, faithful son. A mixed-race wife? That would be even worse. What would Nancy think of such a daughter-in-law? What would his patients think? How would it go down at Eton where his grandson Nanson, son of his deceased favourite son John Miers, was now flourishing?

The third letter was from Teresa. It just confirmed the second. Such strong praise for Pickering. Reminiscences of their own adventures and parallels in what their children were doing. Hopes for seeing more of him in future. This could not be! He could not allow it! He showed Pickering's letter to Nancy again, and pointed out the passages that troubled him and explained why. He did not show her Teresa's letter: he never showed her Teresa's letters. Nancy had not understood the feelings beneath the surface of the letter. It took someone who had felt them himself to see them. But now she was worried. More worried than John, even. What might people say? She demanded that John write to their son to put a stop to it.

In fact, John was not only concerned with what people might say. Since resuming his correspondence with Teresa, he had been thinking a lot and reading a lot about what fellow abolitionists thought should follow emancipation. He had been surprised at what he found.

Benjamin Lay, who all those years ago John had been told considered all slave owners to be apostates, had believed that it would be impossible to assimilate freed slaves into the white population. Anthony Benezet, who had probably done more for the education of black people than anyone else in North America, envisaged a separate settlement for them west of the Allegheny mountains of Virginia. The British had already returned some free black residents of London to West Africa, and although the attempt had ended in disaster, the idea of repeating the operation on a much larger scale after emancipation was still popular amongst abolitionists.

Equal but separate. That notion had begun to appeal to John. Such a philosophy would of course rule out marriages or even long-term liaisons between the races. Sadly, it would have been incompatible with him spending his life with Teresa. His decision not to do so could now be logically justified. And it was completely incompatible with a marriage between his son and her daughter.

John wrote three letters that evening. To Pickering, to instruct him not to see any more of Mary. To Teresa, to ask her to advise Mary not to continue the relationship, with a gentle reminder of his generosity in giving them use of the house and the land on Little Jost, rent-free. To Fothergill, to agree to underwrite his new venture, praising its bold conception and expressing confidence in a positive outcome. One of his sons had died, one had limited mental capabilities, and one was in danger of "going native". He must avoid losing the fourth.

CHAPTER 31

At about the same time as his father was struggling to write three letters, Pickering was approaching Ruth's house in response to a request to come and discuss more of her legal documents. In fact, there did not appear to be very much to discuss at this stage: they were still awaiting replies from her London lawyers before they could take the dispute with Arthur Hodge any further. Pickering sensed that Ruth just wanted to spend an evening in his company, and that the business part would not take long to complete. He was happy to oblige as her conversation was far more inspiring and insightful than that of most of the white residents of the island. He had set out mid-afternoon, hopeful that an invitation to stay for dinner would be forthcoming.

He found the door to the house open, and as there were no servants in sight he walked straight in. The silence of the entrance hall was suddenly broken by a loud declamatory chord sounded on a violin. This was followed by a slow plaintive tune of rising notes repeated several times, becoming ever more mournful. Pickering was transfixed by the poignancy of the music. A quicker passage followed and then a series of loud chords leading to an agitated, spiky tune – then some nasty screeches and discords. "Damn, blast, damn, damn, damn!"

Ruth looked up from the music and saw him through the doorway.

"Did you hear that?" she demanded.

“I was entranced. It’s beautiful. What is it?”

“Impossible, that’s what it is. Just too bloody hard!” She sighed, and put down her violin. Then she took the score from the music stand and slammed it down forcefully on the table: “Take that Herr Beethoven! They may find this easy in Vienna or London, but honestly it is not!” She paused for a while, fighting against her frustration. Then the mood was gone, she saw her visitor politely waiting, and resolved to enjoy his company.

“It really is a beautiful piece of music. The tragedy is, even if I eventually master the violin part – which is unlikely, I’ll never find a pianist to accompany me. There’s not a single piano on the island.”

Belatedly, Ruth’s servant Judith appeared. She knew that music sessions often ended in tantrums, and tended to keep away while they were in progress. Now she offered to bring tea and cakes, and went off to get them.

“I heard that sonata played perfectly in London, by the man for whom it was written: George Bridgetower. The most brilliant and successful violinist in London at the time. You know, his father was a black man from Barbados who claimed to be an African prince. He gave the very first performance of this piece in Vienna with Beethoven himself at the piano. He even suggested some improvements!”

Calm now, Ruth continued to tell Pickering about the sonata as she returned the violin to its case, folded and put away the music stand, and tidied up the score.

“They fell out after the performance. It’s said that Bridgetower made a rude remark about a lady-friend of Beethoven, but I suspect there was more to it than just a remark. Bridgetower had a reputation as a ladies’ man – and I could see why! Beethoven switched the dedication to the famous violinist Rudolphe Kreutzer, but he hates the piece and refuses to play it. Perhaps he just finds all that double stopping in the first movement as difficult as I do."

Ruth, the hostess, now realised that her visitor was still standing. With an apology, she invited him to sit down at her work table and joined him there. But she was still not ready to discuss business: she had more to tell him about the evening she heard the great virtuoso perform.

"It wasn't Beethoven at the piano when I heard him play, but the accompanist was excellent. I forget his name: I was just entranced by Bridgetower's playing. He had such a pretty face. So animated and expressive – a real joy to watch as well as listen to.

"What an evening it was. I went with William, who tolerated music, but was never moved by it. As soon as he saw a black man take the stage, he stood up and said 'Right, we're leaving. I don't want to sit here and listen to jungle music'. For the first time in our marriage, I defied my husband. I refused to leave, he insisted that I did, our voices got louder and people began to stare. Bridgetower was about to start, but he looked in our direction, took the violin from his chin, and waited for us to finish. William went very red, and stormed off. Somehow, the music that followed cut through my fears of what would await me when I got home: it simply took me to another world."

Pickering knew very little about formal music, and Ruth's account made him wonder what he was missing. She continued her story, frowning now.

"When I got home, he was waiting for me with his cane. He would often beat me. Until that evening, I'd always accepted that he was right, and I was wrong. He had the right to beat me because I'd been silly or stupid or wilful. This time, as he caned me, he told me that no black man could ever play civilised music. It would be like the scrapings of a gorilla. I just flipped. I didn't do or say anything: I just realised that I was right and he was wrong. Totally wrong. And having discovered that he could be wrong on one thing, I went on to realise that he could be wrong on other things. On most things actually. I didn't weep as I usually did when he beat me. I didn't feel remorse. I felt anger and resentment. The last years of my marriage were very hard for me. I was so relieved when he died."

At that point, Judith brought in the tea and the cakes, Ruth produced the papers she wanted to discuss, and they got down to business. Part way through, when Judith came to take away the crockery, Ruth asked Pickering whether he wished to stay for dinner. Judith went off to make the arrangements.

*

As Pickering had expected, the paperwork did not take long to complete. When Ruth rose from the table, so did he. Then she sat down again, and asked one more question, pointing to a sentence in one of the documents. Pickering stood behind her, peering over her shoulder, their bodies touching. She reached backwards with her hand, found his, and held it. Then she gently pulled his hand down onto her bare chest, and then pushed it within her bodice onto her breast. Pickering was taken by surprise, but he was also aroused, and made no move to withdraw his hand.

"How does that feel?" she whispered.

"Very warm and soft and pleasant."

"And what about this?" She moved his hand to the side of her breast. He found himself feeling a large, hard, irregularly-shaped lump under the skin. This was less pleasant.

"What is it?"

"A tumour. A cancer." She now pulled his hand out and let him have it back.

"I have breast cancer, Pickering. It was diagnosed in London, before William died, although I never told him. I didn't go to your father. I went to see Gilbert Thompson, because of his reputation for straight-talking. And he was straight. He told me it would kill me in about three years if I left it untreated. That was nearly three years ago. He told me how it would feel, how it would grow and how it would spread. All of those things have happened. He told me about the pain, and now I take laudanum to suppress it. It's partially effective but it affects my brain and my concentration."

Visibly shocked, all Pickering could do was to ask the obvious question: "Is there no treatment?"

"Surgery. They can cut out the tumour, or at least they could have at that early stage. But I couldn't face the pain. I always thought you could get blind drunk, then you wouldn't feel anything. But alcohol makes your heart pump your blood faster and you're more likely to die due to bleeding when they start cutting. The surgery is also hideously disfiguring. I couldn't do it Pickering, and now the consequences are catching up with me."

She stood up, cutting off his attempts to express sorrow and sympathy. She told him abruptly that she had to get changed before dinner, and advised him to go out and get some fresh air. Indeed, after the news she had imparted, he was relieved to be alone for an hour. He walked briskly down to the sea and along the shore trying to collect his thoughts, devastated that he was destined to lose such a good friend so soon after meeting her.

Over dinner, they made stiff and formal conversation, about the food, about the weather, about planting new sugar canes. In the long silences between their bursts of chat, they ruminated silently on cancer, death and friendship. When Judith brought in the main course, Ruth asked her to bring in the fruit for dessert too, and leave it on a side table for them to help themselves later. Then Judith should go home early and clear up in the morning. When they were alone, each with a serving of the meal in front of them, Ruth broke the silence.

"I should like you to marry me."

On a day of surprises for Pickering, this was the biggest. He did not know how to respond, so he waited for her to continue. When she did, it seemed to be on a different tack altogether.

"When I was in London, your father told me about Count Bernstorff."

"Ah, the Danish aristocrat who freed all his serfs. Father talked about him often." Pickering discovered that he still had a tongue.

"That's the one. He gave each man a plot of land, a set of tools and training in how to use them. They all worked together for the good of the estate. As free men with a stake in the land, they worked harder than they ever did when they were serfs. They prospered and Bernstorff prospered. After five years he asked them whether they wished to revert to serfdom. Not one of them did, although many had been frightened of the prospect of freedom at the outset."

Ruth paused to take a sip of the wine, and to allow Pickering to consider this policy. Then she added: "That's what I want to do here."

"What a wonderful idea!" exclaimed her listener, his face alive with admiration. "Ever since I heard father tell me about Bernstorff, I've believed his to be the ideal solution to the problem of slavery. To bringing these people into the mainstream of society."

Encouraged by this reaction, Ruth began to expand on her theme.

"The idea took root on the night my husband beat me for enjoying sublime music. I felt a sudden affinity for all those who are beaten unjustly. My conversation with your father gave it some shape. I own more plantations and more slaves than anyone else on the island: who is better placed to try it? It became a dream, a fantasy. That was all it could be while my husband was alive. But I couldn't stop thinking about it, reading about Bernstorff, planning elaborate details of how it might work. Then William died, and the fantasy became a possibility. But already, this damn disease had been detected, and I knew I had no time to see it through by myself. My son William is too cautious and timid, too much like his father to try such an experiment. My daughter Frances and her husband know nothing about sugar or farming or people. They don't even cultivate the property I gave them."

Ruth paused, and refilled their wine glasses. She was so pleased to have shared her dream with another, although anxious about how he might react. Now to the crux of the project.

"I thought my plan was dead, but then I met you. You share so many of my ideals. More so even than your father. If you were to marry me, then we could start this venture together. When I die, you would inherit all of my land. As my husband, my relatives would not be able contest it. You could complete the transformation, manage the estate, ensure the land was farmed for the benefit of everyone who worked on it. You would be the richest man on Tortola, and I believe your wealth would grow faster than that of the other planters if your workers were free and also had a stake in the land. And after I'm gone, you could marry your true love, Mary."

Pickering blushed a deep red. He had spoken to Ruth about his visits to Little Jost, of course, but he never realised that his feelings of love had shone through everything he had said, without him ever mentioning them.

"As the richest man in Tortola, how could she say 'no'? How could anyone object to anything that you did? I would have absolute trust in you and Mary to see my plan for the estate through to its triumphant conclusion."

*

It often takes a considerable effort to make small decisions. The reasons for taking action will be weighed up carefully, and those against similarly assessed. Once the decision is made, second thoughts will occur and a reversal will often follow. Medium-sized decisions are even more fraught and might take weeks or months to resolve, involving discussions with others and lengthy introspection. The biggest decisions, however, can sometimes be made almost as soon as the case has been put. That was true for Pickering that evening. Inheriting a fortune, pioneering a practical scheme for the emancipation of slaves, implementing humane and modern governance across a large network of plantations, eventually having all obstacles to marrying Mary swept aside. Ruth would be an agreeable companion and a knowledgeable partner in the enterprise, for as long as she was able. Pickering was ready to say 'yes' before they moved on to eat the fruit. It was a feeling that such a quick answer might appear unseemly or even frivolous that led him to promise only to consider the proposal carefully, accompanied by assurances that it appeared to be very attractive and that he was flattered by the suggestion.

By the end of the dinner, Ruth was tired: fatigue was one constant reminder that she was no longer a fit woman. As it had become late, she arranged for Pickering to stay the night in a spare bedroom. He slept well, and when he awoke his resolve was unbroken. Of course he would say 'yes'. He was unable to delay saying so any longer, and told Ruth over breakfast. She expressed her great delight and relief at his acceptance, and confessed to fears that he might have thought her foolish, or unrealistic. She now announced her conditions.

"I should like us to get married in September. That gives us almost six months to prepare. We shouldn't tell anyone at all until the beginning of August. My family will be dead set against us marrying as they'll be concerned about their inheritance: we mustn't give them time to organise against us. I want to show you all of my estates, and introduce you to my main overseers and workers. We need to develop detailed plans for freeing them and transferring ownership to them. Legal documents will be needed, and I shall be relying on you in that respect."

Pickering readily agreed to these conditions. There would clearly be a great deal of legal work to be undertaken.

"We will retain ownership of the sugar refinery and the rum distillery. Buy sugar from our free workers for processing and export. Lead them, mentor them, educate them. We will all prosper as a result.

"You'll need to spend a lot of time here as we prepare, but I accept – nay, I insist – that you continue your visits to Little Jost in the meantime. Your long-term happiness is most important to me, and your eventual partnership with Mary will be central to the success of the enterprise. The time from announcing our engagement until my death will be a test of her love for you. Knowing you as I do, I'm confident that she will come back to you."

Breaking the news of their engagement to Mary and Teresa was going to be the worst part of this, Pickering knew. He wished he could be as confident as Ruth that he would be able to win Mary back. Being the richest man on Tortola would certainly help.

"We must make no mention of our plans for the estates until we're safely married. You must draw up watertight inheritance papers to ensure that everything goes to you when I die. We should also specify what would happen in the event of your death. I was thinking that in that case, everything should pass to your father. He could be trusted to implement the freeing of our slaves."

"I don't intend to die so soon!" protested Pickering, feeling that these preparations were becoming a little too thorough.

"Oh, no", responded Ruth, laughing. "This would be to ensure that you have a long and happy life. We will make this bequest known when we finally reveal our plans so as to protect you. It would become known that murdering you would not reverse our changes. So they will not murder you. I can assure you that there are people on this island, and with interests on this island, who would not be above the odd murder or two to advance them."

Pickering was pacified, but suddenly aware of the dangers this enterprise would involve.

Ruth continued: "You father is old. Who should inherit in case of his death? Should it be your brother Fothergill?"

"He's too practical a businessman. I doubt whether he'd have any sympathy for the workers owning the works. I'll think about it, but probably my nephew Nanson would be the safest bet. He's got his whole life ahead of him. He's a sensitive boy. And there would be time for me to persuade him of our cause, perhaps to have him visit Tortola."

"Yes, that should be feasible. Sadly, there's no chance that I'll be able to bear children with you. There's too little time, too much pain, and it would be unfair knowing that any such child would never get to know their mother. But of course, the children that you and Mary bring forth will be the actual inheritors. So, there'll be no need to excite Nanson too much about his prospects."

After finishing breakfast, and a brief discussion of what a wealthy widow should wear for her second wedding, they rose from the table. A warm embrace and an affectionate kiss, and then Pickering was walking back to Road Town, his head swimming with thoughts about the sudden change in his life's prospects.

CHAPTER 32

"Your father was a keen swimmer too", said Teresa. Pickering and Mary had just returned from another intimate afternoon on Sandy Beach. They had told Teresa about the swimming. "He always told Sam and me that it was good for us."

"Oh, he believes it's good for everyone. Ten years ago, he founded his sea-bathing hospital on the coast. People flock there from London to be cured."

"What does it cure?"

"If you believe my father, just about everything! It's good for your skin and your complexion, it cures sores and rashes, your teeth become stronger and your gums stay sound."

"Do people drink the seawater then?" asked Teresa, incredulous.

"No, but they do swill it around in their mouths. Most people just dip into the sea: they don't generally swim. But it's considerably colder than the sea here. Occasionally though, we do have a beautiful summer. It's dry and sunny and it's warm enough for people to swim."

The three of them were sitting on the sunny side of the veranda, the swimmers still drying out after their dip. Pickering tried to remember whether an English summer ever got as hot as this.

"On a fine summer's day in England, everyone comes out to worship the sun. Here I still wake up, look outside, and think: 'What a beautiful day it is today'. Then I remember that it always is. Maybe there's something missing when it's not so special."

"I don't mind it being warm enough to swim every day", said Mary. "And it keeps my complexion lovely, doesn't it?"

Another weekend visit to Little Jost was slipping by. Swimming, fishing, collecting shells for seafood and for decoration. Helping out with household chores, feeding animals, preparing meals. Spending days with Mary, spending nights with Mary. Growing closer together all the time, as they discovered their own special places, their own secret routines, their own private language. These weekends were numbered, and the supply was becoming thin. As the web that united them tightened, Pickering dreaded his forthcoming severing of their bonds. Yet he grew more confident that Mary would eventually forgive him and return to him.

Over dinner, Teresa asked him about his faith. Was he still a Quaker? Was his father?

"Father still attends Meetings regularly, and he's on lots of Quaker committees. Including the one promoting abolition of slavery. But he's also the physician for the Camberwell Volunteers. That's a company led by his neighbour Henry Smith, ready to resist any invasion by the dastardly Frenchies. He denies any contradiction between Quaker principles and serving a military unit. He insists that his role would just be putting wounded soldiers back together again. As they would then go back and kill more Frenchmen, I'm not convinced."

"And your faith, Cotton?" Mary had adopted the harvest-time nickname devised for Pickering, finding it shorter and softer than his real name.

"Father insisted I join the Volunteers. That was a crisis for me. I wasn't even to be treating fallen comrades, I was to be trained to kill. I knew I couldn't be both a Quaker and a soldier, even a volunteer soldier unlikely ever to see action. I saw a lot to admire about revolutionary France. They even abolished slavery throughout their empire. But Napoleon brought it back. I see nothing but evil in him. I wouldn't be prepared to stand aside and let others resist his troops, and then benefit from their sacrifices.

"So I joined the Volunteers, and accepted the logical consequence: I've quietly allowed my faith to lapse. We drill regularly on the lawn of Henry Smith's house. I'm a lieutenant now! Not so good with the pistol or the musket, but a dab hand with the sword. I'll need those Frenchies to get close to me before I can dispatch them!"

The women applauded. Teresa had a low opinion of the Society that had snubbed Pickering's grandmother. Mary pictured a dashing young man in a scarlet uniform and a sword in hand, protecting her from French invaders.

*

The yard in front of the Belle View plantation house was crowded with slaves. On one side of a platform, built high enough for everyone to see them, stood Arthur Hodge, his overseer McKeough, and his trusted slave Bernardo. On the other side of the platform, two black men were tied to a wooden rail and two more were tending a smouldering fire.

"You all know that I will not tolerate laziness in any form", said Hodge. He was not shouting, but his voice was clear and carried naturally to everyone in the crowd. Pickering could hear him as he approached the yard, bringing the legal papers from London that would settle the land dispute in Ruth's favour. He had walked up to the house from Banger's Bay, and so this time he had no horse to secure. He paused on the edge of the mass of spectators, unsure how to get through them to reach the door of the house.

"These men were late to the fields yesterday morning. That will not be tolerated. They said they needed to bury their children who had died in the night of the fever. That is women's work! That is not a reason to be late to the fields." Then, turning to the men tending the fire, he asked: "Is it ready?" On receiving an affirmative reply, he turned to the black man by his side and simply spoke his name: "Bernardo".

Bernardo then approached the fire and was handed a metal poker. A red hot poker, extracted from deep within in the glowing embers. He walked over to the first man bound to the rail. The man looked terrified, but he seemed to know what was coming as he opened his mouth as wide as he could, ready for Bernardo to thrust the poker down his throat.

Pickering stared horrified. He had witnessed cruelty before, passing by a public hanging at Newgate while pursuing his legal duties in London, seeing sailors being flogged for minor transgressions on the ship coming over, but never anything like this. After what seemed like an age, Bernardo extracted the poker. The victim sagged. The crowd made a curious sound – part scream, part sigh – but they stopped as soon as Hodge turned to face them, trying to work out who was making most of the noise. Instead, he saw Pickering.

"Ah, Mr Lettsom! Do join us up here please. Learn how justice is administered on the islands!"

Pickering made no response. Instead, he determinedly pushed his way to the door of the house, where a middle-aged black woman let him in and showed him to the lounge where he had waited on his last visit. Even there, he could hear Hodge's penetrating voice and the sounds of the second man being tortured in the same way as the first.

The lounge was in much the same state as before, and he carefully chose a place to sit. Before long the woman who had let him in returned with some tea: observing the social niceties despite the commotion outside where Hodge had launched into a rant against idleness, wickedness, theft and any other accusations he could think of to make against his cowering workers. Pickering cleared some unwashed glasses and bottles from a table to make room for the tray. It looked quite out of place in the surroundings: clean, dainty white china with a pink floral pattern. A tea pot, tea cup, saucer, sugar bowl, milk jug, strainer – the whole set. Nothing chipped, nothing cracked. Also three assorted biscuits on a matching plate.

"I'm trying to make improvements", said the woman, reading his face. "Starting in the kitchen, and then working outwards. If the kitchen isn't clean and healthy, then nothing can be. I found this tea service right at the back of a cupboard gathering dust, it's cleaned up very nicely. This is only my first week here: I'll start on this room next week."

"What happened to the other servant? Beverley, I think her name was."

"Oh yes, Beverley", repeated the woman, the smile fading quickly from her face. "She died a couple of weeks ago." Then in a quieter voice she continued: "Suicide, you know. She just walked into the sea and drowned." Then, even quieter: "She had a furious row with the master. He punched her really hard in the belly. Then she lost the baby she was carrying. His baby, the mistress tells me. She never recovered. As soon as she was strong enough to walk as far as the beach, she was off."

"I'm so sorry. I only met her once, but she seemed so sad and lost. And she had had a happy time with your mistress in England." Pickering really did feel upset at this news. The pale white girl had been so pleased to have the chance to confide in him that day. "So what's your name, then?"

"Perreen Georges, sir", this accompanied by a smile and slight curtsey. "A free woman. Sometimes I work in the boiling house here, supervising the sugar refining, but I also skivvy for some of the families in Road Town. That's where the mistress first met me during the days when she used to come into town. She called for me to help here after Beverley passed away. Beverley was her friend first, and her servant second. It's for her that I work here, despite that sort of thing happening all the time."

Perreen nodded in the direction of the yard to make it clear what she meant by "that sort of thing".

"That was very distressing", said Pickering, unsure the extent to which he should let his disgust show.

Perreen continued: "Now Mistress Ann has completely closed in on herself. Apart from me and the master, she sees no-one – except for the children, of course. She's not right in her mind: wanders about talking to herself. But mostly she stays in bed, which is where she is now. I'm so glad that she wasn't up to see what just went on outside. It upsets her so much. The children are locked in the nursery, but they're there much of the time anyway. To keep them from disturbing her, he says. Henry will be sent away to school soon, but I fear for what will become of the girls."

*

"When Hodge eventually came in, I explained the legal situation and gave him a written summary and the letter telling him to keep off your land. He gave one of his arrogant smiles, took the papers and dropped them carelessly onto a dirty table in a puddle of spilt rum. He said he'd be seeing me."

Pickering and Ruth were walking together slowly up one of the steep paths that crossed the main mountain ridge of the island. They were accompanied by four of her slaves, two of whom were leading their horses up this uneven, rocky section. This was part of Pickering's induction into the realities and complexities of growing sugar and managing the people who cultivated it. They were heading for the farthest northwest outposts of her holdings, and she was finding this expedition tiring.

Pickering had told her about the torture that he had witnessed at Belle Vue, and they agreed that this constituted sound evidence of cruel and unusual punishment, witnessed by a judge, no less. He had written a careful record of what he had seen, and suggested taking it to President Thomasson as soon as possible. Ruth advised him to keep hold of his account for the time being. It would be best to wait until after their wedding, and to settle the land dispute first. Reluctantly, Pickering agreed to wait.

"By the way, do you know his new servant, Perreen Georges?"

"Perreen? Oh yes. She was a slave of William's father. Always intelligent, hard-working and honest. He moved her from the fields and into the house, and he was so pleased by the care and support she gave to his wife when she was sick that he freed her. He thought she'd be so grateful that she'd stay in post as a paid housekeeper, but she was off to Road Town the very next day. She was grateful, but not stupid! And that's what we have to avoid when the time comes. We want our workers to stay on our plantations."

"Giving them land and cabins which they can't take away with them, should help."

Now they had reached the crest of the ridge and they were able to mount their horses again. Nevertheless, as the path was rocky with steep drops on one side or the other, they proceeded slowly, in single file. To their right, they could look northwards and see sugar cane extending from the ridge, right down to the ocean a mile away and a thousand feet below. All Ruth's land. At the far end of this stretch of coast, before the headland where the shoreline turned south, was Ruth's most distant possession. A rocky promontory extended into the sea, with Sharks Bay to the left and Hell Hole Bay to the right. Not especially encouraging names, Ruth admitted, but highly productive land. The estate and the peak that overlooked it were named Mount Healthy, perhaps for balance. As they dismounted to negotiate a tricky section of the descent, Ruth resumed their conversation.

"I've spent the year since my return meeting all my overseers and specialised craftsmen and tradesmen. I've dismissed or sold the cruel, the lazy and the drunkards. I've promoted those who work hard, and are conscientious and fair. Some are white, some are black. I've discovered that the traits I wish to encourage and those I'm determined to eliminate come from the soul. They're not peculiar to white or black. The white overseers you'll meet today are just and compassionate in their dealings with slaves, and so are the black ones. All of them are also strict with anyone caught stealing, slacking, fighting or damaging property."

Ruth continued to brief Pickering on the policies she was now following, and gave him examples of what had worked well and what had not. Soon they were able to get back on their horses, but the trail was only wide enough for one animal at a time and this prevented anything but an intermittent, shouted conversation. At last, they rounded a corner and the Mount Healthy plantation house was before them.

They had not arrived at a propitious time. A small knot of people were watching as a tall worker was dragged across the yard to be tied to a wooden frame, while another was approaching him with a whip in hand. A black man, whose clothes were newer and in better condition than most, and whose bearing gave him air of authority, approached the visitors.

"What's going on here, Ebenezer?" asked Ruth, unperturbed.

"Punishment of a slave, Ma'am. Do you wish for us to stop?"

"What's he done?"

"Last night shouting and screaming was heard from his cabin. His neighbours rushed in to find him standing over his wife with an axe. He'd hit her on the head with the blunt end several times, and she was on the floor, bleeding very badly. Their two children had tried to stop him, but he'd flung them across the cabin. The older one had three broken ribs. We can't tolerate such behaviour Ma'am."

"No, certainly not. What's the sentence?"

"Twenty lashes."

"Continue then."

Pickering and Ruth watched as the punishment was inflicted. The man was not at all stoic, and he yelled out pitifully with every stroke. Pickering flinched each time, but Ruth appeared to be unmoved. Women rushed forward to tend to the man's wounds once the beating was over. The punishment was harsh and painful, but to Pickering it did not seem excessive in view of the man's crime. Certainly not cruel and unusual like the punishment he had witnessed on Hodge's plantation.

"It's well known that slaves suffer horrendously from cruel masters and zealous overseers", explained Ebenezer. "It's less well understood that another horror of slavery is having little protection from your fellow-slaves. Some are naturally bad, some are driven bad. Whatever the reason, on most plantations violent men can do what they please provided they don't materially reduce the value of their master's property. There's no protection and no redress. The mistress here is very aware of this. She insists that the weaker slaves are protected and that those who harm them are punished. Twenty lashes is the harshest punishment she will allow. It's enough. He'll be more careful in future, but we'll separate him from his wife and children."

*

It was a very quiet tapping. At first, Pickering thought it might be the wind. No, there it was again: a faint knocking on the door. As if the person knocking was so nervous that they would be happier if the door were not answered. Pickering rose from his desk where he was studying legal papers for a hearing the following day and opened his door. There in the dark he saw someone scurrying away.

"Wait!" he cried out.

His visitor stopped, turned around, and hesitantly approached his door again. It was Perreen Georges.

"I didn't know whether to come, sir. I'm so worried about the mistress."

Pickering invited her in. This evening he was at his Road Town lodgings, alone. He persuaded her to sit down, and poured her a glass of brandy to calm her nerves. It was now a couple of months since he had first met her, and he was surprised to see such a strong and resilient woman looking so frightened.

"Mistress Ann is so poorly", she started. "She hardly gets out of bed, and she's lost interest even in her children. She won't eat, and if she does it makes her sick. The master shouts at her and sometimes he hits her. Then he goes off to spend the night with one of his favourite fancy women. He says she's lost her reason, but that's not it. She knows what's going on, and that's what's driving her mad."

"What is going on?"

"Cruelty, torture, murder, sir."

"Who's been murdered?"

"Many, many people. Slaves of course. He says that who lives and who dies is up to him." Perreen now lifted the glass to her lips and swallowed the brandy in a single gulp. This seemed to steady her. Pickering refilled the glass, but she pushed it away and sat up straight, ready to tell her story properly.

"Prosper was the master's oldest slave. Not the most ancient, but the first he ever owned. He was given to the master by his father. He was cruel to him from the start. Prosper still bore a hideous scar on his forehead where the master had tried to brand him when he was a child. Whenever he ran out of people to torment, it seemed he would go in search of Prosper. He'd given him that name: his idea of a joke. The mistress got to know Prosper. He could tell that she was being mistreated: those who are beaten can recognise suffering in others. He was kind to her, always addressing her respectfully but showing cheerfulness to try to raise her spirits even when he was in pain himself. He was good with the children too – when the master wasn't around.

"A couple of weeks ago, Prosper was passing the mango tree at the front of the house when a mango fell to the ground. He picked it up and saw that it was undamaged. He told me he didn't even know what he was going to do with it – he just didn't want to leave good fruit on the ground where it might be trampled by horses or just rot. Unfortunately, the master came out of the house at that very moment and saw Prosper pick up the fruit. He demanded he pay six shillings for it, there and then. Prosper explained he didn't wish to take the mango, and attempted to hand it over. The master would have none of it. He didn't want it now that Prosper had had his hands on it. Prosper must buy it. The price was six shillings – which of course is unheard of for a single piece of fruit.

"Prosper ran to me at the boiling house. I only had three shillings on me, so I gave it all to him and he ran back with it. The master was not satisfied. He had Prosper held down and beaten with a cart whip for over an hour, and then told him to come back the next day with the remaining three shillings. The mistress saw all this: it took place close to the house and the noise was so much that no-one could fail to notice. But she had no money – the master won't allow her to carry any."

Perreen paused. She was finding it harder to tell the story as the details became more abominable. She reached over and drank the second glass of brandy.

"On the second day, Prosper had found no more money. I had none: I'd gladly have given him all I had. The master was furious. He had him tied to a tree, just in front of the plantation house, and whipped until he had no skin left on his back and he could no longer cry out in pain. He was taken to the sick house and put in irons. Five days later, two slaves who were also there recovering from punishment managed to release their chains and run off. Prosper was too weak to follow. His wounds had crawlers deep inside them and he was surrounded by flies. He dragged himself to his cabin, where he died alone a few days later. It was the smell coming from the cabin that eventually brought people looking. He was buried in a pit by the back door."

Perreen had now almost finished her account. Pickering was himself feeling nauseous. He poured two glasses of brandy, and he downed his in one. Perreen just held hers tight, for comfort.

"The mistress had visited him in the sick house. She knew he couldn't survive. She's talked about it every day since he died."

"Murdering a slave is illegal. That's clearly written into the new legal code for the islands. Getting proof would be the hard part. Testimony from slaves doesn't count. As a free woman, you could testify. Ann Hodge couldn't testify against her husband. We'd need more witnesses."

"There's been more murders", volunteered Perreen. "Some years ago he accused his house slave, Violet, of stealing candles. He had her whipped. Her son ran away, but was caught. He had him whipped. They both died from their wounds."

Now that she had started, Perreen's accounts of the crimes that she had witnessed or been told about came pouring out. She hardly paused between recounting the fatal outcome of one atrocity and starting on the next grim tale.

"Sampson was just a child of ten years. I don't know what he was supposed to have done, but the master had him dipped into a cauldron of boiling water, and all the skin dropped off him. He must have died, but I never heard anything else about him."

"He sent his trusted slave Welcome to recapture some slaves who had run away. Welcome spent five days looking for them, but couldn't find them. When he returned, the master had him whipped, and sent him out again. Again he was unsuccessful. He was whipped again, and sent out a third time. By then he was so weak and in pain that he was in no condition to search for the runaways. He returned a third time without them, was whipped again, put in the stocks and given nothing to eat. He died soon after.

Pickering had started to take notes, and he stopped her there while he caught up. Then she continued with a further catalogue of horror. She explained that McKeough had been instructed to enter those killed as runaways on the list of plantation slaves. She guessed that more than half of the plantation's slaves had been killed through Hodge's brutality over the last four years.

Eventually, Perreen came to the end of her list. She knocked back her third glass of brandy, accepted his promises to see what he could do and warned him to be most careful about whom he told and to mention her name to no-one. Then she departed into the night.

CHAPTER 33

Pickering had to defer discussion of Perreen's visit with Ruth as he was due to visit Little Jost van Dyke the next day. For the first time, he approached the island with a heavy heart, and not with his usual feelings of excitement and joy. It was August already, and his engagement was to be made public the following week. Before that he had to tell Mary. Quite how, he was unsure. He had sent a message in advance to warn that his stay would be one day shorter than usual – just a single night. He could not contemplate staying any longer.

When he landed, he discovered that he had a capacity for dissimulation he had not previously been aware of. He greeted Nanny with a jolly smile when he passed her on his way up to the house, and burst in on Teresa and Mary, full of good cheer and open affection. He gave them presents he had bought in Road Town: cloth from the latest shipment from England that they would turn into colourful clothing, and more wine imported from Madeira. He had also brought more prosaic groceries and provisions from the Road Town market.

Teresa seized the fresh loaves, cheese and salad and set to work on preparing a lunch for them all. Pickering sat on the deck with Mary, swapping small talk about petty misdemeanours of settlers brought before his court and stupidity of goats that wandered off and got trapped on the far side of the island. The lunch was a typical Little Jost affair of fried fish and sweet potatoes, salad and cheese, accompanied by the first of the bottles of Madeira he had brought.

After lunch, Teresa returned to the house to help Nanny with her planned project to repair and renew the chicken coop. Pickering's offers to help were waved away, and he was instructed to take Mary off and give her a break from the hard work she had been doing all week. He dismissed the suggestion of another visit to Sandy Beach, citing the chilly wind that was coming off the sea that day. Instead, he chose Lookout Point as their objective as the skies were clear and the views would be extensive.

Indeed, the view was fabulous that afternoon. To the east they could see the island of Guana, and peeping up behind it, Gorda Peak on Virgin Gorda. On Tortola, the long line of Ruth's sugar plantations was clearly visible, and Pickering told Mary of his recent visit to inspect them. This seemed to set the scene for his bombshell.

"Actually, I have something to tell you about me and Ruth", he began. Mary looked startled, and then afraid. She turned pale and her hands began to tremble. She and her mother had often talked about Pickering's long-term intentions, their predictions taking a well-worn circuit of a proposal of marriage, some settlement for her as a kept woman, and him just walking away to return to England or to take up with one of the white plantation belles. Amongst the latter, Ruth Georges often entered the conversation. Surely too old! But well-preserved and the richest planter on Tortola nevertheless.

Mary felt that the bullet had already left the gun. And then it hit: "Ruth and I are engaged to be married". She didn't fall over. She didn't even flinch. In fact, her hands stopped shaking, and she had a strange feeling of calm. It was as if she was looking down and seeing this couple standing amidst this glorious scenery on a sunny, but rather windy day. The woman was saying: "Congratulations! Ruth is a fine, intelligent woman. And also a very rich one." The woman talking to the man even giggled at this point. She went on to ask details of dates, arrangements, wishing them well. Inside her own head, Mary swooned. She fell to the ground and writhed and screamed and wept. But none of this had any effect on the woman she saw conversing with Pickering.

"Don't tell mother today, please. She'll need some time to adjust, and it'll spoil our last evening. You won't be able to come over here and stay once everyone knows you're betrothed. Can we have one last cosy evening and one more intimate night together? I'll tell her when you've gone. Perhaps, once you're married, you'll be able to bring your new wife to visit us."

Pickering was amazed at her composure. Had she not actually been in love with him after all? Would he be able to win her back later? How he wanted to tell her about his plan, Ruth's illness, his love. But he hid his feelings, just as he had promised his new fiancée that he would, and they returned to the house together. Once in sight of Teresa and Nanny who were hammering together some planks to fix the chicken coop, they rather self-consciously held hands and then gave an enthusiastic account of how far you could see from the top that day and how beautiful everything looked. Teresa suggested that they now relax on the veranda, but instead Pickering insisted on chopping more wood and Mary on starting preparations for the meal. Pickering chopped all the wood he could find: far more than was needed to cook the evening meal, working up a prodigious sweat in the process.

The meal passed off well. The stew was good, spiced with chillies that Pickering had brought from the Road Town market. Another of the bottles of Madeira was emptied. The laughter and merriment was even more intense than usual. Then Pickering and Mary retired to her bed and made love affectionately. Later, they lay side-by-side, each trying unsuccessfully to suppress the tears that flowed, and trying to pretend that they could not hear the other weeping.

In the morning as soon as breakfast was over, Pickering got up to leave. He had instructed the boatman to call early, and the shallop was already at the jetty when he rose. He made some excuse about there being a busy week of court work awaiting him. Mary went with him down to the water. Half way down she stopped.

"I also had something to announce", she said. "I decided not to, but I can't hold it in. Pickering, I'm pregnant." Now it was his turn to freeze. Of course, he had known this was possible. They were always careful, but sometimes in the struggle between caution and passion, the latter won out. "Oh, one slip-up: it won't matter", he had thought. Repeatedly. Well obviously, it did matter. Thoughts ran through his head. Joy to have a child. Reassurance that surely this would bring her back to him when Ruth was ... gone. Confidence that he would have a prosperous family in the long term. Someone to inherit and develop their revolutionary plantation system.

"I will, of course, provide for both of you", was what he actually said. One more hug, mostly for the benefit of any onlookers, and then she turned to go back to the house and he strode down to the boat and was away.

*

" 'I wandered lonely as a cloud/ That floats on high o'er vales and hills/ When all at once I saw a crowd/ A host, of golden daffodils.' " Ruth was in a cheerful mood as she and Pickering walked together to her plantation at Brandy Wine Bay. This was one of her favourite estates, and as it was only a mile away from her house at Fort George she chose to walk. Riding was becoming rather painful these days.

"I used to love the daffodils each spring", she continued. "Here we don't really get seasons at all."

"Just perfect summer all the time!"

"You've not experienced a Caribbean hurricane yet."

Such a pleasant walk, with breathtaking views out to sea and across to the other islands. Ruth reached out for Pickering's hand, and held it tight as they walked, telling him about other poems by Wordsworth that had been in the collection she had just received. Pickering reflected on how delightful this day would have been, had it not been for the searing guilt he was feeling about betraying Mary. Temporarily. But a betrayal nevertheless. And how even more delightful it would have been had Mary been his companion.

They reached the Brandy Wine Bay plantation, and the white overseer greeted them and gave them a tour. Jeremiah Smith was an ambitious young man, enthusiastic about the latest technical innovations in sugar production and estate management. He showed them meticulously compiled records and accounts, and explained that he had taught one of the young enslaved women how to maintain them. He then called Esther in and introduced her to the visitors. She confidently explained her elaborate systems for tracking the workers, the equipment, the sugar and the cash. Pickering was most impressed with both of them, and with the collaborative manner in which they worked, based on mutual respect rather than deference of servant to master. There would surely be key roles for both of them within the new structure to be devised.

On the way back, he told Ruth of his visit from Perreen and of the cruelties she had described. Ruth was shocked at the intensity of mistreatment, but again counselled against acting hastily.

"There'll be a new governor for the Leeward Islands soon, and there's talk it might be Hugh Elliot. He's a keen abolitionist, and someone who could stand up to the planters. We've got the Amelioration Act, but so far no-one's prepared to enforce it. That may change."

“But how long will it take? The situation at Belleview sounds desperate, and Perreen fears for the health of Ann Hodge.”

“At the moment Thomasson and his clique hold all the power on the island. They’re good friends with Hodge and they’ll take no action. But they know change is coming. Thomasson will have to answer to the new governor.”

Pickering was frustrated by this answer. Having seen and heard Perreen tell her harrowing story, and aware of how frightened she had been, he was impatient to take action against Hodge. He was also still distressed by the cruelty he had witnessed himself. However, he bit his tongue. His fiancée was surely right. A good chance of success in a few months’ time would surely be better than risking failure by acting too soon.

Ruth changed the subject: “Meanwhile, the announcement of our engagement will be sent out tomorrow. It’s all getting very close!”

*

Letters and parcels from England had been delayed by storms and by hostilities with the French. Those arriving in early August had been in transit for over twelve weeks, almost twice the usual passage time. As well as poetry books for Ruth, the cargo included two of the letters John had written at the end of April. Mary picked up the one addressed to Little Jost van Dyke at Road Town Harbour while out buying the supplies that Pickering had been in the habit of bringing over. She was worried immediately, as there was only a letter. Usually John’s letters were part of a parcel including a few gifts and treats. She took it, unopened, straight back to her mother.

The letter started pleasantly enough. John had been delighted to learn of Pickering’s safe passage to Tortola and of the warm welcome he had received on Little Jost van Dyke. His son’s description of the island, the house, and above all of the inhabitants, had made him feel as if he too had come home. He had been delighted to read that he had found her, Teresa, looking so well. It was clear that her daughter, Mary, had grown up to be a delightful young woman – a credit to her mother. He was indebted to both of them for the hospitality afforded to Pickering, and gratified that his purchase of Little Jost had allowed them to flourish there.

"When we spoke together, all those years ago", the letter continued, "you accepted that it would be impossible for you to come to England with me as my wife. I was foolishly stubborn in dreaming that it might be feasible, but you were the realistic one, aware that I could not both have a black wife and become a leading London doctor. You also dismissed the possibility of accompanying me as my exotic mistress – not that I ever entertained such a notion! You were so wise and so right. Instead, I married for money and position, and have never enjoyed the same warm affection that we shared with anyone else. You served my mother so faithfully, and have now raised a wonderful daughter. But society has not changed, and I do not think it ever will.

"From his letter, it is clear that Pickering is very taken with Mary. I recognise the feelings he expresses, for I felt them myself. But this must go no further. Your wisdom must once more prevail. Even more than for myself, who was just a poor, unknown planter's son, Pickering cannot come home with a wife of mixed race. He is now part of a family that I have been able to establish within society. He has a distinguished legal career yet to carve out. He will be moving in the highest circles. He will need a wife who understands these things and adds her own social lustre to his talents. Nor would either of us wish our children to embark on an adulterous relationship.

"Teresa, my oldest friend, my one-time love, I beseech you to put a stop to it now. Forbid them from meeting. Explain to Mary the sacrifice that you made, and that she now must make. If she has any regard for my son, she will not wish to be the one who holds him back and prevents him from realising his potential. She will surely find a more suitable partner for her life amongst the growing community of free people of colour on the island.

"Teresa, your beauty and wisdom has graced this world for over sixty years now. In the next world, would that you appear as white as any European and thus able to progress unimpeded to the station in life that you truly deserve."

Teresa stopped reading. She was in tears. All that time ago, she had been strong, she had been wise, she had been right. But could he not have said, "I care not about any of that Teresa, I love you and I must marry you"? She had always thought, somewhere in his heart, he regretted not having had the courage to say so. Now, he had cut the last thread that had seemed to unite them. He had done so by repudiating that which was the most precious of all to her: her daughter.

Mary picked up the letter, and Teresa made no attempt to prevent her from reading it. Her reaction was anger. Rage! Why could he not have written: "In the next world, would that it matters not whether you are black or white at all"? Pickering must have received such a letter earlier. Must have been acting on instruction. He did love her, but his father would not permit it. A more comforting belief, perhaps, than a simple rejection.

*

It was on the following day that Pickering collected his letter. He had been busy with his legal duties but, aware that Ruth had just received her package of poetry books, he made time to visit the harbour and check for any post.

The letter from his father, like that received by Teresa, started pleasantly enough. Indeed, the same sentiments about being delighted that his son had now seen the island on which he had been born and met one of his oldest friends were repeated from a different perspective. Then the tone changed.

"As you have often heard me say, I despise the institution of slavery. I set free my own slaves as soon as I landed back on Little Jost van Dyke, although I could hardly afford to do so. Now my advice to a slave owner would be to proceed more slowly, perhaps allowing a slave freedom to earn for himself on one day per week, then two, and so on. That would give him time to develop the virtues of industry and thrift and to avoid the lure of licentiousness. Or to follow the example of Count Bernstorff, of whom you have often heard me speak, granting freed workers tools, training and land and the opportunity to work with their master voluntarily to create a prosperous estate."

"Good", thought Pickering: "exactly what we intend to do."

"However, as I have got older, raised my own dear children, and learnt more about the outstanding achievements of our European culture, science, medicine and philosophy, I have become more and more concerned about the preservation of our own race and civilisation. I would not wish that the blood of Whites becomes contaminated with that of the Blacks. Although this has already happened to some extent in the West Indies, such mixing will ultimately cease because the issue of such unions will eventually assume the character of mules and cease to breed. The black tinge will then become extinct over the generations as long as no further importation of Africans takes place."

Pickering slammed the letter down, crying out: "What! Mules! How dare you? I never, ever believed that that's what you thought. Free the slaves, you said. Treat them kindly, you said. They can be sensitive, intelligent and genteel. Give them land and tools and they will repay the investment. That's what you said. Never 'mules', never 'contaminators'. You never said that to your children. Stop the slave trade to protect the white race: was that your cause all along? You're not even right about the biology, Dr Lettsom!" Realising that he could be heard from the street outside his Road Town lodging, he stopped shouting and sat down. Then he rose, poured himself a large brandy, and sat down again. He could guess where the letter was going next.

"Your letter dwelt at length on how delightful you found Mary, and what a fine young woman she is. I am pleased to learn that Teresa's daughter has turned out so well. You have spent some pleasant days with her. Now is the time to turn your attention to the daughters of the wealthy settlers, or to bury yourself in your work and come back with a fortune, ready to make a good society match here in London. You cannot return with a mulatto bride, much less with such a woman as a mistress. Due to my unceasing labours these past forty years, our family now has a position to uphold. Your nephew Nanson has just started at Eton College: imagine the gossip that would spread were you to make an unsuitable union. For all our sakes, you must see no more of Mary. I forbid it."

Pickering poured himself a second brandy. He felt an enormous sense of loss. Not the loss of Mary: he was more determined than ever to follow his plan through to the end and to realise his long-term dreams together with her, their child, their family. His loss was of his father. The man he had imagined him to be. The man who had taught him beliefs which it now emerged he did not share.

*

At the same time as Pickering was reading his father's letter, Teresa was drafting her reply. She omitted her usual round up of news from Little Jost and from Tortola. Nor did she mention

Pickering's break from Mary and engagement to Ruth, an act of betrayal that had shocked her even more than it had hurt her daughter. Instead, she went straight to the heart of the matter.

"All of these years I have looked forward to receiving your letters and your presents, and enjoyed composing my replies and selecting shells and sweets and other treats to send to you. Our relationship has been, in my own mind, frozen in the place where we left it forty years ago. Or even, as it had been when we were small children together. I rejoiced to read of the advancements you made in your career: these appeared to vindicate my determination that you return to England unencumbered by a black companion. Throughout this time I nursed the belief that, had things been different, you would have been proud to live your life with me by your side.

"Now I find that such domestic bliss was, in your mind, reserved for another life. And only if I was no longer Teresa, but some woman with a pure white skin who perhaps looked a little bit like Teresa. Now that a perfect union is at last possible in the next generation, you conclude that we are, after all, beneath you. You did have your mark to make, and I would indeed have held you back. Pickering is, thanks to your efforts, already established in society. That makes him free to make his own choices. I shall not stand in the way of Pickering and Mary's developing friendship. I shall support them if it leads to love, marriage and family. It appears that Pickering has more determination to follow his heart than you did at his age, and I admire him for it."

She read it over, and decided that it was complete in itself. There was nothing to add. She did not look for any presents to send with it. She was no longer tearful. Perhaps she was more free than she had ever been. She sat down once more, as she always did, and copied the letter out again neatly and without evidence of her initial poor choices of words or errors in spelling and grammar. She then gave it to Nanny to take to the dock in

Road Harbour. The ship that had brought the post was still there undergoing repairs to damage suffered on the outward voyage, but it would be setting off back to England soon.

CHAPTER 34

When Pickering arrived at Banger's Bay to tell Ruth of his father's letter, he found her sitting at a table pulled up to a window in the lounge to allow the full strength of the daylight to fall upon it. She was making drawings in Indian ink, another of her many accomplishments. A completed picture showed a smiling black woman cutting sugar cane, while she was putting the finishing touches to a second of a laughing black man holding a bottle of rum in one hand and offering the viewer a glass of the same with the other. The first was entitled "Mount Healthy Sugar" and the second "Shark's Bay Rum". Both carried the inscription: "Produced on the Island of Tortola by free men and women – not by slaves".

"What do you think, dear? These are for our trade cards, to be distributed to customers in England in support of our sugar and our rum. During the sugar boycott half a million people stopped buying West Indian sugar. Some turned to supplies from India, but that's not a patch on ours! If everyone who wants to end slavery completely buys our sugar we'll have a formidable position. Might even be able to charge more to salve their consciences."

"But we don't distil our rum at Shark's Bay."

"No. But it has a better ring to it than 'Banger's Bay Rum'! "

"I think they're most artistic and persuasive." Pickering paused. Then he proceeded to the main purpose of his visit: "I've received a letter from my father that I'd like you to read."

Ruth completed a few of the trees in the background of her picture and then carefully laid down her pen and took up the letter. As soon as she had finished reading, Pickering began his rant against his father. Once that storm had subsided, he sat down and awaited her reply. She thought for some time before she gave it.

"Your father is a good man, we both know that", she began. "His father was a kind and considerate slave owner, in the Quaker tradition. Your father went beyond that. He freed his own slaves and campaigned to abolish the trade. Now you're committed to going further still, to work with our freed slaves in partnership, live amongst them and marry Mary.

"Each generation takes the process further than the one before. You should be grateful and respectful to your father for starting you off with such a compassionate outlook. If you're prepared to do more, then that's to your credit. He could look back on his father as just an evil slave owner who lived by exploiting his workers, but I'm sure he remembers him more fondly and realises his own views derive from the start that he was given. You must do the same. Don't forget that your own son might one day look back at you as being too traditional and selfish."

Pickering enjoyed Ruth's generous anticipation of him and Mary having a son. "I don't see how it would be possible to go further than we intend."

"Oh no? We intend to retain ownership of the refinery and the distillery. To buy sugar from our free workers. But we will maintain control over exporting finished products to England. You will still be far richer than them."

"They'll need our connections and expertise. We could do no more."

Ruth smiled. "Your son might say: 'Why not give all the workers shares in the refinery and distillery? Why should you be any richer than they are? Why not allow them to vote on who will be in charge? Why should it always be you?' "

"Do you think that's what we should do?"

Ruth smiled. "I was teasing! I agree with you. They will need our expertise and experience. You'll have a position to maintain, and Mary and your children will deserve a comfortable life. I'm merely saying the job of emancipation is never finished, and that future generations may not see our actions as being as revolutionary as we do."

Ruth may have been teasing, but Pickering took the questions she had attributed to his future son to heart. They reminded him of a conversation with his father when he was about twelve years old. "If all the money now available in England were to be shared equally", his father had told him, "each person would be in possession of forty-five shillings". Pickering had been intrigued by this calculation, and had at once suggested their family give up everything they had except for forty-five shillings each. His father had laughed that off, just as Ruth was laughing at him now. He had explained that, because he clearly possessed more than forty-five shillings, he felt he had to do whatever he could each day to make amends through his medicine and his charity. At the time Pickering had been satisfied by that answer, combining as it did a duty to perform good works with acceptance of a privileged place in society. But how would he react were a son of his to argue for equal shares for all?

"Write to your father", Ruth advised, bringing her fiancé's ruminations to a close. "Admit that you cannot accept his views about white and black people and respectfully question the scientific evidence. Tell him of our forthcoming marriage. Later, you'll be able to write to him about our plans for the estate and our reliance on him should anything happen to you. I still think he's the best, probably the only, person to be entrusted with inheriting our ambitions. Later still, as a rich and successful businessman you'll be able to inform him of your second marriage and of his grandchild. His heart will melt: I guarantee it!"

*

The wedding took place at St George's church in Road Town, and it was a very small affair. A violent storm had hit the island the day before, and on the wedding day itself the wind remained strong and the rain was teeming down. Postponement was discussed, but quickly dismissed as Ruth's strength was fading by the week and her pain was increasing. She bore it that day, as she wished to experience every last detail of her second wedding day and not allow it to pass in a drug-induced haze.

Ruth's son-in-law, Charles Combe was to have served as Pickering's best man. They had met a couple of times at Banger's Bay, although they had not formed any sort of friendship. Just before the storm began, a messenger brought the news that Charles had been struck down by a fever and had taken to his bed. Ruth's daughter, Frances, felt the need to be at his side constantly so she could not come either. Hurriedly, Pickering sent for Jeremiah, the overseer at Brandy Wine Bay who had impressed him so much, and asked him to officiate. It struck him how few men he had found on the island whom he felt able to trust with such a role. A few of Ruth's family and friends from Road Town braved the weather to attend and her physician, Dr West, gave her away. Apart from Pickering, he was the only one who understood just how much support she would need when walking down the aisle.

Despite the storm, despite the small company, it was a truly happy day. Ruth was quite content to have secured the realisation of her dreams for her estates and a gentle and understanding companion with whom to spend her final days. Pickering felt admiration, respect, and indeed love for his wife. The congregation sang enthusiastically, and congratulated the couple sincerely. Outside, soaking wet in the rain, Judith, Ebenezer from the Mount Healthy estate, and Esther from the Brandy Wine estate were among a small group of Ruth's enslaved workers who gave a genuine and heartfelt cheer when they emerged from the church. Afterwards, speeches were short but amusing, the food was warming, and the wine and rum inexhaustible. Eventually, only Ruth, Pickering and Dr West remained. The doctor administered the laudanum that was long overdue, and Pickering helped her into her bed, exhausted.

*

A couple of days after the wedding, when dry, sunny weather had returned to the island, Pickering set out to inspect the effects of the storm on the previously disputed patch of land north of the Hodge plantation. There was no longer any permanent habitation in that area. Some abandoned slave cabins were being used for storage, and they had been due for urgent repair even before the storm. Pickering was to meet Jeremiah from the Brandy Wine Bay plantation there to assess any damage.

Ruth's pain was particularly bad that morning, and her husband spent a considerable time ministering to her needs before setting off. He sent Moses, who usually acted as Ruth's messenger, to summon Dr West. As Moses was also the slave who usually ran with him when he toured Ruth's estates, he set off alone. The rain had washed away sections of the path and turned others into quagmires. It was past midday by the time he finally arrived at the meeting point. He dismounted, and had a quick look around. The hoof prints of Jeremiah's horse were visible, together with the footprints of his accompanying runner, but they had already gone.

"Oh ho! Who's this on my land then?"

Pickering turned round to see Arthur Hodge emerge from one of the buildings, which had indeed been badly damaged. With him were McKeough and Bernardo, whom he had last seen torturing a man with a red hot poker.

"Not your land, but ours, as I demonstrated to you the other day."

" 'Our' land already, is it? Well I don't accept your so-called proof. I've been consulting my lawyers, and they're preparing a counter-claim. In the meantime, you've been neglecting things here. These buildings need repair. We might convert them back to cabins soon. So go away and tell your good wife that we have it all under control and that she need not worry about this little patch of land again."

Pickering stood his ground, unsure what to do next. Hodge made a slow circuit of the buildings, pointing out to Bernardo what repairs needed to be done. Having completed his round, Hodge returned his attention to Pickering.

"Still here. I thought I told you to go. Be off! Get off my land!"

Pickering did not move. It was not bravery. It was not fear. It was indecision.

"So, if you won't go, let's fight for it! The winner can have this land. What could be fairer than that? Pistols or swords? You know I'm the best shot on the island by far. So, I'll be sporting and face you with my sword."

Hodge drew his sword. Pickering realised that he must have been seen setting out in this direction from Banger's Bay, and that Hodge had come up quickly by a route less damaged by the rain, prepared for a confrontation. McKeough also had a sword, which he offered to Pickering.

"You told me you're not a Quaker, didn't you? You're a man of honour. Now show it."

Pickering still hesitated. He remembered his training with the Camberwell Volunteers, and being acclaimed the best swordsman in the company. He contemplated his duty as a husband to protect his wife's interests and honour. He reflected on the amazing chain of events that had occurred since he landed on Tortola: here anything seemed possible. So, he took the sword and felt the weight and the balance of it. It was well maintained and very sharp. Maybe he could do this.

Hodge chose a fairly flat and uncluttered patch of land, and announced that McKeough would be his second and Bernardo would be Pickering's. Both contestants removed their jackets and entrusted them to their seconds.

"En garde!" warned Hodge, and made a lunge at Pickering, which the latter easily parried. Now Pickering slashed down at his opponent, who dodged just in time to save his head but not quickly enough to avoid the slicing open of his ear.

"Perhaps I can do this!" muttered Pickering, feeling a sense of euphoria which was immediately ended by an excruciating pain in his sword arm. Hodge had managed to thrust his weapon clear through Pickering's upper arm. There was much blood and unbearable nausea. Pickering dropped his weapon, swayed and half sat down and half fell down. His second now stood in front of him to protect him from another blow, ripped the shirt sleeve off his uninjured arm, and used that to apply a tight tourniquet above his wound. He raised the injured arm above his head and held it in place.

"Do you concede?" bellowed Hodge. Pickering had fainted.

"My man concedes," replied Bernardo.

"Let's go!" ordered Hodge. "Leave him!"

However, when the party from Belle Vue left, Bernardo stayed behind to watch over his charge. He would lose some of his standing with his master as a result, perhaps take a beating, but he knew he was indispensible to Hodge. Eventually, Pickering's bleeding stopped and he regained consciousness. After an hour, Bernardo carefully lifted him onto his horse and slowly led him down to Banger's Bay. Twice during that painful journey Pickering fell off his mount into the mud and had to be lifted back.

*

Once back at Ruth's plantation house, Pickering was taken to his bed and ministered to by Judith and several of Ruth's other house slaves. Ruth was not at home. When Moses had reached Dr West's home, he had been told that the doctor was away attending to Ruth's son-in-law Charles, whose fever had taken a severe turn for the worse. Feeling a little better by then, Ruth immediately got Moses to take her round to her daughter's by boat. Now, Dr West's apprentice was summoned, and he put in some stitches to close Pickering's wound and advised quiet, rest and continued elevation of the arm.

Bernardo returned to Belle Vue, where he found his master in a magnanimous mood. He praised his slave for understanding the role of a second and for embodying the chivalrous nature of duelling, thanked him for ensuring that the wounded man got home safely, and expressed the hope that Pickering would soon make a full recovery. He felt that the matter of the disputed land had now been settled in a most honourable and appropriate way.

After five days, Pickering began to recover. His appetite came back. The bleeding stopped. He gained strength and began to walk around the house and in the grounds outside where he relished the fresh air. His only complaint was that the skin around the wound was swollen and felt unnaturally warm. On the sixth day, Ruth returned accompanied by her daughter Frances and by Dr West. Charles had deteriorated, and despite West's best efforts of sweating and bleeding his patient, had eventually died. Frances was distraught and Ruth exhausted and in great pain. The doctor had returned with Ruth to advise on her care and treatment, only to find he had a new patient to tend to.

As soon as the bandage was removed, it was evident that something was wrong. It was the rotten smell. The flesh had swollen and the bandages were covered in yellow and green discharge. Had the wound been thoroughly washed? How often had the dressing been changed? Judith admitted that they may not have cleaned the wound so thoroughly and that the dressing had not been changed since it had been applied. West removed the stitches, drained the pus from the swelling and applied liberal amounts of alcohol over the whole wound. He completed his own neat stitches and tidy bandaging and instructed that he should be sent for immediately if the patient deteriorated before he returned to change the dressing in three days' time.

For several days, the Banger's Bay plantation house resembled a cottage hospital. Frances was sick with grief, Ruth brought low with pain, and Pickering suffering from aches and pains that were no longer confined to his arm. After the doctor's first return visit, all three invalids made a determined effort and attended Charles's burial. They were greatly relieved to return to their beds afterwards. Frances was the first to recover properly, realising that although she was grieving she was not actually ill. She was fit enough to tend to the others, and that provided distraction and satisfaction for her. Then Ruth entered one of the better phases of her disease, and began to attend once more to the business of her estate and to engage with Pickering about their longer term plans for its transformation in the belief that such thoughts would help revive him.

They did not. He developed a fever, although he felt cold and despite the heat of his room he was shivering violently. He found it difficult to concentrate and even to stay awake. His wound was now throbbing and felt as if it was on fire. He was pale and his whole body was aching. This time, when Dr West visited, he warned Ruth that Pickering might not recover.

*

"Oh my goodness, he does look poorly!" exclaimed Teresa when she entered the sickroom. "How long's he been like this?"

"Four weeks now", replied Ruth. "It was just after the wedding. He was going to inspect storm damage on one of our properties. He fell from his horse and impaled his arm on a broken tree trunk. It's become horribly infected."

This was the story now. Ruth and Frances knew about the duel, but it was best to keep such matters quiet. Bernardo had visited to enquire about Pickering's wellbeing, and spoken at length to Ruth and Frances about the circumstances of the injury. The victor was not talking about it: he liked people to know that he was formidable in a fight, but was less keen to reveal the names of his victims.

Pickering was asleep. Realising that the end was close, Ruth had sent word to Little Jost. The anger at Pickering felt by Mary and Teresa had softened into resignation – this, after all, was the way of the world. Their commitment never to speak to the deceiver again melted as soon as they learnt that he was close to death. Mary sat down close to the bed and held his hand while tears started to stream down her face. Ruth did not object to their intimacy. She left the two women watching over him and returned to her paperwork.

"Is it you?" muttered Pickering, suddenly waking, his voice sounding frail.

"Yes Cotton, it's me, Mary. How are you feeling?" Both women were now bending over him.

"My love. My own sweet love. What happened? Where are we?" Then a pause, and a recollection. "How's our child?"

"Here my love." Mary stood and took Pickering's hand and placed it on her bump, which was now unmistakable. "Here he is. I'm sure it's a boy, he feels so strong and impatient to see the world."

For a time, all three of them forgot about his marriage to someone else. Here there were just two people in love, anticipating the joyous birth of their first child, watched over by a proud and supportive grandmother-to-be. They said very little. Just smiles, a couple of soft kisses, and some handholding and gentle caresses. Then suddenly, Pickering sat up straight.

"What about Ruth? Why are you here?"

"Ruth suggested that we come and see you", answered Teresa, as Mary was choked for words.

"She's alright then?"

"Yes, she's fine. She's looking forward to you getting better."

"Oh good", and then: "I do love you Mary, you know. We'll be happy together some day. You, me and the child. Girl or boy, I don't care. There will be more children!"

He held her hand more tightly now, staring straight into her eyes. Then: "I'm so tired. Thank you for coming to see me. Thank you." He fell back to sleep, breathing heavily.

"Did he talk to you about the future then?" asked Ruth as they prepared to depart.

"Oh yes, he was very positive", answered Teresa.

*

Pickering died a few days later. Ruth immediately sent Moses over to Little Jost to inform Teresa and Mary and let them know that the funeral would be held the following week. They were not invited to participate in the service. They stood outside the church and watched the coffin being carried in, and then being brought out again to be taken to Fat Hog Bay for burial in a grave close to that of the man for whom the deceased was named: John Pickering. Nanny, Judith, Bernardo, Perreen Georges, Ebenezer and Esther were also amongst the small crowd of black and mixed-race people paying their respects outside the church.

After the funeral, Dr Dawson – Dr West's predecessor, now retired – wrote to John Lettsom to inform him of his son's death. Ruth wrote to her son in London, telling him the same news. She also decided that it was time to acquaint him with her own illness, and the likelihood that she too would be gone within the next six months. In that letter she made no mention of her new will.

A couple of days later, following a bout of pain due to her illness, she wrote to John Lettsom. She told him of her distress to have lost such a wonderful life companion. She informed him of her own frailty. And she described the detailed plans that she and Pickering had developed for their plantations, and his impending inheritance of the estate and responsibility for its transformation. Her letter missed the ship that successfully carried the news from Dr Dawson and Ruth's message to her son. The next ship took Ruth's letter to John, but it was intercepted by the French off Newfoundland and sunk.

CHAPTER 35

Shortly after New Year's Day 1809, Teresa made another visit to Ruth at Banger's Bay. She was intrigued to have received an invitation, and could not guess what the purpose was. She knew that Ruth was gravely ill. She had appeared tired and drawn when Teresa and Mary had been over to see Pickering in his final days, and she had looked distinctly worse at his funeral. Now the gossip in Road Town was that she too would die soon, and a broken heart was the accepted popular diagnosis. Teresa was sufficiently experienced in the matter to know that, although a broken heart could be debilitating, it tended not to be fatal – especially in one with as much spirit as Ruth.

Once Judith had shown her to Ruth's bedchamber, a single look was sufficient to confirm how serious her condition was. This was not solely the effect of mental anguish. She had lost so much weight as to appear skeletal, and her skin was tight and jaundiced. She spoke slowly and softly, and Teresa had to sit close to her to hear properly.

"Thank you so much for coming. Is it only you today?"

"Yes. Mary is busy assessing the cotton, ahead of the harvest next month. It looks like another good year for us." In fact Mary had refused to come, finding all reminders of Pickering to be painful at this time.

"That's all right. I have something to give to her. I hope you can take it to her."

Ruth instructed Teresa to open a drawer in a bedside table and to take out a small wooden box.

"Open it", she instructed.

Inside was a folded silver frame for a miniature portrait. Unfolding it revealed a perfect likeness of Pickering executed in Indian ink on one side, and a neatly inscribed verse on the other: "Shall I compare thee to a summer's day? Thou art more lovely and more temperate."

"Oh, it's just like him! It's really beautiful. And the words are so loving. Such neat and tiny writing. Did you do this?"

"I drew the picture. It's one of my hobbies. He was going to draw a picture of me for the other side, but he was dissatisfied by all his efforts. So he wrote the poem instead."

"I remember: he once told us what an English summer was like. He hadn't realised that we don't have them here – or rather that it's summer all the time. You must have been so happy to read his words."

"Well, not his words actually. It's a well known sonnet. And I don't think it was me he was thinking of when he chose them either."

"Oh, surely he must have been. Anyway, you can't give that away."

"We made several of them, with his head at different angles and with different poems." Ruth now looked straight into Teresa's eyes, and continued with her voice rising almost to its normal level. "I do want Mary to have this. Her child will then see its father, and will know how much he loved its mother."

Silently, Teresa picked up the frame, folded it, and put it back into its box which she clasped tightly in her hands.

"I'm dying you know." This was spoken with such certainty and acceptance, that Teresa knew it would be no comfort to contradict. "So much death. My son-in-law Charles, then Pickering, now me."

Ruth had been sitting up, but now she appeared to be exhausted and she sank back upon the bed and was quiet. Teresa prepared to leave.

"No, don't go yet. Tell me of things at Little Jost van Dyke."

"Well, as I said, the cotton crop's looking good this year. It could be our best since we moved back onto the island." Then she stopped and looked at the floor, before continuing: "It's likely to be our last crop too. I received a letter from Pickering's father. He's going to sell the island."

John's letter had been written in response to Teresa's last defiant message, and before he had learnt of his son's death. He expressed great disappointment that she did not see fit to end the liaison between their children, and was triumphant that Pickering had seemingly followed his advice and done so himself, and that he was now betrothed to the richest woman on the island. He denied that Teresa had ever been anything to him other than a childhood playmate and a loyal servant to his mother. The letter ended with his revelation that he intended to sell Little Jost, as he now had no son who would wish to inherit it.

"Surely any new owner will renew your tenancy", said Ruth. "You've been cultivating the land so efficiently."

"We were living on the island rent-free. We'll not be able to afford whatever a new owner would charge." Teresa turned her head away, hiding her tears. After she had composed herself, she rose again to make her exit.

"Wait!" said Ruth, firmly. "When Little Jost comes onto the market, I shall buy it. I shall then give the title to you."

Teresa opened her mouth to protest, but Ruth just talked over her.

"No. Don't argue! I'm a very rich woman, and this is a small gift for me to make. Pickering was so happy whenever he visited Little Jost. He would have wanted this. I shall make sure my agents arrange it, even if I'm no longer here when the island comes up for sale." She reached out and clasped Teresa's hand with both of hers. Then she let her depart.

A few days later, Ruth died. Breast cancer not being a disease usually mentioned in polite circles, Dr West suggested that the likely cause was grief following the sudden death of her new husband.

*

At Grove Hill in Camberwell, John Lettsom was once more in mourning. The news of Pickering's death hit him hard, and devastated Nancy. He had now lost two sons, one lived on despite enormous mental handicaps and the fourth had suffered financial ruin following his disastrous attempt to extend his tin-plating works in Wales. Only one of his four daughters remained alive. "My path seems to be over the ashes of my children!" he exclaimed to Nancy.

Since the death of John Miers ten years earlier, he had slowed down. His practice declined and his income shrank. His fortune was hit by underwriting Fothergill's foolish business gamble. His generosity to charitable causes remained undiminished and further eroded his wealth.

Another call on his purse was his grandson, William Nanson. Orphaned when his mother died just a year after John Meirs, Nanson was now the responsibility of John and Nancy. Nothing was too good for the boy. He was studying at Eton College, where it was proving expensive to ensure that he was kitted out just as well as – and then even better than – his aristocratic contemporaries. Notions of bringing him up as a devout and frugal Quaker had been swept aside. His passion for English and European literature was indulged, and his disdain for practical professions such as medicine, law or business went unchallenged. John had come to the conclusion that before long he would be forced to sell Grove Hill.

It was against this backdrop that, three months after hearing the news of the death of Pickering, John received another letter from Dr Dawson. This one informed him of Ruth's death. But in the same post was a letter from a lawyer on Tortola explaining that John was the principal beneficiary of his daughter-in-law's will. He was now the owner of nineteen sugar plantations, five sugar refineries, one rum distillery, a dozen plantation houses, and over one thousand enslaved Africans. The annual income from the estates amounted to more than ten thousand pounds.

There was, of course, a snag. Ruth's family intended to fight this bequest every inch of the way. Although Ruth's lawyer was confident that Lettsom's claim would prevail, it would probably take years to settle the matter. In the meantime he would administer the estates in a way that would preserve their value for whoever finally inherited them.

*

Two years later, John Lettsom noticed a report in *The Gentleman's Magazine*.

"On 8 May 1811 on the island of Tortola in the Virgin Islands", stated the article, "Arthur Hodge was hanged for the murder of his slave, Prosper."

John was amazed. He remembered treating that sadistic boy's arm, broken in retribution for a botched attempt to brand his new slave. And he remembered the ironic name Hodge had given to that boy slave who was a birthday present from his father – Prosper.

He read of the testimony given at Hodge's trial by Perreen Georges concerning the death of Prosper and the mistreatment and killing of other slaves on the Belle Vue Estate. The magazine reported that after nineteen hours of hearing evidence and three hours of deliberation, the jury found Hodge to be guilty as charged. The Governor, Hugh Elliot, rejected pleas for leniency and confirmed the death sentence.

On the evening before his execution, Hodge made his farewells to his three children, soon to be orphaned as their mother had already died. In the morning Hodge spent time praying with Methodist ministers. At noon he was hanged in the yard behind the prison building in Road Town. A crowd of about a thousand people assembled to see justice done, comprising stern-faced white settlers, euphoric free people of colour, and a large number of those who were still enslaved but nevertheless managed to attend. A stifled cheer went up as the murderer was dispatched, quickly suppressed as the watching militia momentarily raised their firearms. Then it was over.

The reports did not mention that it had been Pickering's account of Perreen George's testimony, found by Ruth's lawyer amongst her papers, that had furnished the white enemies of Hodge with the weapon to bring down their rival through the law rather than the sword or pistol.

*

Two further years elapsed before legal proceedings concerning Ruth and Pickering's wills were concluded, and John was able to claim his inheritance.

"Grandfather, now you've finally gained possession of Uncle Pickering's estates on Tortola, do you intend to set all the slaves free?" asked Nanson, back with his grandparents in London for the Easter break from Eton. The boy was now seventeen, in his penultimate year at the school and anxiously considering his future.

"Do you think I should?" asked John.

"Well, you've often told us that when you inherited your father's plantation, you set free the fifty slaves he'd left you, even though it left you penniless."

"That was a long time ago, and I had very little to lose in those days. But again, do you think that I should set them free?"

"Slavery is quite wrong and cruel, I'm sure of that. In time, it'll be abolished and we'll be rid of an evil system. But since Uncle Fothergill's business in Swansea collapsed and you had to bail him out, I know that money's been tight. You had to sell our lovely home at Grove Hill, and squeeze us all into this tiny London house. I do so want to go to Trinity College next year. I've set my heart on studying literature and writing my own poems."

"So, what should it be? Freedom for my slaves on Tortola, or the literary life for my favourite grandson? You're quite right: it cannot be both."

"Oh, that's such a horrible choice!"

"Your grandmother and I value your future happiness and success above anything else in this world. Certainly above considerations of people whom we've never met and who live so far away. In time, conditions in the colonies will improve. I'll find a professional and considerate overseer to manage the estates for us. Our slaves – for that's what they are as they'll pass to you along with all of the rest of the property on the island when I'm gone – our slaves will be well treated. In time all slaves will be emancipated and new ways of working will be found. So have no fears, my dearest boy, your future is secure and your conscience can be clear."

With that, Nanson left John's study, looking much happier. His grandfather was pleased to have reassured him. However, somewhere deeper in his soul he felt a twinge of disappointment. Was Nanson really convinced by that argument? He knew he would not have been at that age. The Lettsom family had certainly gained a great deal over time due to his efforts, but what had it lost?

On his bureau was a huge conch shell, a foot long with eleven whorls on its spire. It had rested there for so long, moving with him to every house he had ever owned, that he had quite forgotten about it. But after his conversation with Nanson, it caught his eye and he did remember. Remember, and reach out to hold it once more, and kiss it softly before carefully replacing it.

*

About three months after John's conversation with Nanson, three figures were walking in the sunshine along Sandy Beach on Little Jost van Dyke. These were Teresa, walking quite slowly these days; Mary, restraining her natural brisk pace to stay close to her mother; and her son, running ahead to the water's edge regardless. They had called him Edward Coakley, in memory of his great-grandfather. He was now four years old, fit, healthy and a source of both joy and exhaustion for his mother and grandmother.

"Let's sit here for a while and watch him paddle", said Teresa, sinking down onto a log washed up by the tide.

"Edward! Be careful, don't go in too deep", called Mary before she sat down too. It was a lovely, calm, warm day: a contrast to the previous stormy week that had brought flooding and wind damage to the island. Teresa wondered whether this was what an English summer's day would feel like.

"I've heard that Edward's grandfather has now been confirmed as the owner of all Ruth's estates."

"Will you write to him? Ask him for help?"

"No. We need no help. Thanks to Ruth's generosity, we own this island. There's nothing else I want or need. I've lived here nearly all of my life, and there's nowhere else that I would ever have wanted to be. When I die, which won't be long off now, promise me you'll bury me under the tamarind trees by the house."

Mary protested against Teresa's gloomy prediction, but her mother ignored her. She rose slowly and carefully and walked a few paces towards the sea. Then she squatted down and dug into the sand, rising again with a beautiful conch shell in her hands. She took her place again on the log, holding the shell on her lap.

"I have no regrets", she said. "If my time is near, I don't mind now. Bury me by the great-grandfather after whom our boy is named, and by his great-grandmother from whom you get your name." Teresa made no mention of the other Edward who had so insulted her when they last met, nor of the fourth body resting in that place. "Put this shell, and the best of my other conch shells, on my grave to mark the spot. The Quakers didn't like to decorate or commemorate their graves in any way, but let mine be fancy and colourful."

"Just like you!" laughed her daughter.

Young Edward now ran up to them: "A crab! A crab! It tried to nip me, but it couldn't catch me!" He flopped down in the sand, feigning exhaustion.

"Afterwards", continued Teresa, "you must take Edward and leave the island. Sell it. It'll fetch a pretty penny after all the improvements we've made. Take our savings too: they'll all be yours. Find work somewhere else, find a new life. You can read and write, do sums and keep accounts. You'll be able to find a good position."

"In Road Town?"

"Maybe. But there are other islands, you know. Antigua, Barbados, Jamaica. And the British are expanding their settlement of Trinidad too: capable, English-speaking clerks and bookkeepers will be in demand there. Edward should go to school. His cousin Nanson may be set to inherit the richest estates on Tortola, but our Edward has excellent prospects too. Promise me never to try to contact John or Nanson. You'll not need to, I am sure."

Mary promised, and then continued: "Mother, do you think that, had he lived, Pickering would have married me?"

"Yes, I do. He was so loving at the end. Ruth almost said as much when I went to visit her and she gave me that little picture. I think they both knew she was dying before they got married. And he would certainly have loved his son. Could you have forgiven him for marrying Ruth first? Would you have taken him back?"

"It would have been difficult, but I think so." Mary smiled at the thought of it.

"Can you forgive his father for trying to stop us seeing one another? For stopping writing to you and selling the island, and for writing that horrible thing about wishing you were white?"

"The last is the hardest thing to forgive. It's like he never understood who I really am." Teresa sighed. Then she turned her gaze from the distant horizon and looked her daughter directly in the eyes.

"He is a good man. So much better than the other Englishmen on the islands. He came a long way from how most of them think. I have to forgive him for not being able to shake off all of their beliefs."

Teresa broke off to attend to Edward who was investigating the damp seaweed attached to the underside of the log and getting his hands filthy. She picked him up and seated him on her knee.

"I could never forgive John's brother Ed for the way he treated me the last time I saw him. When I look back at the games we used to play, I can see me and Sam and John, but somehow Ed is no longer there. I can't really remember what he looked like."

Now Teresa was wiping her grandson's hands with a rag she carried for such eventualities and putting him down on the sand with a warning not to get dirty again.

“But John will always been with me”, she continued. “I look at Edward playing, and I see John as a boy. In my mind, I can still see him as the young doctor he was when he visited all those years ago. I’m still grateful for all the things he did for Sam and me. I’m too old to block him out of my memories like Ed. I’d have nothing left. I won’t start writing to him again, but I will continue to remember him fondly.

“In the end we both got what we really wanted. He got his brilliant medical career and I got my beloved island.”

The women rose. Mary took Edward’s hand and led him into the sea, where they jumped together, trying to avoid the crest of each wave as it came in. Teresa kicked off her sandals, and allowed the foam to cool her feet and to lap around her ankles. Then they set off to return to the house, where Nanny had started to prepare the goat stew. Teresa walked behind her daughter and grandson, and paused briefly to look back at the beach where so many of the best moments of her life, and her daughter’s, had taken place.

FACT AND FICTION

John Coakley Lettsom died on 1 November 1815 of septic poisoning, probably due to an infection acquired after performing a post-mortem a week earlier. Within two years of his death, his medical colleague Thomas Joseph Pettigrew had published the *Memoirs of the Life and Writings of the Late John Coakley Lettsom,* a work nowadays accessible online. The biographical account therein provides the essential facts of his life. His birth on Little Jost van Dyke in November 1744 is mentioned and his parents are briefly described. His voyage with Captain William "Lindo" to be received into the care of Abraham and "Hutton" Rawlinson in Lancaster is recorded, together with his meeting with Samuel Fothergill and his little dance for him. Details are given of his time at Penketh School, his move to Liverpool and his apprenticeship in Settle. There is a description of Lettsom's studies in London under Mark Akenside, and of his meeting with James "Beezley". His visit to Tortola in 1767–68 is recorded, his emancipation of "about 50 slaves" even though "he was not possessed of 50l. [£50] in the world", and his "amassing £2000, half of which he gave to his mother" through medical practice. A request to amputate the healthy leg of an enslaved African who was prone to running away is mentioned, but not the way in which the issue was resolved. The acquisition of a degree from "Leyden" University is mentioned, followed by an account of his rise within the medical profession. His marriage to Ann [Nancy] Miers, and the "very considerable fortune" it brought him, are described. His enthusiasm for treatment with Peruvian bark, his warnings of the dangers of drinking tea, and his role in founding the sea-bathing hospital in Margate are covered. Accounts are given of him treating the poor of London and publishing tracts lamenting the conditions in which they lived. The short life of his son, John Miers Lettsom, is documented, as is the move of Pickering Lettsom to Tortola, his marriage to Ruth Georges and their deaths, from "a fever" and from "grief" respectively, within a few months of their wedding. Mention is made of the eventual resolution of legal disputes that allowed Lettsom and his grandson to inherit his daughter-in-law's estates on Tortola, where "there were not less than 1000 slaves". Pettigrew himself attended Lettsom in his final illness, and he describes his funeral.

An especially valuable feature of Pettigrew's publication is the inclusion of about three hundred letters to and from John Lettsom. These relate to correspondence with medical colleagues and other worthy men of the day, but do not include any private exchanges with family. A few of these letters have been important for the development of this book. Letter XXVI to Dr William Cuming, dated 14 October 1784 is crucial to the plot, and so deserves quoting from at some length. It refers to an enclosed gift as follows. "This little trifle of sweetmeats is the present of Teresa, a beautiful mulatto of mine. She has long hair; is a brunette, but has such a pleasing and fine eye, and such symmetry of shape, that many West Indians would have placed her at the head of a black seraglio. I, however, never had a seraglio; and Teresa, though probably proud to have shared the favours of her master, never influenced his passions." The letter concludes: "Poor Teresa! thou little thinkest how much thy master values thy present. He will probably never see thee in this world! In the next thou mayest appear white as an European, and happy as him who has said 'Be free.' " The recipient of this letter had been a close friend of John Fothergill. Lettsom's correspondence with him began soon after

Fothergill's death, and continued until Cuming's own death in 1788, but the two never met in person until that final year. Letter XXVII, written to Cuming the following month reveals that, "Sam's hair was curled, Teresa's is fine long flowing hair like that of a Seapoy's: Teresa is handsome, and Sam was extremely genteel." It also tells of Sam's service on Tortola, his christening as "Sam Coakley" by "Mr Townley, head-master of Merchant Taylors' ", his role as a steward on "a King's ship", his death by drowning and the dispute over his will. Letter XII to Cuming, dated 31 May 1783, contains the calculation that "if all the money in the English European dominions were equally divided, each person would possess about forty-five shillings", and his consequent duty as the holder of more than that sum to disperse some of it to those who have less. Letter XXIX, dated 1 December 1784, mentions that fourteen years previously Lettsom had been to see Garrick in King Lear. Letter LXXXV to Sir Mordaunt Martin, dated 4 April 1791 expresses caution about the sudden freeing of slaves and the need to avoid their descent into licentiousness, while Letter CCXCII to Rev. J Madison mentions Lettsom's belief that the issue of mixed-race unions eventually "assumes the character of mules". The same letter also contains an approving account of the way in which Count Bernstorff of Denmark liberated his serfs.

The most substantial publication concerning John Lettsom is *Lettsom: His Life, Time, Friends and Descendants* by James Johnston Abraham, published by Heinemann in 1933. This is a detailed work of nearly 500 large-format pages complete with many illustrations, and as the title promises it provides insight not only into the life of the man himself but also into those of friends, colleagues and descendants. Much is taken from Pettigrew's volume but Abraham, while adopting a respectful and admiring tone, does include some questioning of the earlier account and some criticism of his subject. He includes a facsimile of Samuel Taine's inventory of eight enslaved people inherited by Lettsom from his father, giving the names used for them in this book, a classification by gender and by old/young/child, and a value in pounds (from £100 for Bentorah to £9 each for the children Myal and Cotto – the online Bank of England inflation calculator converts £100 in 1760 to £16,000 in 2023). The Deed of Sale of Sam and Teresa from Taine to Lettsom is transcribed. He notes that the letters "MD" after Lettsom's name on the latter document were lightly scratched through. He includes a letter from Lettsom dated 4 September 1782 formally freeing Teresa "together with [her] former and future issue and increase", and another freeing three women and their five children, dated 1792. Teresa's freedom was finally registered in Tortola on 19 May, 1785. He quotes at length from *The Diary of Betty Fothergill,* a handwritten journal covering her stay in London in 1769–70 which is held by the Library of the Society of Friends in London. This describes trips to the Queen's zoo, the Guildhall to watch the lottery being drawn, St Paul's Cathedral and the Tower of London. Curtis's demonstration of his electrical machine is mentioned, and some unspecified trick played on Lettsom is alluded to. An intimate conversation with Lettsom, during which he mentioned "his affair with the Tortolan Dame", is recorded. Abraham's book gives the full guest list of Lettsom's wedding. He provides great deal of detail about Lettsom's medical achievements, his interests in natural history and his charitable activities, although nothing is included about his support for the abolitionist movement. A chapter on Grove Hill describes the house and grounds, Lettsom's neighbour Henry Smith, the drilling of the Camberwell Volunteers, lavish entertaining in the grounds and visits to the house by James Boswell. The final chapter provides accounts of John Meirs Lettsom, Fothergill Lettsom and Pickering Lettsom. In an appendix are given various versions of the contemporary rhyme which is included at the beginning of this book.

An archaeological excavation of the Lettsom house on Tortola is described by John Martin Chenoweth in his PhD thesis, *Religion, Archaeology, and Social Relations: A Study of the Practice of Quakerism and Caribbean Slavery in the Eighteenth-Century British Virgin Islands* submitted to the University of California, Berkeley in 2011. He describes where buildings and fields were positioned on Little Jost van Dyke in the eighteenth century and lists finds including a wide variety of shells, a triton (or *Charonia variegate*) shell "hollowed out from below as if to contain something", the skin of a racer snake, "a copper-alloy butt-plate to a rifle or musket", and many shards of "Delft" pottery. At least five human graves were found under the tamarind trees close to the house and amongst them were numerous conch shells. Chenoweth's background material includes mention of Lettsom's Uncle John being criticised by the Quakers for excessive drinking in 1747 and also of the origins of William Thornton's engraving of the Lettsom house on Tortola that forms the basis of the front cover of this book.

Tortola: A Quaker Experiment of Long Ago in the Tropics by Charles F. Jenkins (1923) provides general background information about the Society on the island. The lives of John Pickering and William Thornton are described, as well as that of Lettsom. He mentions that Phoebe Smith and Mary Evans visited Tortola from Pennsylvania to preach in 1750, and provides information about Samuel and Mary Nottingham. Appendices include lists of the adult members of the Society and dates of their births, marriages and deaths. The whole book is available online.

The life and death of Arthur Hodge is presented by John Andrew in *The Hanging of Arthur Hodge: A Caribbean Anti-slavery Milestone* (2000). The book includes the catalogue of atrocities presented at his trial by Perreen Georges, Stephen McKeough and others. These crimes are also listed in a transcript of the trial itself, available on the website of the Library of Congress.

The Story of Quakerism 1652–1952 by Elfrida Vipont and Elizabeth Cazden's article on "Quakers, slavery, anti-slavery, and race" in *The Oxford Handbook of Quaker Studies* (2013), provided background information for dialogue concerning religion. The life of Mary Fisher is described in "Mary Fisher: Maidservant Turned Prophet" by Marcelle Martin in the online publication *Friends Journal* of February 2008, while *The Fearless Benjamin Lay* (2017) by Marcus Rediker describes the preaching and activism of that early abolitionist. Nancy Hornick's article "Anthony Benezet and the Africans' School: Toward a Theory of Full Equality" in *The Pennsylvania Magazine of History and Biography* (1975) provides biographical details of the educator.

Isaac Pickering's map of Tortola, dated 1798, available in the online digital collection of The Huntington Library, locates the position, boundaries and ownership of every plantation on the island. Angel Smith, in his University of Hull PhD thesis *An Anatomy of a Slave Society in Transition: The Virgin Islands, 1807–1864* (2011, available online) provides helpful historical and demographic information about Tortola in general and Ruth Georges' estates in particular. In *Capital in the Twenty-first Century*, Thomas Piketty (2014, pp105, 106 & 207) explains how stable the value of money was during the eighteenth century. He puts average earnings in England at £30 pa. A fortune of £20,000 would yield an annual income of about £1,000 and would allow one to "live comfortably and elegantly, secure proper transportation and clothing, eat well, and find amusement and a necessary minimum of domestic servants". The average wealth in England of forty-five shillings (£2.25) per head mentioned in Chapter 34 and Lettsom's Letter XII is likely to be an underestimate. Table I of "Unequal English wealth since 1670" by Peter Lindert in the *Journal of Political Economy* (1986) implies an average of about

£70 for men in 1782 in contemporary pounds – thus maybe £25 per person (men, women and children).

Samuel Martin's agricultural approach is described by R.B. Sheridan in "Samuel Martin, innovating sugar planter of Antigua, 1750–1776", *Agricultural History,* (1960). Mike Dash describes the murder in 1701 (1697 according to Sheridan) of Martin's father in "Antigua's Disputed Slave Conspiracy of 1736: Does the evidence against these 44 slaves really stack up?" in the online *Smithsonian Magazine* (2013). The Townley map of Lancaster, dated 1684 and the subsequent Mackreth map of 1778, both available online, provide a guide to the appearance of the town at the time of Lettsom's visit. In 1779, 28 years after Lettsom's stay in Lancaster, Abraham Rawlinson and his son Henry were rebuked by the Lancaster Monthly Meeting for taking out Letters of Marque (FRL 2/1/5/72 Lancashire Archive). This meant they were engaged in privateering (licensed piracy) which would involve carrying guns on their ships. The online Slave Voyages database lists three slave voyages from Liverpool of the *Clayton* between 1749 and 1752, owned in part by someone called Abraham Rawlinson, with between 4 and 16 guns mounted. In *Edmund Burke and the British Empire in the West Indies* (2019), P. J. Marshall explicitly links the owner of the *Clayton* with "Abraham Rawlinson, a Lancaster merchant".

Several biographies of Mark Akenside are given on the website *Spenser and the Tradition: English Poetry 1579–1830,* compiled by David Radcliffe of Virginia Tech. These include the 1779 essay by Dr Johnson and a long and informative piece by Alexander Dyce (1835). The incidents on the ward, including the death of the patient who could not swallow willow bark, are described on p39 of Abraham's biography, quoting from Lettsom's own writings. (Incidently, willow bark is related to aspirin while Peruvian bark contains quinine.) Akenside describes his use of ipecacoanha in a paper in *Medical Transactions,* 1768. Borelli's refutation of the theory of animal spirits is described by M. H. Pope in "Giovanni Alfonso Borelli – the father of biomechanics", *Spine* (2005). Joseph Kett describes the role of "men midwives" in "Provincial Medical Practice in England 1730–1815", *Journal of the History of Medicine and Allied Sciences* (1964).

Miers and Kopytoff explain that in Africa "the opposite of slavery is not freedom, it's belonging" in "African 'slavery' as an institution of marginality", an article in the book *Slavery in Africa. Historical and Anthropological Perspectives,* which they edited in 1977. Holly Norton provides the story of the St Jan insurrection in *Estate by Estate: The Landscape of the 1733 St. Jan Slave Rebellion,* a 2013 dissertation for Syracuse University that is available online.

The Natural History of the Tea-Tree, with Observations on the Medical Qualities of Tea, and Effects of Tea-Drinking by John Lettsom was placed online in 2015 by Cambridge University Press. "Ann Fothergill: The Mistress of Harpur Street", by Christopher Booth, *Proceedings of the American Philosophical Society* (1978) provides insight into her character. James and Ann Freeman are referred to in "Thomas Parke's Student Life in England and Scotland, 1771–1773", by Whitfield Bell in *The Pennsylvania Magazine of History and Biography* (1951). John Wesley wrote about electricity in *The Desideratum: Or, Electricity Made Plain and Useful* (1759). The online *History of Vaccines,* maintained by The College of Physicians of Philadelphia states that "Thomas Sydenham (1624–1689), a noted English doctor, had observed that the rich seemed to have a higher mortality rate from smallpox than the poor. This led him to conclude that contemporary medical treatments, largely inaccessible to the poor, might be more harmful than helpful in mild smallpox cases." In *Nelson's Hero: The Story of his 'Sea-Daddy' Captain William Locker* (2005), Victor Sharman mentions that Locker was an old boy of Merchant Taylors' School and that he both became captain of the frigate HMS Thames and was married during 1770. While commanding HMS Lowestoffe in the West Indies, one of his lieutenants was the newly promoted Horatio Nelson. The boarding of the enemy privateer is described by Peter Goodwin in *Nelson's Ships: A History of the Vessels in which he Served: 1771–1805* (2002).

Penelope Hunting describes the gardens of Grove Hill in "Dr John Coakley Lettsom, Plant-Collector of Camberwell", *Garden History* (2006). *The Legacies of British Slave-ownership* database, administered by UCL, provides details of John Fothergill's interests in a plantation on Nevis. John Chance is mentioned in the Lancashire Record Office online document, *Sources for Black and Asian History*. In 2023 an "imagined portrait" of him by Lela Harris was hung in the Judge's Lodgings Museum in Lancaster. George Lillo's play *The London Merchant* about the murderer George Barnwell was first performed at the Drury Lane Theatre in 1731. According to the Wikipedia catalogue of events in Great Britain in 1782, on 24 August on Southsea Common, David Tyrie was the last man in Britain to be hanged, drawn and quartered. The Somerset Case of 1772, in which a judge concluded that the status of slavery had no basis in English law, is described by William Cotter, "The Somerset Case and the Abolition of Slavery in England", *History* (1994). The website of The Abolition Project, under the headings Campaign and Petitioning and Lobbying Parliament provides the list of signatories of the first petition for the abolition of slavery by the Quakers of 1783, including John Coakley Lettsom, Geo. Harrison and James Beesley. *A List of The Society Instituted in 1787 for Effecting the Abolition of the Slave Trade*, a document available online, includes James Beesley, Ann Fothergill, George Harrison, Doctor [John] Lettsom and Mary Miers as subscribers.

The revolt on Isaac Pickering's estate in 1790 is described in five sentences in the history section of the website of the

Government of the British Virgin Islands: these have been extrapolated. Information about Thomas Thomasson is given on the UCL *Legacies of British Slave-ownership* database. Quaker attitudes towards black people are described in *Quakers and African Americans: Their not always FRIENDLY relations,* a webpage by Bayard Rustin hosted by tripod.com, and the views of Benjamin Lay and Anthony Benezet about assimilation are described by Emma Lapsansky-Werner and Margaret Hope Bacon in "Benjamin Coates and the Colonization Movement in America", part of a collection of essays entitled *Back to Africa* which they edited (2005, available online). A potted biography of George Bridgetower is given on the Classic FM website. The article "Breast Cancer in the Eighteenth Century" by George Rousseau appears on the online supplement to *The Eighteenth-Century: Theory and Interpretation,* Volumes 56–57, 2015–16.

The aspects of this novel referred to above, and many more, are therefore true. Or at least, they are reported as true in the sources mentioned. Some may be inventions, but they are not my inventions. Unfortunately, one particularly unreliable source is Lettsom himself. His claim to have freed fifty enslaved people in 1768 appears to be contradicted by Abraham's discovery of Taine's inventory showing possession of only eight people. His claim to have earned £2,000 from his medical efforts during his seven month stay in the Virgin Islands is also suspect. In the book *Thomas Beddoes M.D. 1760–1808: Chemist, Physician, Democrat* by D. A. Stansfield (1984), the author quotes this successful Bristol doctor as stating that it was typical for him to receive "on account of a visit occupying about three days from twenty to thirty five guineas" (or 7–12 guineas a day). To amass £2,000 in seven months, Lettsom would have had to earn 9 guineas a day, every day. Theoretically possible, but allowing little time for travel between consultations, and no time for parties. One questionable claim not repeated in this book is that he and his brother Edward were the seventh set of twins that his mother bore, all previous sets comprising two boys, and all dying during birth or infancy.

In the novel, Teresa eventually becomes the owner of the plantation on Little Jost. This is fiction, and yet it would have been possible. An article in *The Gleaner* by Arnold Bertram dated 31 July 2017 entitled "Jamaica's black and coloured slave owners" discusses such ownership on his island. The plot does not involve Teresa possessing her own slaves, but that too would have been possible.

All of the contemporary historical sources on which this book is based were written by Europeans. Just one sentence allegedly spoken by an enslaved person is included: "I am glad my master is returned safe!" (Chapter 15). Lettsom attributes these words to Sam in Letter XXVII to Dr William Cuming, dated 10 November 1784. There is, however, one invaluable source of first-hand slave testimonies. This is the Federal Writers' project that collected narratives from 2,300 surviving ex-slaves in the United States during the 1930s. Interpretation of these narratives is beset by problems of selectivity, of who survived, who was prepared to talk, and what they were prepared to talk about. Many did describe horrendous cruelties. On the other hand, Silas Abbott (aged 73, enslaved in Mississippi) recalled that his master was "exceptionally good, never drank whiskey", and that he played with the owner's children while growing up, especially the two boys whom he "loved like brothers". Katie Arbery (aged 80, no state given) was raised with her master's children, and called him Pappy. She said that "They treated us so nice that when freedom come, I thought I was always free." Bettice Tolbert (no age given, enslaved in Alabama) felt that her master and mistress were "blessed ole people", and recalled that the slaves followed the former's body to the big house in tears when he died. Nevertheless, she saw her master's brother set the dogs on his own slaves, and heard of an overseer shooting at a runaway slave hiding in a river. James Davis (aged 96, enslaved in North Carolina) learnt the banjo well enough for him to play "for the white folks", and he was a caller for the square dancing. He said that "I had better times than I ever had in my life". Hammett Dell (aged 90, enslaved in Tennessee) told of his grandmother marrying an ex-slave after the civil war, but he whipped her and beat her up until she died.

Although from a later time and another part of the Americas, these testimonies tell of *some* enslaved people being friends with white children (like Sam and Teresa), loving their owners – or at least thinking of them as "blessed ole people" – and mourning them when they died (as the slaves of John Pickering do in my book and in Lettsom's own account), genuinely enjoying playing music for the white folks (like Letitia's musicians), and having worse outcomes after freedom (like Toney). These stories motivated my inclusion of similar sentiments and experiences amongst *some* – but by no means all – of the enslaved people mentioned in the book.

The events of the novel that fill the gaps between those recorded by biographers and historians have been made up. There are a few minor distortions of the truth too. For example, the visit of Phoebe Smith and Mary Evans to Tortola took place several months earlier than described. The Rawlinson children had additional brothers and sisters, who have been omitted from the story. Also omitted are more sisters of the Fothergill girls and the wife, Susanna, of Samuel Fothergill who seems to have suffered ill-health during the time when his nieces were visiting London. Eventually it was Abraham Rawlinson, and then his son Henry, who lived at Grassyard Hall, Caton, but it is convenient for the story to have Thomas Hutton there and Abraham in Lancaster in 1751. Edward Lettsom's sale of Cane Garden Bay has been put back by a couple of years.

More seriously, there is no evidence whatsoever that Lettsom played with Sam and Teresa as a child. Nevertheless, despite being described as a "boy" and a "girl" in their Deed of Sale to Lettsom, the price paid for them and Lettsom's later fantasies of Teresa heading a seraglio are inconsistent with them having still been children when he bought them in 1768. It is not known who the father of Sam and Teresa was, in fact Lettsom suggests they had the same mother and different fathers. The Greenwich May Fair used to be held in Lettsom's day, but there is no record of him attending, nor of the African animals show. Harald Pedersen is an invented character, although Letitia is based on a woman described but not named by Lettsom. There is no record of how or when Samuel Taine died, nor where he is buried. It is not known on which ships Sam Coakley sailed, nor where his voyages took him. The date and guest list of the garden party at Grove Hill has been made up, although he did know the people mentioned. There is no account of Arthur Hodge meeting either John or Pickering Lettsom. There is no evidence that Pickering Lettsom met Teresa, nor that she was living on Little Jost or anywhere else in 1808, nor of the ages or names of any children she might have had. It seems to be well accepted that Arthur Hodge fought many duels, but it is not known who his opponents were. There is no evidence that Ruth and Pickering sought to emulate Count Bernstorff and grant freedom to their workforce – but if the story presented here were true, then there wouldn't be.

The book might be unfair to Samuel Taine and William Payne Georges II as I have made them out to be bad characters based on no evidence. The worst behaviour has, however, been ascribed to Arthur Hodge and as he was arrested, tried, convicted and hanged for a horrible murder, that would appear to be fair enough. Other bad deeds are attributed to known slave traders and slave owners. Despite his own record in that regard, I have portrayed William

Lindow more sympathetically, but merely to provide variety in the characterisations and without any evidence.

Many events have been invented for the sake of the story. I do not believe them to be true. However, each of the things that Lettsom and his circle did, they did for a reason. An account in which no reason is advanced is incomplete, and in some ways just as inaccurate and misleading as one in which the gaps are speculatively filled in.

John Whitehead, December 2023

ACKNOWLEDGEMENTS

I learnt a great deal about trans-Atlantic slavery while studying for an MA in International Slavery Studies at the University of Liverpool between 2017 and 2019. I am grateful to all of the staff who taught me during a course that was both fascinating and disturbing, especially the course directors, Jonathan Lewis and Christienna Fryar. Heartfelt thanks also go to Andrew Paton, Ann Morgan and Novie Younger-Coleman, who all read an early draft of the manuscript and provided many helpful suggestions for improvement. My wife Anne provided some honest appraisals of the plot. The Literary Studio provided an in-depth critique which enabled me to make a series of substantial improvements. I am grateful to Joyce Burnett of British Virgin Islands Holidays for organising a wonderful visit to Tortola, and to the many people there who helped arrange visits to locations mentioned in the book or shared their knowledge of John Lettsom and his contemporaries.